Bella Mellman

Being Oldish

D1738640

Shirley Sacks

Table of Contents

To my wonderful family and friends without whom Shirley would not be me.

About the Author

Shirley Sacks was born in South Africa, and is a long-time resident of Beverly Hills, California. She has been married and divorced twice and has children and grandchildren, all of which have given her an enlightening and amusing perspective on just about everything from life in the new South Africa to life in a condo in Beverly Hills, California. This is her second book about the life of Bella Mellman.

Introduction

Bella Mellman – no middle name – turned seventy-two without fanfare.

"There is no getting around it, seventy-two is not young," she told her twenty-seven-year-old neighbor Nicole Behrmann as they walked Bella's dog Charlie around the block. Bella and Nicole's friendship bonded as Nicole often kept Bella company whilst dog walking. Over the years, Bella found herself playing the role of mentor to Nicole. Though Nicole didn't like talking about her past, she did finally disclose her mother committed suicide when she was already out of the house and working.

"I never knew my father, and my mother told me it was a one-night stand when she was drunk, and she like didn't remember the night it like happened."

Nicole was one of the multitudes of untethered Californian residents who came from somewhere else, somewhere else being a place they never wanted to go back to, other than for notable days, like Thanksgiving or Christmas, or the occasional death in the family.

Nicole – who had no family to speak of – rented a small apartment in a charming Spanish-styled fourplex across the road from The Portland, the Beverly Hills condo where Bella had lived since she immigrated from South Africa thirty years ago.

Bella used to walk Charlie with Hildy Doucet, a friend she'd made at The Portland, who also had a dog. Bella loved Hildy's Southern drawl and way of describing her once super luxurious life in Dallas before her divorce. However, the second husband Hildy thought would be easier to find in Beverly Hills rather than in Dallas didn't materialize. So, exit Hildy, back to Dallas, where, at least, she had grown children and old friends.

Shelly Davidson – who moved right next door to Bella's condo on the fourth floor at The Portland a couple of years ago – came to Los Angeles for the same reason as Hildy Doucet. So far, she had the same lack of success. Nevertheless, she was optimistic and told Bella, "I'm an active seeker, and if you came from Stockton like I do, you'd understand. Everyone knows everyone's business there. My first husband was having an affair with his secretary, who couldn't wait to marry. So unoriginal. My second husband had no children and was never married. I had to marry him to discover why. People thought I was lucky to lure him into marriage. They were wrong."

"You're not old," Nicole told Bella. "Seventy is not old. You look like sixty,"

"That's not young either, darling," Bella replied.

"Whatever... You look amazing. My friends can't believe you are over seventy. I want to be like you when I get old."

Bella tried to see this as the compliment it was.

Shelly arrived at Bella's front door with her delicious banana bread. She sang the happy birthday song in its entirety.

"Don't look so glum," Shelly said. "Eat cake, it'll cheer you up."

"Are you channeling Marie Antoinette? I'm trying to lose weight, not gain it." Bella could not help laughing at the way Shelly looked in her white satin robe trimmed with feathers, her dyed blond hair still in overnight orange rollers. She wore full makeup.

"I am never seen without my face on. I learned that from my mother," Shelly told Bella when they first met. Bella didn't inform Shelly she always wore blusher, which she thought was the one bit of color that made her look so much better.

Bella's daughter Jessica, a successful interior designer, and son Ivan, a successful movie producer, were out of town. Bella knew Jessica would arrive back from her trip with a thoughtful gift. Probably a pair of earrings. Bella loved earrings and was never without them. Most of Bella's earrings, bangles, and necklaces hung on a wall of hooks inside her walk-in closet; they made a colorful testimony to her style. Her more valuable jewelry – a few pieces she'd hate to lose – she kept in a locked drawer built into her closet. One of these was a ring Guy Rufus, ex-husband and father of her children, once gave her. It was a heart-shaped emerald surrounded by diamonds, an 'I am sorry gift', after she'd discovered one of Guy's more blatant indiscretions.

Bella, once Bella Rufus, and for a short time, Bella Varelly changed her last name back to her single name before she became a citizen of the United States. "I don't want to carry around my past," she said, having discovered she could use any name she had legally.

Bella didn't consider her marriage to Guy Rufus a failure. It didn't last, but with time, the bad parts faded. As for her second short marriage, she said, "I never even think of the time I was married to Phil Varelly. It was a whoosh in and a whoosh out.

As Bella knew he would, Guy – who moved to Los Angeles around the same time Bella did – called to wish her happy birthday. Guy lived in an Italianate mansion, once owned by a famous actor, in the best part of Beverly Hills.

Once, both Bella and Guy emigrated to live in Los Angeles. Bella became part of Guy's family, which included Wife Number Two and child Hayley. Despite being divorced, neither she nor Guy wanted to be completely untethered, and so she was integral for family celebrations and holidays.

After Guy's divorce from Wife Number Two, he quickly found his European Mongrel, who, being childless and thirty years younger than him, had a good body. Bella dubbed Guy's second wife, Wife Number Two, when she wrote about her, which Bella understood was about claiming position and not very nice. Bella was also not nice calling Guy's much younger lover, 'A European Mongrel'. "I'm not being mean, but Irina is a mix of Serbian, Belgian, Spanish and Macedonian. She's like my dog, Charlie. He's a mix of terrier, poodle, corgi and who knows."

According to Edna Feather – Bella's therapist – Guy Rufus was, "The man in your life." Bella loved Guy in a way Dr. Feather surmised, "You and Guy have a karmic connection. You could have been his mother in a past life, the way you love him."

Bella agreed with Dr. Feather. She'd been connected to Guy from the moment they met at a party. Bella was seventeen and Guy was twenty. Guy Rufus drove Bella Mellman home and that was the beginning; dating, breaking

5

up, getting together again, marriage, children, divorce, moving from South Africa, first to London, then Los Angeles... their lives were entwined in a way Dr. Feather decided, "You are so clearly fashioned from the same cloth."

The day after Bella's birthday, she and her close friend Greta Mallory had their mutual birthday celebratory lunch at Mariposa, the restaurant at Nieman Marcus.

Greta – now in her mid-fifties – and Bella bonded at a mutual friend's party at Chasen's, a restaurant frequented by movie people. Famous for its chili, Chasen's – closed in 1995 – was now the site of an upmarket grocery store.

Bella and Greta met, as usual, in the shoe department, where Bella didn't mind waiting whilst looking at the latest in fanciful foot ware.

Once Greta arrived, Bella led her to a display of embellished sneakers sporting famous designer names. "Feel the weight of these sneakers. It's like wearing ankle weights."

Greta found a grey suede shoe she loved. "This would be perfect for a dinner I've been invited to."

Bella pointed out, "I don't think you could walk in them. They're so high."

Greta said, "I can walk in them for dinner."

Bella announced, loudly enough so a salesman and a few browsers could hear, "Until women stop wearing high heels, we won't be free."

Bella always looked underneath the shoe at the sticker price, noting none of the other potential customers did.

Was this, she wondered because the price was immaterial, or they wanted others – people they didn't even know – to think it so?

Greta proclaimed of a shoe, "It's a work of art."

Bella asked, "Who can afford to pay so much for a pair of shoes?" It was more a statement than a question.

Greta replied, "Very, very rich people. The kind who go to charity events and own yachts." She added, "Russian oligarchs, Chinese billionaires, movie stars, though actors usually must return the shoes." Greta sighed, "And mistresses, obviously not ones like me!"

Greta was referring to her long-time affair with Glen Short.

Before they sat at their table, they perused the houseware department adjacent to the restaurant. They had their usual fun imagining which set of gorgeous and plates they would buy. Greta always went minimal. Bella always chose the most exuberant.

After they sat down at their table, Bella gave Greta a scarf she'd knitted. Greta gave Bella another one of the handmade Florentine notebooks she knew Bella liked. "You must continue writing."

"Writing?"

Greta replied, "Another screenplay. And, of course, the episodes of your life. I love those, even when I don't come off well."

Bella said, "What's the use of being a screenwriter when your script doesn't get made into a movie?"

Greta said, "The Lions of Amarula is a wonderful story. Being from Africa, it is so authentic."

"You're a fan. Nobody else is."

Like many people who moved to Los Angeles, Bella tried writing a script. She had an excellent story to tell, and from all the How to Write Script books she'd bought, she was pleased how 'The Lions of Amarula' turned out.

The script was bought by IR Films. The film production company was owned by Bella's son Ivan and Ivan's friend, Farrel Bootch. The company was founded by Farrel's billionaire father Digby Bootch. People who hadn't read Bella's script might think the sale was due to motherly nepotism. However, it had an excellent plot, mesmerizing characters and a lightly executed shout-out against racism. It could and should be made in South Africa, which would be a good thing for the country's flagging economy.

Greta said, "Your script is not the only one gathering dust." She added, "Don't get me wrong. I think it's timely, and with the charismatic villain, it's a part actors would love to play." Greta mused, "Why do I prefer villains? You know, those old cowboy films? I always fell for the bad guy, the one with hooded eyes and deeply furrowed cheeks? The way he looked down from his saddle as if he knew what a woman wanted."

"Like your Glen?"

"He's not my Glen," Greta replied.

"I know. He belongs to his wife," Bella retorted. She wished her friend would get rid of her long-term married lover.

Changing the uncomfortable subject, Greta said, "Seriously, you have a talent. Write another script."

Bella said, "When I write about my life, the words come easy, but script writing is so constraining; plot points, specific page count, three-act structure."

Greta said, "You can make money with a script, especially after Ivan and Farrel make 'The Lions of

Amarula' into a movie. They will, not because they should, but because it's fucking good. And you know I don't curse. But it is! Then other people will be interested in you, so you'd better have another one to show after Lion is a success. Also, you'd be less dependent on Guy. On the other hand, dare I say you like being dependent on him. It keeps you connected."

Greta was astute when it came to her friend Bella and her connection to her ex-husband, the father of her children, Guy Rufus. Greta, more than any of Bella's American friends, understood how much Bella still loved Guy without wanting to be married to him.

"You could try writing a comedy?" Greta suggested.

Bella replied, "What about the awful state of the world? All the injustice and unfairness and the sheer horribleness of it."

Greta said, "Don't go all grandiose, Bella. People must laugh. And if you really don't want to do another script, so what. You're not a young thing embarking on the road to glory. You're seventy-two. Life isn't over, but you can relax a bit," Greta teased, "Take up a hobby. Oh, I forget you already have a hobby."

"Are you referring to my art or my knitting?"

Greta replied, "You can do both. I adore my scarf." Greta had hung the finely knitted taupe scarf around her neck.

Bella said, "It looks good on you. It's cotton, so it's washable."

Greta said, "I wish I could knit. I'd like to knit, but I don't want to learn how."

Bella teased, "I'd like to be a marine biologist and I also don't want to learn how."

Bella said, "Thank goodness I had to learn the basics of knitting at primary school in Johannesburg. Imagine that, in today's world! The boys did carpentry, and us girls learned to knit, crochet and cross stitch. I don't regret learning it all. I once made the most exquisite needlepoint evening bags. I sold them in a fancy shop in London when I lived there, for those three miserable years after I got divorced from Guy. I kept one, but where it is, I have no idea. I think I brought it here, but it's years since I've seen it. I learned here a purse is a bag, and for me, a purse was a wallet. Odd differences in the same language, in different countries. I thought I might have given it to Jessica, but she says she doesn't have it. If she says she doesn't have it, she doesn't. You know how tidy her house is."

Greta said, "I am mad for her house. I heard rt5rtf Jacoby's loved what she did for them. I'd love to see their house."

Bella said, "You can, it will be featured in a magazine. I think Architectural Digest, but she won't tell me which one till it's certain."

Greta said, "I love your place, too. You know that. Nobody has décor like you. Who do you know who collages all the kitchen cabinets?"

"It cost too much to redo the kitchen, so I collaged it, and it's aged so well. Over the years, it's developed a patina from cooking. It never looks dirty."

Greta said, "I remember when you lifted the old fitted carpet and decided to do stencils on the bare concrete."

Bella said, "Now that was difficult. I had to wear a mask to spray on the paint. Every now and again, I spray over the old ones. It's not got a pattern, as you know, but like the kitchen, it's developed a patina. I love it."

Greta said, "Who writes quotes on doors. And what about all your collections? Your place is unique. It's like living in an art installation. It's quite something, your home!"

Greta said, "I'd like to be artistic, like you, so I've done the next best thing. I do love finding art for my clients."

Bella said, "My grandmother on my mother's side

helped me with knitting and crochet. She was a very good knitter. She made twinsets for herself and sleep socks for my brother and me. They laced up down the center and were made with thick wool. Her socks were our armor against the icy Johannesburg winters, and we treated them as valuable gifts, which I suppose, they were. Knitting is a type of meditation for me."

Greta said, "I still want you to teach me, even though you won't."

Bella laughed, "If there's one thing I refuse to teach anyone to do, that's to knit. If you go to a yarn store. They'll show you how. The staff is so helpful, and people sit around a table and knit and chat. You'd like it."

Greta said, "I guess I don't really want to learn to knit. But aside from knitting, painting, or any of the things you do, you should not stop writing about your life. And your memories."

Bella said, "I'm still doing that."

Greta said, "Continue!"

Chapter 1: Violet Blooms

Flowers have the prettiest names.

Bella thought of writing a novella about Violet Mawela, the black maid who worked for her in South Africa. How Violet also ended up living in Los Angeles was so unlikely that it was worthy of a screenplay.

After Bella – living in a flat in Killarney, Johannesburg – was sure she wanted to make Los Angeles her home, she rented her place. Violet's maid service came with the rental, and Bella felt perfectly happy, leaving Violet in charge. Violet was an inspired cook; she kept Bella's flat spotless. When Bella still lived there, she teased Violet about how often she polished and re-polished the brass findings of the old windows.

"I like to see them shine," Violet said.

When – after a couple of years – Bella sold the flat, Violet went to work for the Gerbers, who lived in the same building. The Gerbers decided to emigrate to live in Los Angeles and they brought Violet with them as a nanny for their new baby. The Gerbers had their Green Cards. Violet came with them on a six-month tourist visa and stayed.

"I am very excited to be coming to America," Violet

called Bella to tell her the news.

"What about your family?" Bella inquired.

Violet's daughter Gracie was an under-educated South African woman. She'd dropped out of school when she got pregnant with Lazarus, who was now an adult. Lazarus' father was never in the picture. This was accepted as normal. Apartheid, the iniquitous system the Afrikaner government put in place to keep black and white people separate, was mostly to blame. Men left wives and children to come work in the big cities. They went back 'home' once a year. Bella's gardener told her, "Us men, we have country wives and city girlfriends."

Gracie didn't make the same mistake in her choice of a new husband. She was now married to a policeman, and they had one daughter, Patricia. Gracie did part-time housework when she could find it but mostly stayed at home with her daughter.

Violet called Bella as soon as she arrived in Los Angeles, where the Gerbers had rented a house not far from The Portland, Bella's condo.

"Welcome to America!" Bella said, "I can't believe you are here."

After effusive greetings, Violet launched a tirade about

how bad life in South Africa had become.

"Haai, Shirley, the crime is terrible! It's the Zimbabweans. They take our jobs and commit terrible crimes."

Xenophobia was as rife in South Africa as anywhere else in the world. Mandela's Rainbow Nation was shattering with the influx of Zimbabweans, Swazis, Malawians, Ghanaians, Kenyans, Ugandans, and Ethiopians, all hoping to find a better life in South Africa. Yeoville, where Gracie now lived, had become an immigrant hub.

In the days of apartheid, Yeoville was a middle-class white suburb and integral to Bella's ex-husband Guy Rufus' life story: struggling immigrant parents, lots of scrapping in a rough neighborhood, making it out of poverty big time.

When Bella met him, Guy still lived in Yeoville with his family. He lived there – as was common – until he married, sleeping in a narrow porch bedroom. Bella lost her virginity in that tiny space, which Guy dubbed, 'The Bird Cage'.

Guy now lived in a home in one of the best parts of Los Angeles. His house was both luxurious and understated. It would not be out of place in a glossy home decorating magazine. Not that Guy would never allow his home to be published. He wasn't that kind of person, which was one of the reasons seventeen-year-old Bella fell in love with him.

He was contrary in ways Bella found endearing or, depending on his mood, terrifying.

Yeoville, when Guy grew up, was adjacent to the upper-class suburb of Houghton, where Bella lived in a large double story mansion perched on the wrong side of a hill, so the sun didn't warm through the diamond-shaped leaded-window panes. The house was icy in winter, and it was just as well every room included a fireplace, where, in the winter months, the house 'boy' set a coal fire; first in the living room, then, before everyone retired, in the adult's rooms; the adults being Bella's parents, Joyce and Speedy Mellman and her grandparents on her father's side. Bella did nag to have a fire set for her bedroom, but she was never allowed, and she and her younger brother Derek were left to eiderdowns, extra blankets, and Granny's handknitted bed socks to keep warm. Bella remembered the extra blankets were peach-colored, and the eiderdowns were pink paisley. They were kept in an upstairs built-in linen cupboard.

The solid, square double-story house, built by Bella's grandparents, was no more when Bella was last in Johannesburg. Abandoned by a developer who planned to build apartments, then taken over by squatters and finally demolished, all that was left of the terraced acre garden, swimming pool, grass tennis court, orchard, and the rose garden was a wretched tumble of unkempt red earth entwined with rooted out shrubs, and mounds of dried out vegetation laced with plastic detritus. The parable seemed obvious, and Bella wondered whether she should write about South Africa, from its inception as a trading post for the Dutch, to an English colony, to an embarrassing example of the white man's inhumanity to his darker fellows, to the present government's destructive corruption was a vast subject.

Some of Bella's memories were vivid, but she didn't like reading about other people's childhoods, even when their adulthoods were exceptional, and though she wished it was different, she had not discovered anything, done anything remarkable and her contribution to society was in no way so memorable that her childhood would be of interest. Bella thought her teenage years would be boring to anyone other than those with whom she shared them. Who would care that she still harbored a deeply ingrained grudge towards Erin-Anne Friel for ruining her best friendship with Yael Kahn with a blatant lie Yael chose to believe? Or that nobody could believe Anthony Jacobson asked her to be his date for his sister's twenty first birthday party until the very evening of the event. She was white and privileged, loved, well fed, and had an excellent education. Her interests were encouraged. She was a pupil at Madam Vanya's art studio. Madam was Hungarian. When Russia invaded Hungary after the Second World War, Madam was so upset that she canceled classes for a while. Bella also attended Milly Marais' elocution classes and took part in the annual Eisteddfod, though she was never comfortable on stage and once got such stage fright when reciting a monologue. She forgot the words and left the stage in tears

Nobody – not even her daughter Jessica, and certainly not her son Ivan – would care how thrilling it was when the 'boys' from the coal truck ran up the raised stone path on the side of the house, singing and huffing as they heaved coal in hessian sacks from their backs into the coal-cellar in the backyard. Bella wondered why it was some memories – so inconsequential – stuck. It was mystifying, this thing called memory.

The back yard was the service yard. Servants lived there, in a row of small rooms with a short stairway up to each door, as if the room was important, rather than a tiny space, big enough for a single bed, a clothes cupboard and a small table and chairs. The staff shared one shower and a toilet. The staff's enamel mugs and plates were kept in a cupboard above the sink. They ate their own food, mostly mielie pap, which was a staple. Pap was akin to Italian polenta. It was eaten for breakfast with milk and sugar and for supper with meat stew and gravy. It was a treat when the cook spared some for Bella and her younger brother Derek. Like the staff, they ate with their fingers, swooshing the pap into the delicious meat gravy.

That Speedy Mellman, her father was an alcoholic, and her parents divorced and remarried could be stuff to write about. Divorce was not common at the time. And who cared? She didn't like her stepfather, her stepmother was sometimes the proverbial witch, and she was devastated when her grandmother on her father's side died. No, childhood memories were best left to lodge in the part of her brain where such recollections were stockpiled.

Bella wrote in her notebook, "How Violet Mawela morphed from a South African black woman into an African American." But she didn't feel inspired. She hoped her forthcoming trip to Africa, not only South Africa but also East Africa, where she'd never been before, would be inspiring.

Chapter 2: Birthday

Some gifts last forever.

When Bella turned sixty, Guy presented her with a check. She used the money to purchase a pair of gold and silver earrings, plus a ring designed by John Hardy. Bella liked Hardy's work from the moment she saw it under the glass counter on the ground floor of Nieman Marcus. His pieces were handmade in Bali; different – yet not outlandish – and not heavy, which Bella appreciated. She did not go for heavy artistic pieces, nor did she wear feather-light chains with a charm barely visible. Greta helped Bella choose after their yearly birthday lunch at the Mariposa, the restaurant in the basement of Nieman Marcus in Beverly Hills. Bella often wore the earrings, but the ring was now tight. The finger on which she liked to wear it was bent and swelled with arthritis.

Arthritis was a bane of old age. Fit or not, healthy or not – with age – joints become worn out, stiff and painful. Bella's Granny Lil also suffered from sore hands, and she gave up her ever-present crochet after she'd finished making each of her four grandchildren a fine tablecloth made from alternating crochet and embroidered linen squares. Bella would forever feel guilt that somewhere along the winding path of her life, her tablecloth had been stolen.

Bella wasn't big on birthday celebrations. She once asked her therapist, Dr. Feather, why she didn't pay much attention to them, and they had a session on why marking certain times was not important to her, which illuminated nothing much.

Guy made out he didn't like birthdays or birthday gifts, but Bella knew that was not true. What he didn't like was being beholden. It was something in his character, and it was never going to change. "Buy me colored socks," he said.

When Guy turned forty – he and Bella were divorced by then, and both still living in South Africa – Bella thought socks were too unimportant and so she gave him one of her drawings, framed. He seemed grateful, that is until Bella infuriated him with something she said. She could not recall what. Guy became so enraged that all she remembered was leaving his house in tears as he smashed the drawing to the ground, breaking the protective glass.

That Guy had a quick temper – a temper that cooled almost as quickly as it flared – was something Bella learned to accept after their divorce. Nevertheless, she went back to buying him socks.

When Guy turned seventy, socks again didn't seem sufficient, and so Bella gave him a very small painting, which he accepted – age having done its mellowing – most graciously. When it was time for the cake, Bella – as requested – made her famous red velvet cake (from a box) with colorful, artistic icing. There was another professionally made cake which Wife Number Two had ordered. Bella thought that her cake might have looked a bit unkempt due to the layers not being centered and the artistic, expressionist icing, which gave everyone a laugh, but Bella knew her cake tasted better. Wife Number Two gave Guy a monogrammed Hermes blanket.

Before Bella turned seventy-two, he offered herself, Jessica, and Chloe a trip. "Anywhere you want to go, after you've been to South Africa," he said, aware Bella was going to visit her brother Derek, who hadn't been well.

Guy's generosity caused endless debate, seeing as he so munificently offered, "Go wherever you like."

There was a whole world and many places Bella hadn't yet seen. India beckoned, but the time suitable for Jessica and Chloe to travel was monsoon season. Jamaica was considered, but Guy said, "It's not safe for women on their own." And neither Jessica nor Bella wanted to push it.

"What about Kenya or Tanzania?" Bella suggested to Jessica. "I've always wanted to go to East Africa. Maybe we could see The Migration?"

Jessica laughed. "If Dad thinks Jamaica is dangerous, what's he going to think of East Africa?"

Shelly – who thought anywhere east of La Cienega was dangerous – could not understand why Bella wanted to go to Jamaica, East Africa, or India. "They're all so…" Shelly didn't finish her sentence, but what she meant was dirty, unsafe, unsanitary and not Western.

The Gods were with Bella when someone told Guy about a trip he and his family made to East Africa, which was organized with streamlined precision by the son of a mutual friend who was trying to build up his travel business. Thus, when Jessica cautiously mentioned East Africa, Guy said, "Yes."

Guy was incredible that way. He helped friends – even people who weren't friends – like Peter Granger, who Guy heard was totally broke and living in Cyprus. Peter was not deserving of charity. On reflection, Bella realized it was Guy's way of showing Peter he'd made it whilst Peter – who briefly dated Bella just before she began dating Guy – hadn't. Men had their own ways of demonstrating one-upmanship. And so, after a visit to South Africa, on her own, Bella was off to meet Jessica and Chloe in East Africa. Starting off in Arusha, the town near Mount Kilimanjaro. Then the Ngorongoro Crater and the Serengeti. If they were fortunate, they might see The Great Migration. Finally, ending up at a beach resort on the island of Zanzibar.

"Lucky Guy still loves you in a very generous way," Shelly could never get over the relationship between Bella and Guy. Her two husbands wanted little to do with her. She didn't want to have anything to do with them.

Bella agreed. "I love you, Guy," she whispered once the trip's itinerary was finalized. "I love you, Guy," she murmured as the finest needles pricked sufficiently for tears to well. "I love you for what you are and what you aren't and what could have been and what isn't."

The tears neither spilled nor lasted as they were replaced by thrilling words, 'Zanzibar, Ngorongoro, Serengeti, Arusha…' The words sounded like a mantra. Bella had been on a few safaris in South Africa and Botswana in the past and loved every one of them.

As a child, she'd been to the famous Kruger Park on the days when you had to stick to the road in your own car and be back at camp at five. Two families went regularly during the July school holidays. The children played games at night, running around the unfenced and unlit camp, swinging gas lanterns, with no adult admonishing, "Be careful!" The adults played their own games.

Nowadays, both safaris in Kruger and elsewhere in

Africa have been supercharged as far as the camps and services and costs go. As an adult, Bella had been to Londolozi, in the Sabi Sands private game park in South Africa with Ivan and Jessica when they were younger. With Jessica and Chloe, she'd been to Botswana, where most of the time was spent on chairs on a river boat, or a dugout, watching elephants, waterbuck, and birds, hoping they'd not disturb any hippos. Hippos are easily the most dangerous animals in Africa. A disturbed Hippo can chomp a man in half. Their jaws open one hundred and eighty degrees, and the pressure when they close is enormous. Even today, Hippos kill about five hundred people per year. Bella had been to Zimbabwe, once with Guy not long before they parted, and once with Jessica and Chloe. Shortly before Bella came to live in Los Angeles, she'd been on a fishing trip along the Okavango River with Ingo and Dawn Sterling. The Sterlings didn't tell her that Don Vincent was also coming – without his wife – which Bella knew was no accident. Bella spent every night persuading Don to go to his own rondavel, despite Bella being terrified of insects as the rondavel had no panes in the windows. Bella remembered weighing up her terror of insects, despite a mosquito net or savior Don. The days – however – were glorious. They sat on a large barge on chairs, casting their rods, drinking beer, seeing the odd elephant, lots of water buck and marvelous birdlife. As crocodiles abounded, there was no swimming in the water, but their pilot, who flew them to the lodge and remained with them for the duration, undressed and jumped into the river.

"There's no better holiday for me than going on safari," she told Nicole.

Nicole asked Bella as they walked Charlie, "What do you do on safari?"

Bella tried to explain. "There's a pattern, we get woken up before sunrise. Everyone meets for tea or coffee or delicious hot chocolate and rusks; very little conversation at that time of the morning. Then everyone goes out with their ranger in an open vehicle to search for game. Sometimes we stop and have breakfast. The ranger and the lookout – there are always two people – cook eggs, sausages, bacon, and fried tomatoes. Or we go back to camp where there's a great breakfast set up. We hang out till lunch, eat a light lunch, rest again till four, then off again for the evening drive, where the best part – aside from seeing nature – is stopping for cocktails before the sun goes down. We get out of the truck and wander a little bit. I try to feel the presence of my creator. I think everyone does as they observe how the sun goes down and the first stars show up. Without city lights, there are so many stars. I've been in the bush when there is a full moon. It's glorious. There are snacks, like biltong and nuts. We order what we want to drink before we leave. I order a tomato cocktail which comes ready mixed in a can. It's one of the few times I wish I could have a proper drink, but the feeling passes quickly."

Bella, sober for over twenty years, attended Alcoholics Anonymous regularly. "Then we drive back to camp in the dark, with the tracker shining a powerful light back and forth in the hopes of seeing something interesting. The light picks up animals' eyes. Even a hare's eyes shine bright. Then back to camp for dinner. There is a lot of eating."

"Are you ever scared?" Nicole asked.

"Occasionally, my heart jumps, but the rangers are very careful, especially around elephants. They can tell when the elephant is angry or posturing from the way the ears flap. When we were in Botswana – on the river – the ranger was very careful about hippos. They can be very dangerous. They have big teeth and bad tempers."

Nicole said, "I so want to like to go with you next time if you go."

Bella said, "If I were rich, I'd take you."

"There are so many things I'd do if I were rich," Nicole

said, "I often think about what I'd do if I were really rich."

Bella said, "If I were rich, the first thing I'd do would be to bring my brother and his family here. I'd buy them a house. Or maybe a condo in The Portland. I'd love them to live close. I'd buy my housekeeper Julietta a house, and I'd give a large donation to PETA."

Nicole and Bella played the dream game of what they would do if they were very rich. Nicole said, "I'd come on Safari with you and buy a condo in your building. I'd tell my boss she's thoughtless, and of course, I'd resign. I think I would go back to school. I'd go to a top-rated cooking school in… I don't know, somewhere in Europe. Then I'd open my own restaurant."

Bella noted that not one of Nicole's wishes included settling down with a man and getting married.

Chapter 3: Home Invasion

"Home is where you feel safe."

The flight to Johannesburg was long, twenty-four hours of flying time, not counting waiting around at airports or sitting in the plane whilst waiting for its turn on the runway.

There were different routes to get there, via various European capitals or via Atlanta, Georgia. It made no difference to the length of the flight. Though going business class, as Bella did, the flight was still something to be endured, and she cursed the airlines for their greed every time she glimpsed those in Economy who had to suffer in tiny seats that barely reclined.

When Bella arrived, she first called her brother Derek and his wife Josie, who were already on their way to the hotel to see her. She adored them both.

Bella packed so well. It took hardly any time to unpack. She hung up most of her clothes on thin hangers and lifted them from her suitcase to the closet. Make-up was in a brilliantly designed, simple bag that laid flat and could be gathered into a sack and her shoes were in shoe bags.

Who to call once she'd settled in?

As the years passed, there were less and less old friends

she wanted to see. Serena Hickey was one of the few people with whom she still felt a close connection. They'd known each other through marriages and divorces. They could now laugh and reminisce about what life was like then, which is what they did when they met for lunch at Tasha's in the fashionable Hyde Park shopping center.

"Remember all those memorable meals on Monday night?" Serena asked. "You were sterling the way you supported Adaline Exeter."

Adaline – a well-known sculptor – was pregnant and chose to have the baby without acknowledging a father. She'd had one abortion and then – almost past child-bearing age – decided to have the child. At the time, in conservative South Africa, this was extraordinary.

Bella reminisced, "That's how my Monday dinners began. Nobody had Monday night plans." I told Adaline she must come for dinner every Monday. "It started with a small group; Adaline, you, Marina Painter usually came – without her husband – and that divine Luke French. He was such a wonderful artist, totally self-taught and unabashedly certain he was painting masterpieces. He lived one building away from me, so I often popped in to see what he was up to. I used to sit and watch him paint those tiny canvasses. He had such an air."

Serena said, "He was exotic with his long curly hair."

Bella said, "He followed the teachings of Rudolf Steiner and tried to convince me the answers to life were to be found in Steiner's writings, which I simply could not understand. I tried contacting him. He has no email, and he doesn't answer his phone."

Serena, who knew everyone and what they were up to, told Bella, "The last I heard, he found a rich French woman to support him. I believe they live in Namibia. You know how impressed he was by foreigners. He thought they were so much more sophisticated than us South Africans, even though he was one of us and came from a very ordinary family."

Bella said, "How those dinners expanded, especially when I bought that extra table from Luke. I thought he was mad to sell it, but he said he didn't want it. He liked living more as an ascetic with no furniture but a bed and his art. It was a fabulous art deco table with matching chairs. I sometimes had twenty people for a sit-down dinner with those two tables."

Bella then lived in a much-admired art deco building. Her dining room – with wrap-around windows – provided excellent light for the space, which also functioned as her studio. Her easel – with whatever canvas she was working

32

on – loomed large in the corner of the room.

Serena said, "Oh, the days! Your dining room, and the way it led to the living room and then on to that small, comfortable study that led onto the porch where we often sat. It was like an old-style atelier. You had such interesting guests. I almost ran off with that Indian Doctor. He was to die for."

Bella said, "We got into an argument. I told him, as an Indian, he was hypocritical when he berated South Africans for apartheid, seeing as India had a much longer entrenched class system. Did you see him after?"

Serena was a man-eater. That she was married didn't much matter. He'd be another notch in her belt, which included other women's husbands. "Do you expect me to tell you?"

"Why not? It's years ago."

"I was dating John. He would be very upset to think I went to bed with anyone else then."

Bella's dinners took place during a time of upheaval in South Africa. Apartheid was ending. Mandela was released from jail after twenty-seven years. The conversation around the dinner table – often political and heated – was fueled by copious amounts of wine. Bella bought a mounted photograph of Mandela from a sidewalk hawker and hung it in the dining room. Mandela, though he did not know it, received endless toasts. Despite being pregnant, Adeline drank and said – Bella was sure untruthfully – "My doctor says it's fine to have a couple of glasses of wine with dinner."

In trying – as ever – to explain life in Los Angeles to Serena. Bella said, "I've lived in Los Angeles for so long, I'm a sort of native. But I will never feel as if I belong because I don't. I'm an immigrant, and though I speak English – thank God for that because you know how bad I am at other languages – there are times I feel as if I have a schism deep in my soul, like the moving plates under our earth, that occasionally shift, and rearrange themselves, and never quite settle. I'm being poetic."

Serena added, "That's a good metaphor for Los Angeles with your earthquakes."

Serena had lived in many places with many husbands. With her final one – the charming English-born John Hickey, they were forever contemplating where to move, away from South Africa. They'd got as far as Cape Town, where Serena decorated one of her gorgeous homes, but they didn't like living there and returned to live in a Cape Dutch style house in Houghton, not far from where Mandela lived where he made his home, after his twenty-seven-year imprisonment.

"Nobody entertains in Cape Town," Serena said. "We hated it. Nobody wants to go anywhere. We lived on one side of the mountain, and nobody who lived on the other side would ever come to us. That damned Table Mountain, it's in the way," Serena laughed. She knew she sounded ridiculous complaining about the position of the mountain, which gave Cape Town its glorious beauty. "I mean, how long can one look at that bloody mountain."

Where to move was the bane of white South Africans long before South Africa gave up apartheid and became a democracy. There were those who moved because of the injustices of apartheid. Others moved for fear of being massacred by angry black hoards. Some realized they would be living in a black-run country, which would go the way of other black countries when colonialism ended. The example of neighboring Rhodesia – now Zimbabwe – wasn't reassuring.

Bella was accustomed to moving. After her divorce from Guy, she moved to London with Jessica and Ivan. Four years later, she moved back to Johannesburg after what she now understood was an alcoholic breakdown.

Bella found her footing, briefly married Phil Varelly, who she didn't realize was gay, then fell for a sociopath whom she casually called 'My gangsta lover' before moving to Los Angeles. Guy facilitated the move. He decided Los Angeles was the place for him and Wife Number Two and his first family – which always included Bella – to make new roots. Guy's second marriage – like his first failed – and Wife Number Two received a significant lump sum in a settlement, which oddly didn't bother Bella.

Dr. Feather explained when Bella wondered about this in a therapy session. "It's Guy you love. You loved him before he was so successful. It's a pure love you have. It is truly karmic. You can't fight it."

Serena asked, "How's Guy?"

"He's fine, happy as a prince with his new European mongrel," Bella said.

Everyone who knew Bella knew Guy Rufus was the love of her life. It did not matter that Guy was married and had a daughter, Hayley, with Wife Number Two. It didn't matter he and Wife Number Two divorced, and Guy now lived with Irina, who Bella knowingly and unkindly dubbed The European mongrel, to those who'd understand where she was coming from.

"How long since I've seen you?" Serena asked. "I think I was in Los Angeles two years ago? I can't remember a thing these days. I suppose it's better than falling off the perch, but I'm not so sure," she laughed.

Serena had a way with words, which never failed to amuse her many friends, whom she entertained with casual and sophisticated pleasure. Dinner parties, lunch parties, drinks parties... these were the celebrations giving Serena an excuse to dress up in her stylish finery and show off how she still retained her continuing beauty.

Bella, having what she herself called"Eagle Eyes," noted Serena's skin showed not one single brown spot, or if she did indeed have them, they melted into her constant tan in which any wrinkles barely showed. Serena wore lightly tinted sunglasses. She said, "So I don't have to bother with eye makeup." She did need readers to look at the menu. They were a pair of antique tortoiseshell, which folded in half and came out of a small case with Serena's initials embossed on the front. Maybe not seeing clearly was a choice! She also wore no makeup other than her tan and pale lipstick, which she reapplied without looking. Bella did full makeup in front of a 10x magnification mirror. There was no mercy there.

Serena's breasts were pert – Bella knew they were done – and her arms looked thin and shapely under the thin, cotton, long-sleeved fitted t-shirt. Serena claimed proudly that she'd had a tummy tuck even though she didn't have children and her stomach was flat to start off with. "The best thing I ever did," she said, pulling up her t-shirt a bit to show off her flat bronzed middle, which Bella, with her glasses giving her perfect vision, was pleased to notice was wrinkled. Serena must have known her stomach, though flat, showed signs of age, but she had the confidence of a woman who felt comfortable making a joke about her great beauty's gentle demise and the adoration of her husband, John Hickey.

"Do you exercise?" Bella asked.

"God no! Never."

Bella glanced at Serena's well shaped calves sticking out from a slightly above the knee length black skirt. Through her tan – which Serena wore like a comforting shawl – there was but a hint of broken veins. But in general, Serena's body retained a youthful appearance. Bella admitted she was envious of Serena. She had a magnetic way about her, which was attractive to both men and women. Bella exercised, she lifted weights. Still, she was aware her old arms were old arms, and there was the unavoidable puckering as the upper arm met the trunk. Serena had some of that, but it was skinny, puckering, and tanned.

"I finally got it right," she said of John.

Serena lowered her voice, "Oh my God, there's Gideon Fellows?"

Bella turned in her seat. She waved. Gideon returned the wave. Serena also waved and said, "He's got no clue who we are." She said this as if it was the most amusing thing that Gideon Fellows – never the brightest – was now completely dimmed by Alzheimer's. "He's gone, quite gone. His brother, David, remember David – he was the taller one – he dropped off the perch last year. Heart attack, his third."

Bella said, "Those boys grew up with Guy in Yeoville. I went there yesterday." Bella knew this would shock Serena.

Since the fall of apartheid, which permitted black people to live anywhere, Yeoville had morphed into an over-populated and run-down black suburb, which attracted foreign Africans.

Serena rolled her eyes. "Yeoville! What on earth for? It's not safe to go there."

"I brought some clothes from America for Violet's daughter. Violet lives in Los Angeles now."

"Violet, your old cook, the one who made the gnocchi?"

"Yes, that, Violet. She came as a nanny for the Gelson's when they emigrated; they lived in a flat in my old building. I don't think you knew them."

"Violet lives in America! And you went to Yeoville!" Serena was amazed. "On your own? You could be killed there, robbed and mugged. I bet you didn't see a white face there."

Bella said, "I didn't."

Serena still could not get over Bella's trip to Yeoville.

"Weren't you scared?" Serena enquired. "The place is unrecognizable."

"I was a bit scared, but I wanted to give Violet's daughter and her granddaughter a lift back to her place. She came to my hotel to pick up all the clothes Violet sent for her. I couldn't let her take a bus or even a taxi back, she was so laden. She even said she was afraid she would be robbed, seeing some people knew she was coming to see me. You know there hasn't been any water in her building for weeks. I told her and her daughter to go shower in my hotel bathroom. They were so grateful."

"So, what did you think? I mean, about Yeoville?"

"I wasn't shocked because I was there a few years ago with Jessica to show her where her father grew up. Where Gracie lives, families live in rooms, not in whole flats. They share a kitchen and bathroom. There is a definite sense of danger with so many young men hanging about, obviously with no jobs."

Serena said, "Well, Violet landed with her bum in the

butter. Everyone wants to go to America. John and I considered it, but it is too expensive, with the value of our pathetic Rand so low against the dollar. We would have preferred living on the East Coast. We have tons of friends who live there," Serena said with a sense of superiority.

Bella always saw her old friend Marina Painter.

From a distance, Marina looked twenty, having never lost her skinny figure. Closer, with her long, highlighted brown hair in a low kind of bun, she looked half her age. After her husband died, she sold her rambling thatch-roofed home. She bought and renovated a smaller home nearby. The house was divine. Marina had exquisite taste.

"It's a house only for me," Marina said as she showed Bella around. "I didn't even make a proper guest room. I love it. I can do what I want when I want. Just in case Bella thought she didn't miss her man, she added, "I miss Harry, but my life is so much more... mine."

"At least you feel safe here," Bella said. "The guard at the street entrance looked fearsome."

"The guard didn't help when I was robbed. I was walking down the stairs one morning after I got dressed to find two thieves nonchalantly walking upstairs towards me."

"We want money and jewelry," one said, waving a gun.

"'Come with me,' I said – equally calmly – as I walked them upstairs. I opened the door to my dressing room and showed them a drawer in which I had money especially stashed, in case of such a situation. Another drawer had some jewelry. Not my best. Afterwards, they told me to lock myself in and count to three hundred. The two of them walked in with the workers planting the new garden. They didn't notice a thing. And neither did that fearsome guard."

"They were probably in on it," Bella suggested.

"Everyone's in on it," Marina replied, "Even inadvertently. My maid chats to her friend about how much money or jewelry I have, the friend talks to her boyfriend, who talks to his uncle, who talks to his brother who is part of a gang of robbers, and so it goes. I don't even blame them. For instance, what must my maid think when she sees the difference in the way she lives and how I live? I pay her well above the going rate, too, with extras. But you know what it's like here. Money is needed for the children's school uniforms… the aunt's funeral. Oh, those endless costly funerals. It's a huge industry and completely absurd. People take out insurance to pay for them. They save money on Burial Societies, which could be used for education or something more useful than a fancy coffin for a dead person. It's all about status. Status of those alive and those passed on. When my maid's mother died, she paid for a cow to be slaughtered, all the drinks, plus a group of singers for a three-day event. She baked for days. Her mother's funeral cost her almost a year's wages, and nobody helped her. Except for me, of course. Friends are not expected to contribute."

"I'm not even having a funeral," Bella told her friend about how she'd donated her body to science.

Marina said, "That's so brave."

Bella said, "I'm not so brave. I don't like any of the ways we're got rid of when we die. If there's an autopsy on TV, I have to peep through my hands. But the way I am doing it is trouble free, and I can't see myself buried in Los Angeles, and I don't think I'd want to be flown back to Africa to be buried near my family. They come and take you, and that's that. Then after six weeks – if you want – they cremate what's left and send it to whoever you choose."

Everyone Bella came across during her trip was the victim of a crime, some more serious, like poor Naomi Barrow's husband, who was stabbed to death in the Barrow's holiday home in Knysna. "Take what you want," Naomi heard Sam say. He offered no resistance. Still, they killed him, then tied up Naomi, who had just stepped out of her shower, and stole her old Jaguar, which was found abandoned with its innards removed.

Bella always made time for her friend Dinky Lawson who was an architect. Dinky was the only one of Bella's old friends who knew how to work Facetime, and so Bella and Dinky sometimes chatted, both in bed, due to the different hours. Bella's morning, Dinky's night or vice versa.

Dinky lived in an old Houghton home with the most exquisite acre garden, lovingly tended by Joshua, manservant and gardener. Dinky was ironically held up whilst discussing plans for a guardhouse outside a home she was renovating.

"Two men walked by and held a gun to my head. They stole all the builder's tools. I couldn't even call the police as they grabbed my cell. Anyway, the police don't do a thing. We drive with our handbags stored in the trunk of the car, our cell phones well out of sight, the car windows firmly shut, and doors locked. And still, they smash the window when cars are stopped at the light, even in heavy traffic. People merely remain in their cars, note what happened and thank their lucky stars it wasn't them this time."

"That's terrible," Bella said.

"It's the way it is. It's all about poverty. I don't know how most black people manage. I find things expensive, and I am, well, I am sort of… very rich in comparison. I sometimes think we are like the frog in the pot of water, which is gradually heated, so the frog does not notice until it's too late. There's been a trash-collectors strike for over four weeks now. Haven't you noticed?"

Bella said, "Of course, I've noticed. I know some areas have hired private companies to collect the trash, but there's nobody hired to collect the trash in Yeoville. It's horrific; overflowing, piling up in the streets, which are filled with trash at the best of times. I went there a few days ago to drop off Violet's daughter and granddaughter. They came to see me and to collect a whole suitcase of stuff Violet sent for them."

Dinky said, "Yeoville is dangerous. You're lucky you weren't robbed." Bella said, "They have no water in Violet's daughter's place."

Dinky said, "It's our useless government, our corrupt government. We often don't have electricity. We go into emergency mode if we're having a dinner party and the electricity goes off. It's quite fun. It's called Load Shedding. We know exactly what to do. My neighbor, he's one of the black diamonds. He's got his own generator."

Rich black South Africans – known as Black Diamonds – now also lived in the most desirable suburbs. They went for designer labels and were as unconcerned about Yeoville as was Serena. They lived in mansions hidden behind ten-foot walls topped by lines of electric wires – like a jail – many with the added protection of a sentry in a purpose-built security post. The endemic crime – which followed the end of apartheid – was a profitable time for security companies. Derek, Bella's brother, and his family lived in a charming middle-class suburb, no stranger to burglaries, often with violence and murder. Derek's house was one of the very few properties without deterrent electric wires, iron spikes, or embedded glass shards on top of the garden wall.

Derek said of his wife – whom everyone adored – even the thieves, "Josie makes sandwiches and gives them to beggars who come to the front gate. That's our deterrent and it works."

Serena Hickey called to invite Bella to dinner later in the week. "I haven't had a party for a while," she said. "It's not like the old days when everyone entertained. I am not sure if it's because we're all getting older or if things have changed so much. I suppose it's a bit of both."

However, Serena rang Bella the day before to cancel. "I was held up. They cleaned me out. They took the fridge. It was full of food. They removed the stovetop from the granite counter and the oven from the wall. Nobody's heard of them taking a fridge! Of course, the TVs are gone and the computers too. They took art off the walls, not rubbish

46

either. Good pieces only and they took my shoes! New ones! I bought it in Paris when John and I were there a couple of months ago. And my lovely antique linen sheets, I suppose to wrap the art. That's what I'm most upset about. I can't replace them."

"And you, how are you?"

"A bit wobbly," Serena said, managing one of her wonderful throaty laughs.

"How did they get in?" Bella asked.

"They rang at the gate and told Hobson, our manservant. There was a DHL package delivery for Mrs. Serena. He knows not to open the gate unless I've told him someone is expected. I suppose when they gave him my first name... they're smart. He opened the gate. When I arrived home, there were two men standing by a pickup van."

"'Who are you and what are you doing here?' I asked, but I knew instantly that something was wrong. They tied me up with plastic ties. Hobson was already tied up in the sitting room, facing the wall."

"You're lucky they didn't harm you," Bella said.

Bella went to visit Marina a few days later. She'd heard about the robbery at Serena's house.

"She's lucky she wasn't raped. I have a friend who was."

Bella pointed out Serena's house was safe, and the home invasion was a result of human error in that Hobson opened the gate.

"Everyone's moving to Cape Town," Marina said. "It's the last bastion of civilization before we all collapse into the ocean. Tons of friends have moved already. Suki Dugraigh moved after Belan dropped dead. Tina de Waal moved when Leslie dumped her after twenty-five years of marriage. Cape Town is beautiful."

"Not everywhere," Bella corrected. "What about Khayelitcha? There's no way into the city from the airport other than driving past that eye sore. I can't believe it still exists."

Khayelitsha was a vast spread-out slum, easily visible on the road from the airport into the city. There, shacks made from corrugated tin, plastic sheeting, and cardboard were 'home'. Murder, rape, and every sort of crime was endemic. Vicious gangs ruled.

"It's really shocking," Marina agreed. "I can't imagine why the government doesn't do something. It gives tourists a terrible introduction to our country. They should plant trees or a big hedge or something to hide it."

Marina's maid showed up with a perfectly set tea tray – white linen tray cloth with monogrammed initials, silver teapot, milk jug, sugar bowl, and tongs, with solid squares of both brown and white sugar plus a platter of open-faced smoked salmon sandwiches set upon another linen cloth covering the silver platter. Bella noted the excellent quality of the salmon. Marina still lived well.

"Hiding Khayalitcha won't mean it doesn't exist."

Marina knew her friend had moments of showing off an annoying moral authority. "There are poor people in America," Marina huffed.

"It's not the same."

"What about Detroit? I've seen poverty there."

"You've been to Detroit?"

"No, but I've seen Detroit in movies and TV shows. There are lots of homeless people." Marina pointed to the large television set subtly embedded in the paneled wall.

Bella tried to explain, "Our homeless are mostly mentally disturbed or drug addicts. It's true we don't have enough facilities to treat them, even though many don't want to be treated. But it's not a young mother with her baby begging for food like I saw yesterday. Or teenage boys hawking cheap Chinese earphones at a traffic light, so they can buy a loaf of bread."

"There are hungry people in America."

Bella took the last salmon canape, noting Marina ate but one.

Bella wanted to tell Marina how the deep poverty of Africa was different from that of a Detroit slum that in America, poor people were obese as they could only afford to eat fat-making junk food, but she knew she wasn't going to convince her otherwise. South Africans needed to equate their country with others and find them equally wanting, which in different ways, they were. Instead, she changed the country, "Imagine living in Syria?"

Marina said, "Or Saudi Arabia, where women have to wear a black shroud in the heat. I see more and more women dressed like that around here. And underneath it's La Perla and Chanel… but only for the husband, or more likely the lover?"

"You get stoned to death for a lover," Bella quipped.

"Half my friends would be dead," Marina laughed.

"If you renounce Islam, you're killed. Being an apostate is a death sentence."

"Oh, I never knew the meaning of the word Apostate. I'm an apostate. I refuse to set foot in a Catholic Church. Not until they allow divorce, and abortion, and women priests, and allow them to marry and have kids."

Bella was both astounded and impressed by Marina's vehemence and – seeing Bella thought Marina was Jewish – her Catholicism.

"I thought you were Jewish?"

"I am, or I was. I converted when Harry and I got married, but I never felt like I truly belonged."

"Do you know why they stopped allowing priests to marry?" Bella asked.

"No, but I'm sure you're going to tell me," Marina knew her friend.

"Because of greed. Married men have children and wives who inherit their property. In days gone by, priests married and became wealthy estate owners. A single man leaves all he has to the church."

Marina shook her head. "Jesus would be turning in his grave."

Bella replied, "He's not in a grave."

Marina moved on. "Harry and I adored India. We stayed in the most unbelievable hotels. But there's no escaping the poverty there. It's in your face… and the stray dogs."

Marina, like Bella, was a dog lover, but just in case Bella thought she didn't care about people, she added, "And to see little children begging – deformed on purpose – made me weep. Our guide said not to give them money, as it only encourages the adults who send them out begging. He told us about small children who are drugged, and a doctor is paid to amputate a leg or even worse. Begging's an industry in India. I tried to concentrate on the colors of India. Even poor Indian women look divine in their saris."

Bella agreed the colors of India were magical, though they masked the fact that many poor people have no access to toilets and are forced to defecate wherever, or the inequities of the ostensibly illegal caste system, which – though outlawed – still exists and keeps the low-class Dalits – who clean the toilets and such other dirty jobs – in their place.

Bella hopped onto Afghanistan. "Imagine living in a blue burka looking at life through a face grill. Do you know more opium poppy is farmed in Afghanistan than before we went to war? It's the only crop that gives those people a living. When I read about things like this, I get mad."

Marina traveled South. "How about your side of the world? There are some dreadful places there, like the favelas in Brazil. And Mexico with all the drug wars."

It was becoming a sort of 'how to impress' conversation.

"Then there's Kiribati. That's another big-time problem for all of us." Bella grinned, certain Marina wouldn't know of such a place, but Bella was wrong. Marina and Harry once holidayed in Fiji, which was near Kiribati.

Marina told Bella, "When I was there, we went on a boat around a few other islands, and the guide said some of the islands would soon be inundated, and the entire population would have to move. It's global warming and we're all going to suffer for it. I hate seeing photographs of the poor Polar Bears with nowhere to go. Is that the Arctic or the Antarctic? I always get them mixed up."

Bella laughed, "The largest animal living in Antarctica is a flightless midge. If it had wings, it would get blown away."

"That's useful to know," Marina laughed.

Returning to Africa, Bella asked, "Did you know Kinshasa is the world's second-largest, French-speaking city in the world."

"Oh, so that's why you've been learning French? In case you have to move to Kinshasa."

Whilst having this serious conversation served, with dollops of flippancy and smoked salmon canapes, Bella thought how lucky she was to live in The United States of America, California, Beverly Hills, The Portland, with its minor vicissitudes. An officious Portland Homeowners

Board, silly rules and regulations about having to have only beige at the windows, and beige or white umbrellas on the patio. Best of all, she lived close to Jessica and Chloe, and of course, Guy and Ivan.

Ivan kept an apartment in Hollywood, which he used when he was in town. Bella prayed he would end up living in Los Angeles. She didn't approve of the American way of children moving as far away from their parents as possible and then having family dramas on Thanksgiving and Christmas. There were so many scripts using that scenario.

Marina said, "At least South Africa is energetic, and there are men here who still look at us women. You'd be married if you lived here. Look at Serena."

Serena's multiple marriages made the point. "I suppose practice makes perfect," Bella said.

"You could find a husband here if you wanted?"

"I don't want one, and I don't want to live here." Bella was irritated.

Marina defended her country. It was the same as a parent berating a child but defending anyone else who did the same, and Bella felt she'd done wrong to the country of her birth, the birth of her parents, her children, Guy, and most of her friends. It was the country in which she was formed. As it is said, 'Africa is in my blood' and Bella felt this to be true. She might have an American passport, but Africa was cleaved to her soul, something only another African – no matter what color – could understand.

And so, Bella went on to praise. "I must say South Africa is an extraordinary country. It has a vibrancy one doesn't feel in America."

Marina softened.

Bella continued, truthfully, "There's so much creativity. The craft markets are filled with true artistry and not mere tourist tat. I could fill a container with stuff to take back with me and I've seen two plays that were extraordinary."

"Yes, our theater is wonderful."

Bella found more things to praise. "There is no such thing as Mozambique prawns in the whole of America. We have tasteless things they call shrimps, with the heads removed. Americans are squeamish. They'd faint if they had to suck into a head."

Marina said, "That's the best part."

Bella added, "We don't have gem squash. They're my favorite. We have every other kind, but not gem squash."

Marina said, "Next time you come, I'll make them for you."

By the time Bella finished extolling the pleasures of South Africa… its lively restaurants, its spectacular beaches, its wildlife, trees, vast skies, and above all, its friendly people, Marina said, "Why don't you come back here?"

Bella replied, "For one thing, my children live in The United States and my darling Chloe."

Marina cocked her head knowingly and gave one of her Cheshire cat smiles, "And so does Guy."

Bella ignored Marina's comment and went on about her ongoing trip to Tanzania and Kenya. "Jessica and Chloe are meeting me in Arusha. We're staying a couple of nights on a coffee plantation before we go on safari. We might see the migration."

Marina said, "I wish your children came. I would have loved to see them."

Bella said, "Another time, maybe."

Chapter 4: On Safari

"Africa is in your blood."

Bella always felt sad when she said goodbye to her brother and his family. This time the sadness was mitigated by her excitement at meeting Jessica and Chloe in the Tanzanian city of Arush, the gateway destination to Mount Kilimanjaro and Mount Kenya in the northeast and to the Serengeti National Park in the west, which was where they were going on Safari.

In Arusha, they spent the first two nights in a cozy bungalow, part of a tourist lodge, on a working coffee plantation. Meals were served in the main house. Dinner sharp at seven. In the lounge – leading to the veranda – pre-dinner drinks were set up on an antique mahogany table, where a large silver tray showed off sparkling cut glass decanters with name tags, whisky, gin, vodka, and so on. They were the only guests there. It felt like sitting in a private lounge. Jessica sank into the feather-filled pillows of the burgundy brocade-covered sofa in front of the fire after pouring herself a diet coke.

"This is heaven." She picked up one of the coffee table books. "These coffee table books are really about coffee," she joked.

Chloe said, "I'm hungry."

The partial wrap round veranda leading from the lounge overlooked green lawns, magnificent old trees, a rose garden, and a pool beyond.

The waiter beamed, "Welcome to our home." He wore a white twill suit with a red sash and took their order from a small menu.

Bella said, keeping her voice down, "The way our waiter is dressed reminds me of the old days in South Africa. Imagine, when I was married to your father, Jessica, Freddy served dinner every night dressed just like that. He changed from khaki pants in the day, when he tended the garden, to a white suit and red sash just like our waiter here. However, I changed the look and had him wear African patterned tops. Mandela style. He was delighted, and it began a happy new trend."

Jessica said, "I remember."

Coffee was served back in the lounge, where again, they were alone. "I can't have coffee this late," Jessica said. Bella agreed and they ordered chamomile tea. When they returned to their cottage, a real fire burned in the brick-lined fireplace. It was a warm welcome as the night turned chilly.

Jessica's Australian friend suggested a visit to a school

in Arusha, which was mostly funded by Australians. Jessica told Bella, "It will be good for Chloe to see how much she has." Bella didn't disagree.

The next morning was taken up by first a visit to the school. "I know this is going to be upsetting," Bella said.

"Why?" Chloe asked, "It's just a school."

Bella bought loads of colored pencils with her to donate to the school. Chloe bought books.

A neatly dressed woman welcomed them. "I will be showing you around. You will be able to see our classrooms, our dormitories, and even our kitchen. You may be able to join a class," Bella's sighed, resigned.

"Our school is one of the finest in Arusha. It enrolls only one member from a very poor family, the idea being with one person educated, he or she would be able to assist the rest of the family."

When Bella saw the children's worn backpacks in a pile outside a classroom, she felt a physical ache. At Chloe's school, backpacks were new almost every year. A new backpack was a rite of passage moving up a grade.

"These children and their families consider themselves fortunate," the guide said. "The school has such a reputation that we have rich families pretending to be poor, so their children can be accepted here."

When the tour was over, Chloe told her grandmother before Bella had a chance to give a little lecture on gratitude. "I get it, Gran. It's sad we have so much, and they have so little, but we bought them lots of stuff. Mom packed one case with all my old books, and you brought so many pencils and crayons."

After school, they went to another tourist venue to tear the heartstrings. Their first thought was lunch and the setting was glorious. A large, sloping emerald-green lawn with scattered seating led to an open-sided tent, where a delicious lunch was served.

"Now's the hard part," Bella said as they walked back across the lawn to the various stalls where disabled craftspeople demonstrated how they made their fare.

"This is the place to buy gifts to take home," Jessica said.

Bella told her, "You'll have to post them. You know our instructions from the travel agent were to take very few clothes. We were told washing and ironing is done daily at camp and remember when you're hopping around on small planes, only soft luggage. With weight restrictions in mind, they bought earrings and bracelets. After this, it was back to the coffee plantation, where they were picked up by a ranger who drove them onto the extraordinarily decorated camp – a mix of Glitz and Safari – overlooking the Ngorongoro crater.

"Ngorongoro means 'gift of life'," they were informed by their ranger on the first outing.

A couple on their honeymoon – with loads of camera equipment – shared their vehicle. "We're going on to see the Gorillas in Uganda next."

"Ngorongoro is a caldera," the ranger explained. "It was created about three million years ago after an enormous volcano exploded and then collapsed on itself."

Chloe asked the ranger many questions, which delighted Bella, and might have irritated anyone else but a honeymoon couple.

"How big is it?"

"One hundred square miles."

The ranger was both knowledgeable and patient. He told Chloe how elephant and buffalo herds climbed up the slopes of the surrounding thick forest at night, where it was safer from lions and that lions didn't leave the crater and thus, the gene pool was small, which wasn't a good thing, which got them talking about early man. "We are not far from The Olduvai Gorge."

Bella blurted out, "That's where the Leakeys found those fossils." Jessica rolled her eyes. Her mother knew a bit about just about everything.

Bella defended herself. "I've always been interested in where we come from. Sometimes I think of myself going further and further back to being a creature like Mrs. Ples... even further back, way, way back to being a Coelacanth with little arms helping to drag me onto land... or to being an amoeba." Bella impressed the ranger and irritated her daughter.

"Who's Mrs. Ples?" Chloe asked.

"Don't you remember when we once went to The Cradle of Africa?" Jessica asked her daughter. "We saw all those bones?"

"It's also a World Heritage site," Bella added. "Imagine, you've already seen three World Heritage sites."

"How many are there in the whole world?" Chloe was impressed.

That stumped Bella. However, she did later find out that there were one hundred and twenty-five deemed both important and worth protecting for different reasons by UNESCO, which Bella did not know, was the intellectual arm of The United Nations.

Bella explained further, "Those early bones were from people called Australopithecus. They found a similar skull in Ethiopia, and they named her Lucy. She was alive more than three million years ago."

"How did they know she was a girl?'

"Scientists can tell from the size of the bones. Females were smaller."

"Why was she called Lucy?" Chloe asked.

Bella was stumped and Jessica was delighted to fill in. "There's a song by the Beatles called *Lucy in the Sky with Diamonds*. The archaeologists were playing Beatles songs to celebrate their find. I'll play it for you later."

Bella announced, "We, who are alive in this truck, all came from Africa. Every single person in the world comes from Africa. We are all connected."

Bella's mind was far from finding a way to turn her African experiences into a screenplay, though she forced herself to make notes when she got back to camp.

o   A honeymoon couple on safari.

o   Ther new bride realizes she's made a mistake.

o   A tourist goes missing.

o   Was he killed or murdered?

o   A tourist falls for a ranger.

o   Will she stay, or will he leave with her?

o   It's a disaster any which way.

Bella wrote and underlined *NO GOOD* IDEAS!

In the days that followed, Bella kept on saying, "We are all connected," Until Chloe said, "Granny, you've said that a million times!"

"Well, it's true," Bella resolved to be more careful about what she said.

The next camp – built on a hill – overlooked vast pale gold grasslands. It was situated on the Tanzanian side of the Serengeti and was less overwrought in its décor but just as luxurious in a laid-back style.

With an already practiced eye for the nuances of safari décor, Chloe pronounced, "This camp is much more Africa."

"I'm in heaven." Jessica flopped down onto yet another fabulously comfortable king-size bed, dressed in high thread count white linens.

From the private patio outside their room, Chloe shrieked, "Come quickly. There's a giraffe."

Over four nights, they saw elephants, huge buffalo herds, and many more giraffes on game drives or whilst they relaxed on either their patio or the stone walled lounge and bar overlooking the Serengeti.

Darlene Coats, an American tourist from Miami,

discovered Patty Heller, her best friend, was at school with Bella. "Small world," she said, delighted to find a mutual connection.

"The Serengeti is very different to the bushveld in South Africa."

"How?" Darlene Coats from Miami asked.

"South Africa's wild animals have to contend with trees, shrubs and thorny acacia bushes. There aren't huge herds of animals and these great sweeps of grasslands like here on Serengeti." Bella paused, "Every time I say the word, 'Serengeti', I get a thrill."

"Me too," Darlene Coats agreed.

"We're all connected," Bella said.

Chloe, playing Mancala – an ancient game played in a wooden palette with grooves for stones – with the ranger looked up, "Granny, you keep saying that."

"Well, it's true," Bella replied.

A small plane was waiting for them on the runway to take them to the next camp. This was tented.

Bella declared, "Oh my God, that's the smallest one yet!"

The four-seater plane was one of many tiny planes – bush taxis – ferrying tourists to and fro. This time they were off to a tented camp on The Serengeti, from where they hoped to see The Migration. Almost a million wildebeest, plus other animals like zebra, join up to move from one side of the Serengeti to another in the search for better grazing. This requires crossing a boundary river, which can be a trickle or a torrent, depending on where the animals choose to cross.

Thousands of calves are born on the way. They are easy pickings for following predators. For thousands of newly born calves – who can walk a day after being born – the migration is a rite of passage where life can so easily be lost.

When they got to their camp, the charming young lady, with a posh English accent – showed them to their accommodation. To call it a tent did not describe a barn-sized space; big enough to enclose a line of three single beds, made up with clouds of bright white puffed duvets and pillows. There was a free-standing copper bathtub, an open shower, two sinks and a separate toilet at one end of the tent. At the other end, a sitting area done up in immaculate safari style was the perfect place to sit at the desk and write postcards or read from Safari-themed books on the coffee table. A strategically built viewing deck – leading from one side of the tent – overlooked a shallow pool where a wounded male hippo, showing bloody pink gashes on his body, was resting.

In her clipped English, the young manageress informed them of camp rules. "No walking alone at night, not even if you think it's safe. This camp is not fenced." She also announced, "You're in luck. The migration has begun."

The next morning, their ranger was waiting for them, ready to set off on the drive to The Grumeti River, where the animals would cross. In the distance, as far as anyone could see, long lines of wildebeest marched determinedly through endless golden grasses, their impetus towards the river embedded in their DNA. "There must be thousands," Bella declared.

Their ranger Lebo, corrected, "Hundreds of thousands."

Nearing the river, the herds became denser. Calves gamboled close to their mothers as they made their way towards their first migration. For some, it would be their last.

The Grumeti – at the juncture where they hoped to see The Migration – consisted of a series of pools and channels. By the time they arrived at the viewing point, five vehicles were already parked, claiming what they hoped would be the best viewing rights.

On rocks on the far bank of the Grumeti – which at this juncture was not running large – two gigantic crocodiles basked. They were so well fed their girths were almost as wide as their length. In the shallows – legs up in rigor mortis

– were two swollen, wildebeest carcasses. The animals had tried their luck the previous day. Every now and again, one or two vultures, from hundreds perched on the far bank, flapped down to feast. Certain vulture species were adept at puncturing tough hide; others had to wait for the hide to be breached before they could eat. Two unconcerned hippos lay sleeping at the water edge. They had nothing to fear.

The air was thick with dread as the herds began to mass behind a clump of bushes adjacent to the riverbank. Dust clouds rose as they pawed the dry earth with fear-filled anticipation.

Once Lebo negotiated their vehicle into a better position, Jessica hoisted herself onto the roof for a better view.

"Come up here, Mom," Jessica whispered.

"I don't think I can," Bella said.

"Yes, you can," Jessica encouraged.

With Jessica pulling and Lebo pushing, Bella made it. Chloe ignored the tension and read from her kindle.

Everyone was warned to keep silent as the herds moved forward, then startled by the slightest disturbance, moved back.

Finally, the herd surged.

A Chinese tourist, dressed in bright pink and blue –

despite the directive to wear dun color – let out a screech, and the herd immediately retreated.

Bella glared disapprovingly.

"She doesn't understand glaring," Jessica laughed,

It was another hour – in absolute silence – before the wildebeest braved another approach.

This time there was no hesitation, and the tightly packed herd moved forward in unison. One after another, they jumped and tumbled from the high riverbank into the water. The dry red earth of the far side riverbank became slippery. Animals struggled desperately to hoist themselves out of the water as the mud became slime. When successful – as if granted a stay of execution – the animals danced madly, momentarily free from fear.

Bella and Jessica fixed on one young animal as he failed to pull himself up the bank. Repeatedly he heaved his body... almost... almost... but he slipped back into the shallow muddy water. Bella thought his leg must be sprained or worse, broken.

"Please, God, help him." Bella and Jessica willed the animal to succeed. Chloe stopped watching. She didn't want to see how the animal hobbled to the middle of the river and turned to face both death and the riverbank from where – moments before and filled with hope – he'd jumped. What if the wildebeest had jumped a moment later, or sooner, or from one foot or maybe as little as one inch down from where he chose to leap? No amount of Bella's pleading to a Higher Power could change this animal's life trajectory, and Bella felt the essence of powerlessness in the face of life's frequently disturbing directions. The only thing she could do was pray and hope to find strength in her idea of God, which was to search. "God is a search!" Bella believed, and at moments like this, she searched and came up with no answers other than life did what it did, and she was part of life, as was everything else.

Bella would never get the picture of the plaintive wildebeest out of her head. *Why, oh why did her God condone such suffering? Why did creatures have to eat others in order to live? Why must the spider entrap the fly? Why must the lion bring down the Impala? Why? Why was there sickness and cruelty? What was the reason for suffering? Why are we born and why do we die?*

Bella was well aware great minds – throughout the ages – addressed the very same questions. Bella found it oddly comforting that luminaries such as Einstein, Darwin, Michelangelo, Shakespeare, Marie Curie, and Queen Elizabeth died. Death was part of living. Perhaps death merely altered the position of atoms?

Chapter 5: Valentine's Day

"The color of holidays punctuates the year."

After Bella got back to Los Angeles, she read through the jumble of notes she'd made when she was in Africa. Her handwriting was so bad that even she couldn't work out what she'd written, and she thanked her lucky stars she could easily type on the computer.

She laid out some ideas and themes for a screenplay, but life in Los Angeles intruded; what went on in the land of her birth faded as life in Los Angeles showered her with its easy-going abundance.

As she walked around the large drug store, where she'd come to buy a tonic for the persistent cough she caught on the plane back to Los Angeles, she could not help noticing all the paraphernalia for Valentine's Day. The year was punctuated by holidays, and Bella acknowledged them by at least wearing their festive colors. After the red and pink of Valentine's Day came St Patrick's Day. Bella kept a bright, emerald-green scarf, despite having no Irish in her blood. Bella liked occasions and honored them accordingly. Easter came next and the drug store would be inundated with chocolate eggs and pastel decorations, mostly of bunnies. Bella had an embroidered yellow Indian kaftan for Easter. It was a bit tight for her now, but she kept it anyway. July 4th, Independence Day, was next. Bella had no problem dressing in red, white and blue. Then came Halloween, which was the children's favorite holiday as they could dress up and indulge in candy. Bella didn't like any of the artifacts connected with Halloween; revolting masks, fake blood and gore, and the hideous combination of black and orange. For her first Halloween in America, she bought a skeleton romper from the drug store, which had served her well every year since she bought it. It was super comfortable, with one tie at the neck.

The holiday Bella liked best was Christmas, even though she was Jewish. Her father's second wife always hosted a fun Christmas lunch. Bella carried on the tradition as her father and his wife got older, and she carried on – even more so – when she lived in Los Angeles. Christmas crackers were essential, and old-fashioned Christmas pudding studded with silver coins, which weren't easy to find in Los Angeles. Crackers were not an American thing. Bella kept decorations – collected over the years since she came to live in Los Angeles – in her storage room at The Portland.

As for New Year's Eve, with its tinsel sparkle, Bella never liked the forced gaiety. She also had nasty memories of Guy both disappearing or kissing someone else as the bell chimed in the New Year.

Nicole came out to accompany Bella as she gave Charlie his last walk of the day. "It's soon Valentine's Day and I don't have anyone," she complained.

Bella told her, "When I grew up, Valentine's Day was the day you could send a boy you fancied an anonymous card, professing affection. I think I might have sent a card when I was in primary school."

Nicole said, "I haven't had a romantic Valentine's Day like ever. I don't think men my age send flowers anymore. They don't know how to be romantic."

"Don't worry," Bella said. "I've never had a delivery of red roses or any other more lasting demonstrations of adoration on Valentine's Day. Any man I happened to be involved with on February 14 was obviously not romantic. I suppose I'm not either."

Greta shared Bella's low opinion of the day for similar reasons.

On the other hand, Shelly declared, as she and Bella walked down the passage to their respective condos, "I love Valentine's Day."

"That's because you make sure you have a date on February 14," Bella teased, and it was true. Whenever a major day loomed, there was Shelly scrounging around for a date on Match.com or JDate or whatever was her currently favored dating site. True love didn't come into it.

Bella thought Valentine's Day was now made too all-encompassing. In the current climate of nobody feeling left out, Chloe had to make a Valentine for every single member of her class.

When Bella picked Chloe up from school the day before Valentine's Day, Chloe told her grandmother, "I'm giving everyone love potions. But I have a secret. Promise you won't tell anyone." Chloe didn't wait for Bella's promise and gleefully announced, "I'm going to put pepper in the love potion for Sebastian and Phoenix."

It was during the run up to Valentine's Day that Bella toyed with the idea of having a party for her single friends. No couples. One day she thought she should. The next day she imagined all the effort required. Was she in the mood, or not? Bella wasn't accustomed to being so indecisive, and she waited four days before inviting everyone.

Ivan said he'd come and asked if he could bring Farrel Bootch. This surprised Bella until he added, "We're going on to another party at The Chateaux, but that'll be much later."

Chateaux Marmont was affectionately known as The

Chateaux by those well-known enough to regularly frequent its comfortable lounge, bar and terrace. Celebrities and stars lodged there, deals were made there and – mentioned every time the hotel was written about in the press – John Balushi died there of a drug overdose.

Bella liked Farrel. Though he was brought up in extreme wealth, there was something about him that made Bella think of Oliver Twist asking for more. She could see why Digby hoped Ivan's naturally buoyant spirit would rub off on Farrel. But nothing would ever turn Farrel into the kind of debonair individual Digby wanted as his son and heir. The occasional snort of cocaine sometimes helped Farrel lose his natural diffidence, as did a couple of tots of scotch, but he didn't like the feeling, and neither did Ivan, who fortunately didn't like the effects of drugs or alcohol. This was one of the reasons Digby trusted Ivan with both his son and his money.

Bella invited Violet, who said she would come if she wasn't working. Jessica was bringing Chloe, of course, and Chloe asked if she could bring her friend, Tiara. Tiara's mother was single, and the poorly named child had no father as far as anyone knew, though it was rumored the sperm donor was a famous and very married film director. Chloe was more than excited to be wearing her new red denim skirt.

Bella asked guests to wear one thing, either red or pink.

Shelly wasn't enthusiastic about her date. "I don't think he's my type," she informed Bella. But he was male, and that was what counted for Shelly.

Bella told her, "If it doesn't work out, come over. It will be fun. But don't even think of arriving with him."

"Don't worry, I won't, but I don't know why you want to have a party. It's so much work, and just for..." Shelly realized she should have kept her mouth shut, but Bella didn't get upset, instead she smiled. "I like preparing. That's the fun part. It's sort of like what Robert Louis Stevenson wrote: *"It's better to travel hopefully than to arrive."*

Bella could see Shelly didn't get what she meant.

"You know Robert Louis Stevenson, the one who wrote Treasure Island and Dr. Jekyll and Mr. Hyde. He was a sickly child and spent days in bed dreaming about going places. He understood the pleasure was often in the dreaming and not the realization of the dream, which could disappoint, like getting married."

"And so, what's that got to do with your party?" Shelly asked.

"I like planning what to serve, making things look festive."

Shelly had never been to a party since she moved into The Portland. Her idea of entertaining was taking guests to a restaurant.

Bella further explained, "Being the hostess is a bit like being a frantic Monarch butterfly trying to find a milkweed plant on which to lay its eggs. And because of urban development and Monsanto's Roundup weed killer, there's hardly any milkweed left."

"What's milkweed got to do with your party?"

"A hostess can't relax." Bella realized her comparison was not sound, but she'd been reading about the poor Monarch butterflies in the morning newspaper.

"Well, you're not serving milkwced, whatever that is, are you?" Shelly shrugged.

Greta was delighted about the party, and so was Bella's young neighbor Nicole who sighed, "I wish I had a nice date to bring."

"If you had one, you couldn't come. It's only for singles.

"I wish I had a boyfriend, like a soul mate."

"You will, one day," Bella assured her, "You could have more than one."

"Do you really think so?" Nicole looked forlorn.

"Of course, I do."

When Nicole informed Bella the day before Valentine, her best friend Abby had been dumped by her longtime boyfriend. Bella offered, "Bring her too. The more, the merrier."

Bella listened to the sad story of Abby's dumping.

"Abby waited for him for eight months to make up his mind, and then he did."

Bella didn't bother to comment.

Bella enthusiastically threw herself into planning the party. Off she went to Costco to find pink and red edibles: smoked salmon, shrimps, pink lemonade, pretzels covered in red and white chocolate, and strawberries. She would make her red velvet cake. Everyone thought she made it from scratch, and she never told anyone she made the cake from a mix not available at normal supermarkets.

Rather than red roses, Bella bought puffy pink hydrangeas from the downtown flower market. She arranged a magnificent display in an antique tureen she'd once bought – for very little – on eBay. Others, she massed in front of the fireplace. With so many people plus clement weather, it would be too warm for a fire. Bella loved her gas fire. It made the room inviting, and in Winter, it did give quite a bit of warmth, mostly enough for Bella without resorting to air-conditioning, which Bella didn't like in her apartment.

Closing the windows and doors made her feel boxed in.

At Bristol Farm – the morning before Valentine's Day – Bella bumped into her old friend Hankey Sussman and invited him to the party. She'd lost contact with Hankey; his phone number had been disconnected and emails to him were returned. Bella occasionally wondered what happened to him.

Bella first met Hankey (Herbert was his given name, but everyone called him Hankey) years ago at a wedding in San Diego. Both being without partners, they were seated with older singles at a table where nobody knew each other: a couple of widows, single relatives, the bridegroom's tennis coach and the bride's mother's Ukrainian facialist.

Bella's heart sank when she first sat down at the table for ten, and then Hankey arrived and sat next to her, and it was one of those rare cases of instant friendship.

For starters, Hankey was familiar with South African politics. He told Bella, "I was a reporter and covered the first multiracial election in South Africa when Mandela was elected."

Then they found out they both lived in Beverly Hills. Hankey lived almost within walking distance of The Portland, on the top floor of a charming old duplex filled with artifacts and memorabilia from his travels.

Bella told Hankey, "I am thrilled you live so near to me. It's not that I am a snob and want friends who live in Beverly Hills, but I am tired of finding people I like who live in places like Altadena or even Malibu because, with the best intentions, we never get to see each other. I want friends who are geographically desirable."

Hankey's biggest talent was a genuine interest in people. He had a prodigious memory and remembered everyone he'd ever met and everything he was ever told. He knew a lot of people and knew about a lot of things. Hankey and Bella never ran out of conversation.

Hankey had his quirks and was more than a little phobic when it came to dirt. He was fastidious in his dress, his cashmere sweaters never had balls, and his shoes looked new, even if they weren't. An inadvertent stain acquired whilst wearing something was an abomination and sent him into a tizzy. With no hint of shame, Hankey also claimed celibacy. "I don't like sex. It's…" he shuddered. "All that exchange of bodily fluids!"

Bella found this rather strange, seeing as Hanky maintained he lived on the fortune he'd once made publishing trashy romance novels.

Hankey was a Birder, which he explained was the reason he traveled to exotic places. "I know it's weird, but seeing a new bird species for the first time in its natural habitat is sort of like having an orgasm."

However, after knowing Hankey for a while, Bella worked out he must work for the CIA or some other clandestine outfit, as his travels took him to countries where conflict was either imminent or ongoing, like Afghanistan and Ruanda. He'd been in Argentina and Brazil during troubled times and his knowledge of South Africa came from the violent period prior to the fall of apartheid.

Hanky once arrived at Bella for dinner bearing a gift, a small blue burka from Afghanistan.

"The Afghani women must be tiny," Bella observed as the garment fitted Chloe – who must have been four or five – far better than it did Bella or Jessica. Hankey maintained he'd gone to Afghanistan to photograph rare birds, at which time Bella blurted out what she suspected, "I know what you really do. You work for the CIA."

"What gives you that idea?" Hankey laughed so loudly that Bella thought it must be true

"Who travels to Afghanistan for pleasure?"

"You don't understand the lure of birds," Hankey replied. "CIA? That's plain silly!" he insisted as Bella continued to tease him about his undercover associations. It was shortly afterward that Hankey vanished.

When Bella saw him at Bristol Farms, he told her, "I've given up traveling. I must take care of my mother. She has dementia."

By the time Hankey accepted Bella's invitation for Valentine's Day, he'd gotten out of Bella what mixed feelings she had when Guy got involved with Irina after his divorce from Wife Number Two, what Jessica was up to, and that Ivan was working with Farrel Bootch. Bella was not one bit surprised when Hankey told her he attended the same college as Digby Bootch, Farrel's billionaire father, or that he knew Digby's second wife, a couple of his mistresses, and was acquainted with other members of the Bootch family.

"You haven't changed a bit," Bella told Hankey. "Is there anyone or anything you don't know something about?"

"I pay attention," Hankey replied with a captivating, serpent smile. Remember, I've been around."

"In some strange places," Bella said.

On Valentine's Day – as she'd done for some years – Bella called Guy. He either wasn't at home or didn't pick up the phone and so she left a message. "I am calling to wish you Happy Valentine's Day," she paused and added, "I love you." It was a well-worn love, one that had survived – in its unique way – through years of separation, further marriages and divorces. It was a love born of familiarity and trust. It was the truest love she had ever known, and it was the kind of love that needed them to be separate. Almost as soon as Bella put down the phone, Guy called to wish her the same. He'd not even had time to listen to her message, and that pleased her. Guy never acknowledged the day when they were young and dating, let alone when they married.

Bella's therapist, the astute Dr. Edna Feather, never quite understood how Bella and Guy were bonded together. She told Bella, "Guy needs nothing material from you. He simply wants you in his life. And you need him in your life, though it's not merely financial. It's karmic."

Shelly – when she popped in later in the day – suggested, "Perhaps Guy called you back because of his new girlfriend?"

"Why would that have anything to do with his call?"

Shelly thought for a minute and giggled, "Maybe she made him all mushy," Shelly stopped. "And that made him think of you."

Bella shook her head. Shelly meant well, but she could be idiotic.

At the front desk of The Portland, bowls of red roses

arrived all day. Keisha at the reception desk told Bella, "My husband brought me pink roses. I wonder what pink means?" Keisha answered her own question. "I think pink is less expensive."

Keisha and Bella often chatted about their respective families, especially since they found a common cause in grief when their mothers died within a few weeks of each other. "I never realized I'd miss her so much," Bella said, and every year, as the anniversary of their mother's death came around, they were united in their mourning.

Keisha had four sons. Two were married and two were single. She did not like her daughters-in-law. One was particularly difficult, but Keisha told Bella, "Whatever she says, no matter how much I disagree with her, I keep quiet."

Keisha told Bella how her late mother had taught her the mantra of WAIT (Why Am I Talking?) as a way of overcoming the fault lines of words, especially when it came to families.

"I wish I could tell your mother how much that mantra has helped me," Bella told Keisha.

"You can," Keisha said. "She is here. I feel her around."

"I sometimes feel my mother here, too. It's funny. No matter how old you are, you miss your mother."

Later, Bella bumped into Shelly as they were both collecting their mail. Shelly sighed,

"Do you know one hundred and fifty million Valentine cards are exchanged today, and I haven't received one."

"Me neither," Bella said. "But I didn't send any either, what about you?"

Shelly replied, "I sent it to my kids. I sent one to both my exes, though I am not sure why."

"Well, once you've loved someone, you always do," Bella replied.

"No, I don't love either of them. Not like you love your Guy."

"I didn't send him one and he didn't send me one. I doubt he's ever going to send anyone a card for Valentine's Day. He pretends he doesn't like special occasions, even birthdays, but God forbid anyone forgets his."

Bella didn't mention she'd called Guy or that he'd called her back. A call wasn't the same as a bowl of flowers. She didn't want to admit it, but it would have been nice for one of the many bowls of red roses delivered to The Portland to have been for her, and out of the blue, she felt teary.

In the elevator, Bella rode with Edith Binder, who was carrying one of the flower deliveries.

"From an old friend," she said before Bella made any comment. "He never forgets."

Previously Bella did toy with the idea of inviting Edith to her party, seeing she was single but decided against it. Now, she spontaneously asked, "If you're not busy, pop over at four, I'm having a small Valentine's Day soiree, only for singles."

Edith gazed into the heavens of the elevator, "Oh, thanks, Bella, but I'm going to The Peninsula for dinner."

Bella felt flat, but her mood lifted once she began organizing the party. She dressed the dining table with yards of dusty pink damask she bought years ago at a yard sale with the idea of making pillows. She arranged the repast on antique tin trays she once collected and covered the food with tin foil and kitchen towels, which she would whisk off like a magician once guests began to arrive. She expected around twelve if nobody let her down.

Bella couldn't make up her mind what to wear, black pants and a red silk tunic from Govinda's, a treasure trove store adjacent to the Hari Krishna temple in Culver City, or a patterned kaftan. She decided on the kaftan. It was more comfortable and though not solid red, it was red enough.

Bella made the usual attempt to blow her hair and gave up as she always did before it was quite dry. She took care with her make-up, which she also always did, not that anyone ever noticed, for she had the kind of skin that managed to slough off whatever she applied within the shortest time.

Makeup and hair complete, Bella mixed a glass of orange juice and powdered greens and sat down on her favorite armchair to relax for a few minutes before her guests began to arrive. There was a time she'd have opened a bottle of champagne. Now, she was over twenty years sober and her life much better for it, so nonalcoholic had to suffice.

Nicole and her friend Abby arrived first. Neither wore anything red nor pink. "I'm sorry I forgot," was Nicole's lame excuse when admonished by Bella.

Abby rightly claimed, "Nicole didn't tell me."

Bella gave Nicole and Abby each a length of red silk ribbon to tie around their necks.

Jessica arrived wearing red pants and a flounced red blouse. Red was Jessica's favorite color, so finding something to wear wasn't difficult. Chloe looked adorable in her new red denim skirt, as did her friend Tiara in red shorts.

Greta wore all black accented by red patent high heels. "I didn't even think I had anything red in my wardrobe, and then I remembered these shoes. I've never worn them. I don't know what I thought when I bought them." She added, "I am wearing red lipstick."

"You always wear red lipstick," Bella replied.

Bella expected Hankey to wear red cashmere socks and he did. Ivan wore what he claimed were red jeans, but they were tan.

Farrel wore a marvelous pair of red suede Tod's moccasins.

Bella said, "I want those shoes."

The mood was festive, and everyone complimented Bella on the food: smoked salmon, baked salmon, salmon eggs, beet salad, red bean salad, various pink dips for raw vegetables, raspberries, and strawberries. Bella's red velvet cake was eaten with gusto. Farrel had three slices and Bella offered to make one for his birthday. He blushed and seemed delighted but said, "I probably won't be in LA that time of the year. My birthday is two days after New Year. We're usually away."

"Snow or beach?" Bella asked.

"Probably beach," Farrel replied. "I hate the snow, though father likes it."

Not that Bella was party to all conversations, but she did not hear one word about anyone being unhappy about not having a date or partner on Valentine's Day. There was no mention of loneliness, feeling left out, or sad. Even dumped Abby had a good time and declared, "I am like really cool my boyfriend left. I'm totally chill about it now."

Shelly arrived as the party was winding down. "I should have come here," she said, sinking into the sofa.

"You didn't have a good time?" Greta was unable to prevent a smirk.

"Let me count the ways... that's from a poem by Elizabeth Barrett Browning." Shelly felt triumphant with what she knew was a refined quote.

"The restaurant was packed with couples forcing themselves to act as if they were having a good time. The service was bad, and the food was bad. My date drank too much. Actually, so did I. It was the only thing to do, and I am regretting it already," Shelly paused and asked Bella for some aspirin.

"I should've left when he explained why he wished his ex-girlfriend would move from Atlanta to marry him."

"You should have come here," Greta, Nicole and Abby said almost in unison.

"Next year, you will," Bella said, contemplating an annual event.

Two days after the party, Bella received a delivery. It was from Farrel, a pair of red suede women's Tods. The note read, "I had a lovely time. Thank you for including me."

Bella caressed the supple suede, then slipped on the shoes, which were so beautiful she almost didn't want to ever wear them, and the first day she did, she bumped into her neighbor Edith Binder in the elevator.

Edith remarked, "Tod's?" Bella nodded.

"I've never seen them in such a great shade of red."

"They were a Valentine's Day gift." Bella gave a discrete smile.

Chapter 6: A Piece of Meat

"It's not easy to be humane."

When Bella signed up for The Conference on Animal Rights, her eyes were wide open to the thoughtless abuse humans inflicted on animals, especially those eaten, worn, or used for experiments and entertainment.

Greta agreed when Bella said, "This is something worthy to write about."

"But you can't be heavy-handed," Greta warned.

"I know," Bella agreed, having forced herself to watch videos of animals suffering so that not eating meat, not drinking milk, and not wearing leather would be easier.

Greta said, "You could make a children's book. How many writers can paint and draw like you? You could make one about not eating meat. About the poor cows and chickens."

"I suppose that's something I could do. I know the drill of children's movies as I watch so many with Chloe when she sleeps over. There's always a parent who has recently died, a move away from home, horrible children in the new place who tease, an animal who provides succor and is then taken away, sold, lost, or stolen by the horrible people. Usually, the bereaved parent finds the perfect partner. It's the beginning of the Cinderella complex."

Bella always felt she should do more like those remarkable humans lauded in the back of The Christian Science Monitor, a magazine to which she subscribed. The section was titled *MAKING A DIFFERENCE* and was about those who did a myriad of helpful things, from cleaning up the filthy Ganges in India to risking their lives to nurse Ebola patients. However, Bella knew she didn't have it in her to clean sewage or do the truly challenging things deserving acclaim in the magazine. There was something ironic in that Bella was invited to a barbeque to watch the finals of a football match at Digby Bootch's home on the day she was to attend the Conference on Animal Rights. Fortunately, she could fit in both events. She thought as she drove to Digby's Beverly Hills home after leaving the Animal Rights Conference. She'd never been invited to Digby's house before and was interested to see how he lived when he was in town, which wasn't that often, seeing as Digby spent most of his time in either New York or London.

Bella thought Digby's abode would not be ostentatious and she was correct. The house was naturally in the best part of Beverly Hills, that is, 'above Sunset'. Houses below Sunset were priced less. Fanny Moskowitz, a fellow resident at The Portland, alerted Bella to this subtlety when she said proudly, "We used to live on Palm, on the eight hundred blocks." This wasn't the best address, but it beat slumming it on the fourth block or, how demeaning, the second block before Palm melded into the famous shopping streets of Beverly Hills.

Ivan told Bella, "It's not a huge house, but it's perfect. You know Digby is not showy."

This was true, Bella could see as she parked outside and ventured up the path, framed by manicured boxwood hedges and blooming double white begonias, to the front door, which was opened as she approached by a manservant,

Bella was partly correct in her expectations of beige and off-white furnishings, down-filled sofa pillows, large bowls of white orchids – which Greta never stopped telling her should be called by their correct name Phalaenopsis – in antique blue and white bowls. She didn't expect Digby would have such contemporary art pieces quite shocking: a life-size sculpture of a woman with holes where her heart and womb should have been, or an enormous sculpture of a tennis ball with eyes embedded, plus startling paintings demonstrating that, whilst Digby was old school in the way he'd made his money in finance and real estate, in his immaculate manners, but his art showed a wildly adventurous taste.

As a host gift, Bella bought something from the Animal Rights conference; a black t-shirt against the crime of elephant poaching. She also bought t-shirts for Farrel and Ivan and one for Chloe. She chose carefully, not wanting to shame Digby for his carnism. The message on the front of everyone's t-shirts said, *Save the Elephants.* Just about everyone – other than the subsistence farmers whose crops were being flattened and eaten by elephants – could agree upon that.

Carnism. This was the word Bella learned at the conference. Carnism was the ideology or belief system conditioning people to eat certain animals. They don't see it as a choice and don't wonder why they eat cows, pigs, and chickens and yet cherish dogs and cats.

Bella also carried a bag of literature from the conference. She brought the blue bag with a picture of a cartoon pig with a speech bubble saying, "Don't eat me!" into Digby's house, thinking she may have an opportunity to awaken someone to the horrors of carnism, but only if the perfect moment presented itself. She learned at the conference that shaming people who ate meat was counterproductive. As one workshop leader pointed out, "When you ask people if they love animals, 98% say they do. That's the love that needs to be brought out."

Farrel adored his t-shirt. "I'm going to put it on right now."

Ivan didn't follow suit, and Bella didn't expect him to change from his soft, lime green linen shirt. Ivan would no more wear the t-shirt than wear anything not exquisitely designed, which was one more reason Digby so liked him and his association with his son, Farrel. When Bella arrived, Digby was in his study, apparently on an important call.

"You're in great shape," Bella observed as Farrel took off his well-worn grey t-shirt with the words, 'Beat It'.

"Thanks to your boy, who makes him work out with him." Digby appeared out of nowhere, it seemed, and Bella barely recognized him. He'd shaved his balding head, grown a short beard, and looked rather like a slightly chubby Mahatma Gandhi.

"And what can I get for you, Madam Bella?" Digby asked, almost snapping his fingers to summon the waiter. Digby added before Bella made her choice, "I've got vegetarian dishes for you, so no panic."

As if he knew Bella would ask him when he'd fund making *The Lions of Amarula*, Digby managed to tell Bella soon after she arrived. "Your story is clever, thoughtful and truly fascinating, but the boys (that's what Digby called his son Farrel and Bella's son Ivan) have a hit on their hands with *Juke Box Highway,* and whilst there is this buzz, I think they should do *Juke Box, The Sequel,* before *Lions of Amarula.* I assure you, my dear girl, one day, and very soon, the boys will make your movie."

"I'm not a girl," Bella replied, thoroughly irritated. But Digby was not the kind of man to take offense. He was formal and exceptionally polite, a result of his Swiss upbringing.

"I use that term only as one of endearment, not to diminish you in any way. How about 'my dear friend', is that better, for that is what you are, and of course, your wonderful boy? Had your brilliant son Ivan not taken my profligate Farrel in tow? I don't know what might have happened to him. And before you berate me, my dear, I know I am at fault. I have not been the best father. I can admit that to you as a dear friend."

Bella softened. She touched Digby on his hand, a hand with elegant long fingers tipped by manicured nails. She noted his fine, cream silk shirt with double cuffs held together by simple gold knots. "I'm fine being called a dear friend," she said.

Bella might have been mildly shocked to see Digby's art and his new shaved head, but when Digby asked, "Is your ex-husband usually a late arrival?" Bella almost fainted.

That's not quite true, but that's how she described her feelings to Greta the following day. Apparently, Ivan told Digby Bella would be fine with Guy and Irina at the barbeque and told Digby he'd warn her they were coming. Bella was getting used to the two of them at family events, but she would have liked a heads-up so she could more calmly either rise above her feelings or bury them.

"I forgot, mom," Ivan said, not looking one bit remorseful. "I've been so busy."

Bella wondered whether Ivan was too scared to tell her they were coming or had truly forgotten, but whatever, she had a bit of time to compose herself before Guy and Irina arrived. And by the time they did, she was relaxed or as relaxed as she ever was in the company of Guy.

"I might have been shocked to find out Guy and Irina were invited," she told Greta, "But nothing was as shocking as watching the enormous steaks everyone ate once we finally sat down."

"I'm not a vegetarian, but I never eat steak," Greta's disdain for red meat could be heard over the phone. "What else did Digby serve?"

"Chicken. But I learned at the conference that chickens have cognitive abilities more advanced than those of cats, dogs and even some primates. They have cultural knowledge that they pass on from generation to generation."

"They do?" Greta knew if Bella said so, it was probably true.

"In one experiment, they fed chickens blue and yellow corn kernels. The blue made them sick. So, when the next generation grew up, the mothers kept their chicks away from the blue kernels, even though they were now harmless. That's culture, the ability to learn and pass on what you've learned."

"It's not exactly Shakespeare," Greta teased.

Bella carried on, "When they're not factory farmed, chickens have social hierarchies. You know the term pecking order? Chickens have social dynamics, at least when they're allowed to be raised naturally. There's the head honcho rooster…"

"Like Guy?" Greta teased.

"Hens have their ranking also. And the rank is established early in the chick's life."

"Obviously, you're the head hen." Greta continued teasing.

"Obviously," Bella confirmed.

At the barbeque, Bella pointed out that chickens were at least as smart as dogs to a sharply bearded young Italian actor ironically named Berdi, who was seated next to her at the long table set up on the patio.

"But Madam Bella." Berdi had taken the lead in calling her so from Digby. "Hens don't come when they are called."

"That's because they're smart," Bella whipped back and went on to explain that chickens over the millennia were not taught by man to respond to their commands like dogs.

As if to demonstrate, Digby's dog appeared.

"Come here, Ophelia. I need to put on your sunscreen." Digby's face expanded with affection as the dog bounded up to him. "I'm allergic to dogs," Digby explained, "But Ophelia's got no hair to be allergic to," he laughed. "She's my third Ophelia."

Ophelia was an acquired taste. She was uniquely ugly, with a muddy brown spotty body and tufts of red hair on top of her head and at the end of her tail.

"She's a Peruvian Inca Orchid," Digby announced before Bella could ask what she was. "Isn't she a beauty?" he said without a trace of sarcasm. "And she's so sweet." Ophelia demonstrated this by standing quietly whilst Digby sprayed her with suntan prevention, all the while soothing, "That's my beautiful girl."

With the appearance of outlandish Ophelia, the subject

inevitably turned to dogs.

Svetlana, a gorgeous Russian model, said, "I luff my dog. I weesh I could keep him. But I had to geef him to my neighbor."

"Why?" Bella asked.

"Travel!" Svetlana's reply implied so much more.

Bella thought of saying something, but Ziff – a member of a well-known band Bella hadn't heard of – did it for her. "That's why I don't have a dog."

Ziff then launched into a sad tale of his first dog.

Bella thought dog conversation was only marginally more interesting than recounting dreams and tried to switch the conversation to politics. When that failed, she was forced back to the canines.

"It started with wolves."

Ivan knew his mother was about to explain something most people did not know. It seemed to him she knew something about everything, and it annoyed him intensely. He wished she would keep quiet. But then he looked at his father at the end of the table, kanoodling with Irina and decided to listen to his mother was better than watching his father.

"Some wolves were naturally less afraid of humans, and

they began to scavenge after humans had eaten; a bone gets thrown, and a brave wolf grabs it and then one wolf gets so used to grabbing bits of food it doesn't mind eating in front of the human. It's called flight distance. That is the distance an animal will allow humans near before running away."

"It's like some abandoned wolf pups started it all," Ivan hoped his mother would not tell Farrel not to use the word like. She did it all the time, to everyone.

"Do you think you are the Like Word Police," Ivan complained.

Guy did not even glance Bella's way. He could not take his eyes off his Irina, which Bella noticed, even as she spouted on about dogs and how – once domestication and selection for certain traits – we now have dogs that hunt, herd, and sit on laps, dogs with legs so short they are crippled, dogs with so much loose skin. They are heaven for skin parasites, dogs with eyes almost popping out, and dogs with faces so squashed flat they can barely breathe.

During the luncheon, Bella did learn more about the relationship between Digby and Farrel, and she was pleased, for she wanted to know more about them, seeing as Ivan's life – at least for the moment – seemed so inexorably bound with theirs.

"Farrel had everything a son could wish for," Digby told

Bella. "I grew up dirt poor. My father often didn't have money for rent. It was survival."

Bella knew about Digby's early life. She'd read about his career, first a bouncer in a club, then a club owner, then the owner of the building that once housed the club, and finally the owner of so many enterprises nobody could quite say what Digby did any longer, other than he made money.

Farrel also shared some information Bella didn't know. "My mother died in a car crash. It was my father who was driving."

Bella made no comment. She sensed this was the time to wait for more information. "Nobody knows, but I know. And don't ask me how I know, but I just do."

"How terrible," Bella wondered why Ivan hadn't told her. Perhaps he didn't know?

"I've had years of therapy about what happened. I must let it go – every therapist says so – and I have. The thing is, my father did love my mother. I know that because I've read some of his letters to her."

"How old were you when your mom died?" Bella asked.

"Twelve."

"That's young to lose your mother. My mother died when she was in her nineties. And I was devastated."

"You had her around for a long time. More time to have memories, more time for her to love you and for you to love her."

Bella thought Farrel wise to make this observation. She didn't like it when people asked her how old her mother was when she died, as if having reached an advanced age, there was no need for mourning.

"What about your stepmothers?" Bella knew Digby was married multiple times.

"All three of my father's wives were interchangeable: blonde, young, and avaricious. Nothing like my mother, who was with my father long before he made his fortune. She was dark and everyone said she was smart and funny. I wish I remembered her better."

Farrel then said something so perceptive, at least in psychological terms, "Ivan is the son my father wanted. He's amusing and bright. He's fun to be around. It's not as if he tries. He is that way. He's self-assured and confident. Girls love him. Men love him. I love him. But don't get me wrong. I'm not gay. He's the older brother I wish I had. You know, I almost wish my father had more children. But after my mother died, he had a vasectomy. His fourth wife almost persuaded him to get it reversed, but before he did, he discovered her having an affair with her tennis coach, and they divorced."

"It's odd how many women have affairs with their coaches and trainers," Bella said.

Farrel replied. "They devote all their attention to their pupil. They know how to make the ladies feel good about themselves."

After the main course, it was time for the game.

"We'll have dessert afterward," Digby announced as Bella's sweet tooth kicked in.

Viewing was set up in the den.

"I'll have a proper viewing room when the contractor decides to work," Digby said. "Seeing as I am now a bona fide producer. I will have to have a bona fide media room."

"This is good enough for me," Bella said graciously, choosing the most comfortable chair, leaving a long sofa with a back too low and a selection of designer chairs to the others. Guy picked the next most comfortable chair and Irina perched in front of him on an ottoman. Bella noticed how she pressed her back against Guy's legs. She noticed how Guy looked down on her straight blonde hair and stroked it with what to Bella looked like fatherly affection. Not that Guy was ever affectionate towards his children in that way. Maybe he was making up for it now, with Irina, young enough to be his daughter?

Bella had no interest in the sport. On occasion, when unavoidable, Bella managed to get mildly interested in a tennis match. Golf; how boring was that? Rugby – popular in South Africa and other colonies of the once powerful British Empire – was an excuse for burly men to violently rub up against fellow players and only marginally better than American Football, which was for similarly powerful men who accepted their brains being pummeled, despite wearing protective helmets. Soccer was an excuse for rowdy drunk behavior. Boxing did inspire movies – the man from the poor background makes good – but the real result was mashed brains and concomitant neurological disorders. Basketball was more about height than anything, as far as Bella could discern. "It is obvious sports are a substitute for man's desire for war," Bella commented. When nobody responded – their eyes glued to the game – she added, "I suppose it is better to kick a ball around a field than go to war and murder each other."

Ivan shook his head. He was well aware of his mother's opinion.

Digby agreed. "The battlefield equates with the sports field. But there are other battles, battles for dominance in business or especially politics. The results can be just as bloody."

Bella didn't laud – as most Americans did – those who joined the army. She would never say, "Thank you for your service," as she'd heard others voice gratitude to people dressed in uniform. Those poor sods either thought they were fighting for a noble cause or hoped to fight themselves out of poverty, frequently returned from the battlefield more damaged than those they sought to kill. She thought if America found itself having to go to war, there should at least be a draft, so everyone had to take part. However, Bella knew – as did the billionaire armaments corporations – that wasn't going to happen any time soon. The draft was one of the many reasons she chose to leave South Africa, for in the days when Ivan was of that age, he, like all boys who finished school, had to do a two-year stint in the army. This didn't sit well with Bella.

"It's one of the reasons I left South Africa," she told those who were interested enough to ask. "Boys had to go into the army after school or after they'd gone to college. I was not going to have Ivan fighting for a cause I didn't believe in."

An older guest whose name Bella couldn't remember asked, "Was that like draft dodging? You know we had boys who went to Canada rather than fight in Vietnam."

Bella explained the difference, but she could see he didn't quite understand. "Africa is one baffling country to most Americans. They have no idea the African continent is so big that The United States, Portugal, Spain, France, Germany, Italy, Switzerland, Eastern Europe, and India. Japan and China could fit into its land mass."

"I am in love with Kip Dervish," Svetlana declared from the depths of the sofa, where she was splashed between Ivan and Farrel.

"He's married," someone piped up.

Though Bella didn't have a clue who Kip Dervish was, she assumed he was one of the players.

"I love him too, love his dreads," said Ziff's model companion.

Bella had never loved anyone she didn't know. She thought it strange how adults could be so invested in the lives of strangers: movie stars, models, singers, and sports people. She did find some movie stars sexy, but that was because of the parts they played. Billy Bob Thornton was sexy until she watched him in an interview, and he became himself. The same went for Al Pacino and Michael Douglas. They were merely men and not the charismatic characters they played. There were certain literary figures she once found attractive, like George Plimpton, who founded The Paris Review, but when she discovered his second wife was twenty-six years his junior and that he had twins with her, she realized he was just like every other man and not special at all.

As if anyone cared, Bella picked her team. "I am for the English."

"The Germans will win," Guy stated. It was the first words Guy directed at her.

"Well, I'm for the English," Bella declared more firmly.

She tried to focus on the game and cheered as the teams ran up and down the field vying for a goal, which nobody was able to score. Occassionally, she asked a question, but she truly could not work out the rules of the game even though Farrel did his best to explain offsides, back fours, and the reason for free kicks, which made her eyes glaze over. Farrel would probably feel the same way if she tried to explain knitting stitches like plain and pearl or yarn over the front or behind to him, though it was highly unlikely he'd ever ask, but just for fun, she asked out loud to everyone in general, "Has anyone thought of taking up knitting?"

Either nobody heard, or nobody chose to reply. Undaunted, Bella carried on. "Do you know, someone told me George Lucas knits, and Russel Crowe took it up to help with anger management and somewhere I also read they promote knitting in jail. Nobody was listening. "I think more men would knit if they thought it was cool." This prompted a different tack in Bella's ever-agile mind. "And why is it that women have fought for the right to do men's stuff traditionally, like play soccer and fight in wars, and men don't fight to do traditional women's work, like knitting?"

Farrel picked this one up. "Women think they can do anything men can do, and they can. And they do." Farrel might have been politically correct, but this wasn't what Bella was getting at.

Bella thus, gave up attempting conversation, though she wished she'd brought something to knit, which she knew would keep her relaxed whilst watching young men risk their lives to play this war-like game. Especially dangerous for developing CTE, scientific name, Chronic Traumatic Encephalopathy, was an American football, boxing, ice hockey and wrestling. The brain was not developed to be knocked about on purpose.

When the game went into overtime, Digby said, "Dessert is now served on the loggia. We'll watch the finals afterward. It'll be recorded."

The long aluminum table with sharply angled corners that had already stabbed at Bella's hip – a bruise was certain to appear – was now cleared by Digby's staff and set out with platters of fresh fruit and silver bowls containing different flavored ice cream.

Bella knew ice cream was made with milk. Milk was from cows who were treated with overdoses of antibiotics so their mammary glands wouldn't suffer from severe mastitis. They were also pumped with hormones to make them produce more milk. Even before The Animal Rights Conference, Bella was aware of how cows were kept pregnant by artificial means so they would continue to produce milk, and the moment their calves were born, the poor babies were removed and placed in veal crates where they would spend their short and miserable time on earth before being slaughtered. Cows mourned for their young. Calves were terrified. All this she knew and still she could not resist the strawberry ice cream.

Bella noticed Irina only ate the fruit. There was a reason – aside from her youth – for her slim figure. Even Svetlana and the other young women loaded their dishes with ice cream.

Bella served herself a second helping, this time vanilla and coffee mixture. After dessert, they went back into the den to watch the end of the match.

With not long to wait before the match ended, Bella found herself genuinely caught up with enthusiasm for her team. "Go, England, go!"

As she cheered for England, she noticed not only Guy but also Ivan giving her odd looks. And then she had a moment. She realized she had made a mistake and it was England in dark blue shirts and not Germany.

"I don't care a damn who wins," Bella tried to save face. "As long as the best team does."

When she got back home, she contemplated a script using Digby, Farrel and Ivan as characters. She made notes. Bella took care with her handwriting, remembering how she was taught to write cursive with a dip pen in grade two. Pencils were used in grade one, thus ink was a huge step up. The teacher filled the porcelain inkwells, which fitted into a hole in the wooden desks. The desks had flip tops for storing books and papers. Bella loved handwriting, but her thoughts were too fast for her fingers. Thus, her writing was illegible, even to herself, unless she made a conscious effort to properly form words, which she did now as she made notes.

- *Spenser and Pricilla Becker are a golden couple with a daughter of four called Kim.*
- *Pricilla's starts to drink more and more. She is an alcoholic.*
- *Spenser and Pricilla have a huge fight and leave a party.*

- *Pricilla begs Spenser to drive slower, but he is enraged about her dancing with another man at the party.*

- *Pricilla grabs the wheel and the car crashes. She is instantly killed. Spenser is lightly wounded. Everyone blames Spenser as they saw he was in a rage as they left the party. Spenser is distraught. He must live with the knowledge he was initially responsible for the death of his wife.*

- *He pays his grieving daughter Kim, scant attention.*

- *Soon after Pricilla's death, Spencer remarries.*

- *His second marriage lasts six months.*

- *He marries twice more and is presently single again.*

- *Kim grows up believing her father caused the death of her mother.*

- *Kim confronts her father and Spencer does the best to explain what happened.*

- *Spenser is lightly wounded,*

- *Kim goes off to college on the East Coast.*

- *She won't speak to her father.*

- *After many years of study Kim gains her Doctorate in Evolutionary Biology.*

- *Not only that, but she has discovered something new to do with sea sand.*

- *Spencer, now an old man who lives on his own, reads about her discovery and asks Kim if he can visit her.*

- *Spenser tells Kim what happened.*

Bella then drew a line through what she'd written and wrote:

This is a pathetic plot!

Digby and Farrel will see right through it. Ivan won't speak to me, ever.

Chapter 7: Questions

"Let me think about it is often the best answer."

Bella managed to displace most thoughts about a screenplay to plan Passover, which this year was at her home.

Normally celebrated at Guy, this most significant Jewish holiday required Bella to sling all feelings of jealousy into a heavily guarded vault and effusively compliment Wife Number Two on her excellent catering and hostile hospitality, all in the name of family togetherness. Now, with Wife Number Two gone, Ivan called his mother. "You are going to have Passover?" It was more a statement than a question, followed by, "I'd like to bring Farrel. He's never been to a Seder and wants to come."

"I'd love to have him," Bella replied. She joked, "Maybe I'll get a pair of blue suede Toms afterward."

Ivan kept quiet.

"What's wrong? It was a joke."

Then Bella realized the reason why Ivan kept quiet had nothing to do with her joke but rather with the following statement. "You will, of course, invite Dad, and he will want to bring Irina."

"Can't your father have the Seder at his house, as usual?"

I already asked him, and he said no. I think he wants you to do it so that he can show Irina your home."

"Why?"

"You know, Dad."

Yes, Bella did know Guy. He might have teased Bella that her house looked like a junk store, but in truth, he admired her eclectic and uniquely creative taste. He wanted Irina to know what an artistic woman he married. This was hard for Bella to explain to anyone other than Dr. Feather, who, over the years of listening to Bella confronts her relationship with Guy, kept telling her, "Your relationship with Guy is one of the most interesting I've ever come about, and I have heard many unusual relationships."

The last time Bella did Passover, she was drinking and not fazed by anything. So, the brisket didn't turn out right, or the matzo balls were either rock hard or falling apart soft; it was all about family being together with lots of red wine, not that ghastly sweet kosher stuff but decent Burgundy, which Bella said – incorrectly – never gave her a hangover. Now that Bella didn't drink, she was a different woman. She wanted perfectly proportioned matzo balls with just the right amount of binding, so they were soft but not soft enough to fall apart.

The traditional brisket would be a definite no-no. She couldn't serve chopped liver. She might do gefilte fish? She did succumb to fish from time to time, even though she was recently made more aware fish were as sentient as cows, chickens, pigs, and for that matter, humans.

"You can use that fake chicken soup mix," Greta told Bella. "I do it all the time and it's delicious."

Bella did a lot of thinking whilst she walked Charlie at night. During the day, it was normally too bright and hot. The sun didn't encourage thought other than, "I should have worn a hat to prevent more sun damage, and let's get this over fast."

Nights were different.

As Bella waited for Charlie to sniff the origins of what passed before him, she found herself contemplating the origins of existence, which never failed to send her into a state of panic-peppered wonder.

She looked up to find what phase the moon was in, then fixed on the bright light of Venus. There were nights Venus shone, so she thought it must be a passing airplane. She admired how – even in darkness – leafy trees showed off subtle dark color gradations, how branches formed sculptured silhouettes and how pearls of water from timed irrigation glistened on the tips of grass spears. The night was her time to meditate, to marvel, to pray to the great unknown, and to squelch her all too human fears, "What am I, why am I here, where am I going, why is there anything?"

This night – after she told Ivan she'd do the Seder – she thought of the four questions traditionally asked by the youngest person at the table, starting with, "Why is this night different from other nights?"

Passover was the one Jewish holiday she clearly remembered from her own childhood, and she imagined it was the same for most Jews. In the retelling of the story, the struggle from bondage to freedom was universal. "Let my people go," was a powerful refrain.

When Bella was a child, she learned the four questions in Hebrew. She'd been forced to attend Hebrew school, which took place half an hour before regular school began. However, after a year of early risings and wondering why she had to learn a language she not only didn't understand but wasn't expected to, she conducted a successful rebellion. Her second rebellion was giving up piano lessons. Her grandparents had a baby grand piano. They probably wanted their sons to play. Speedy, Bella's father, wanted her to learn.

Mr. Ballofski, known as Mr. Ball, the Hungarian piano teacher – well named for his physique – informed Bella, "If you don't practice when I come here for your next lesson, I will not teach you." Bella hid in her nanny's room. "Tell Mr. Ball I didn't practice."

At the Passover Seder, Bella's late grandfather read from a prayer book. He spoke as fast as possible so that the meal – served only after the whole Passover story was told in Hebrew, a language nobody understood, could be finally enjoyed. Thankfully, since those days, the story could be now told in English, so Jews who didn't know Hebrew could follow the travails of their people and their exodus from the Land of Egypt.

Who would be the youngest? Chloe would be out of town with Jessica. She'd invite Nicole.

Nicole was Jewish. She was, according to Jewish law, as her mother was Jewish even though Nicole told Bella, "My dad is a like a sort of a Buddhist and my mom was like an atheist."

Greta would have to come, despite the fact she was not only not Jewish but normally went to a Seder held by friends who lived in Pasadena. Greta always joked, "I think they're the only Jews who live there."

Bella needed Greta's support. Guy and Irina, in her house! Together.

Bella watched as Charlie took his normal and inordinate length of time to pick the precise position on the grass to receive his defecation. Would residue from Charlie's poo – after she'd scooped it up in a plastic bag – make a difference to the blades of grass upon which he'd eliminated? Does that butterfly's wing flapping in the jungle truly make a difference in the scheme of things? What about the Hadley Cells drying up California?

Hadley Cells were in the news. Thus, Bella looked them up on the Internet but couldn't quite understand what they were other than they could cause havoc with both drought and monsoons. Hadley's cells made Bella think of Guy's daughter, Hayley. Ivan hadn't mentioned Hayley. She was probably with her mother and her mother's new husband Lew Pinto – the Brazilian tango dancer – whom Bella heard from Shelly was now in commercial real estate and doing very well for himself.

"What about inviting Hankey Sussman? He's fun," Greta suggested.

Bella thought this an excellent idea. Hankey would surely know someone who knew Guy. He might even know someone Irina knew, for Bella had never known Hankey not to find some connection. Hankey had already met Farrel at her Valentine's Day party. "So, there's you and me, Ivan and

Farrel, Nicole, Hankey, Guy and Irina. That's perfect."

Bella could sit eight comfortably, ten with a squeeze at her mid-century table which for the Seder would be covered by a vintage white linen cloth Bella once bought on eBay.

"I don't think Irina will come," Greta said, "Maybe there'll be only seven?"

"Let's have a bet. If she comes, you pay for lunch at The Ivy. If she doesn't, I take you."

Greta laughed, "You know how to make lemonade out of a lemon." The Ivy was one of Bella's all-time favorites, and one way or another, they'd have lunch there.

Bella researched vegan Passover. Maybe this wouldn't be so difficult? There was even a recipe to make vegetarian chopped liver, and Bella did a practice run, blending lentils, mushrooms, onions, and walnuts. Shelly tasted the faux liver mix and declared, "It is surprisingly delicious." She asked if she could have some to offer her latest date, who was coming over for a drink before they went to the opera. "He's an opera buff and I don't even like opera, but he's kind of cute for his age."

"How old is he?"

Dr. Dennis Davis was eighty.

"He's young in spirit," Shelly declared. "And he's a

widower, so there's no bitter ex-wife and his kids want him to find someone."

"He's about twenty-five years older than you," Bella pointed out. Bella was not quite sure of Shelly's age, for she kept this a deep dark secret as if keeping it would make it not so.

"So, Irina is about thirty years younger than Guy," Shelly flung back.

"That's ridiculous, too. What can you possibly have in common?"

"We're both single and we both want someone."

"Ah, that dreaded someone!"

Shelly left with enough fake chopped liver to charm her eighty-year-old, though the next day, she told Bella, "He loved the fake chopped liver. I told him it was a new kind of recipe, more nouvelle and not fattening. I didn't even think to tell him it was made with nuts. Only after he felt sick, and we had to leave the opera, did he mention he wasn't allowed to eat a whole lot of foods because of his irritable bowel syndrome and these included nuts."

"How irritating," Bella joked. "But maybe not, seeing as you don't like opera."

"I was enjoying the opera. I sort of got into it. But I'm

not going out with him again. He told me about his diarrhea all the way home, and it put me totally off."

Bella said, "At eighty, every man has something not working well."

"So long as it's not his…"

"You really still want sex? With an eighty-year-old who most likely needs medication to do it."

"Not everyone's like you, Bella," Shelly declared.

"I suppose not," Bella replied.

Bella unearthed the old Seder plate at the back of an unused top cupboard in the kitchen. It once belonged to her grandmother, then her mother. Joyce passed it on to Bella when she moved into the retirement home and as Joyce said many times before, "It must be worth a fortune. It's very old."

The Seder plate was old and worth nothing. It had indentations of worn blue enamel for the symbolic edibles and was trimmed with brass. One indentation was for the lamb shank. According to tradition, this was either a reminder of the tenth plague when all first-born Egyptian boys were killed or the sacrifice of the lamb that was slaughtered and eaten during the days when the temple stood in Jerusalem. Both memories were gruesome. Vegan

Passover info suggested a beet, which looked bloody enough. Bella wasn't quite ready to give up eggs, so she didn't have a problem with hardboiled eggs on the plate. Jewish practices were filled with contradictions; thus, the eggs were symbolic of fertility or mourning the loss of the two Temples; the first was destroyed by the Babylonians in 586 BC, the second by the Romans in 70 CE.

The remaining representational foods were by nature vegan: charoset, a mixture of apples, nuts, wine, and spices representing the mortar Jews used whilst building the pyramids, bitter herbs representing the bitterness of slavery, parsley to be dipped in salt water to symbolize tears. Bella wondered whether parsley was included to prevent bad breath, seeing as the plant was known to remove the smell of garlic. Jewish law was – in its origins, if not in its practice – practical. Eating dairy products after meat did make for unpleasant gastric confusion, and seafood could easily be suspect, especially in days before refrigeration. The Sabbath, the day of rest, was surely an ancient mode of stress management. That orthodox Jews were now not supposed to drive, switch lights on or off, do outlandish practices like an elevator programmed to stop at every floor, leaving lights and the stove on so they didn't have to be switched on, or even gardening on the Sabbath, was to Bella a demonstration of the typically illogical and absurd bureaucracy influencing the spiritual zone of all religions.

Greta asked, "Should I make my turkey? I don't think Guy will like all those veges."

Despite her best intentions, Bella agreed it might not be a bad idea. Greta made the best turkey ever. She smothered the bird – it had to be a hen turkey – in a pound of butter, placed it in a deep roaster with water one inch below the top of the pan and it turned out moist and tender with copious amounts of delicious gravy. It was a recipe from a long past lover who cooked well.

Even though Shelly wouldn't be there, Bella accepted her offer to make Tzimmes. "I make it with carrots and potatoes and raisins. It is delicious, but I use butter, or it won't taste good."

"Make it taste fabulous."

Bella ordered matzo ball soup from Greenblatt's deli. She didn't ask them what was in their broth. She didn't want to know, but she did know their matzo balls were perfectly light and fluffy, seeing that's where Wife Number Two bought them in the days when Guy held the Seder at his house, though Wife Number Two accepted all compliments for creating their perfection. Bella also discovered shmurah matzo.

This particularly holy matzo has been guarded against coming into contact with water from the time the wheat was picked to the time it is packed, all this to prevent the slightest hint of fermentation. Regular matzo only needed to be guarded against the time the wheat was ground. Both varieties memorialized the same event; how the Jews left Egypt in such a hurry that their dough didn't have time to rise. Bella was a very wayward Jew, otherwise known as a Secular Jew. For her, this meant she didn't attend services, ever. She didn't follow the dietary laws or, for that matter, any laws with which she didn't agree.

Shelly was a mildly observant Jew in that she attended synagogue on the High Holy Days: The Jewish New Year and Yom Kippur, the Day of Atonement. She didn't eat shellfish or pork. "Those laws are why the Jews prevailed for three thousand years," Shelly said.

"Maybe they shouldn't have prevailed," teased Bella, knowing Shelly wouldn't find this amusing.

"That's a terrible thing to say," Shelly huffed. "You're so judgmental." Shelly shook her head. "And very intolerant."

"I can't work out why intelligent people do silly things. For instance, it is contradictory for a married orthodox woman to wear a gorgeous wig, so no other man can see the real beauty of her hair when the wig makes her look better than she would with her own hair. And you know the law says, "Not to eat blood, surely it means being a vegetarian?"

"Really?" How do you know that?

"I looked up the laws on the internet. They are divided into things to do and not to do."

"And what did you find out?"

"There are 613 commandments. This is what Moses brought down from Mount Sinai. That is excluding the famous ten."

"So many?" Shelly was amazed.

"Some are so out of date they are absurd. Most commandments concern basic morality be charitable, do not cheat in business, don't be greedy, praise God, and so on. Men are commanded not to wear women's clothes and vice versa; being gay was a big no-no, so much so that a commandment was made for it. Do you realize this means we have five thousand years of intolerance behind us?"

"And now anyone can marry. We've come a long way, baby," Shelly added.

"As for the priest class, they lucked out with commandments. They were to receive the first shearing of sheep, dough as in bread, and money after the firstborn son was born. The best parts of slaughtered animals, and after a firstborn, they were given a donkey. The Kohen's, the priest tribe, was also given a lamb."

Shelly said, "My grandmother, on my mother's side, was a Cohen."

Bella laughed. "So was mine, much good it did us. But seriously, there are excellent commandments; leave the land fallow every seven years, place a guardrail around a flat roof, help others to load and unload their beasts of burden, pay wages on time, and lend to the poor and destitute. They understood a lot about sustainable methods of farming."

Shelly laughed, "They were also careful to stop people from falling off the roof."

Bella continued, "There are some strange commandments, like not being able to wear garments made from a mix of linen and wool."

Shelly wondered, "Maybe it was scratchy?"

Bella said, "I can't wear wool next to my skin."

"That's because it's never cold here," Shelly replied. "If it was cold, believe me, you'd wear wool."

"No, I wouldn't. I also don't like the way they treat sheep."

"Oh my God, Bella, you're too much. What about

circumcision?

It was at this point Nicole arrived and managed to hear the tail end of the conversation. "What's this about circumcision?"

"Funny how you manage to show up the minute anything to do with sex is being talked about," Shelly joked.

"They say it's healthy," Nicole announced.

A brief discussion took place, in which the verdict was unanimous. A circumcised penis was more attractive. "What about female circumcision?" Nicole asked. "That's dark. One of our models had it; she's from Ethiopia. She told me how her mother held her down when she was a little girl. She can't ever have an orgasm. Not from anyone or anything? And she accepts it. She says she's Muslim and all the girls have to do it."

"Now that's an abomination as it is said in the bible," Bella declared.

Nicole added, "It's worse than that. It's mutilation, so men can have their fun and women can't. How did women ever allow themselves to be so abused? That's like what I find amazing."

Bella set the table the evening before Passover. One less stress for the actual day. She surveyed the white tablecloth with cutwork and matching napkins, which she bought on eBay, at surely a fraction of what it once cost. She briefly wondered what was its story. What hands stitched the rough edges of the cut patterns, so they didn't fray? What tables did the soft white linen once cover?

She positioned her pair of simple silver candlesticks and remembered the extravagant pair belonging to her grandmother. What happened to them? What happened to the Clarice Cliff vase?

"The pattern on the vase is known as Bizarre," her grandmother said every time she used it. Bella thought the word magical and utilized 'bizarre' in an English essay in third grade. This so impressed her teacher – that forever after – she was known as an excellent English student.

This got Bella thinking of valuable things she'd lost: the diamond earrings left to her by her grandmother on her father's side, the Piaget watch with the jade face and an eighteen-carat gold bracelet. The extravagant timepiece was a guilty gift from Guy after she discovered one of his first transgressions. It vanished after Jessica had a birthday party. The jewelry box was on a table in her bedroom. Bella never quite got over the loss of both the earings and the watch. "It's material, I know," she told Jessica, "But I would like you to have had them."

"I would like to have had them, too."

Bella was married to Guy for around a year when she lost her wedding ring. She considered this an inauspicious event seeing as the marriage ended up failing. The ring was twenty-four-carat gold – a thick, simple band – and once belonged to her late grandfather on her father's side. It was swept off her finger by a wave as she gamboled in the surf on the South Coast of the province of South Africa called Natal, which is now known as Kwazulu.

Guy didn't care. Not only did he not buy the ring, but he also didn't care about other aspects affiliated with marriage, like being faithful. Bella wondered why Guy – for whom one woman was never enough – bothered to marry again, but then as she always said, "Men aren't capable on their own."

Nicole called Bella on the morning before Passover. "I know this is last minute, but I have this friend who lives in London, and he'll be here and he's Jewish…"

Bella didn't let her finish. "And you want to bring him? Of course, you can."

In Bella's personal law book, when someone was without family on any holiday, they must be made welcome, and so, it came to pass Bella added one more to the table. "In a way, I'm glad. It'll make it less awkward with Guy and Irina coming."

"Awesome," Nicole replied. "Can I bring something?"

"No, just your cheerful self and your man. What's his name?

"Christian Smith."

"That's a good Jewish name."

"He wasn't born Jewish. He converted."

"Good. He'll know what to do, more than any of us."

On the day, Greta arrived early after picking up the matzo ball soup from Greenblatt's. She'd brought her almost ready turkey over earlier in the day. Bella's eagle eyes immediately noticed Greta's perfect bangs were now swept slightly to the side. "I'm growing them out," Greta fiddled with her hair before Bella could say anything.

"You look …" Bella searched for an appropriate word … "younger." Greta grinned. Her married lover Glen was leaving his wife.

"This time, I mean it," he said. "I can't take it anymore." He gave Greta a thin band of diamonds. "Wear it on your ring finger."

Greta tinkered with the flowers casually arranged in several of Bella's collections of vintage stem vases. She kept taking steps back to view her work as if moving one blossom left or right made a difference. "That's better," she kept saying.

Julietta was employed to help in the kitchen. When she came in the afternoon, Bella said, "Thank goodness you're here." Bella was relieved, even though Julietta was the most reliable of individuals and had never ever let her down in all the years she'd worked for her.

Bella was pleased Hankey arrived first. Hankey was so easy going his presence would make everyone more comfortable. After an effusive air kiss, he plopped a large flat box of matzo in Bella's arms. "It's made by a sect in New York," he laughed. "Probably with the blood of Christian children mixed in."

Ivan and Farrel arrived next. Farrel pushed a large bunch of yellow roses into Bella's arms, which she took into the kitchen. She stood up on the kitchen steps to fish out a vase from the cupboard above the stove hood. She didn't cut the stems, which she knew she should.

Guests never seemed to realize cut flowers need to be arranged or at least put in water. Another chore for a stressed-out host.

Julietta, in charge of the kitchen, said, "Don't worry, Ms. Bella."

Julietta was forever telling Bella not to worry. When

Bella couldn't find her glasses, her handbag, paper, a book, her iPhone, her regular phone, her earrings, it was, "Don't worry Ms. Bella."

By the time Bella – with Julietta's help arranged the three dozen yellow roses – Nicole and Christian Smith had arrived. From the kitchen, she could hear Hankey confidently managing introductions.

When she returned to the living room – the roses arranged in a large Dorothy Thorpe rose bowl bought on eBay – she did a double take. Christian Smith was black. He was also, as Hankey described afterwards, "Drop dead divine."

Christian quickly told everyone, obviously used to the discombobulating, "I converted to Judaism when I was at college."

"Black and gay aren't enough of a cross to bear," Bella said. "You had to add to it by becoming Jewish."

Everyone laughed, including Christian.

Bella said, "You will have to tell us why later," which Christian did in a truncated manner. "I fell in love with a nice Jewish boy. I fell more in love with his family… three sisters and a widowed mother who is still my Jewish mother. I kept the religion and lost the boy, but I gained a family, and he became a good friend only." Christian smiled as he used the Yiddish word. "It was meant to be. It was bashert."

Bella thought of her relationship with Guy and how in its very odd way, it too was 'bashert'. Guy arrived last, without Irina. Bella almost danced the Horah!

"She was coming until the last minute," Guy said... his voice trailed as he muttered something about a sore back. Bella removed the ninth place. Eight it was, as best suited the size of her table.

Whilst everyone was well dressed – including Guy, who looked like a handsome old movie star – Farrel excelled in a navy suit. When everyone complimented him on the suit, he told them, "It was made by the Pope's tailor in Rome."

He explained, "I was in Rome and sitting beside me at a restaurant, I saw a man wearing the most exquisitely cut jacket," Farrel began, "I asked him who made it? And off I went."

Hankey, who knew everything and everyone, exclaimed, "Gammarelli made your suit! I thought they only tailored for the clergy."

"I convinced them to make this for me." Farrel, being the son of a billionaire, was used to paying for what he wanted.

In Bella's opinion, that Hankey even knew of

Gammarelli was further evidence he was a spy. Farrel also wore red socks; not any color red socks, but a most particularly rich cardinal red, bought from the Pope's tailor. "They had purple, too. But this is red like no other," Farrel proudly declared.

A lively discussion ensued about which clergy wore the red socks and which the purple. "I'll look it up," Ivan said, taking out his iPhone.

"No electronics. Not tonight."

Ivan put the phone back in his pocket, for once listening to his mother.

Guy, accustomed to being the most elegant man in the room, complimented Hankey. "When we're next in Rome, I'm going there, at least for the red socks." The reference 'we' was like a sharp pinprick to Bella, even though Irina wasn't there.

"I'll give you a pair," Farrel offered. "I bought a dozen. I liked them so much." Farrel addressed Ivan. "Remind me."

Ivan replied, "I'm not your secretary."

Guy instructed Ivan, "Remind him!"

The Seder went off perfectly. Everyone took turns in reading the story from an abridged Haggadah, explaining the celebration with its food and wine accoutrements. Christian being the youngest, asked the four questions in both English and Hebrew, which was impressive. As a convert, he was clear about Judaic lore and explained things to Farrel.

Farrel adored the evening. "This is what I call a family. I want to come again tomorrow night."

Bella said, "Our family celebrates the first night. Lots of people do two nights, but one night is enough. When I was young, we did two nights and two luncheons. There is so much cooking and preparation. After my parents divorced and my mother moved to a flat with her new husband, my grandmother on my mother's side arrived at our flat and took over the kitchen, which wasn't large. She spread out to the adjacent dining room. The smell of fish cakes, gefilte fish, pickled herring, and her specialty, sweet and sour fish – which I didn't like – permeated down the outside corridor. She also made chopped liver. My mother's sister brought the brisket. Cooking was the main event, and my grandmother expected and received much praise."

Guy was more relaxed than Bella had ever seen him, at least in her home. He'd been there a few times in the past for birthday parties with Wife Number Two. They came late and left early.

Since Wife Number Two was out of the picture, Guy's demeanor changed for the better. Both handsome and fit, he believed he didn't age like other men. That the body of Irina – the age of his daughter with a body unblemished by childbirth – had a lot to do with this. Nevertheless, Irina had to live with Guy and that gave Bella a secret satisfaction, seeing as she knew how difficult this was.

Afterwards, Bella told Greta, "The Seder gave me some ideas for a screenplay. But I don't want to do the same old same old Grown Children come home, and what dramas can be squeezed from that familiar scenario."

Bella saw everything around her and outside of her had possibilities for a screenplay.

Marina called her from South Africa to inform her, "Ivy Marcus dropped dead of a sudden heart attack."

Bella said, "I bet her husband killed her."

Marina laughed, "Don't be silly!"

Bella said, "I never liked that doctor husband of hers. There was something creepy about Dr. Graham Marcus. He was a liar, too. He told Guy he'd slept with me. Remember Ivy's sister's husband had a heart attack when he was so young, and then the sister came to stay with them. Now his wife has a heart attack, and he and the sister are together in the house. Who knows what's going on there? He's a doctor. He knows how to make people die. And I bet there was no autopsy. He probably signed both death certificates."

Marina said, "It couldn't ever be proved. If you told anyone but me about your suspicions, they'd think you've lost it. I never liked him either."

Bella thought of making this scenario into a script. She'd use the real names to make the story simpler for her as she wrote. Then change the names when the script is done. Maybe she'd turn it into a novel? The setting was South Africa. She could write about the country where she was born easily. Bella thought what power an author had to make people live or die or fall in love, or walk down the street, or be smart or stupid, careful, or careless. In the case of Dr. Marcus, she'd make him brilliant but a tad careless. Careless enough to get caught. Bella wrote:

- *Dr. Graham and Ivy Marcus have been married for around seven years.*
- *Dr. Marcus is an expert in his field of cardiology.*
- *Rick Stafford is married to Lucille, sister of Ivy.*
- *Rick Stafford dies shortly after he and Lucille marry, of a heart attack.*
- *Their whole group of friends and family are devastated.*
- *There was no sign of prior heart failure.*

- *Graham and Ivy take Lucille into their home.*
- *It's a happy three some, though not sexual.*
- *Lucille meets a man she wants to marry.*
- *Graham must keep Lucille in the fold.*
- *He has a long-term plan to win her, since he first met her, when he married his wife.*
- *He will poison his wife Ivy. He will examine the body and sign the death warrant as a heart attack as he did with Rick, Lucille's husband. That was a practice run many years prior.*
- *Now he will poison his wife as he did his brother-in-law.*
- *A distraught Lucille will fall into his arms.*
- *Dr. Graham Marcus sets his plan in motion.*
- *He will administer the poison before Ivy and Lucille go to the movies.*
- *It will be disguised as a vitamin shot.*
- *Ivy will succumb to what seems to be a heart attack.*
- *Nothing goes wrong. Nobody suspects Dr. Graham Marcus.*
- *Lucille duly falls into Graham's arms.*
- *She is the one who tells him never to leave her as her husband and sister left her.*

- *She is oblivious to anything he might have done.*
- *Graham asks Lucille to marry him. She accepts his proposal.*
- *The happy couple goes on honeymoon. Lucille begins to suspect something is not quite right.*

Bella closed her notebook, tired of thinking.

Chapter 8: What About Sex?

"What about apples?"

Bella could see Violet was miserable when she came for a Sunday visit.

"Haai, I have spoken to Gracie this week and she is sick. She has a very bad cough. I think it's bronchitis."

Bella said, "She must go to the clinic. She must not do nothing! Though Bella didn't say it, she knew Violet understood her daughter might also be HIV positive or have active AIDS. I want you to call her now," Bella said. "If she is sick, there is new medicine she can take."

Violet promised to call her daughter later due to the time difference. South Africa was either nine or ten hours ahead of Los Angeles, depending on daylight saving time.

After Violet left, Bella couldn't stop thinking about Gracie and what would happen to thirteen-year-old Patricia if she died.

Patricia was not old enough to live on her own, and there was no way she would be able to get a visa to come to The United States. Unfortunately, Johanna – Gracie's bad daughter – could not be relied on to fill the role of parent. Violet did have an extended family, but families rejected those who were sick. It was shameful to have the disease, which was the reason, so many of those afflicted refused to get help. Merely attending a clinic could turn a person into a pariah.

Bella wondered why the awful disease started at all. Did the virus jump from monkey to man? Whatever the theory, the disease took hold in South Africa like it did in no other country. By 2012, over six million people were living with HIV in South Africa. Nearly one in four South African blacks carried the virus in 2001. Orphans were created at a steady rate. A report revealed the number of deaths from AIDS rose by a massive 93% between 1997 and 2006. The statistics always horrified Bella, and now Gracie might be a statistic. Bella called her good friend Serena Hickey. "Has AIDS affected you?" she asked.

Serena told Bella, "My gardener got sick and died. He went back to his home in Swaziland and never returned. His cousin called to tell me he was dead. I asked him what he died of. He said it was stomach sickness. I'm sure it was AIDS. My maid is forever going off to funerals. It's an aunt, uncle or cousin… and they always die of something vague concerning the stomach, or the heart or a cough. Babies and children die, not only older people. There is so much bloody denial. It makes me so damned furious. The poor sods drop off the perch by the hundreds… what am I saying, by the thousands, maybe the tens of thousands! Then – and this makes me so bloody angry – the men explain why they won't wear condoms. They like skin to skin and the women agree, which I don't fucking understand. They know unprotected sex can cause AIDS, but they do it anyway."

Bella was aware Thabo Mbeki, vice president to Mandela and president from 1999 – 2008, did nothing to stop the spread of AIDS in South Africa.

Mbeki challenged the link between HIV and AIDS. He insisted AIDS was a disease of poverty and not caused by the HIV virus. He said AZT, the new drug to combat HIV/AIDS was toxic and its use was part of a plot by imperialists to kill black people. He found crackpot scientists who supported his opinion and withdrew government support from clinics beginning to offer drugs to prevent mother-to-child transmission. Mbeki supported testing the drug, Virodene and even paid for unethical tests using government funds. In its secret formula was a dangerous industrial solvent.

At the sixteenth global AIDS Conference in Toronto, The South African Department of Health presented a display of garlic, lemons, and beetroot as cures.

Jacob Zuma – president after Mbeki – showed his ignorance by claiming – in a trial where he was accused of rape – he prevented AIDS by having a shower after sex.

Serena told Bella, "It's bad enough AIDS might have been purposefully spread, but Mbeki and his cohorts did nothing to help. They set in motion a mindset and now people are scorned if they are even seen at the clinic. The poor sods become outcasts."

"I know," Bella replied. I think Violet's son-in-law had it. He was a policeman."

Now we have a constant barrage of ads, hoping to change attitudes. Wherever I look, it's something about AIDS. Do they help?" Serena answered her own question. "No, they don't. And the worst thing is that there are quacks getting rich from a variety of cures."

Bella said, "When people are desperate, they take help from anywhere. It's like having a broken heart and going to have your fortune told. Usually, the fortune teller manages to say just the right thing. When we want to believe, we do. Faith can move mountains. I don't know. I don't have enough faith to move off the phone to go down to the gym to do my cardio before Sven shows up."

After Bella's session with Sven, he asked her to come with him to buy a particular hair coloring he wanted to use for an event. Sven was forever doing things with his hair, and he wasn't gay. He dyed bits, he shaved patterns into it, and he cut and grew top and sides regularly.

As Bella walked through the isles at the drug store, she noted lots of both St Patrick's Day and Easter decorations on sale. This past St. Patrick's Day, Bella could not find the bright emerald green scarf she'd had for years.

Meandering down the aisles, whilst Sven looked for hair coloring, Bella thought she should buy some adorable pastel bunnies, which were half-price. Easter wasn't even over. She considered buying some, but then she thought, *what if I die before the next Easter?* Would I have wasted money? Usually, Bella made a big fuss hiding Easter eggs amongst the low hedges around The Portland. Chloe and a cousin on her father's side came and searched the hedges as if the one who found the most eggs was a Supreme Being. This year, Jessica and Chloe were away and Ivan, as usual, wasn't around.

Bella invited Shelly and Greta for a very casual Easter Brunch. "It's just the three of us. Nicole might come later. I'm making scrambled eggs and there will be bagels and smoked salmon. That's it. And orange juice.

After brunch, Bella said, "I want to run something past you about this screenplay I'm sort of working on."

Shelly didn't wait, "I hope you put in lots of sex. A movie or a TV series must have sex. Naked people. They usually show the woman's nipples. And I am quite pleased to see some really young actresses don't have the best boobs."

Greta said, "I haven't seen a movie lately that doesn't show a man or woman enthralled by oral sex. As if it was the best thing ever, which it isn't."

Bella said, "I close my eyes, or half close them during sex scenes. It debases the reality of the act, showing off fake simultaneous orgasms, and afterwards bodies replete with mutual satisfaction."

Greta said, "They still don't show the man's private parts."

Bella said, "Yet. They show the man, naked, his back facing the audience."

Shelly said, "Or if he's naked, he's far off from the front of the screen."

Greta said, "They show the woman pulling on the flies of his pants. Then he throws his head back in apparent ecstasy. Or the man is kissing the woman and then... he kisses her going down her belly etc. Her head is also thrown back in ecstasy."

Shelly laughed, "You know what, Bella. I think you're a prude. I can describe some things to you. Then you can write it in your own way. I'll only describe what happens."

Bella could not imagine writing how one of her first boyfriends went down on her in the back of his car and how dismayed she'd been. With parents who never told her anything at all about sex – despite themselves indulging in extramarital affairs – she'd never imagined such a thing and was so shocked she couldn't relax and enjoy it. She never truly did after that, though she pretended she did and wondered why she was different from other women but didn't dare ask. It was obviously a thing.

Once Bella had sex – with Guy the first time – there was the added stress of 'falling' pregnant. The very words 'falling' implied being clumsy and careless, which she was. So, she fell pregnant when she was at college and had an illegal abortion. Bella wouldn't wish that on anyone for the ensuing guilt. The pill hadn't yet arrived on the shores of backward South Africa until after Bella was married. Condoms were it, or the Dutch Cap, though when Bella saw the contraption – the possession of the older sister of Bella's friend – she knew nothing so obscenely large would fit inside her body.

As Bella matured, she realized she wasn't so abnormal as far as sex went. Men and women were – in the main – incorrectly assembled, at least for simultaneous sexual satisfaction. Parts, which meant to connect, didn't. Sizes could be mismatched. Men wanted what women didn't, and vice versa. The whole thing was fraught with performance anxiety, ignorance, and embarrassment. When love entered, the ramifications were further complicated. Bella envied women with satisfactory sex lives. Who the hell were they? How did great sex last? Did it ever?

Once she was divorced, sex was even more of a minefield. There were one-night stands, brief dalliances, and a few ongoing forays, which due to copious amounts of alcohol – and on occasion, mood-enhancing drugs – gave her the illusion of gratification. There was also her mistake – due to a lack of experience – equating sex with love, a residue of her hard-to-dispense-with-fifties morality. And what about Mistake's Second Husband, Phil Varelly, who refused to have sex with her after a few weeks of marriage?

Something interesting could be written about being married to a person who isn't interested in a sexual relationship but loves you anyway: gay, in the closet, or otherwise? Her good friend Marina Painter was content with her charming, intelligent husband, whom everyone knew was gay. She even had a child with him. "It works for us," she claimed. When Harry died, Marina was devastated.

From what Bella heard, sex was not important in long-term marriages. Personally, she'd experienced how sexual desire diminished with familiarity, although Bella's English cousin Biddy Lovejoy did tell Bella her husband thought she was still – after years of marriage – the sexiest woman in the world and wanted sex every day. "But I don't," Biddy declared. "I do it, gritting my teeth."

What about lust? How was it different to love? Bella's crazy affair with sociopath JP had a lot to do with lust – but in retrospect, Bella came to understand – this was partly a reaction to being rejected by Second Mistake Husband.

Bella asked Shelly what she thought was the difference between love and lust. Shelly gave the question some thought, and her answer was unusually poet. "Lust is like an electric storm. Love is like a gentle rain."

Greta said wistfully, "I am in love with Glen, and we have good sex."

Bella said, "He's married. Forbidden sex is more exciting."

Nicole's idea of love was lust.

Bella said, "You've never had a long enough relationship to know the difference."

Shelly, very much sexually active, said, "What about old sex? When I date a man more than once, he expects sex. Old single men want sex."

Bella teased, "I hope you know how to handle a Viagra-infused organ for three hours and fifty-nine minutes, and then – if the erection lasts longer – rush to the Emergency?"

Once, as an ad for one of those types of drugs droned in the background on the television in the gym at The Portland, Bella joked with Sven, "Imagine how embarrassing it would be to show up at the emergency with an erection?"

Sven, fast as a whip, quipped, "Or you could call another woman." He added, "Or a man."

Bella didn't discuss with Sven how necessary it was or wasn't for women to use estrogen cream to keep their parts oiled when estrogen could cause cancer. Was the risk worth it?

What about the influence of porn on sex?

Whilst porn was once viewed in discrete books, well-fingered cards and dark booths, Internet Porn – as graceless as deep-fried cheese wrapped with bacon – made up around 30% of all Internet traffic. Bella found the percentage astounding. She googled 'free porn'– she wasn't going to pay for it – to see what it was about. She quickly grasped that 'free' usually led to a paying site. But there were people who did it for fun and for free, and though Bella wasn't shocked, she felt dirty merely scouting around. She clicked on one site and saw a little girl – penis height – standing in front of a fully dressed man with an open fly. The picture was blurry, but Bella got such a shock she shut the link. Bella remembered reading about a woman who dedicated her time to finding kiddy porn and reporting it to the authorities. Bella thought castration was a suitable punishment for men who so partook.

Bella watched a few videos touting enormous members, which surely made more normal-sized men feel lesser. It was men who thought women wanted large, not women, for whom large could prove painful. One video showed a woman lying on a red, plastic-covered mattress in the center of a small room surrounded by naked men sitting on upright wooden chairs set against the wall waiting for the show to begin. The woman used a bright red dildo, larger than any real organ, whilst she indulged her Eastern European audience in doing hand jobs until she'd satisfied everyone, except surely herself. The absurdity of naked grown men – seated on cheap upright chairs around the perimeter of the room – still wearing shoes and socks – waiting their turn was beyond pathetic.

When Bella asked Nicole if she'd ever watched Internet Porn, she said, "I have. Not often, but I have. It's a rabbit hole you don't want to go down."

"Thanks for protecting me, darling, but I agree with you. I was doing a little research, and I felt…"

Nicole added the words, "Dirty, ugly, sick. I know. But there are professional and amateur. That makes a difference. Professionals are like better looking." As if she was an expert, Nicole added, "Better production values."

Bella was sure her trainer Sven was familiar with internet porn, but then Sven's life was so different to anyone else's she knew. He'd posed naked in his youth and many of his once ever-changing girlfriends showed off their Professional Bodies on social media. This meant: silicone breasts, apple-round bottoms, washboard stomachs, long, swinging hair, come hither expressions, and revealing bits of clothing. Sven and his friends frequented strip clubs, especially when they went across the border to Tijuana. Sven told Bella he'd been to high-profile sex parties where people showed up wearing masks.

"The thing is this. You have to come with a partner. No partner, they won't let you in. You both have to be into it." He explained.

Bella asked, "What about older people or a woman on her own?"

"Do you want to go?"

"That's not why I asked," Bella laughed. "I'm doing research. I might write about it."

"Ask me," Sven grinned and continued explaining how some partygoers are voyeurs, others are participants and how frequently such events take place all over Los Angeles. Sven added, "And in New York. I've been to some great parties there, but I'm so over that kind of stuff now. Having my son, Adam, changed me."

"For the better!" Bella added.

Sven was the most extraordinary father. His relationship with Adam's mother failed, but he was an active and present dad and the two parted amicably and were maturely – so far – bringing up Adam together.

Bella imagined porn might not be that difficult to research, seeing as The San Fernando Valley – a few miles over the hill from Portland – was known as The Porn Capitol of the world. On bleak streets stretching for uninviting miles, Porn Studios proliferated behind unsightly fifties and sixties stucco walls.

At the so-called Porn Oscars, which Bella came upon whilst searching for something to watch on TV, porn stars looked as thrilled and proud to be announced "Best Anal" or

"Best Girl/Girl Sex Scene" as any actor on the Hollywood Oscars red carpet. What happened to shame? Or humility? Or dignity? Or respect?

Sven told Bella about the live-in girlfriend of one of his friends – she called herself Deep Sea – who made a fortune streaming.

"What do you mean, streaming?" Bella asked.

"She masturbates in real time for men who subscribe to her channel."

"Her boyfriend doesn't mind?"

"He wants her to stop. But she makes so much money."

As Bella struggled through leg lifts, the thought of men in wife-beater vests masturbating to Deep Sea's streaming porn made her almost retch, and she knew she could simply not write about sex, no matter how much money she might make.

"I can't write about sex," she told Greta. "I have to find something else people think is important. I don't know what. It's driving me crazy."

"Carry on writing about your life." Greta was so encouraging. Bella knew she was fortunate to have such a friend. "Another idea for a script will come, I promise."

"You promise? So now you're like an angel or God?"

"You said you had some ideas when you came back from your last South African trip."

"What seemed inspiring then doesn't now."

"Get with it, Bella. You know you always tell me life is in the doing, not the feeling or the thinking."

Chapter 9: Violet's Travails

"Green does not always mean go."

The Gelson's, for whom Violet worked originally in Los Angeles, were unable to find a way for Violet to overstay her tourist visa. When, after a few years, the Gelson's children grew up and no longer needed a nanny, they offered to send Violet back to South Africa, but Violet was having nothing of that. For a woman with barely a standard five education, she was open and enterprising and wanted to become American.

At Bella's suggestion, when Violet first arrived, she joined a Baptist Church in West Los Angeles. Bella took her to her first service, though she didn't stay. Violet joined the church and participated in their choir and in church events. Violet once invited Bella to the church for a special Easter choir celebration. Bella was very much welcomed and the only white person there. For a nanosecond, she wondered if she should attend the church more often.

Being Jewish wasn't a problem for Bella; a place of worship was a place of worship. The churchgoers were so embracing and invited her to return. However, Bella did not like organized religion of any variety, though she almost wished she did, for religion was a comfort to millions.

She'd once gone to the Agape church and once to a service at the Self-Realization Lake Shrine Temple, but she preferred her own way of worship, which was a search for her God everywhere: in the trees, the sky, the wind and in the words of people and in her own time.

For Violet, the church proved disappointing. "Nobody has asked me to their house," Violet told Bella. "They are very nice, but nobody asks me any questions about Africa, and I have not made friends there."

Bella understood this congregation was one that was affluent and well educated. They didn't relate to Violet, which Bella understood. Africa was a huge continent, with many countries, and within those countries, tribes and clans. Some Africans were well-educated, some barely, many not at all. They did not all follow the same religion. It was wrong putting all black people from Africa in one basket, like thinking all white people were the same… those from Switzerland, the Ukraine, and Italy or France and so on. They were all white but totally different in their cultures. However, Violet persisted in attending the church, and one Sunday, a man showed up who'd also come from South Africa.

According to Moses Dube, he was one of the young revolutionaries who left South Africa to join the external anti-apartheid resistance in the late seventies.

Moses didn't normally attend church but was persuaded to go with a friend in the hopes he'd like the congregation, which he didn't. What he did, was become friendly with Violet.

Moses might have once been an anti-apartheid fighter, a noble youth fighting for equal rights, which was how he got into America at the time. When Violet met him, he was overweight, had issues with his heart and drank too much. Bella met him one weekend and told him he should meet her at an AA meeting near where he lived.

Surprisingly he showed up a couple of times.

Moses was bright, he knew how to use the system and when he met Violet, he devised a way for her to be his caregiver and for her to obtain a Green Card. Both would benefit. He would marry Violet. She would become his caregiver and whatever money she was given by the state to take care of him would be paid to Moses. Thus, Violet became Mrs. Moses Dube.

There was a wedding ceremony – with photographs to prove it wasn't purely expedient, and a small get-together afterward. Bella was out of town on the date, but she did see the wedding album. There were other proofs necessary to apply as the wife of an American: bank accounts, electricity accounts and so on. Moses guided Violet through the bureaucracy, and on the days she had off, she lived with Moses.

Violet's first job – once the Gelson's children were grown and they no longer needed a nanny – was taking care of the elderly mother of a friend of the Gelsons. As a parting gift, the Gelsons gave Violet their old van, one they bought for Violet to drive the children to school. Bella was impressed with how Violet learned to drive at her age. Violet also made friends with the driving teacher Ramirez. Violet said he was good to her, took her out for meals, and let her drive his car often. Violet told Bella, "His daughter is grown up and doesn't live with him. She wants him to marry me. She is a very nice somebody. When I go to his house, I cook for him and her, and sometimes a friend."

However, the potential romance came to naught, which both Bella and Violet thought was a pity, as Rameriz was American and made a decent living.

Violet complained about Moses, who, in addition to her stipend, expected her to buy groceries.

"It's two years of having to deal with Moses, and then you can apply for a Green Card," Bella said. "You have to remember that."

Bella and the Gelsons helped Violet with money for an

immigration lawyer, but even with a lawyer, the process was complicated. Violet quickly learned how to hang in and deal with endless documentation, constraints of time and money, plus the job of being the caretaker to a woman with Alzheimer's.

Shelly and Greta were on the patio going through the Sunday papers when Violet arrived, as she sometimes did, before going to church. As usual, she filled Bella in with her latest travails. This time she was worried about her oldest grandchild, Lazarus. "He can be killed when he drives the Uber."

Lazarus, who Violet said was no longer sick, lived with Gracie and Patricia and presently worked as an Uber driver.

"The taxis are fighting with the Uber drivers. They can kill you," Violet told Bella.

Shelly piped up, "He can be killed for driving an Uber?"

Bella said, "You have no idea how things are in other countries."

Greta said, "It's like the mafia."

After Violet left, Bella tried to explain the ins and outs of getting around in Johannesburg.

"The Taxi Wars began before the end of apartheid when the government deregulated public transport. Black people used to take Putco busses… they were painted green and a menace on the road. After deregulation, the taxi business exploded with sixteen-seater mini-busses. In South Africa, they are called Kombis. Now, instead of the Putco busses, Kombis are the main source of transport for black people. They are a menace on the road and have horrible accidents. They also take passengers long distances. Those are the profitable routes. That's what they mainly fight over."

Nicole asked, "What happened to the buses?"

"I don't know what happened to the buses. There are still some, but taxis have taken over. Taxi drivers were forced to become part of Mafia-like taxi associations. The wars were brutal and still go on to this day. Contract killings and extortion is business as usual. Now Uber is added to the violent mix. It's a subject I've considered writing about, but from a distance, it's impossible. I'd have to be there."

After Violet left, Bella said, "Violet is amazing. It's difficult to negotiate life here and she's done it, and her life isn't easy."

"Why?" Shelly asked with a hint of disdain.

Bella replied, "If you knew where she came from and how she managed to get a driver's license at her age and find a man to marry… you can't even do that!" Bella knew she was a little mean towards Shelly, but she deserved it.

Bella said, "Violet found her way around Los Angeles

using public transport; she made a life for herself with few resources." Bella's voice rose, "Remember when you first arrived in Los Angeles, how you got lost all the time, driving your car? And you have an education and were born in The United States and understand what's what."

"OKAY, OKAY, I get it. Violet is amazing!" Shelly agreed. Bella would not hear of anything said against Violet.

However, Shelly could not help herself. "I don't get how she doesn't want to go back to South Africa. Her family is still there, aren't they?"

"Her daughter says she'd hate it back there. Now she's got used to America. And her daughter hopes she will find a way to come here. I don't know how. I helped Violet with some of the legal fees, and the lawyer told her it would take time. I know these things do."

Shelly was dimly aware of the situation in South Africa. She knew from Bella that South Africa was not a safe place. She had no idea how epic-style corruption spread over the great pride of what was once called The Rainbow Nation. Mostly she switched off when Bella spoke about Africa. Africa was beyond Shelly's sphere of existence.

Bella did occasionally ask Violet, "Don't you want to go back to South Africa?"

Violet was firm, "No, I don't want to go back. Gracie she says, "Mama, you will not like it here.""

Having been back to South Africa a few times since Violet arrived in Los Angeles, Bella agreed.

Violet – a changed person – would not stomach the litter-laden streets, the lack of facilities, the fear of being robbed no matter where you were or whatever time of day or night. She knew her life in South Africa would be one of poverty. As an older woman, she would struggle to find work, and if she did, she'd be paid a pittance in comparison to what she earned in America. Not that she was a big earner, but everything in life is relative. Violet was almost American. She would one day – in the not-too-distant future – become a naturalized citizen. As time went on and phones became like computers, Violet could more easily keep in contact with her family, though Mavis, Violet's older daughter, changed jobs and telephone numbers so often Violet couldn't keep up.

Violet told Bella, "Mavis, she has very good jobs, and she does not help Gracie and Patricia. Never! She is terrible."

Mavis was clearly the bad daughter. Bella met her when she lived in South Africa and paid for her to have driving lessons. At the time, Bella was sure Mavis would go far in

New South Africa. She was charming, personable, and landed excellent jobs, but she was flawed and was, thus, regularly fired. Bella thought she was a sociopath. She once borrowed Gracie's car and returned it only after Gracie threatened to go to the police and tell them it was stolen. Gracie was frequently unable to contact her sister. Violet knew Mavis was in trouble.

Shelly said, "I don't think I could bear to not see my children for so long."

Bella replied, "You hardly ever see your children. And you don't understand anything about what it's like in South Africa now. Violet's daughter Gracie doesn't want her to come back to South Africa. She wants to come here. It's not only the Taxi wars. It's crime in general. Criminals get away with murder. This affects the rich and, more so, the poor. When I was last there, a car followed me until, thankfully, I got back to the hotel. Criminals work in unison. They block you on the road, and there's nothing you can do. Usually, they want your car or your cell phone. It's so common nobody even talks about it. A crime has to be really bad for anyone to take notice."

Shelly asked, "do people still go there for vacations?'

Bella said, "They do, but living there is different. Remember I told you about my friend who was killed."

Greta asked, "I sort of do. Tell me again?"

"He was shot outside a friend's house as he waited for the electronic gates to open. He didn't resist. He was murdered for an old Mercedes he borrowed from his sister as his new Mercedes was being fixed from a little accident he had. The trouble is in South Africa, they rob, but they also kill you for no good reason." Bella continued, "The streets are dirty, and the infrastructure is breaking down. They have electricity blackouts because the government didn't spend any money improving the electricity, but they found money to buy three submarines they don't need and can't operate. Who is going to attack South Africa by sea? But they do need domestic electricity, and that is often sporadic. They call it load shedding. One traffic light I noticed near my hotel was broken. It's been out of order for three years!"

Shelly said, "It's like Mexico City."

"I thought you've never been there?"

Shelly replied, "I've been to a resort on the coast. I've never been to Mexico City."

Greta said, "I've been begging Bella to come with me. It's exciting, and there is so much art to see. I have good clients there."

Bella wanted to go with Greta to Mexico City, but so

far, this hadn't worked out.

Greta said, "My Mexican clients have a bodyguard for their kids. Imagine that! And when they go out, there's another bodyguard. He followed us around whilst we looked around the art fair. They have kidnappings."

Bella said, "Johannesburg houses – small and big – have huge walls, many with electric wire across the top, like a prison. Some housing complexes have a guard house at the front, with electronic gates, but thieves still manage to get in. Some neighbors get together and have a sentry in the street to let you in. There are also farm murders. Gangs go to the farms and kill the farmer. They kill the farm workers. And they are brutal. They rob, but why kill? I think I've told you before how my friend's husband was stabbed to death when they were at their holiday home in the Cape. She was in the shower, and when she got out, she heard her husband say, 'Take what you want'. He didn't put up a fight, but they stabbed him to death anyway. It's no wonder Violet never wants to go back there. She says she would rather find a way for Gracie and Patricia to come to America."

"Why is it so difficult?" Shelly asked.

"What's the matter with you?" Bella sounded irate. "You know how difficult it was for me, and I had the money for a lawyer and family here to help me. Can you imagine how difficult it must be for Violet? You Americans don't get how hard they make it to get in here. You accept you live in a free, safe country and think other countries are similar and they aren't."

"Okay, I get it, I really do," Shelly replied. "It's just that I'm tired of hearing the travails of Violet. There are so many Mexicans in her position. My housekeeper's mother wants to come here. So does her sister and her sister's friend, and cousins and everyone. America is a honey pot and there are so many bees. We can't take all of them."

"I know, but I'd like Violet and her family to be one you take." Bella corrected herself, for she was now a citizen of the honey pot, "One we take."

Later that day, Bella made some notes about a potential screenplay about the Taxi Wars.

Bella wrote:

- *Tobias is thrilled to be given the opportunity to work for Uber. He is one of their best drivers and helps his mother and younger sister.*
- *His girlfriend Betty is pregnant. Tobias and Betty plan to marry.*
- *Whilst off work, Tobias is accosted by a man who informs him he can no longer work as an Uber driver unless he pays this gang part of his earnings.*

- *Tobias does not know what to do. The police are corrupt and in on everything.*
- *Tobias discovers his girlfriend has been unfaithful to him. She does not realize she has contracted HIV.*

Bella scribbles through her notes.

In bold puffed-out letters, she writes the name Tobias.

It is the only good thing about this.

Chapter 10: Naturalization

"Belonging isn't fitting in."

Bella felt such relief when she finally became a naturalized American. "I'm an American citizen! I am legal."

Her route to citizenship came through her daughter Jessica who married and divorced an American. Jessica obtained her green card, which enabled her to apply for citizenship. Once she was a citizen, she could then apply for Bella. After the customary bureaucratic delay, Bella received her green card. There was a five-year wait before she could apply for citizenship.

Bella said, "I am finally here, legally. It's such a relief. I feel safe."

Bella will never forget the day she became an American for a number of reasons.

In her case, the naturalization took place at the Los Angeles Convention Center with around another three thousand people.

Bella was excited. She dressed in red, white, and blue: white, embroidered Indian cotton kaftan top, blue jeans, and a red, white, and blue silk scarf she'd had for years and wore every July 4th. She imagined everyone would be wearing red, white, and blue, yet she was one of the very few who did.

For the big day, Jessica drove Bella downtown.

"I will be so relieved when I'm American," Bella told Jessica. "They won't be able to kick me out. Even if I commit a crime."

"What are you planning?" Jessica joked. Mother and daughter's easy and jovial camaraderie was interrupted when, as they approached downtown. Jessica spotted a stray dog running terrified down the street. Without a second thought, she pulled ahead to the curb.

"Grab him, Mom!" Jessica screamed and without a thought, Bella opened the car door and scooped the disheveled mutt onto her lap.

The dog – mid-sized, scruffy-brown terrier mix – was soaking wet and filthy.

"And now what?" Bella asked Jessica, looking at her once pristine white top.

"You can call him Citizen," Jessica said.

"What do you mean I can?"

"He's yours! It's sort of like you saved Charlie, isn't it?"

"I'm not having another dog. No way! And you know damn well I've tried with Charlie. He doesn't want another dog. Neither do I."

The panicked dog jumped madly from the back to the front of the car, further dirtying Bella's clothes, not to mention the seats of Jessica's car.

"He's thirsty," Jessica stopped to buy water. Fortunately, she already had a collapsible water bowl in her car.

The dog refused to drink but managed to upset the bowl all over the car seat.

"I can't be late," Bella said.

"Don't worry," Jessica replied.

When they arrived, there was the added concern of finding a parking space near a source of fresh air for the anxious animal. Jessica's car had a sunroof, so that could be left open.

"What were we thinking?" Jessica said.

"You weren't thinking," Bella accused.

When they finally found an airy spot, Jessica parked and aside from opening the sunroof, left the windows half open.

"Maybe someone will steal him?" she said, hopefully.

In the great hall at The LA Convention Center, Bella sat between a sullen young man from Turkey and a wizened Asian woman, the kind seen in photographs in National Geographic. The young Turk told Bella, "I've had my green card for twelve years, but next year they're going to make it more expensive to apply for citizenship."

"That's your reason for becoming a citizen?" Bella's tone could not help showing disapproval.

He shrugged and went back to his Turkish magazine. The Asian woman spoke no English, despite the fact proficiency in English was claimed to be a requirement for citizenship.

"How did you pass the test?" Bella asked.

The Asian woman smiled and repeated, "No good English."

After the exceptionally well-organized ceremony was over, Bella Mellman, plus more than three thousand others, became naturalized Citizens of The United States of America.

She was elated in a way nobody who hasn't been through the trials of becoming an American Citizen can understand. She chose to apply for a passport there and then, which was an option. Jessica would have to wait a bit longer as no guests were permitted in the hall. The whole affair took ages, but finally, Bella and Jessica made their way to the parking lot, hoping against hope Citizen might have disappeared.

"What are we going to do with you, Citizen?" Jessica looked at the dog, who was – thankfully – worn out on the back seat.

Bella had an idea, "Let's take him to The Fisher Foundation. They take in strays."

"Not ones off the street. They go to the pound."

"So, the worst they can say is 'no'."

And so, off they went to The Fisher Foundation. Jessica remained in the car with Citizen while Bella went to the front office to enquire.

She reported back, "Nobody is at the front desk. It's deserted. Maybe they're having lunch?"

Simultaneously, mother and daughter had the same brilliant idea.

"You do it. I'm driving," Jessica said.

And so, Bella took Citizen – with makeshift leash fashioned from Bella's red, white, and blue scarf – into reception, and heart beating madly ran back to Jessica in the get-away car.

The Fisher Foundation would never find out who left the smelly wet dog in their waiting room with the lovely scarf attached, but if they did, nothing serious could happen to Bella, seeing she was an American Citizen and they couldn't deport her, whatever she did. This, Bella, found out later, wasn't true. A Naturalized citizen can have citizenship revoked if they do something very egregious. Dropping off citizens didn't fall into that category.

The following day, when Bella went to her regular volunteer job at the shelter for women with substance abuse problems, one of the long-time residents – a keen baker – had baked a cake iced in red, white and blue.

Everyone asked, "How did it go?"

Bella wanted to tell them about her escapade with the dog – these were women who would not be aghast at minor moral shortcomings – but she decided against it.

Chapter 11: The Black Swan

"Anything one can imagine can happen."

Bella told Dr. Feather, her long-time therapist, "I don't feel as if I am getting anywhere with a new screenplay. I have ideas, which seem, at the time, worthwhile and then I just..."

Dr. Feather suggested, "Why don't you leave it alone for a while? Write a short story, don't give yourself such a mammoth task."

Bella said, "How is it possible that so many people write screenplays. It's difficult to write even badly. How do people do it? And most movies they make are so bad. I wonder how they ever get made?"

Dr. Feather suggested a slight increase in the dose of her antidepressant, and Bella agreed. "I am a big believer in modern medicine, as you know."

Bella recalled the first time she took what she thought was a miracle drug – Prozac. Six weeks to the day she started taking the drug, she felt normal. That was years back when she was still living in South Africa and horribly depressed after the failure of her marriage to Husband Number Two, who was surely gay, though hidden firmly at the back of a deep closet.

Greta was also depressed, but Bella knew she wouldn't take anti-depressants. Greta said, "I like my emotions undiluted."

People who didn't suffer from depression couldn't understand how someone like Bella could descend into an unbearable blackness. The feeling was beyond melancholy, beyond sadness. Those who'd never been afflicted didn't understand.

When Greta heard from a meddling acquaintance that Glen – Greta's long-time married lover – was seen in his black Mercedes outside the gym, kanoodling with one of the young trainers, she said, "I'm not sure if I want to kill myself or kill him. If it's true." Greta wanted to believe it wasn't.

Bella said, "Don't even make a joke about killing yourself. Glen is flattered by a young woman paying him attention. Anyway, I wouldn't trust anyone who tells you something sure to upset you. What's their motive?" Bella replied to her own question. "It's to ingratiate themselves with you."

"I don't think Glen has time for anyone else. Between me and his family…" Greta's voice trailed. She didn't want to acknowledge the likelihood Glen might be on the prowl.

Bella, in her cynical best, said, "It takes two years for the sexual passion for waning, and you've been with Glen so much longer than that. How many years is it now?"

Greta shrugged, "Long enough."

Bella said, "He's sort of married to you, too. You've become like a boring wife."

"You know I don't want to marry Glen," Greta said, "I like things the way they are. But if he's fooling around with someone else, that's unacceptable!"

Bella said, "Married men can be opaque when it comes to being out of reach."

The day after this conversation, something untoward happened, and Glen dropped dead. He literally dropped dead of a heart attack on the golf course in Hawaii, where he'd taken his wife. He told Greta, "To keep her happy."

Greta found out Glen was dead when she finally plucked up the courage to call his office. He hadn't called her for two weeks after she knew he'd returned.

"It's like a Black Swan," Bella told the extremely distraught Greta.

"What's that?" Greta said weekly. She didn't feel like one of Bella's elucidations.

"I read a book, The Black Swan. It was about finance, not ornithology, but the premise was swans are white, but every now and again, a black swan shows up."

"And?" Greta didn't get Bella's drift.

"The scenario completely changes with a black swan. Like 9/11. Or like Glen suddenly dying."

"Sort of like a curve ball," Greta mused.

Fortunately, Glen Short – beloved husband and father – was already buried by the time Greta found out he'd died, so she didn't have to obsess about whether she could attend the funeral service. However, a couple of weeks after she found out about Glen, Greta asked Bella if she would come with her to the cemetery. "I don't think his wife will be there," she said.

Bella replied, trying to make Greta see some light, "Glen's wife is probably already clearing out Glen's closet and making more room for her things, as well as planning her life as a merry widow."

And so, off they went to the cemetery where they found Glen's final resting place near a tree.

It was a very hot Summer Day; Greta said, "I'm glad he's in a sunny spot." He liked having a tan.

"It's cold underground," Bella could not help herself, "Unless you get to the center of the earth, where it's boiling hot."

Instead of – as usual – berating Bella for being so cynical

or irreverent, Greta started to laugh. She couldn't stop, and then Bella joined her, and they had one of those pants-wetting laughs, which was like a gift from God.

A gardener walked slowly past. He ignored them.

His presence made them laugh even more.

Afterward, they went to lunch at a hole-in-the-wall Mexican restaurant where Greta felt she could now sob and wail and wonder why it was she couldn't find a decent, unmarried man and reflect – in one way – it was a good thing Glen had died since her life consisted of when or if he could be with her.

Bella said, "If you were married to Glen, he would have been unfaithful to you."

"I know," Greta agreed.

"No, you don't. You thought he'd be different from you. But from what I know of men, they are not made to be faithful. Women would probably be happier if they accepted this fact. I never could myself, but I do think if the husband is good to his wife…" Bella remembered how Guy's philandering affected her, but then Guy didn't make her feel loved. When she came to think of it, being so young, she had no idea how to make him feel loved either.

Bella said, "You had the best part of Glen. It was

exciting, as it was."

"He did make me happy," Greta's face softened.

Bella said, more to comfort her friend, "I can't think of one married couple I know who is happy. Oh, other than my old friend Eleanor Lewis. She and her husband adore each other, but they've both been married several times before. Horace Lewis was a catch. All the divorced women wanted him after he left his third, or maybe the fourth wife. But he fell madly in love with Eleanor. She said she kept him happy by feeding him well and allowing him a long leash. She also said by the time she got Horace. He was too old and tired to make an effort necessary to stray. The problem is he died. Oh, there's one more. My friend Serena Hickey is in South Africa. She's been married five times."

Being less cynical than her friend, Greta disagreed. "There are men who would never look at another woman like my father."

"That's the exception proving the rule," Bella said firmly, adding, "Anyway, daughters have no idea what their fathers get up to. An old friend of mine told me her father could never be unfaithful to her mother. I didn't mention how he tried feeling me under the dinner table. We were both Fine Arts students. He once called to invite me to lunch. Lunch! Lunch is a euphemism for an assignation."

"It's so final, death." Greta returned to Glen, though she'd long stopped crying. "In a way, it's easier Glen died rather than me finding out he was unfaithful. It doesn't hurt as much."

Bella said, "That's a wicked and most excellent observation."

By the time Greta dropped Bella back at The Portland, they were both drained. They'd exhausted themselves discussing love, romance, death, and what life did and didn't mean. Greta's tear ducts were thoroughly drained, and Bella shed a few tears too when she spoke about Guy, who she still loved, in that strange way she and nobody else could understand.

As Bella expected, the shock of Glen's untimely and sudden death took time for Greta to get used to, and being a good friend, Bella listened to Greta turn Glen alternatively into a thoughtless bastard who'd died without informing her, to the only man who ever understood her.

For the first time since Bella met her, Greta's sliced black bob was not regularly trimmed and Bella noticed a chip off Greta's nail varnish; only one chip, but enough for Bella to know her friend was not over Glen's death. Greta was also not eating.

"You're becoming anorexic." Bella was concerned.

"I have no appetite."

Bella knew Greta was secretly glad to be so thin. She suggested a therapist and for once, Greta, who'd never been to one and decried such help, agreed though she didn't do anything about finding one.

It was the oddest thing that seemed to help Greta the most in getting over Glen's death. It was seeing Glen's wife at Costco. "She was buying wine, lots of it. Like she was having a party. She looked happy. I think she might have had a facelift. Of course, she had no idea who I was, but I smiled at her as we passed each other down the aisle. She smiled back at me. I almost started a conversation about what wines I should buy, seeing as she looked like she knew what she was doing. But I decided not to."

"And?" Bella waited for more.

Greta grinned. It was a real grin, not a smile, but a grin. "Do you know what I felt afterward when I was driving back home from Costco? I felt happy I was not married to Glen, and I could see – even though I am sure she was shocked he died and probably sorry about it – she was glad she wasn't married to him either."

"You saw all that whilst passing in the aisle?"

"Yes, I did. I sort of felt Glen laughing at us, or maybe

with us, at how unimportant this all was; how unimportant we all are, no matter what color swans swim around."

"You sound cured," Bella said, delighted to observe that Greta, the perfectly groomed, intelligent and amusing Greta was back.

Chapter 12: The Donation

"How to give yourself!"

Bella thought she could possibly write a script about a woman like Shelly who still searched for that elusive 'someone.' The last 'someone' was a con artist who almost convinced Shelly to invest in a soon-to-be-launched non-existing IT Company. Had Bella not done some research on the Internet, Shelly might have lost money.

Bella told her, "I have a nose for knowing when something doesn't look or sound right. I am observant. I notice things most people don't. I can tell a fake Gucci, a fake Hermes and a fake emotion, not so much from the way people look but from the way they behave. I knew when Guy was unfaithful, and unlike Wife Number Two – who shut her eyes and went shopping – I made it my business to find out. One time I went to Guy's office, I convinced the night watchman to open the door and when I rummaged through a closet in his office, I found a bunch of letters from a woman he'd met whilst on a business trip to America."

In a childish scrawl, Astrid Carell plagiarized Ernest Hemingway and wrote about their lovemaking, "The earth shook." Bella was shaking when she read them.

Guy's protestations of it being nothing important were a

lie. But what was appealing in a hotel in Las Vegas didn't stand the travel test and buyer's remorse set in when she showed up in Johannesburg and so, Guy palmed Astrid off to one of his friends – who was married and equally unfaithful – until she left South Africa to return to her home in Las Vegas.

Shelly was glowing when she popped into Bella early one evening. "You've met the love of your life?" Bella grinned. "Again!"

"It's not a new man. I went in an isolation tank." Shelly added, for clarity in case Bella didn't know what she meant, "A floatation tank. And I have made an appointment for you and me to go together next week. My treat."

Bella was usually up for new things. But she had a natural antipathy towards anything that was airy-fairy, and you could not deny that lying down in a tank of body temperature water filled with Epson Salts with no sensory input was airy-fairy or rather not airy at all, for the tank had a cover and air had to be filtered in.

Shelly, on the other hand, was forever hoping that one thing or another would enlighten her or, better still, help her to find the man of her dreams.

She'd done The Forum, attended – for a while – Kabala, and tried out various methods of meditation, none of which gave her anything but a veneer of enlightenment, which rubbed off the instant a new man was in sight.

The Relaxation Index was on the seventh floor of one of those ugly fifty's office blocks, passing for modern architecture. Genesis, the proprietor in his doctor's coat, was handsome. He told Bella he came from Bulgaria, "But I have been in The United States for many years."

In a forceful yet mellow voice, he instructed, "You must relax, don't worry. This will alter your consciousness forever."

Bella said, "I don't want to alter my consciousness forever?"

Genesis said, "I promise you will like it. Ask your friend how wonderful you feel after."

Serenity, Genesis' assistant dressed in all white, like a nurse, offered fluffy, white toweling robes to wear once they'd undressed. She then led them to the flotation room, where two tanks ominously sat in the center, one in front of the other.

"It looks like a coffin," Bella declared.

"Everyone says that when they see it for the first time," Serenity said.

"You will love it once you're in," Shelly enthused.

Once divested from their clothes – which they placed in a locker in a luxuriously appointed changing room – and completely naked under their gowns, Shelly, familiar with the process, took off her gown, handed it to Serenity and stepped into her tank. "Bye for now," Shelly smiled. "Have a good trip."

Serenity gave an encouraging smile and shut the top.

Bella handed her gown to Serenity.

Serenity lowered the cover. "See you in an hour."

Not one sliver of light pierced the tank. The only sound Bella could hear was her breathing and her heartbeat. She wiggled her hands and feet. In what was about one foot of water, her arms floated weightlessly beside her. She opened her eyes and slammed them shut. The dark was... utterly dark. She imagined this was like being a fetus in a womb. She focused on visualizing: a clear brook bubbling over well-worn stones, an expanse of calm turquoise ocean, gulls flying in a blue sky, and sunset in the African bush. She drifted, returned, drifted, trying to alter her consciousness. Bella pondered on what exactly that meant and went on to tree roots and how they communicated with other trees via root ends coated with fungi. The trees were so smart. They made a callous around the wound from a torn-off limb to prevent infection. They were their own doctors. Was there some conscious decision-making when flowers turned to the sun or closed, depending on the time of day? And all the time, the pulse of her heart beating, almost like an echo.

Bella had been in the tank for around forty minutes when claustrophobia wiggled into her consciousness. She lifted the top a bit. She expected it to be heavy and was pleasantly surprised to find it wasn't. She peeked out. Nobody was in the room, but if necessary, she felt relieved she could get out of the tank without help.

Earthquakes arrived in her consciousness. What would it be like to be in the isolation tank when an earthquake hits? She imagined being in the middle of surgery as the earth began to shake or being in the dentist's chair with a root exposed. What if she was in the tank? What if something heavy fell on the tank and she couldn't lift the lid and she was injured and couldn't call out to be rescued? What if the earthquake was so big that her body wouldn't be discovered for millennia, like the dinosaurs? What would the new species think of this human soaked with the residue of Epsom Salts? Would they imagine she was a special person? After all, how many people would be stuck in an isolation tank when an epoch came to an end? Stop! Think of a waterfall, birds, clouds, the African bush, the Milky Way… stop thinking about being in a coffin. Stop it. Is this what it's like to be buried?

Bella could take it no longer. She opened the cover.

"Are you okay?" Serenity was there and smiled sweetly.

Bella said, "I've had enough."

It was the coffin-like experience in the floatation tank, followed by the expected death of Greta's much older sister, that finally decided Bella on The Donation.

"Cassandra donated her body to science," Greta informed Bella. "When they are done with whatever they do, they are going to send us the ashes of what's left, and we are going to spread them in the ocean. That's what she wanted."

Bella dwelled on this. She did not like the idea of being buried or burned. But she also didn't like the idea of being sliced. She asked Greta to find how Cassandra – who lived and died in Hawaii – did it. Greta gave Bella the information, and Bella was surprised when searching the internet, to find several companies doing the same thing. That was all she did, though she kept on reminding herself to do more research. Then Bella found herself having to attend two funerals, three weeks apart from each other.

The first funeral was for Max First. Bella hadn't seen the Firsts for years, but she knew them when she lived in South Africa and decided that attending the funeral was the right thing to do. She expected Guy would be there and so she outfitted herself with care. Bella knew she still loved Guy as she dressed for him. She thought this was pathetic.

There were a few people at the funeral whom Bella hadn't seen in ages. They looked so old. Bella knew to them she'd also aged, but at least she'd bought her clothes in recent years. So many women remained styled in the era in which they once looked their best.

The widow, Joanie First, wore a black jacket with huge shoulder pads from the eighties. Charlene Cohen's short shag reddish hairstyle hadn't changed in either color or style for more than forty years. Bella could not stop noticing what people wore, how their hair was done, their shoes, and their make-up. She also noted glances and whispers and made-up scenarios between people that may or may not have been true. Bella wondered whether there was some obsessive behavior in there, though she didn't think so. Still, she spoke about this to Dr. Feather.

"It's because you're an artist," Dr. Edna Feather explained. "It's not like flagellation or obsessively washing your hands."

Bella thought some of Dr. Feather's patients must do those things.

Joanie's sister Helen, who'd come from New York, was

immaculate, understated and up to date in a pale grey Armani suit. She had far too much Botox and a taut face, which removed all expression.

"Do you still live in New York?" Bella asked.

"Manhattan," Helen corrected. "I could never live anywhere else," she said in a manner informing Bella she was superior to anyone living in Los Angeles.

Joanie and Max's two adult daughters sat together, apart from their respective spouses and children. One was blonde, and one was dark. Bella watched how the back of their heads, both with long straight hair, melded together as they sat leaning into each other in grief. They were devastated, having recently decided not to have anything to do with their father unless he stopped drinking. Bella hugged them both and whispered, "Do not think for one second you could have done anything different. Do not blame yourself."

The eldest daughter was overcome and could not finish reading the poem she'd written about her father when it came to her turn at the podium. The younger daughter didn't speak. A friend of Max spoke about how much he would miss Max's sparkling personality.

Behind Bella, a mourner whispered to her companion, "The only thing sparkling about him, in the end, was the champagne he drank."

Guy arrived late. Bella noticed him at the graveside. Irina was with him. She wondered why he'd brought her, but she had no problem greeting them both as the coffin was about to be lowered into the freshly dug grave.

Guy was still introducing Irina as 'the love of his life.'

"That won't last," Greta said when Bella told her how annoying this was.

"She's in it for the long haul," Bella's son Ivan said. "And you have to admit. She could be worse. She could be a rapacious Eastern European hooker."

Irina reminded Bella of Guy's mother, though she was, in her sweet and accommodating personality, nothing like her. But there was something about the way she stood, arms crossed as if she was waiting for something, as well as the shape of her brows, or maybe it was her thin ankles. Dammit, she had good ankles.

It was said men went after women like their mothers and Bella wondered what woman Ivan would go for. At this point in his life, he went only for a short term. His main focus was his work and making it a success. Ivan and Farrel were already producing their fourth movie and Digby didn't stop letting Ivan know how grateful he was for managing to turn his son around; the latest demonstration of gratitude was a black Jaguar.

"I wish I had friends like that," Bella said.

"Nothing comes for nothing," Ivan replied.

Bella stood at the back as the mourners settled themselves around the grave, waiting for the coffin to be lowered. She waited for the sound – so distinctly final – of the first shovelfuls of the earth as they hit the coffin. *Poor Max*. She wondered if she'd seen Max more often, she might have been able to demonstrate – in her own person – how a sober life was possible. By the time her turn came to shovel earth into the grave, the sound was muffled. Max was buried, and the living moved on to the funeral feast at the First's home in Brentwood. Bella chose not to attend.

Bella wore the same black linen jacket – with subtle cream embroidery on the front – to Max's funeral as she did to the funeral of a young man she'd met at an Alcoholics Anonymous meeting.

Byron – in AA, there are no last names – had been in and out of hospitals and rehabs, but the lure of oblivion was too great, and after six months of shaky sobriety, he overdosed and died. Bella bought the jacket about a week before Max's funeral, thinking it would be for cooler summer days, but she knew she'd never be able to wear it again without thinking of death. And so, Bella gave the jacket to a delighted Keisha, who, with a remarkably affable attitude, manned the reception desk at The Portland. Keisha admired the jacket when Bella passed by after both funerals. "It's tight under the arms and not comfortable," Bella explained. She didn't want Keisha to know where the jacket had been.

It was the week after the second funeral when Bella requested information from *Gift of Research*.

A large envelope promptly arrived in her postbox at The Portland, which she finally opened after staring at it on the side of her desk for weeks. The procedure wasn't complicated. There were forms to fill in: age, diseases, and surgeries. Two people – not relatives – had to witness her signature. Bella chose Julietta, her housekeeper, and Keisha. She hoped she'd filled in the forms correctly. Form filling was never the simple exercise it should be.

A couple of weeks later, Bella received the okay. *Gift of Research* deemed her body acceptable for medical study. A credit card-sized paper press out – to be given to the person who would call when she died – accompanied the acceptance letter. She made copies of the card and covered them with clear tape for protection. One she placed in her wallet. She gave one to Jessica, who looked at it as if it were covered with the Ebola virus. Children do not like to think of their parent's death. She planned to give one to Ivan and one to Dr. Fehrer, her internist, when she next saw him.

Oddly, she felt exhilarated, as if she had accomplished a daunting task, which she supposed she had. She'd taken control of her own demise.

A short while after, Bella asked Jessica, "I hope you've put that card about my death in a safe place. I don't want a mess up."

"Oh my God, what have I done with it?"

Bella did one of those maternally disapproving sighs. "Maybe it's still in your wallet?"

Jessica rummaged, and there it was. "Don't lose it!" Bella warned.

One evening Bella watched a TV drama in which a donated body– an elderly man – was about to be cut open by a group of medical students. Bella usually shut her eyes when there was blood or gore on screen. Her brother Derek passed out once when he cut himself. Now – with her hands over her face to control the image and with her donation in mind – she forced herself to peep. The professor, looking somewhat scornfully at his young students, asked, "Who would like to make the first cut?"

A female student – she was the star and going to be the first one – took the shining scalpel and made a firm and deep cut from the top of the chest down to the stomach. There was no blood. Bella realized blood congealed in a dead body. Bella half permitted the image of herself lying there, dead. Of course, it wouldn't hurt, she knew, but the idea was sort of painful. When she cut her nails, she looked at the tiny slices of discarded keratin laying in the sink before she collected them to throw away. They had no feeling in them whatsoever, and yet they had been part of her. *Is this what it feels like to be dead?* Bella wondered, *What about hair?* Like nails, the only part considered alive was hidden. Yet hair stood up on arms, and eyelashes were super sensitive. Nails and hair were both dead and alive. They were rather like Schrodinger's Cat – a scientific thought experiment she could never get her mind around – in which a cat in a box could be dead or alive depending on the manner in which you looked in the box. This had to do with Heisenberg's theory of uncertainty, another scientific concept she wished she could comprehend; something was a particle and a wave at the same time and the more precisely you were able to pinpoint the particle, the less you knew about it. It was amazing that there were minds that understood such implausibility. Bella wished she possessed a more scientific brain, but her brain was decidedly artistic. She could not fathom how – when multiplied – fractions become smaller. Her brain understood that multiplication meant more. If you had two apples and multiplied them by two, you got four apples, so why, when you multiplied two quarters, did you get one sixteenth? Bella knew Quantum Physics concerned itself with minute things and had to do with the wave and particle conundrum and she could not count the times she tried remembering exactly what photons, neutrons, and electrons were and why – if atoms were supposed to be the smallest things – there were things inside them much smaller. And what if you cut that small thing in half repeatedly, there must always be something – however minute – left to cut in half. She was familiar with terms like electromagnetism, the strong and weak forces, space-time and string theory, and the Higgs bosom, but she didn't remotely grasp their meaning. She'd read many books and watched hours of documentaries in the hopes of enlightenment, believing that physics and religion – at their core – were attempts to answer the meaning of life. Both asked the great question; why is everything? And what is nothing or infinity? What happened before the beginning? And after the end, then what? Bella read how mathematicians 'see' their symbols. When they make those little squiggles and numbers, they visualize shapes in space. Einstein saw his theory of relativity. He wrote the famous $E=mc2$, and it made sense to him. Bella watched a number of programs explaining how E = energy and m = mass, but what was c2? Occasionally, she felt she almost got it, but then the concept slipped from the neurons, axons, neurotransmitters and synapses and the rest of the matter that constituted her brain. Even that marvel of scientific clarity, Neil De Grassio Tyson – whose passion was to make science less confusing for the layman on TV – couldn't do that for Bella. Bella adored the man. He was the kind of man she would like to have around; erudite, amusing. He was also black, which somehow pleased Bella. However, she had no idea whether he was married or a decent husband.

Would her brain show how she loved, how depressed she'd once been until modern medicine stepped in? And how was it that most doctors treated the brain without looking at it? There should be a yearly brain scan, like a pap smear or a mammogram. It was one thing to research schizophrenia or dementia using an MRI, but what about regular normal depression, the kind for which anti-depressants were copiously prescribed without one little peek inside. More than likely, the brain didn't show a thing, just as a dead hand wouldn't show what it touched during its tenure or the eye what it had seen. In fact, probably, horribly, terrifying, all she'd thought and felt, everything she'd done, would be done with. But then she tried focusing on those times when she felt connected to something outside of herself, or better still, when she had some personal 'message' from her Higher Power, like when she found a small porcelain angel lying on the sidewalk as she walked Charlie one Sunday morning. She was at the time suffering from debilitating tinnitus, which almost made her not want to live, when she found the angel, and shortly afterward, the tinnitus began to abate. The angel ornament sat on her bedside table, ever reminding her how her prayers were answered.

Bella finally had reason to make an appointment to see Dr. Fehrer. She reminded herself to give him the card from *Gift of Research*.

Bella had a bladder infection. Cystitis. In her past libidinous life, she had two bouts of incredibly painful cystitis. Anyone who has had the experience will understand how awful this was. However, having been celibate – which she thought prevented such infections – she was certain she had something more serious. Of course, she went to the Internet.

According to Dr. Google, The Mayo Clinic, and other experts, she had chronic noninfectious cystitis. This was difficult to cure. Certain foods exacerbated the condition. Bella immediately stopped coffee and, for three days, had dreadful headaches. Orange juice was out, as was spicy food.

She drank copious amounts of water.

When Bella informed Dr. Fehrer, "I have noninfectious cystitis, he replied, "I don't think so." He added, "Some people don't even think it's a real disease."

Bella didn't like that. She didn't want to suffer from a disease doctors thought wasn't real.

"You probably have a mild bladder infection," Dr. Fehrer said. "A urine test will show that I'm sure."

Bella gave Dr. Fehrer the card from *Gift of Research*. He took a few moments before speaking. "That's a really, very fine thing to do," he said. "I will keep it safe." He slipped the card into a pocket in her file.

Though Dr. Fehrer didn't ask, Bella explained, "They will send Jessica my ashes when they're done with me. Jessica was also a patient of Dr. Fehrer. "She says she will scatter them on the African bushveld, maybe on Londolozi."

Londolozi was a private Safari camp near the famed Kruger National Park.

When Jess and Ivan were young, Bella took them there. This was long before it became all gussied up with chic African-themed décor and electricity. The first time they went, they slept on iron beds with stiff springs and lumpy mattresses, the lights were fueled by paraffin and there were no luxury bathtubs or bath goodies sitting on snowy white towels for the use of privileged guests. Bella loved it, as did Ivan and Jessica. Nobody warned them not to relax on the large boulders on the riverbed in case a lion, an elephant, or more likely a crocodile showed up.

Dr. Fehrer – like Bella – had also been on safari in East Africa. There were photographs taken from his trip hanging on the walls of his waiting room and down the corridor to the surgery. Dr. Fehrer was a fine photographer. Like anything he undertook, he did it with passion. One of his photographs – two giraffes in silhouette – won a prize in National Geographic.

Bella was pleased she'd given the card to Dr. Fehrer. It felt safer than leaving it with Jessica or Ivan.

"My death will not cost anyone a cent. When I die, someone calls and they pick me up, at their cost," she told Sven, her long-time trainer.

"Put death out of your mind and live well." He handed Bella a set of twelve-pound weights. She usually worked with ten-pounders.

"Wow, this is heavy!" Bella exclaimed as she began to lift. Sven always lifted weights with her; he was twenty-five pounds.

"We have to make sure there's a muscle to be studied," Sven grinned.

Sven had a way with words. He knew how to make Bella feel better when she was upset over just about anything, especially suspect symptoms and weird non-diseases like chronic noninfectious cystitis. Three days after seeing Dr. Fehrer, the urine test confirmed Bella had a mild infection. Dr. Fehrer prescribed a course of antibiotics, which, to Bella's surprise, seeing as she was still convinced she had something much more serious, worked.

"I told you, it was just an ordinary infection. I know about these things," Sven said.

"Well, I am happy I can go back to coffee and orange juice. I don't care about spicy foods. I don't like them anyway."

Sven said, "But what about some other kind of spice?"

"If you think I need some spice, find me some," Bella taunted.

Bella also told Greta she'd finally signed the papers to donate her body to science. Greta said, "Don't think this means you can stop living."

Chapter 13: Sunday

"Rest or Wrestle."

Sunday brunch on Bella's patio was becoming a thing, at least during the Summer. Bella put out the Sunday papers and bought smoked salmon and cream cheese for the bagels, which Greta bought. Shelly came with People Magazine, orange juice and either chocolates or ice cream. Shelly didn't have far to go, and neither did Nicole, who usually showed up with laments about her Friday and Saturday night ventures. Violet also often showed up and usually complained about Moses, who made extra financial demands, like expecting her to buy more food. Moses managed to have his sister Dudu come live with him. She had a green card. Violet didn't know how Moses organized this. Violet liked Dudu, she made Moses less surly.

This Sunday, a particularly lovely summer morning, everyone arrived early, except for Violet.

Shelly, undaunted in her quest to find Husband Number Three, said, "I had an interesting date last night."

"Do tell," Greta said.

"He's younger than me and never been married. He's a composer. More than six feet and very handsome. He's Egyptian, but he lives in London. He's trying to make it here."

"How much younger?" Bella asked.

"He's thirty-five."

"And what does he compose?" Greta asked.

"He's working on the music for a movie."

Greta and Bella laughed.

Shelly said, "Don't laugh. You're also working on something."

"Does he have a Green Card?" Bella asked.

"I didn't ask him."

Violet showed up before she went to church and as expected, began by complaining about Moses. "Haai, he is terrible. He wants more money and more money. I cook for him and I clean. Still, he wants more." Almost as an after thought Violet said, "Moses has a baby."

Bella exclaimed, "What do you mean, he has a baby? He is a father of a child?"

Violet said, "The mother is a drug addict. She is terrible. She left the baby with Moses. It's terrible."

Bella said, "What's he going around impregnating drug addicts? He should know better. He's an old man. What's wrong with him? How's he going to care for the baby?"

"Dudu, she will take care of the baby. It is like her own.

She can't have children, so she thinks God has given her this baby."

"What's the baby's name?" Bella asked.

"Niala."

Greta said, "It's a pretty name."

Violet said, "She is very good. She loves me like a granny."

"How's your family in South Africa?" Bella enquired.

"Haai, there is still no water where Gracie lives. It's terrible."

Bella asked about Patricia, Gracie's daughter, with the policeman.

"She is very clever at school." Violet's face perked up.

After Violet left, Greta said, "Bella, why don't you write about Violet? There's a screenplay there, at least I think so. She's an example of someone who faced big changes and challenges and managed against the odds to flourish."

Shelly said, "I don't think she's such an interesting person. She's black and from Africa, that's all."

Though Bella didn't want to write a story about Violet's life, she would not hear anything negative about her. "She upped and left the country where she was born. She left her children, who have no way of coming to live here. She managed to marry an ex-revolutionary and become legal."

Shelly wasn't impressed. "Lots of immigrants come to live here and have a hard time fitting in. Even you did."

Bella said, "It was comparatively easy for me."

Greta said, "What about your compatriot, Oscar Pistorius – a man born with no legs – who take part in the Olympics and then murders his girlfriend in a blind rage? There's definitely a story there."

Bella said, "There is, but everyone knows it already."

Bella was getting aggravated. "Why don't you worry about yourselves and not what I should write about?"

Nicole arrived soon after Violet left, and the mood changed. The older women all had lots to say about what Nicole should and shouldn't do regarding her job, her diet, her desire to change her lovely nose, and her latest potential amour.

The next week, when Violet showed up, her face was a study of misery. Shelly rolled her eyes. She didn't want to hear about Violet's travails yet again. But this time was different.

Violet blurted out, "Gracie's husband is dead."

"The good husband, the policeman?" Bella asked. "What happened?"

"He was sick. He went to the hospital."

"What kind of sickness?" Bella asked, and she knew, without Violet having to tell her, which she wouldn't, that he died of AIDS.

Violet said, "It was his stomach."

Bella asked, "Was it AIDS?"

"No, it was his stomach. He was a good man. He was a good husband. I think Gracie will get a small pension from the government because he was a policeman."

Not long after this, Violet showed up with further bad news. "Lazarus is sick. He is in the hospital."

"Is it AIDS?" Bella bluntly asked. "No, it is his appendix."

"Do you want to go back to South Africa?" Bella asked Violet.

"No, I do not want to go back there. Gracie says, Mommy, don't come. You will not like it here."

Bella knew AIDS exploded in South Africa in the early two thousand. It was so sudden and so deadly. How had it happened? When Bella was last in South Africa, the red AIDS motif was ubiquitous. In the crafts market, there were pins made of beads with the red motif for sale in almost every stall. Bella bought a few, thinking she'd give them out as little gifts, but what seemed so apt in the craft market did not seem right in Los Angeles as a memento. Fortunately, she also bought dozens of key rings fashioned into various beaded animals, which were much appreciated by friends and the staff at The Portland. She always gave everyone a choice when she returned from Africa. No matter who, people get more excited about gifts when they can choose from several similar things. Maybe there was a story in this?

After Violet's news about Lazarus, Bella called her old friend Marina Painter, as she often did, since overseas calls now cost nothing. "You know Violet, the lady who came to America with the Gerbers, the one who used to work for me."

"How can I forget her broccoli gnocchi," Marina said. "Those were magical days, those dinner parties. We've all got old now, and the country has changed so much. Hardly anyone entertains. Even Serena's mostly given it up, and you know how much she loved throwing parties."

Bella announced grimly, "Violet's son-in-law died. He was a policeman and married to her daughter, Gracie. I'm sure it was AIDS. Now, I'm worried about Lazarus. He's Violet's son or Gracie's son, I'm not sure which. I think he's Gracie's son, born when she was very young."

Marina didn't sound phased. "There is so much AIDS

here and here. It's not gays, it's men and women, and women who have it give birth to babies who become infected in the womb. One of my friends – you don't know her – works in a clinic where they try to get pregnant mothers to take the anti-virals so their babies, at least, don't come out sick."

Bella did some research on how AIDS spread so virulently in South Africa, so much so that one resource claimed almost 20% of the population aged between fifteen to forty-nine were HIV positive.

Bella found other frightening statistics. In 1990 HIV prevalence in women attending an antenatal clinic was around 0.7 %. By 1994 it was 7.6% and in 1998 it reached 22.4%. That's only eight years! Why exponentially so much more? Other African countries had the disease, but South Africa had it worst of all. Was it possible AIDS was introduced on purpose? There were many who thought so.

Bella read a lot about AIDS, when and where it was first found and how it became so contagious in South Africa. This was worth a screenplay, and she had an idea. She would pass it by Greta when they next met for dinner.

Usually, their dinners began with Greta filling Bella in on what was going on in her romantic life. Having finally gotten over Greg, Greta was having a long-distance affair, which Bella thought suited her fine, seeing as Bella knew

Greta could never stand a man full-time. For now, she'd settled on an Italian, Marco Vitali. She met Marco at a dinner party. He was on business, visiting from Milan.

Greta said, "We got on so well. It's funny how that happens, but we liked each other instantly. We found lots to talk about. I showed him around, Los Angeles."

The affair deepened with a misunderstanding when he messaged Greta after they'd had a romantic dinner at the restaurant at Marco's hotel. Marco wrote: "Come, Stai."

"He wants me to come to Milan and stay with him," she told Bella.

"Go! It will do you good," Bella encouraged.

"I don't want to stay with him. I don't know him well enough. I'd rather stay in a hotel," Greta said.

"So, stay in a hotel, but go," Bella encouraged.

Marco and Greta had been messaging for some time when Greta showed Bella one of his many messages where he'd written Come Stai.

Bella shrieked with laughter. "Come Stai means how are you?

Greta and Bella had a good laugh at the miscommunication.

"So, I've been sounding or rather messaging more

intimately because of what I thought he said. Now, he's coming to LA again, and he's invited me to go with him to Carmel… I told him separate rooms and he's fine with that."

"Maybe he's gay?" Bella said. "You know you're not good at noticing that."

"I don't care," Greta said. "He's thoughtful and intelligent. I think he's an honorable person. He exports Italian food. He's a foodie, so he likes going to the best restaurants."

"Messages are not the same as seeing a person in person," Bella said. "Remember how crazy I was about that faux English professor who lived in Arizona. I was brokenhearted for about… a month or maybe more. But I learned how people – including me – open up in the email. He was so seductive online. I could not see he was living with a woman who was supporting him."

"I remember it well," Greta said. "You were pathetic. Remember, we went to a lingerie store in Beverly Hills. You bought a turquoise bra and matching panties."

"I still have them. They're much too small now. I wore them once. And he didn't notice. And he had some health issues, so he was… and he was so cheap, he didn't pay for my valet parking, and I noticed he parked across the road. We met at an Indian restaurant. I think it's still there. Then he disappeared and emailed he had an emergency. I was brokenhearted. I can't even think why now. But I have some good news. I have found something that might work for a script."

"That's marvelous," Greta said with a swift flick of her perfect bob.

Bella told her friend, "Basically, it's a story about AIDS and how I think South African black women were deliberately infected."

"A conspiracy story? That's good," Greta was encouraging.

Chapter 14: A Story Is Born

"Giving birth isn't easy."

It took Bella many discarded pages and 3 x 5 cards to work out how her story might be told. She would embellish later.

The year is 2000.

- *Dr. John Beadel – the evil protagonist – is a brilliant, well-known gynecologist in Los Angeles.*

- *Going back to his childhood, in the hopes of understanding his behavior: Beadel's father, a military man, was typically domineering.*

- *His mother was once Miss Ohio.*

- *When he was a teenager, Beadel discovered his mother having an affair.*

- *His mother begged him not to tell his father.*

- *That was a turning point for him to distrust and even hated women, and most importantly, he had power over his mother.*

- *He didn't have many friends. He worked for a medical lab during the school holidays. There was one young girl who also had a holiday job. She rejected his advances. He ruined one of her experiments.*

- *After high school, he got a degree in Microbiology and after that he obtained a medical degree in Gynecology. At college, he met the beautiful Ilene Smith, who was a devout Catholic. He converted before they married.*

- *Beadel liked outward demonstrations of wealth. He wore only Ferragamo or Gucci shoes, had a collection of watches, some vintage, some new and at the time of his death, drove a Cadillac de Ville. He didn't like foreign cars.*

- *The Beadles have two children.*

- *Aside from his Gynecological practice, Beadel and his wife Ilene started a biological company devoted – in the main – to invent a cure for AIDS. They are equal partners.*

- *Ilene oversees the office. She is not a doctor.*

- *If the product works, the Beadels will be incredibly rich.*

- *Beadel has an ongoing affair with his assistant Paige, whom he often took with him on mysterious trips to South Africa.*

- *He told Ilene it was easier to do research there.*

- *Now to Johannesburg, South Africa.*

- *Black prostitutes ply their trade in different areas of Johannesburg. This will give the viewer some idea of the dark undertones of the city. A voice-over will explain. Something like a flashing travelogue showing palatial homes, luxury shopping malls, and adjacent slums.*

- *Dr. Beadel and Paige, in their respective homes, get ready for a trip to South Africa.*

- *Dr. Beadel and Paige – in first class – on the plane. In her bag, Paige has toxins hidden in lipsticks.*

- *The plane lands in Johannesburg.*

- *Scenes at the airport. A driver holds up a card announcing he is there to pick up Dr. Beadel and Paige and take them to their five-star hotel.*

- *Beadel unpacks and goes down to the hotel bar, where he meets Bossman, his South African contact.*

- *The next day, Dr. Beadel and Paige are picked up by a driver in a large black Mercedes.*

- *They are driven to an unassuming office block. The suite of offices is set up to have a luxurious entrance with lots of leather chairs, fresh flowers, a bowl of fresh fruit and a bowl of fine chocolates.*

- *One by one, black prostitutes arrive. They are offered tea, wine, or beer. Once everyone is accounted for, Dr. John Beadel appears in a white doctor's coat. He is welcoming and charming and does some talking about his aim in life, to cure AIDS. He illustrates certain things on a whiteboard set up on an easel. Paige also wears a white doctor's coat.*

- *Dr. Beadel informs them he is going to help them with a new drug he's developed in America.*

- *Dr. Beadel explains that it takes around twelve years and billions of research dollars to bring a drug to market, even if it's proved safe, and they are having the privilege of a drug that prevents and cures AIDS before anyone else, even people in America.*

- *Dr. Beadel requests the ladies go around the room and announce their names.*

- *Paige hands each woman an impressive folder. Inside, there are a few pages of information, plus a large amount of cash, tied up prettily with a red ribbon.*

- *The women are thrilled.*

- *Dr. Beadel notices Mabalell, the most beautiful of the prostitutes.*

- *It's now time to do the dastardly deed.*

- *One by one, the women enter the surgery.*

- *Dr. Beadel mixed his deadly brew and assisted by Paige, inserted the mix into the prostitutes.*

- *Mabalell lies on the doctor's table. She is flirtatious and promises Dr. Beadel a good time.*

- *Dr. Beadel gets the AIDS virus ready to insert, then he hesitates. He gives Mabalell some excuse for not giving it to her and promises her he will do so before he returns to the States.*

- *Dr. Beadel makes plans to see Mabalell the following day at his hotel.*

- *The prostitutes leave the building, excited.*

- *Some of the prostitutes are already working the street.*

- *Mabalell arrives at Dr. Beadel's five-star hotel. When she is sent up to his room, he is waiting for her, dressed only in a hotel toweling robe.*

- *A sex scene here.*

- *Nine months later, Mabalell gives birth to a baby boy. Dr. Beadel is the father.*

- *Sometime later, most of the prostitutes are sick.*

- *Back in Los Angeles, Ilene starts to suspect her husband is having an affair with Paige.*

- *She finds out her husband has bought a condo, which he tells her he bought as an investment.*

- *She spies on the condo and sees Paige, who obviously lives there.*

- *Beadel tries to convince his wife that Paige pays him to rent and he is not romantically involved with her.*

- *Dr. John Beadel wants to get rid of Paige, as she is pregnant and threatening to tell his wife about their affair.*

- *He waits for the right moment. It is July 4, and he suggests he and Paige go up to the roof of the condo building where they can better see fireworks displays.*

- *He also tells Paige he has a surprise for her. Paige has noticed a wrapped box from a Jeweler in Dr. Beadels office.*

- *They go to the roof. Nobody else is there. It's very dark. They walk to the parapet.*

- *Beadel seats Paige on the ledge.*

- *She peeps and sees Beadel with the jewelry package.*

- *Beadel tells Paige he is divorcing his wife and wants to marry her.*

- *Paige is sitting on the parapet, legs up, looking at the fireworks,*

- *"I have something for you," he says and instructs her to close her eyes.*

- *He rustles the paper and tells her to reach out her hands, palms flat. She does so.*

- *Paige thinks he is going to give her an engagement ring.*

- *Beadel places the package in her hands, then in one quick movement, he removes the package and pushes her over the edge into the dark alley.*

- *With all the noise from the fireworks, Paige's body is only found the next morning.*

- *Beadel tells the police Paige has been depressed. They find bottles of anti-depressants and sedatives in her bathroom.*

- *The police believe Beadel, when he tells them he was having an affair with her and wanted to break it up. He told her to have an abortion, and he thought she had, as he had given her money for it.*

- *One early evening as Ilene leaves the office and walks to the open parking lot of their office building, a man called Matt Moritti shoots her. She is only wounded as the bullet was deflected by a file she was holding.*

- *A local passerby sees what happened and takes down the number of the getaway car.*

- *Police discover Dr. John Beadel and Matt Moretti had been in contact for days and also on the evening before the attempted murder.*

- *They have known each other for years, which Ilene does not know.*

- *The next day John Beadel shoots himself. (is this suicide or murder?)*

- *The police searched Beadel's office.*

- *Inside a storeroom in the office complex rented by Beadel, police find a refrigerator filled with dangerous toxins: Anthrax, Ricin, Botulism, and many others. On shelves, there are many containers filled with further toxins.*

- *Questioned by the police, Dr. John Beadel's wife, Ilene, tells them she is suspicious about her husband. Ilene believed her husband wanted to take over her share in their business.*

- *Moretti is arrested and charged with attempted murder.*

- *The driver of the getaway car is never found and Moretti refuses to divulge his name, which would ensure a lesser sentence.*

- *This indicates how afraid Moretti is of these person/persons.*

- *Moretti is sentenced to twenty-five years.*

- *Moretti is murdered in prison.*

Bella might have written all night had she not had to have dinner with Greta, their usual every other week arrangement.

Bella was always the first to arrive. No matter how late she was, Greta came later. This time Greta came almost at the same time as Bella.

"I need this," Greta said. "I am in a mood. I hope you don't mind if I have a huge vent before we order."

"Of course, I don't mind," Bella said. "Vent away."

"I have a job hanging art for this big legal firm downtown. Four floors of a high-rise, yards of blank walls. It's all going perfectly well. No fuss about prices. They love what I am doing. My artists are thrilled and then the wife of one of the partners decides to take an interest. Enough said. I am meeting with her and her husband and who knows who else wants to stir the pot on Friday morning."

Bella said, "I once helped a man decorate his house."

"You were a decorator?"

"I had a few jobs, but I wasn't of the right temperament for dealing with clients who didn't like what I liked."

"I can't see you dealing with clients."

Bella said, "You're right, I have no patience, but I have some phrases you can use with the wife. *You may be right,* or *I didn't think of that,* or *let me think about that,* or *that's an idea.* Nod your head and listen. Don't disagree with her. She will lose interest, especially when you show her a blueprint of plans for where to place the art."

Greta said, "It's four whole floors and so complicated to hang. I can't go changing things around. I've been working on the job for months now."

Bella said, "Agree with her and do whatever it is you were going to do. I bet you a lunch at The Ivy. You'll never hear from her again."

"I hope you win," Greta said.

Bella didn't tell Greta about her idea for a screenplay. She didn't feel like answering Greta's questions before she had the story further worked out, not only in her head but on paper.

When Bella got back home, she couldn't fall asleep. She gave up trying and went to her computer to make notes on the potential screenplay.

Chapter 15: Detective Mellman

"An enquiring mind is of great value."

Bella notated the way Violet spoke about AIDS. She used some of her words in the very rough draft of her script.

"It is the Zimbabweans; they bring the disease."

Bella said, "I don't think that's true, Violet."

Bella wrote down her exact words to use in the script.

"Some people say it's the white people. They want black people to die. But I know it's the Zimbabweans and people from Nigeria and especially Congo. They come to South Africa to commit a terrible crime. They bring their germs!"

Violet also told Bella, "Gracie is better now. And Patricia is doing very well at school, but Lazarus, he is still sick. He said when he had his appendix out, the doctors did something to him."

"He must go back to the hospital. They'll check him."

Violet shook her head. "He is going to a witch doctor. He says she is the only one who has the powerful medicine."

Bella said, "He can go to the witch doctor, but he must also go to the hospital to get the right medicine and he has to take it as they tell him."

Bella wondered whether her words would be taken

seriously.

Another Sunday on her patio, Bella outlined the basis of her new screenplay to Greta and Shelly. Nicole was coming later.

Shelly said, "My cousin died of AIDS. He was gay, of course. His parents didn't know. They didn't want to know."

Greta told Bella, "I'm often for conspiracy theories, you know that. This one is a doozie."

Bella said, "From what I've read about AIDS in South Africa... It's something I've been wondering about for a long time but didn't think I could write about it. I'm opening wounds. It's like a birthing. It's painful, but I think the head has almost pushed through."

Greta said, "God, Bella, the way you describe things!"

"You're not a writer. You don't know how it feels."

"I'm not a mother either, but don't you think AIDS is sort of history? It's Ebola now."

Bella replied, "So you're against historical stories."

"You're right. What I said doesn't make sense. I don't know why I said it. If it's true, it's worth writing about. I wasn't thinking."

At this point, Nicole arrived with her new neighbor, Undrew Gault-Jones. Undrew altered the A of his first name to make it distinctive when he came to Los Angeles from London – like thousands of young people – to make his way into the movie business. His name matched his distinctive looks: thick and slightly wavy, long auburn hair, pale skin, chestnut eyes, and sharp features. Bella met him before when walking Charlie with Nicole. He was a charmer all right, and Bella told him if he persevered and didn't get caught up in drugs, he might make it. From his hot potato accent, Bella could tell he came from the English upper classes. Undrew went into the kitchen to deposit the ice cream he'd bought; salted caramel, which Nicole told him was Bella's favorite.

The discussion returned to the validity of an AIDS conspiracy story.

Shelly said, "I told you to write a sexy story, not one against sex."

Nicole said, "I think it's amazing."

Undrew agreed, "It could easily be true."

Nicole said, "I hope you're not stopping writing about your life. I love your stories. Undrew has read some of them."

"They should be made into a sitcom," Undrew said.

Shelly changed the subject. She was so bored with Bella's endless ideas for her screenplay. She asked Undrew,

"Do you like Los Angeles?"

He leaned back and put his arms together behind his head to demonstrate the pleasure of his reply. "I am so happy to be away from the constraints of my pompous family," he sighed. "And their drafty, old pile."

Bella imagined a large country house with impressive family portraits, comfortable sofas with down-filled cushions, armchairs covered in worn chintz, marvelous antique furniture, silver, and porcelain. The house set in rolling green lawns, fringed by gentle forest.

She said, "I'd love to live in a drafty old pile."

Undrew said, "It's so big my family only uses a few rooms. It's too expensive to heat the whole house. I think it might have to be sold or cut up into flats, I mean apartments or condos, whatever you call them. It's a better way to make money than selling the silver."

Bella said, "I'd love to live in the English countryside."

Undrew said, "No, you wouldn't. It's constricting. Everyone knows your business."

Bella said, "I'd rather like that. Los Angeles is a callous city. It's spread out, and the friendliness or rather a helpfulness is spread out thinly. Nobody cares about what you do unless you can help them get into the movies or fund their movie or help them in some way. Those born here are distrustful of immigrants and keep their doors closed. It's a city of immigrants, and you are the right kind of immigrant movies gobble up and discard. You have to be careful."

Undrew said, "That's what I so adore about LA. Freedom! I can be whoever I want to be. Everyone here is acting in some kind of role in the drama of their own life. Your life can become a sitcom. There is only one caveat."

"What's that?" Bella asked.

"You must believe in yourself, and I do."

Bella said, "I've started planning a screenplay about something so dark it's making me depressed."

Nicole said, "Maybe like write a comedy."

Undrew said, "Not any comedy, but a comedy about your life. It's an interesting life, so Nicole told me. She thinks you're the bee's knees."

Bella said, "A sitcom is a special craft. I have no idea how to write one."

Nicole said, "You sold The Lions of Amarula."

Bella said, "A sitcom is different."

"That's maybe where I come in," Undrew said.

Bella laughed, "There isn't a starring role for you."

"I will make one," Undrew said, blithely, as if writing a comedy starring himself was easy as pie.

Chapter 16: Glass Slippers

"Shoes are meant to protect, not hurt, the feet."

Bella rarely took Chloe to the movies. She didn't like movies geared towards the young, but she promised Chloe she'd take her to see the new live-action Cinderella movie.

Bella was looking forward to seeing the film, curious to see what could be done with that phony old myth of being saved the drudgery of an ignominious life by a Prince.

Bella knew – unlike frogs turning into princes – it was more usual for the transformation to be the other way around. Evidence was the high divorce rate even amongst Princes, like English Prince Charles.

In 1981, whilst living in South Africa, Bella watched Charles and Dianna's wedding on TV with her friend Marina Painter. They oohed and aahed together with seven hundred and fifty million others when Dianna exited the glass coach in her puffy silk taffeta wedding dress decorated with lace, hand embroidery, sequins, ten thousand pearls and a twenty-five-foot train.

"The only reason I'd have forever getting married again is to wear a dress like that," Bella said.

Thirty years later, Bella thought the dress looked dated and the enormous skirt far too voluminous.

To say the new Cinderella movie was about the dress wasn't an understatement. Articles were written about how the customer made the skirt with layers and layers of lightweight fabric so that when Cinderella moved, danced, and ran up and down the stairs, the dress – painted in washes of watercolor – would float as if it was made by a real Fairy Godmother. The dress would make Disney ever richer as facsimiles were sold to millions of little girls so they could flounce around feeling fabulous – or if they were anything like Chloe – itchy. Thankfully Chloe was over the dress-as-a-princess phase.

The movie was better than Bella expected, mainly because of the sumptuous gowns worn by Cate Blanchett as the wonderfully wicked stepmother. Chloe loved the movie and made no mention of the Cinderella myth, and Bella chose not to explain the fairy tale of finding a Prince within a modern society that encouraged women to forge their own Kingdoms.

When Bella got back home, she did some searching on the net and discovered the original Cinderella story was one of the hundreds of folk tales collected by the German brothers, Jacob and Wilhelm Grimm. The way they wrote the story was not dissimilar to the Disney version, but in the original tale, the glass slipper was made of gold and the ugly sisters were blinded when white doves pecked their eyes out. The doves also took the place of Fairy Godmother and they hovered beside Cinderella and the Prince on their wedding day. There was no pumpkin carriage. To escape the prince, when he chased Cinderella as she left the ball, Cinderella jumped into a pigeon coop. The prince destroyed the coop, but Cinderella was gone.

The original fitting of the shoe was gory. One ugly sister chopped off parts of her feet to fit into the gold slipper, and just before the prince was about to marry her, he noticed the blood from her wounds, after which Cinderella, with her tiny feet, was found.

"What is it about having small feet?" Bella exclaimed after she and Greta discussed the enduring Cinderella myth at their usual dinner.

Greta – who never wore sandals because she thought her toes unattractive – told Bella, "I once had a client who sent me to an auction to buy up a collection of those tiny shoes Chinese women wore. They're called Lotus shoes."

"Those beautifully embroidered little silk shoes?" Bella asked.

"Yes, they may be beautiful, but the practice was horrible. Chinese women, mostly of the upper classes – or those whose parents wanted them to get there – had their feet tightly wrapped when they were as young as four years old. Their toes were broken and curled under their arches by the tight bindings."

"My foot's aching at the thought," Bella grimaced.

"I also had to find antique frames for a series of old photographs my client had, showing Chinese girls with their deformed feet. A couple of the photographs showed the bindings being removed, so the nails could be trimmed and the foot bound over again. He wanted those in his bathroom. Weird, I know. But he was a sweet man and never queried prices."

Bella said, "It never ceases to astonish me what we women allow to be done to ourselves, to please men. I presume it was men who liked those tiny feet. But I can't imagine why other than it prevented women from running away."

Greta laughed, "Believe it or not, those crippled feet were considered erotic. Of course, men never saw them without the pretty shoes or satin wrappings. No man set eyes on the horrible infections caused by the binding and breaking. Sometimes whole toes broke off, which was considered fortunate. It was believed by some that bound feet strengthened vaginal muscles! My client knew all about it. I suppose he was something of a foot fetishist."

Bella said, "You suppose!"

"He lived alone, with some marvelous art and old photographs, but these particular ones were only for his eyes, in his bathroom suite."

"He sounds most odd," Bella declared.

Greta then proceeded to tell Bella about a potential new client, "He's as rich as Croesus, and gossip says he's about to divorce his second wife."

Bella chose not to make a witty comment about Greta's romantic prospects with Croesus, for, despite her bravado, Greta was still hurting after Glen. Bella knew because Greta kept on gossiping about Glen's wife, whom she quite strangely kept on seeing, even though the widow didn't know who Greta was. The Cosco sighting was repeated at a car wash on Sunset Boulevard.

Greta said, "I wish I could go up to her and tell her that her loving husband wasn't as loving as she imagined."

"What makes you think he was loving?" Bella asked.

When Bella got home and walked Charlie, Nicole came with her. She wanted to know whether Bella enjoyed Cinderella. "I heard it was awesome."

"Really? From whom?"

"Abby. Remember she came over when her boyfriend

dumped her on Valentine's Day."

"How's she doing?"

"Looking for her prince. I told her if there are any princes, they're gay."

Then, as if to reinforce the Cinderella theme, Lydia, the cleaning lady at The Portland, invited Bella to her daughter Rosa's Quinceanera.

In another life, Lydia would be the director of a bank, or at least the Manager at The Portland, but in this life, having been born in El Salvador, she cleaned the brass in the elevator, vacuumed carpets in the corridors, made sure the gym, the pool chairs and so were spic and span for ridiculously demanding residents. She manned the front desk when a valet was absent. She was kind and efficient, and Bella sometimes cried on her shoulder, which always elicited an uplifting response.

"I've never been to a Quinceanera."

Bella was thrilled when Lydia asked her, "Would you like to come?"

"I'd love to." Bella hoped when the time came, Lydia would remember, which she did when she proudly handed Bella a thick pearlized envelope. Inside was a heavily embossed ivory and turquoise invitation. Bella felt extremely privileged.

As the day of the Quinceanera approached, Lydia told Bella, "You don't need to come to the church, only the party."

Bella replied, "I wouldn't think of missing any of it."

"If you do come to the church, you must come later, one hour after it says on the invitation," Lydia warned. However, as usual, Bella arrived early. She was always early, no matter how hard she tried not to be.

"At least I found a parking place," Bella said to herself as she chose an aisle seat in the cavernous hall, which sufficed for a church.

With her eagle eyes, Bella had time to take in everything a hundred times over, for when Lydia said the church ceremony would not start on time, she was serious. Bella noted the decorations, both fresh and fake flowers, gold drapes, decorative ribbons, and swathes of turquoise netting. A piano sat on a small stage to one side, waiting for its player. This wasn't going to be a short ceremony. Bella took out her iPhone and played Scramble. The game made waiting somewhat tolerable.

Very slowly, the church began to fill with family and friends. Like Bella, most women were dressed in black.

Almost all the men wore jackets and ties. Only the children were dressed in color. Bella wondered why ethnic cultures foreswore their gorgeous clothes and replaced them with pedestrian, unimaginative Western style black. Why did she choose to wear black? How did black become the hallmark of elegance? Why had she not worn one of her colorful kaftans?

A family arrived and chose to sit in the aisle in front of Bella; mother, father and two well-behaved children. Bella imagined Chloe nagging, "When does it start?"

The family was Spanish speaking. Why did she take French lessons for all these years? Why learn French when Spanish was almost the lingua franca of Los Angeles? It wasn't as if she even knew anyone French. French made no sense here in Los Angeles, where Spanish would be not only useful but also convenient to practice. Why had she not switched to Spanish instead of carrying on with a language she couldn't get her tongue around? When she watched French movies with subtitles, she could barely understand a word. She could have practiced Spanish with Julietta, her long-time housekeeper, or with the valets at The Portland, with Lydia, or any number of Los Angelinos who spoke the language.

Around an hour after Bella arrived, Julietta – Bella's

housekeeper – and her husband Otto showed up. Bella knew Otto. He worked as a carpenter and did occasional work for Jessica at her decorating company when he was available. Otto made a joke about the late church ceremony. "Mexican time," he said, even though he was from El Salvador.

The pianist finally showed up and began tinkling on the keys. The priest, church elders and deacons gathered. The church was around half full, which was as crowded as it would become.

Eventually, the celebration began. First, Lydia came floating down the aisle in a turquoise chiffon dress with pearls and beads decorating a sweetheart neckline. Her glossy black hair – always in a ponytail at work – flowed in bouncing curls. Radiant with pride, she greeted her guests. This was as much her day of glory as her daughter's, and she'd done it alone. There was no father in the picture. Bella never asked why.

It was at least twenty more minutes before – to applause and piano crescendos – Rosa's eighteen attendants – nine girls and nine boys – walked down the aisle. They were dressed in theme colors; girls in shades of turquoise, boys with turquoise cumber bands and bow ties. Bella wondered whether Lydia forked out for all their outfits. She'd paid for a makeup artist and hairdresser and each girl was coiffed and made up. The girls looked so much older and more sophisticated than the adolescent boys.

Finally, all eyes were on the entrance as Rosa – in a dress on par with Disney's Cinderella – posed for the photographer – before making her way down the aisle.

Her dress was an extravaganza of gold, ivory and turquoise with frills, flounces, laces, beads, and sparkles. The bodice was laced at the back with a gold ribbon – like an old-fashioned corset – giving Rosa an hourglass waist, very much like the Disney Cinderella whose corseted waist was so tiny it was more like Barbie's.

If Barbie was a real woman, she would be 5'9 feet tall, bust 39 inches, hips 33, waist 16, shoe size 3. Her 3.5-inch wrists couldn't carry a handbag and her head – too big for her body – would be heavier than her slender neck could carry.

The ceremony went on and on in Spanish. Bella understood, nada. Was the Quinceanera more like a wedding or a coronation? Did Lydia have a Quinceanera? Bella hoped Rosa wouldn't have a baby before she finished school like Shelly's housekeeper's daughter. This made her wonder why so many educated women waited too long to have babies so that they needed fertility treatments.

The loud piano music – more disco than church bothered

Bella's ears, reminding her to always keep earplugs in her purse, in case. Bella feared the terrible tinnitus she once had might return and she kept away from loud music.

Finally, the service was over. A dinner and dance were to follow at a separate venue not far from the church.

After parking in the lot opposite the party venue, Bella approached the entrance of the hall where two security guards – handsome, impressively fearsome and dressed in sharp suits – stood sentry. Gatecrashers must be a problem and the physical invitation was necessary to enter. Bella was thankful she hadn't left hers in the car as she was politely waved into the party, which was in full swing; hot, crowded, and very noisy. Obviously, she judged harshly, most guests didn't bother to attend the lengthy church ceremony.

In the center of the dance floor, surrounded by her attendants, was the Quinceanera in her impressively frilled apricot, gold, and ivory dress. Bella did a double take. It wasn't Rosa, but another Quinceanera, wearing a Cinderella dress in a different color scheme.

"Leaving so soon?" The guard quipped as Bella walked out. "I'm at the wrong party."

Let me see." He looked at his clipboard and, without a trace of humor, said, "Your party is around the corner, facing the main street."

There were four different halls in the same building, all of which were booked for Quinceanera parties. Four different fifteen-year-old girls – originally the age when a girl was introduced into society and available to marry – were being celebrated by family and friends. All over the Latino world, wearing different variations of Cinderella gowns, Quinceaneras were taking place with lavishly designed cakes, meals, music, flowers, and decorations. There were even destination Quinceaneras nowadays, like destination weddings, where guests had to fork out – not only for a gift – but also for travel and hotel expenses. The Quinceanera – a mélange of the debutante ball, sweet sixteen, bar mitzvah and wedding was Big Business.

Chapter 17: I Can Get It for You Wholesale

'You get what you pay for.'

When Bella admired a soft, long-sleeved, navy-blue t-shirt Shelly wore, she was informed, "I buy them wholesale. It's one of my clients, Veronique Padilla. I sold her house in Culver City and moved her into a condo on Wilshire. She's doing so well. She sells at all the top stores now."

Bella did not like shopping wholesale. She'd never appreciated the thrill of a bargain when accompanied by shabby surroundings and inferior service. Buying wholesale meant buying more than you anticipated or needed, plus no returns. Nevertheless, when Shelly asked, "Want to come down with me to buy t-shirts?" she decided to go. She told herself she needed a break from working on her script. But the truth was, she hadn't been working on it, although she told herself, thinking about her work was working on it, which was true.

"You're driving too fast," Bella complained as Shelly negotiated the ever-present road works diversions whilst showing off her new, white BMW.

"If you don't like the way I drive, you drive next time." Shelly knew how much Bella hated driving.

Once they arrived downtown, the street fronting Veronique's building was closed to traffic. A security guard positioned outside the ground floor jewelry store informed Bella, "There is going to be a protest march." He didn't know what it was.

The elevator of the scruffy office block where Veronique's factory was housed on the fifth floor wasn't working. "The elevator is always out of order," Shelly said. "When Madelaine Moore and I came, it also wasn't working."

"You came here with Madelaine Moore!" Bella was astonished. "Do you mean to tell me that Madelaine Moore – who buys couture – treks down here to buy t-shirts?"

Madelaine Moore was Shelly's rich friend. Madelaine's husband Marvin made a fortune left to him by his father even bigger still when he invested in a quasi-health product known as ThinR, which was a kind of pyramid scheme. Marvin had a bad reputation. Only his political connections helped him skirt the law, yet Shelly was impressed to have them as friends.

Bella was delighted to note she was less out of breath than Shelly by the time they reached the airless factory showroom, where Veronique waved to Shelly from her tiny office and shouted, "Hi honey, you know your way around."

The t-shirts – enclosed in plastic sleeves – overflowed from cardboard boxes stored under a clothes rail hung with paper patterns in a room that had neither air-conditioning nor windows. A mirror was propped against one wall.

There were five styles, all of which had sleeves too tight for Bella. "I've developed my late grandmother's arms." Bella grimaced as she gave up. "I was always fascinated by her upper arms as they went into her elbows and her lower legs – like piano legs – into her ankles. Now I've inherited them."

With a most irritating shimmy, Shelly tried all five styles in all four colors, as if she could not make up her mind whilst she showed off her newly slimmed down body, gratis Weightwatchers. Bella was disheartened, though Shelly managed to convince Bella that one style was flattering.

"Black makes your arms look thinner."

Bella's day was saved when they finally exited the building to find an all-female protest for Immigrant's Rights had begun right by the entrance to the building.

"You're mad!" Shelly said as Bella – with enthusiastic determination – strode into the center of the crowd of mostly women and young children, many in strollers. She marched in one place as the marchers passed onwards.

Bella could identify. It had taken her many years to obtain a green card and a five-year wait after that to be eligible to apply for American citizenship. Violet also had to wait forever. Being illegal wasn't a nice feeling.

Shelly took a video with her iPhone. "I am going to post this on Facebook," she warned with glee as if this might stop Bella. Instead, Bella marched with even more intensity and kept posing for Shelly with her arm raised in a fisted salute.

After Shelly was persuaded to buy a dollar American flag, even she became caught up with the moment and throwing caution to the wind, marched beside Bella. Then, with increasing bravado, she marched ahead, waving her little flag.

The march was, in its way, charming, if you can call a protest charming. Mothers wheeled infants in strollers and children held placards, "I want my dad to live with me and my mom." This wasn't a group of violent, angry people. They were heart-sore, expressing with undeniable passion their wish to be included in a system that wanted their cheap labor but nothing else of their lives.

On the way back to Beverly Hills, Bella said, "We are so lucky, you and I."

"Why?" Shelly asked.

"We're lucky because we're white, middle to the upper class. We've been educated. We have a pleasant roof over our heads and more than enough food and if something goes wrong, we have people who will help us. We have medical insurance and," Bella pointed to the plastic bag filled with Shelly's t-shirts. "And we can afford to buy new clothes."

Shelly didn't like it when Bella went on one of her social rants. She teased Bella. "Do you know how much shoes cost these days? I mean like good shoes, like from Nieman's and Saks and Barney's. $300 used to be like a fortune. Now I can't find a shoe I like under $500."

Bella said nothing but noted how many times Shelly said, "Like."

Shelly lived in a luxurious cocoon and was proud of it. Unlike Bella, Shelly did not suffer from even a smidgen of deep-seated Jewish Guilt.

Shelly continued, "If Madelaine Moore likes a shoe, she buys two the same, in case one wears out. She has like, I don't know how many Louboutins, you know, the ones with the red soles."

Shelly was now using the word 'like' like the teenager she wished she still was.

Bella said, "I am aware Louboutins have red soles. You

know I get all the latest magazines. So, did Madelaine Moore wear her Louboutins when she came with you to Veronique's?"

Shelly ignored the question. "She's like a nice person when you get to know her."

When they got home, Shelly – as she threatened – posted the video of Bella marching. Bella rather proudly reposted it on her Facebook page.

Marina Painter sent Bella a private message. "I'm laughing. Did you realize you were making the ANC salute?"

This was the raised fist, the one Nelson Mandela gave after the trial that ended with him being found guilty of treason and sentenced to life in prison; the one he gave when he was freed after twenty-seven years; the one the whole country gave when Mandela became the first black president of what was called, *The Rainbow Nation*. The raised fist was accompanied by the shout *Amandla,* meaning 'Power,' followed by the refrain *Awethu,* "To the People."

In her anti-apartheid days in South Africa during the late eighties, before she came to the United States, Bella could proudly say she was a small part of the revolution. She went to anti-apartheid meetings, where there were usually disputes between the various attendees about what action to take. She made a petition to be sent to the President. She handed it out and had it printed in the newspaper and certain magazines. She sent it to various educational institutions. People could cut it out and sign it and send it to her address. She wasn't hiding. The words of the petition were straightforward.

I am not a revolutionary. I am an ordinary South African. I want all South Africans to have equal rights.

Bella was sure her phone was tapped. She could hear her strange clicks. A young man called to discuss how he and his friends could help. He was part of the state security apparatus, which became apparent when he said, "President Botha is not so bad." The address he gave her to drop a newly designed petition didn't exist. Bella had calls from people asking who funded her work and what group she belonged to. It was only Bella. When she gathered 5000 signatures, she sent them to the president in a pretty box. She received a polite reply.

She attended on her own – for none of her friends were interested – a protest held in the Witwatersrand University Hall. This made her realize how trifling her white protest mattered. Desmond Tutu, Anglican Bishop, a potent anti-apartheid figure, spoke. After the speeches were done, the mostly black crowd toy-toyed from the hall, chanting

Amandla Awethu. She couldn't join in. She would look ridiculous. She understood – no matter how much she abhorred the racist system – her protest was colored by her color. She watched the toy-toying demonstrators as they danced past her, understanding not only was she white, but she would feel ridiculous toy toying.

Shelly decided to hang out with Bella after their downtown protest. "Do your own thing. I want to look through your magazines."

Bella received almost all the fashion and home decorating magazines. They arrived, month after month. Occasionally Bella received a bill to extend the delivery, which she paid. However, even publications she could not remember ordering arrived.

"I won't bother you," Shelly said.

"Sure," Bella replied. "I am going to do some work."

"Work? What work?" Shelly asked.

"I need to do more research."

"You're always on your computer. I don't know how you do it."

Bella said, "Firstly, I write on the computer. Secondly, I find out all sorts of things as I wander around the internet. It's like being dunked in an enormous pool of knowledge I didn't know existed."

Shelly was happily paging through Vogue whilst Bella was working on the back story for her characters. She was also working on a title. *The Lions of Amarula* had come easily, but this was much more difficult. So far, *The Malevolent Dr. Beadel* was the best she'd come up with.

Shelly called Bella, "Come look at this."

"It was a photograph of a man she thought looked interesting. He was not as famous as his very rich ex-wife. He lived in The Pacific Palisades, which was near enough for Shelly to find him. "Look here. He says he doesn't date young women."

Bella glanced through the article, which was about men who married famous or very rich women.

"He looks a bit like a farmer," Shelly added. "Not that I know any farmers. He looks like my cousin Alfie. Maybe you should meet him? He's never been married and he's very nice. He's not that handsome, but he's got a good sense of humor."

Bella simply could not get Shelly to understand she had no desire to meet 'someone,' including Shelly's cousin Alfie who'd never been married and had a good sense of humor.

"He looks sort of boyish," Bella tried to sound polite.

She was practicing tolerance and understanding. "I'm going back to my work."

Shelly kept on interrupting Bella with something she found interesting in a magazine. "Look at these shoes. Do you think she's had a facelift?" and so on. Eventually, Bella said, "I have to make some private calls."

"Oh, mysterious," Shelly said. "Maybe you do have a hidden lover after all?"

There were times Bella had to find an excuse to get rid of Shelly, or she'd just about move in. Bella could see why she needed to find a husband. She could not stand being alone.

Chapter 18: The Schnitzel

"Follow the recipe."

It was the anniversary of Bella's mother's death. "I wish granny was still alive. I miss her," Jessica said in a teary voice when she called her mother. Jessica adored her grandmother.

"You are my first and so far, only granddaughter," Joyce told her. "You have that special place."

Bella felt tears stinging. "She could be so irritating, but I miss her desperately. There's not a day I don't think of her. Remember the Vienna Schnitzel?"

This was one of those stories that would – with glee – be recounted repeatedly by Bella and Jessica.

The Vienna Schnitzel story was from the days when Joyce was well enough to come to Los Angeles and took place at Spago – one of the finest restaurants in Beverly Hills.

When Joyce came to town, Olivia Blauss, Bella's older, rich, and incredibly chic friend, always invited her and Bella to lunch at Spago, where they were seated at the best table in the room and Joyce usually said something along the lines of, "This is the kind of restaurant my friends in South Africa wouldn't understand. They're not that sophisticated."

Though Olivia was in her late seventies, she'd never lost the self-assurance of being a natural-born beauty, and it was without effort she charmed especially men, but women, too. She was thoughtful and generous and always presented Joyce with a gift. This time it was the perfume; Shalimar by Guerlain.

"Bella told me it was your favorite scent at one time. I hope you still enjoy it."

Bella said, "When I smell Shalimar, it takes me back to being ten years old, watching you getting dressed to go out for the evening."

"I don't remember using it," Joyce said.

Joyce took forever to make her choice from the menu, eventually announcing as if she'd made the decision to declare war, "I will have the Vienna Schnitzel."

Joyce never found LA food up to her high standards, and on the drive, back home after lunch, her criticisms surpassed the more usual grumble.

"My Vienna Schnitzel was terrible. Did you notice I left half of it on my plate?"

"What was wrong with it?"

Joyce huffed, "It was not Vienna Schnitzel."

"What was it?"

"I don't know what it was, but it was not Vienna Schnitzel. It was coated with puffed batter, and it wasn't served correctly."

"How should it be served?"

"Vienna Schnitzel has to be served with thin slices of hard-boiled egg, a slice of lemon and an anchovy."

"I am sure there are lots of ways to make Vienna Schnitzel," Bella offered. "You know Wolfgang Puck – the owner of Spago – is Viennese. I am certain he knows more than you do about Vienna Schnitzel."

Joyce was unimpressed. "I don't care where he's from. Vienna Schnitzel is Vienna Schnitzel."

The next day Bella overheard Joyce asking Jessica to find out the telephone number of Spago.

"What are you going to do?" Bella asked.

"I am going to complain."

"You can't be serious, mom," Bella laughed.

"I am," Joyce replied.

"You're not calling when I'm around.

"I'll call when I want to call."

And so, with Bella removing herself to her bedroom, Joyce called Spago to complain about the Vienna Schnitzel.

The Public Relations lady was polite, "You know, Mr.

Puck is from Vienna."

Joyce countered, "I have traveled around the world, and I have had Vienna Schnitzel in many well-known restaurants, and it is always served with slices of hard-boiled egg, a slice of lemon, and an anchovy on top, and the veal is coated with crumbs not batter."

"I'm so sorry it wasn't to your liking, but Mr. Puck makes it this way."

Joyce was nonplussed. "If you call a dish Vienna Schnitzel, it should be Vienna Schnitzel."

"I will pass the message on to Mr. Puck and come back to you."

The next day the PR lady called. She told Joyce exactly what Bella told her mother; there was more than one way to make Vienna Schnitzel. She was very sorry Joyce was so dissatisfied, but there was nothing to be done.

Bella wondered what her mother hoped to gain by making such a fuss and then remembered how Joyce complained so that she received refunds and better still, the offer of something for nothing. "Did you seriously think they would offer you a free meal?" Bella enquired.

Joyce's expression and voice turned girlish. "Yes," she said, without a trace of shame.

Bella wondered how her family would remember funny incidents when she was gone.

They might recall the night she left shrimp on the patio to thaw and served them smothered in pink sauce, not realizing they needed cooking. She was teased about that for months.

Jessica and Ivan might remember the time she put a dishwasher in the washing machine when they all first went to live in London after she and Guy Rufus divorced. "Soap is soap," Bella said, pouring a cup full of dishwashing liquid into the machine, which was housed in the basement of the rented house in Chelsea.

Biddy Lovejoy, a distant cousin, arrived at the same time as the bubbles – having reached the ceiling of the basement – bubbled their way up the stairs. "What did you do?" Biddy was disdainful. "Well, I suppose when you've grown up with servants, you really don't know the difference between dish soap and dishwasher soap," she said as Jessica and Ivan shrieked with delight in the bubbles.

Then there was the first Sunday lunch in London.

"We are having a proper Sunday lunch," Bella told her children as she worked out how to use the gas oven. "I am not going to let our standards drop. We are having roast chicken, roast potatoes, peas and gravy."

Bella invited Terrence Higgs, an irreverent bachelor she'd met when he was in South Africa, on a business trip. He was helpful starting off the gas oven, but when he carved the chicken, there, still nestling in the cavity of the bird, was the plastic bag with giblets.

Terrence thought it was hysterical and Bella's ineptitude made him even more in love with her. Unfortunately – though Bella adored his sense of humor and accent – she wasn't in love with Terrence. When he was eventually married, she sometimes wondered whether she should have given him more of a chance, seeing as he – unlike any of her chosen men – proved to be a kind, witty, patient, easygoing and devoted husband to his Gertrude.

Bella hoped Jessica and Ivan wouldn't remember too much about her behavior when they lived in London, for it was a period in her life when she was adrift.

"I almost drowned," she told her therapist, Dr. Edna Feather. "I was trying to fit in like the proverbial square peg in the round hole. I was a nice Jewish girl trying to conform to a louche upper-crust society that didn't value education, morality, or anything I thought important. I needed alcohol. It was my salvation."

"But you left that behind," Dr. Feather reminded Bella. "You eventually came to America. You got sober. You turned your life around. Not everyone does. They stay in that ocean and flounder. Look at your screenplay, *The Lions of Amarula* … and your writing."

"I don't know if it will ever get made."

"But you did it. You finished a project. What happens to it is not something you can control, but you did your best. And you're working on another one. More important, you have a grandchild who has never seen you drink."

"Yes, that's true."

"You've made memories with her she'll treasure. Think of those."

Bella's mind flashed to expressionist decorations on birthday cakes she and Chloe made together; how she'd taken Chloe to protest the use of wild animals in the circus; watching BBC comedy programs when Chloe slept the night; eating slices of strong cheddar cheese and chocolate in bed; allowing Chloe to mark her height on the door jamb in the bathroom with added drawings.

"Knowing you as I do, I assure you everyone in your family will remember you with enormous fondness." With that, Dr. Feather stood to motion. Bella's hour was over.

"That compliment cost me $250," Bella said to herself as she wrote out a check.

Later that day, Bella and Nicole walked Charlie together. Nicole was trying to bump into Undrew without seeming to stalk him. She simply would not believe he was gay. "I think it suits him to say he is."

"Why would he say he is if he isn't?" Bella wondered.

"Maybe then he doesn't need to reject me?"

Bella said, "That's a fair deduction. Now, instead of thinking about Undrew – really, his name sounds silly to me – you can help me work out parts of my new screenplay."

Nicole was intrigued by the story. She gave Bella suggestions and did her best to have some input, which Bella appreciated.

At this point, whilst they were walking Charlie, Undrew Gault-Jones – waving a cheery greeting – did jog past.

Nicole blushed when he stopped briefly to kiss both her and Bella on each cheek. "He's not worthy of you?" Bella wished she was able to help Nicole have more confidence.

"He's to die for. He's so handsome," Nicole sighed. She corrected herself. "I know no man is worth dying for."

Charlie stopped for the twentieth time to mark his territory.

Nicole asked Bella, "Can I tell Undrew about your script? It will give me an excuse to talk more to him."

"Of course, you can. I doubt he's going to copy my ideas."

A few days later, there was Undrew and Nicole waiting to accompany Bella and Charlie on the dog walk.

Undrew, having heard a garbled story of Bella's screenplay from Nicole, said, "It sounds like a thrilling movie. The doctor has a marvelous name."

Bella said, "Dr. John Beadel."

"That's right. He is a depraved individual like Winston Agadees, the main character in *The Lions of Amarula*. I hope you don't mind. Nicole has a copy and she gave it to me to read. I'd love to play the lead. He had an English accent, didn't he?"

Bella replied, "Yes, he did. My back story for the accent is that he went to boarding school in England."

"Perfect," Undrew said. "Maybe I can show it to… Bella said, "No, it's been bought."

Nicole added, "And paid for."

Bella said, "Lions of Amarula are sitting on a shelf. Probably beneath twenty other scripts."

Nicole said, "Bella, don't be so like negative."

"Yes, Bella, don't be negative," Undrew agreed. "So, when they cast *Lions of Amarula,* please let me know. I'll let my agent know and voila. I might be Winston Agadees, the evil protagonist of *The Lions of Amarula*. And whilst I am dreaming, I will become a big star, and the movie will make millions and I will win an Oscar."

Nicole said, "You've got such a like sense of your own importance since you got the part in the daytime soap."

Undrew was cheerful, "That's where stars begin."

Bella said, "You already know my new script is based on the idea AIDS was deliberately introduced in South Africa. It was there already, but the way the disease exploded was highly suspicious, in my opinion."

Undrew said, "It's a conspiracy theory. It can't be proven or not. I get it. I think if you were younger, you'd have done something in the movie industry."

Nicole butted in, "She has done something in the movies. She sold her screenplay."

Undrew said, "You might have been an actor."

Bella said, "No, I don't like being in the spotlight. Maybe I'd have been an art director. Maybe costumes? I do love fashion, old and new. I always notice clothes in movies?"

Nicole insisted, "You did sell your screenplay. That means you're a screenwriter."

Bella rolled her eyes. "There is not one person who

comes to LA who doesn't write a screenplay, and as you know, mine is languishing in Ivan and Farrel's office, waiting for Godot."

"Who's Godot?"

Undrew explained, "He's a character in a famous play by Samuel Beckett... and the thing is that Godot never comes."

Bella said, "In my new script, I keep making my character more and more evil. I have to give him one redeeming feature."

Andrew suggested, "Give him a dog. There's a couple who live somewhere near here who have two of the biggest Dobermans I've ever seen. They both have stick-up ears. It's so cruel. One of the dogs is pale gold. I've never seen one that color. When the woman walks both dogs, she looks like she can't handle them. So maybe give him a pair of golden Dobermans."

Nicole said, "Bella wants a redeeming feature, not like vicious dogs. He should have something unexpected, like a tiny Chihuahua."

Undrew draped his long arm over Nicole's shoulder as they walked. Bella could see this intimacy pleased Nicole, though she could see, for Undrew, it was merely a gesture of friendship.

"Maybe you should be careful," Undrew suggested. "I know you're looking around the internet for scary things. You could make the FBI wonder. They have people looking for leads. You know, if you are researching toxins and murder and AIDS, and all that, Big Brother is Watching You."

Undrew's warning made Bella think of two requests to join her Facebook she'd recently received and rejected. Both – a month apart – were from an American soldier stationed in Afghanistan. Their Facebook front page showed them happily posing with other soldiers. When Bella asked one of them why they wanted to be friends, both men said she looked pretty and had a lovely smile.

She refused both requests realizing they were not bona fide. After Bella told Greta about the soldiers wanting to be her Facebook friends, Greta said, "Don't imagine you're special. I've had lots of similar messages."

Chapter 19: Life Weaves a Pattern

"Even the weaver might not know how it will turn out."

Greta arrived for what had become a regular Sunday brunch as Violet was leaving to go to church. Bella had already put out a tray of smoked salmon and bagels on her table, which served as a combo dining/library table.

"How are you?" Greta asked, relieved Violet was leaving.

"My daughter Gracie still doesn't have water. Haai, it is terrible! She must buy water and it's very expensive. She has paid the rent, and still no water. How can she have a shower with no water? Haai, this is terrible!"

After Violet left, Greta said, "I couldn't live without a shower every day. Sometimes I have two if I have to go out!"

Bella said, "There are women all over the world, on their haunches, washing the dishes, the clothes and themselves from a bucket of water they have carried from a distant well."

Greta didn't want to seem uncaring. "How do they do it, sitting like that?"

Bella said, "I don't know, and they do it with apparent ease. In South Africa, I used to often see women with a huge basin of washing on their heads. They walk as if it's not there. Rural women have a workout merely by living. I pay Sven to force me to exercise. We have whole industries to keep us fit. It's so…"

Greta didn't wait for Bella to find the right word. "I have a new man in my life."

Bella immediately picked up on Greta's tone of voice, which indicated something not quite right.

"What's wrong with him?" Bella asked.

"I feel embarrassed even telling you."

Bella knew she'd get whatever it was out of Greta.

"He was…" Greta paused "…he's been out for a few weeks."

"Out of what?"

"Fraud. He took the fall for his partners. It wasn't a big fraud."

"You mean he was found guilty of a crime and was in jail or prison? I never know what's the difference here. For how long?"

"I'm not sure. I think two or three years."

"What did he do?"

"He told his brother about something that was going on in this company, and his brother told a friend and so on."

"You mean insider trading?"

Greta stressed, "He made a little mistake."

"You're about to make another," Bella warned.

"Anyone can make a mistake."

"Is he single?" Bella inquired.

Greta almost whispered, "He doesn't live with his wife."

"That means he's still married."

Greta sighed. "He is separated. Remember, he's been in jail for the last few years. His wife wants money he doesn't have. She thinks he's hidden his money and it's not true. I've seen how he's living in a small studio apartment in Hollywood. But he's confident he can build up a business again. He's one of those men who knows how to recover."

Bella said, "I'll do some investigating later."

Nicole arrived and Greta said, "I'm so happy you're here. You saved me getting flagellated."

Nicole brought Undrew with her. She did ask Bella if she could. Undrew had been to Bella once before and being English and brought up not to show overt enthusiasm, refrained from commenting on her astonishing décor. Now, knowing Bella a bit better, he asked if she might show him around.

"This place is like a work of art. Wherever I look, there's

something so fabulous to see. It's an art installation and you live in it."

Recently Bella papered the walls of her bathroom with pages torn from a book of botanical ferns. Some of the illustrations partly covered the previous 'wallpaper', pages torn from a vintage Japanese book written on rice paper. She was also a collector of sorts. There were plates hanging on the dining area wall, a collection of porcelain dogs, which began when her beloved Pekingese died. There were mirrors and bookshelves in every room. Coffee table books, not for show, but because she was interested in something, were piled up on a sitting room table. Some walls were completely mirrored, making her home look larger than it was. Ornamental rugs covered the concrete floors, a few on top of each other. Bella wrote on some of the door quotes she liked. The front double door was collaged with tarot cards, cigar bands and Japanese decorative papers she once collected. The door to the guest bathroom was collaged with flower illustrations.

Bella was always flattered when anyone appreciated her unique flair for decoration. "It's so comfortable," Nicole said, sinking into one of a pair of armchairs.

Bella was particular about comfort. Every chair had a surface nearby on which to place a glass or cup. There were footstools to be pushed around for tired legs.

Bella told Undrew, "When I first moved to Los Angeles and into The Portland, I chose quality. My ex paid for everything, and I knew what I chose had to last. The sofa and chairs are on their third upholstery incarnation. I originally chose taupe linen. I was enamored of the spare Japanese style I saw here. But I'm not a minimalist, as you can see. The taupe linen was replaced by blue and cream toile, and now..."

Undrew enthused, "I love this flowery linen. It reminds me of houses in England, but more interesting."

Undrew was effusive about Bella's kitchen office. The desk and bookshelves were built shortly after Bella moved in by a handsome young carpenter who had a crush on Jessica, hence his competitive pricing. Bella drew out the curved shape of the desk sweeping along one wall to the window overlooking the street.

"I never feel cut off from civilization when I'm at my desk working on my big screen iMac. From my vantage point, the comings and goings of the street keep me from feeling isolated."

Greta teased, "She spies on her neighbors."

Greta was referring mainly to the neighbor with a long

dark beard and shaved head. "I think he's an Islamic terrorist," she told Nicole, Greta, and Shelly.

"There is only one odd thing. He has a dog," Bella said. "Fundamentalist Muslims don't like dogs. In Mohammed's hadiths – the spoken words of the prophet – he called for all dogs to be killed especially black ones. There was an outcry, and working dogs were thus permitted. More inventive religious scholars found ways to discount the dog-hating hadiths, seeing as many Muslims wanted pets."

Nicole and Bella discussed whether they should call the FBI.

Greta told Bella, "You've lost your mind. Lots of men have beards!"

Shelly, on the other hand, agreed the man looked like a terrorist. "It's not a trendy beard," she noted. "It's a terrorist beard."

Then Nicole discovered he was an actor, playing a part in a movie.

The bearded young man was from Nevada, loved dogs, and was adopting another. He and his girlfriend were engaged to be married and he would be moving out soon. All this made Bella more aware of how appearances could be misleading.

Bella announced, more to Undrew than anyone else, "I feel a bit shameful having given my imagination free rein to envision bringing down our poor innocent 'terrorist'."

Undrew said, "I understand. I am a suspicious person, myself."

Bella said, "I think in some ways I am a bit of a bigot."

Nicole said, "No, you're not. Not at all. You are like nothing like a bigot."

Bella said, "Maybe bigot is not quite the right word? I might judge, but I don't act differently upon my judgment."

"How do you mean?" Nicole asked.

"I have an extremely negative feeling towards women wearing a hijab. But if I had any interactions with a woman wearing one, I'd be perfectly polite."

Undrew said. "I feel sorry for them."

Greta said, "I believe they feel sorry for us, having to subject ourselves to the male gaze."

Bella added, "I'm an equal opportunity bigot. I don't like Orthodox Jewish women who dress drably and wear wigs to cover their real hair. It's sort of like a hijab but made of hair, not a scarf. And don't get me on the ridiculous garb men wear who belonged to some orthodox sects with their fur hats... the odd thing is I don't feel the same way towards nuns, and I'm not Catholic."

Nicole said, "I've never noticed you being rude to anyone. In fact, you're quite nice to that crazy woman who we see on our street. You're much more tolerant than I am."

Undrew agreed.

Bella said, "I have a tolerance for 'off' people. I feel for them. They can't help being what they are. It's as if God forgot to wrap them up in pretty packaging and tie the bow."

Undrew said, "That's awesome the way you like to think about them."

Bella grimaced. Undrew was picking up Nicole's descriptive go-to, plus the use of 'like'.

Bella said, "I once took a course in marketing when I lived in Johannesburg. I was a copywriter in an ad agency. None of the other copywriters or art directors wanted to do it with me. It was their loss because I learned some very valuable things."

"Like what?" Greta asked.

"The four Ps of marketing. If one is missing, the product or service, whatever it is for sale, fails. You need to have the right *Product*, in the *right Place*, with the right *Promotion* at the right *Price*. So, for example, my screenplay might be the right product, and I sold it at a price I was willing to accept.

But it languishes in the wrong place, in an office, where it's under a pile of other screenplays, and it is not being promoted."

Nicole said, "That's so awesome. I want to remember the four Ps."

Bella continued, "I also learned about how important it is when it comes to presenting ourselves. We are what we eat, but we're also how we get ourselves up. How we choose to show ourselves to the world says so much about us. For instance, if a man wears a white wife-beater vest, showing off a good body, it says something about him. If it's a man who hasn't got a good physique – flabby and hairy – it says something else.

One says, "I am hot."

The other says, "I don't care."

Both Nicole and Greta said almost in unison. "I hate wife beater vests."

Bella said, "The world has changed so much. I didn't dare show a bra strap, for instance. Dresses sometimes had little hooks inside the shoulders to keep bras in place. When I was sixteen, I wore a two-way. That's what we called a girdle; it was meant to keep your tummy and bottom all smooth."

"Like Spanx?" Nicole asked.

"Yes. Totally constricting. Imagine a sixteen-year-old body needing to be kept smooth. And the two-way had clips hanging down to keep up stockings. There was no such thing as pantyhose or tights. A two-way kept the boys out. I can see myself dressed in a pink and white striped sailor suit... tight skirt with a slit on the back, and a blouson top walking from the bus stop to my mother's office in town. That's what we called the center of the city. *Town* was where all the fancy departmental stores and shops were. I wore white kid wrist-length gloves and I felt enormously grown up. I could go on and on about what I wore. I think someone's written a book like that. Clothes bring on memories, like songs, and scents, and photographs."

"Why do we remember some things so vividly and others not at all?" Undrew asked.

"It's a miracle we remember anything," Bella replied.

Undrew said, "I remember the oddest things, like my aunt peeling an orange for me."

Bella said, "I remember my grandmother making me beef tea. She boiled a piece of meat in hardly any water and gave me the broth. It was delicious, a big treat. I suppose that's why I remember it, but I remember almost nothing about my first wedding to Guy, other than his stupid best friend, who was the photographer, who didn't put film in his camera. There is not one photograph of me and Guy. Only ones that were taken by a photographer we hired to take pictures of me, my mother, Guy's mother, and my maid of honor before the wedding at my mother's flat."

Nicole added, "Funny, I remember having Jello-O at my friend's house. Her mother made it with pieces of canned peaches. I don't want to talk about food. I'm like trying to lose weight." Nicole picked up the latest Vogue from a pile of fashion and high-end decorating magazines that arrived at Bella every month. She paged through the magazine until she came to a photograph of a model posing on a hay bale. "See her boots. I love these boots! I've gone to visit them at Barney's twice."

"You visit boots?" Bella thought this amusing.

Nicole said, "It's almost as good as owning them. Better. My boots will never get old or hurt my feet."

Bella added, "Or get you in debt."

After Shelly showed up, Nicole showed her the boots. "I'm like dying for them, but they are like stratospheric... the price!"

Referring to her rich friend, Shelly said, "Madelaine Moore would buy two pairs."

Bella said, "She'd look ridiculous in them."

Shelly ignored Bella and picked a magazine from the pile, "I'm so glad you get all the magazines." Greta and Nicole agreed.

Bella often left them piling up on the table, and then, almost like a chore, she looked through the lot. Just as she wanted to know about the politics of the day – not only in The United States – Bella wanted to be up on fashion and home décor. Glossy magazines were inspirational for her art and even her writing. She also subscribed and paid for magazines she regularly read, like The Economist and The Christian Science Monitor. The LA Times was delivered every morning. There were online newspapers she received and paid for. Bella liked to be up to date on things other than fashion.

Shelly, paging through one of the fashion magazines, said, "These clothes are weird."

Greta, referring to the Nancy Sinatra hit of old, sang out, "These clothes aren't meant for wearing."

Shelly laughed, "Look at this! How can the model use her hands if the sleeves go down to her knees? And here's a tailored jacket with only one sleeve. Imagine wearing that in New York. One side freezes and the other stay warm."

Greta said, "There's a big difference between fashion and clothes. Designers are artists. And imagine they must make new designs at least twice a year. Some designers make up to five collections. Clothes for Spring, Summer, Autumn, Winter and Vacations."

Bella said, "I like to see what's in vogue, even if I can't wear it, which makes me feel a mixture of sadness, anger, jealousy and admiration all in one glance."

Nobody picked up on discussing this further.

Shelly piped up, "Look here; this woman lives here in Los Angeles. She's from Sudan."

Bella said, "That gives her voguish clout. Also, Sudanese women are generally gorgeous."

Shelly continued, "She married... guess who?"

Greta was quick. "A billionaire banker."

Shelly laughed, "Spot on. She wants her home to be like a sanctuary for her four-year-old twins from this marriage, plus his four grown-up children."

Bella said, "Of course, he's been married before. He's traded in his old wife for something new. Rich men do that."

Shelly broke into another song, "If I were a rich man..." She didn't know the rest of the words, and nobody else did, either.

Bella said, paging through yet another high fashion magazine, "Imagine being the daughter of a company that's been around forever, like Hermes. It's like being a sort of royalty."

Greta teased, "Instead of being the daughter of a drunkard and a working mother."

Bella said, "In a past life, I think you were a courtesan."

Greta didn't take this as an insult, nor was it meant to be.

Greta dispensed with magazines and stitched the needlepoint she'd again taken up. "Who was that Queen who embroidered until her king showed up? It's one of those old Greek stories. I know you'll know, Undrew."

"She was Penelope, the wife of Odysseus. He left her and promised to return. He was presumed dead, so Penelope was supposed to remarry. She said she would wed after she'd finished the shroud she was making for her father-in-law. She undid what she sewed in the night so she didn't have to remarry. Finally, Odysseus did return."

Nicole was impressed. "That's so like rad."

Bella said, "I used to do a lot of needlepoint, now my fingers hurt, but I loved placing one stitch against another and seeing it turn into a pattern. I made up my own patterns. You know me, I can't follow patterns or recipes, which – I must admit – results in some flops. Yet there is an occasional triumph."

Greta risked it and asked Bella if she'd come with her to a big art show later that day. "It's an important show and I need support. You won't have to talk to anyone. You can walk around and look at the art and move down the aisles of galleries. You can people-watch. There will be lots of young arty people."

"What's important about it?"

Greta said, "Galleries are participating from all over the world. It should be interesting. You never know. You might meet someone."

"No, I won't. I mean I will come with you, but I won't meet anyone interesting. In all my life – and it's not such a short one now – I've never met a man interesting or otherwise at an art show. Never. And I've tried. Believe me, I have asked interesting-looking men – of all ages – what they think of a piece of art, and I have never had more than a cursory reply. It's as if I have the measles should I attempt further conversation."

"So, you'll come?" Greta was pleased.

At the show, Bella happily wandered around on her own, leaving Greta to conduct business. There was a lot to see, both artworks and people. Bella made going to these big art shows with Greta fun by asking various people if she could take their photographs. She'd never been declined by anyone. Bella thought the subjects imagined themselves splashed across some arty website and they were far too cool to ask who Bella worked for. Bella also engaged certainly approachable gallerists.

"What medium does the artist use?" Bella enquired of an emaciated gallerist of indeterminate sex with curly red hair, shaved off on one side, and a narrow-cut, purposefully crumpled black suit.

"She uses crushed coal, used motor oil and slashes them across the canvas. Then she scrapes the surface with old tins. She does this many times to achieve the resulting patina."

Moving on, Bella found no coherent answer to a thick line of red paint cutting a canvas into two areas, with a square drawn badly in black paint in the top half and a circle painted as badly in the bottom half. The gallerist said the painting was about both simplicity and division.

"It does show that," Bella agreed and moved on to a large gallery space where a kitchen door in a frame stood in the center.

An art lover – with intense Japanese tattoos covering skinny arms – swooned to his companion. "This gels with me, big time."

He was one of many imaginatively dressed people clustered around the door. Another viewer muttered, "Extraordinary!"

Bella could not help herself and asked him, "What's extraordinary about an old door leading to nowhere? Where would you put it if you owned it?"

The gallerist, pale and ethereal in ubiquitous black, stepped in.

"It's a conceptual piece," she said politely. "The artist is interested in the relationship between the continuous process of entering and leaving. The door is very old. It's been used many times. The artist found it discarded in a building site."

Bella refrained from further inquiry, moving on to find herself confronting a huge colored photograph – slightly out of focus – of a pimply young man lying naked on a nondescript bed, sporting a gigantic floppy penis.

"That looks like porn to me?" she said to nobody, seeing as she was the only one looking at the work.

Bella wanted to ask the gallerist to explain, but though she kept on returning to the photograph, no gallerist made an appearance. And as if the art going public were embarrassed to even stand before it, nobody other than Bella looked at the photograph other than furtively in passing.

At one gallery space, old postcards in elaborate gold frames were hung haphazardly on a wall. Bella asked the gallerist – another androgynous creature with white bleached hair – whether the cheap office chair beneath the postcards was a chair or art. Bella was joking, but without a trace of embarrassment, the gallerist replied, "It's part of the whole. It comes with the pot plant beside it."

Bella was thus made aware of the struggling rubber plant in a fake terra cotta plastic planter beside the chair.

"So, the art is the chair and the pot plant and the postcards?" Bella kept all sarcasm from her voice.

"Yes. The artist always demonstrates how the ordinary has a presence." The gallerist gave a wide smile. He was delighted he'd managed to get across the significance of the piece.

Further along, Bella stopped to watch a young woman with voluminous, tousled purple hair looking at a pair of purple boots dipped in a bucket of purple paint. "You match," she said and asked if she could take her photograph. She was, as everyone else Bella photographed, thrilled.

Greta finally completed her business. "This was most productive. Thanks for coming with me."

As they drove off, Bella said, "The people were more interesting than the art."

Greta said, "I bought a fantastic piece for my client. Everyone at the show was talking about it. There were better-known art dealers wanting it. But I have a relationship with the gallery, so it's mine. I mean, it's my clients."

"Which one?" Bella asked.

"Did you see the door? Everyone was crowding around it.

"Yes, I did. I was stopped from walking through to the other side of nothing."

From Bella's tone, Greta could hear Bella thought it was crazy that anyone wanted it. Bella was always going on about how some art clearly demonstrated the story of *The King's New Clothes.*

Bella said, "Maybe I should paint again?"

"You could. Find a studio, get yourself in the groove and paint!"

Bella said, "I'm not in the painting groove. I'm in the writing groove."

Chapter 20: NY NY

"New gets old."

When Bella's daughter Jessica asked her to come with her and Chloe to New York, Bella was relieved. She had a good excuse put her screenplay aside for a while.

Jessica was invited to attend her good friend Poppy Rapinski's housewarming party in Manhattan. She wanted Bella to join her on the trip so she could babysit Chloe during the night. This was no hardship for Bella, for she liked New York, as well as babysitting her granddaughter, and she was excited. "We can go to The Frick Collection and the Guggenheim. Chloe will love the Guggenheim."

"I don't like museums," Chloe piped up the moment she heard the word.

"I don't like flying, but I'm coming with you," Bella countered.

Bella might have been more of a traveler had she not feared flying. Sven, her long-time Swedish-born trainer, always told her when she expressed her fears before a trip, "You are NOT flying. The pilot is flying." This line never failed to make her smile as the plane took off when there was turbulence, and before it landed, though she still – at take-off, turbulence, and landing – furiously rubbed the belly of the gold-mounted jade Buddha charm her mother gave her when she turned twenty-one.

The charm – one of many talismans keeping Bella aloft – hung on a gold Gucci-style linked necklace her ex-husband Guy Rufus gave her after one of their many turbulent tiffs. Besides Buddha, there were four Saint Christophers. Bella was Jewish, but all the help she could muster was fine. She also had a gold Chinese good luck charm, a gold heart with the initial S given to her by an old lover, a Hebrew lucky charm and a silver Turkish shoe from who knows where.

Bella read somewhere that the most dangerous moments in flight were the two minutes after the plane took off and before it landed. Her cousin also told her he overcame his fear of flying by learning to fly, but she didn't want to go that far.

Jessica and Poppy once worked for the same design firm in West Hollywood. They were planning to start their own interior-decorating firm when Poppy fell for a man in the diamond trade who lived in New York. And so, Jessica branched out on her own. Poppy's romance ended, but the experience gave her a jumpstart in the jewelry business. Poppy's creations were now sold not only at Barney's but also in boutiques in Milan and Paris, though most of her income came from high rollers in Las Vegas whose wives and mistresses snapped up her more extravagant pieces. Poppy also – thanks to information from the said boyfriend – invested in townhouses in Kosovo, which she sold for a decent profit, enabling her to purchase her New York Soho Loft.

"Who knew there were townhouses in Kosovo?" Bella said.

"People live everywhere, mother," Jessica replied. "Not only in Beverly Hills."

Bella didn't like the tone, but she said nothing. She'd decided before she left not to complain about anything nor to react nastily to anything Jessica or Chloe said. She would keep all moans and groans to herself. It was a challenge she almost lived up to, especially seeing her punishment for not doing so was doing twenty squats there and then, which, when she did it in the oddest places, made Chloe thoroughly embarrassed and Jessica hysterical.

"What are you doing, mother?" Jessica exclaimed with horror when Bella began squatting in the airport concourse.

"Keeping fit," Bella replied. She wasn't going to let Jessica in on her challenge, which she'd already failed when she shouted at Chloe, who whizzed around on her scooter, wearing a rainbow-colored helmet with turquoise spikes.

At their hotel in New York, the upgrade the manager offered Bella at no extra cost was the result of Poppy's influence. Bella thought Poppy looked decidedly influential when she arrived to take them all out for dinner. She wore a sharply cut pale peppermint green linen shift, the highest heels imaginable, plus a strategic scattering of her jeweled pieces.

Chloe insisted on bringing her scooter and swooshed along the sidewalk, even though the restaurant was a short walk from the hotel.

"Can I pet your dog?" Chloe asked late-night dog walkers with their pedigree animals. This gave Chloe the opportunity to explain her dog in Los Angeles was a rescue.

Bella and Jessica were exhausted when they got back from dinner, but Chloe maintained she wasn't tired and wanted to read on her Kindle.

"I've read fifteen books so far this vacation, and I'm not tired. You always tell me that's how to learn from reading."

Bella fell asleep remembering her brief affair with Eli Burns. She called Eli her Literary Stallion as he claimed everything he knew he learned from books. He was extremely erudite and gave her books to read by Freud, Jung, J. D. Laing, and Herman Hesse.

The next morning, whilst planning their day over breakfast, Jessica warned ominously, "We have to do things Chloe likes too."

Thus, after breakfast, there they were inside FAO Schwartz, the famous toy emporium from which Bella knew they would never exit in time for The Frick or The Guggenheim, especially as they were to meet Poppy and her boyfriend for lunch at a restaurant twenty blocks away.

Bella's heart sank. But being creative, she decided to make the best of it. She was not going to do squats in FAO Schwartz. She was going to take selfies. Had she known the store would be no more, she might have taken a photograph of her family in front of the store.

Bella leaned into a display of life-sized stuffed animals; she draped the chimpanzee's arm over her shoulder.

"What are you doing?" Jessica exclaimed.

"Taking a selfie."

"Let me see," Chloe grabbed Bella's iPhone. Bella grabbed it back.

"I look like my father!" Bella was horrified when she looked at her picture. She always thought she looked like her beautiful mother Joyce, but no, here was Speedy Mellman with a bulbous nose, a vast lined forehead, and a halo of frizzy hair.

"You have to hold it up higher," Chloe instructed with the scorn of the proficient and whooshed off on her scooter to *Build Your Own Bear*. She chose a deflated furry bear, had it stuffed to her preference – she could even install a heartbeat if she so desired, which she didn't – and dressed it in an outfit from The Bear Bootique.

The lengthy procedure gave Bella more than enough time to take selfies with newborn Madam Alexander dolls. In case you don't know, these are premier dolls and look quite real. She held her iPhone up and angled her face beside a life-size panda, a life-size lion, and various other soft offerings. She thought she'd do an art project; Bella Mellman posing with the soon-to-be detritus of modern consumerism keeping China afloat. However, no matter how she posed, she still looked like Speedy Mellman at his drunken worst. And so – being vain enough to care what she looked like to others, even in an art project – she trashed the lot and resolved to make an appointment to have Botox injected into her furrowed forehead. For her nose – drooping, as all noses did with age – only surgery would help, and she wasn't going to do that.

Finally, after looking at her emails, her Facebook, and playing all the word games permitted by the makers of an addicting word game, her heart soared when she saw Jessica in the pay-up line.

Once she left the store, Bella knew Chloe would not play with the bear with the fake leather chaps, sneakers, and aviator sunglasses, which took eons to choose, but it was almost impossible to leave the store without buying something. Even Bella, for one rash moment, thought it might be nice to have Penelope the pink and white plush dog, or Penelope's brother, Patrick, in the large size at $299 – made from a material that felt like a mixture of clouds and chinchilla – to cuddle on her bed.

Outside FAO Schwartz, the heady air of Bergdorf Goodman beckoned.

Bergdorf surely catered mostly to the 1%. And a good percentage of those were buying shoes in the expansive shoe salon. One tiny young Arab woman – her eyes well made up – wearing the black shroud to spare lusting males from their debasing instincts – pranced around in a pair of stiletto boots costing more than two iMacs. Bella often compared excesses to the price of a computer. "Perfect for the desert," she whispered.

Jessica warned, "Shut up, mom, people can hear you!"

Whilst Bella and Jessica looked at shoes, Chloe whizzed by on her scooter, pausing now and then to look at a pair of boots. Chloe had big feet and could fit into an adult size five, which delighted her no end.

"Maybe I can find shoes for me?" She showed Jessica a pair of soft black biker boots.

Jessica laughed. "They're too expensive for me. And your foot's still growing."

Chloe looked at the price of a few more boots and pronounced, "I think they make them expensive so rich people can feel good about themselves when they buy them."

And with that priceless comment, Chloe whizzed off down the escalator to find the glittering party dresses she had admired on the way up. She managed to get lost, but a smart child that she was, she decided the best place to be found was on the ground floor by the escalator.

"You don't run off like that. We've been looking for you! I was about to go to customer service to announce you were lost," Jessica admonished Chloe.

Bella told Chloe, "You're really smart to wait by the escalator. You knew we had to come down this way."

"What if we took the elevator?" Jessica asked.

It was twenty blocks to the restaurant for lunch. "We need a taxi," Jessica said.

"Let's walk," Bella was shocked to hear herself.

Normally she hated walking, but that was because, in Los Angeles, the city wasn't walking friendly. Narrow streets with something to look at were conducive to walking. New York, London, Paris, and Rome were walking cities. In Los Angeles, it felt like a half-mile long walk just to cross a road.

"It's twenty blocks!"

"We need the exercise," Bella added, feeling strong and powerful and filled with New York energy.

Chloe whizzed off again, managing to avoid pedestrians as well as elicit complimentary remarks about her extraordinary space-age helmet, the likes of which had not been seen on the streets of Manhattan.

Jessica screeched constant warnings. "There's a bus! There's a taxi! Be careful! Watch out!" But Chloe managed the streets of New York with aplomb.

Bella told Jessica, "I once knew someone who really did get run over by a bus in New York. I can't remember her name. She was engaged to Lenny Ziff."

Lenny – with whom Bella went out once after her divorce from Phil Varelly – was a nice, though flaccid man. He claimed he was in love with her after the first date. "I want you to come on Friday night for dinner at my parent's. You will love them," he told Bella. "You'll love my sister and her husband too."

That was enough to make Bella run a mile. Friday night dinners with someone else's family sounded like torture.

Chloe was exhausted from her day in New York and wanted room service dinner.

Bella and Jessica left her happily watching TV and walked to a nearby restaurant recommended by the concierge of their hotel.

The restaurant was both cozy and modern at the same time and populated by sophisticated and chic-dressed New Yorkers of all ages. Bella noted a few older women with sharply cut steel grey hair and resolved there and then to stop streaking platinum blonde highlights in her going grey locks. "People look so different here," Bella sighed, "I've seen a whole lot of really attractive men and elegantly dressed."

"Gay," Jessica replied, gesturing towards the bar.

Bella said, "It's nice to see people dress with a sense of occasion. New Yorkers do look more stylish and better put together. They make an effort."

Jessica agreed, "LA Casual can be taken too far."

"We are going to the Frick tomorrow," Bella reminded Jessica as they happily shared a lemon soufflé. And then we can go to the Guggenheim Museum."

Jessica said, "We have to think of Chloe. You and Chloe have to be at the theater at seven."

Bella and Chloe were going to see Kinky Boots whilst Jessica went to Poppy's housewarming party.

"Maybe just the Frick?" Bella sighed.

However, as they were about to make their way to The Frick, Jessica said, "Chloe needs some exercise, so let's go into the park for a bit before." That's all Chloe needed to hear before she whizzed off again, with Jessica and Bella shrieking for her to be careful as she brilliantly negotiated the sidewalk.

"The last time I was in Central Park was with my mother," Bella said. "I miss her so much."

It was spring. Joyce had never been to New York and the park was at its best. Joyce adored New York. That trip was the last time Joyce would be able to travel so far, as age made a more serious grab at her heart and lungs.

Joyce adored the illicit adventure of buying fake designer handbags in a basement showroom in China Town. By the time she got back to Johannesburg and told her friends at the retirement home about her fabulous trip to Los Angeles and New York, the adventure of how she bought a fake Hermes – in a basement showroom guarded by the Chinese Mafia –

was well embellished, as were the lives her American family. Ivan was brilliant at making movies: Jessica designed interiors for movie stars and well-known restaurateurs. Bella had her pick of eligible men, unfortunately, none of whom she liked well enough. She was soon making a movie. Of course, Chloe was both adorable and brilliant.

As Bella and Jessica, with Chloe speeding on her scooter, approached Central Park, they found themselves, inadvertently, at the gate that led directly to The Central Park Zoo.

As zoos went, it was a fine one. Bella didn't mind the Tropical Zone with its exotic monkeys and birds, but there was the Snow Leopard Exhibition, The Temperate Territory, The Sea Lion Pool, The Polar Circle, plus a Petting Zoo, and Chloe had to see all of them and that put paid to The Frick, for they were to meet Poppy for lunch in Soho.

Chloe was unimpressed by Soho. The streets were torn up, and there was lots of scaffolding preventing her from scooting. Worst of all, after lunch at Café Habana, Chloe was forced to go shopping.

"We've done things you like," Bella pointed out, believing logic was applicable to a ten-year-old. However, Jessica thoughtfully brought Chloe's kindle with her, so whilst they shopped, she could read.

"I love New York," Jessica said as she tried on various Italian-made linen dresses with subtle details, perfect for New York, finally picking one that was, fortunately, on sale.

Bella bought a soft cotton kaftan, also on sale, plus a pair of raffia earrings. Earings were the one accessory Bella found hard to resist. She had dozens of pairs, mostly for pierced ears and most of them hanging on hooks and nails on a wall on the side of her walk-in closet. Bella did have a few pairs of vintage clip-ons in a drawer, plus some left-over heavy dangles from the eighties. An unflattering photograph of herself wearing a jacket with enormous shoulder pads and hair that cascaded to her shoulders in a layered frizz never failed to remind her of the dreadful fashions of that time.

After they got back to the cool of their hotel and flopped on the bed, exhausted from their day, which had not included The Frick, let alone The Guggenheim, Jessica had an idea. "Carolina isn't so far from here…"

"And so?"

"Let's find out if we can change our tickets and go."

"North Carolina or South?" Bella asked.

Jessica was not sure, but she remembered reading Carolina was a great state in which to bring up a child.

"It's the one with Charleston," Bella replied.

Bella always wanted to visit Charleston, which now Google on her iPad informed her was in South Carolina. Veranda, a magazine showing off mainly Southern décor, was one of her favorites, and she had once researched property in Charleston on the internet, which was fabulous for dreamy meanderings. "Once you have moved to another country, it's easy to imagine moving again," Bella always said.

Bella once investigated Oregon and Seattle. She liked rain and cloudy skies and could never understand Los Angelinos, who complained about a single cloudy day. The endless blue of Summer combined with the heat of global warming was tiresome. Bella considered any hint of actual weather a treat. She missed the huge cumulus clouds that banked in the summer in Johannesburg. When they darkened sufficiently, there were storms with lightning and thunder and sheets of water running down the streets. As cars drove, their tires splashed out huge sprays. The storm quickly passed, leaving the land with the inimitable scent of wet earth. Johannesburg winter was rather like Los Angeles Summer; endless boring blue skies, only the temperature was cool. Occasionally there was frost on the ground and winter flowers perished.

On line Bella looked at property in Nice, France and Bath in England. She'd never been to Bath, but she had a friend who once lived there, and it did look charming. Bella thought the English countryside was idyllic. When she lived in London for those four years after her divorce from Guy, she always thought about how much she would like to live in an English Country house. However, inexperienced and naïve as she was at the time, it didn't dawn on her that she could, without a man.

In those days, property in London was affordable due to a drop in the market. As the downslide moved upwards, Bella bought and sold three different homes before she went back to South Africa, cowed by depression and her yet unrecognized alcoholism.

"If only I had bought that house in Chelsea... if only I had kept that flat in Kensington."

She had a few materials if onlies. "If only I had looked after my grandmother's one and a half carat diamond earrings and not left them on the bathroom counter to be stolen, probably by the masseuse who came to my house every other week when I was married to Guy."

On vacation on Hawaii's Big Island with Jessica and Chloe, Bella went so far as to call a realtor who showed her a divine newly built cottage that was part of a development on land adjacent to The Four Seasons hotel. The home had rights to use the nearby private beach club and the sheltered cove. Bella called a private school on the island and schlepped a reluctant Jessica and Chloe to see what it was like. Unfortunately, Jessica did not find Hawaii as captivating. Bella would not move there without her family.

Bella never understood the American way of seeing family; twice-a-year visits, Thanksgiving and Christmas, and complaints at even that. Jessica adored her brother Derek, and his angelic wife Josie, and their children and grandchildren. She loved her cousins. She wished they all lived in America instead of Johannesburg. Bella didn't have a big family, but she liked what she did have.

"That's because they live on a different continent," Greta quipped.

Greta's parents were dead, her older sister was dead, and she didn't talk to her two older brothers. It had to do with money. Of course, most family feuds do. According to Greta, her brothers ganged up on her ailing mother after their father died and persuaded her to exclude Greta from the will because she was not married and didn't have children. The amount of money was not significant, but Greta was justifiably hurt. "It's so unfair to punish me for my choice."

But, as Bella often quoted, "If you want fair, go to

Pomona." Bella loved the quote, having never been to the Pomona Country Fair.

Jessica called her travel agent, changed their tickets, and booked a hotel in Charleston, South Carolina."

Bella checked her iPad: what to do in Charleston. "Thank god for Google." Then she asked Jessica, "Have you ever noticed god is dog spelled backward?"

"Yes, you've mentioned that before," Jessica added what she had heard so many times from her mother. "And if you add a zero to god, you get good."

"Funny that: god, good, dog and Google."

"What's funny about that?"

Bella said, "I remember the first time I saw the word Google spread out on a giant billboard near the Beverly Center."

Bella wished she had bought Google shares, not to mention Amazon and Netflix, though wishing was silly, seeing as she didn't invest in the stock market.

"The stock market is for professionals," Guy always said. "You need nerves of steel."

Guy had those. He knew when to buy and sell, when to cut his losses and when to wait things out.

"I love New York. I could stay longer," Jessica said as

she dressed for Poppy's party.

"It's dirty," Chloe was unimpressed, though she was looking forward to seeing Kinky Boots. "Milo's seen it. His dad took him when he was in New York. His mom was furious with his dad for taking him. That's so lame," Chloe said. "Milo knows about gay people and sex."

Bella wondered what Chloe did know about sex, other than pulling a face and saying, "EEEEWW," when anything even vaguely sexual came up in conversation or if something as simple as a kiss was shown on the TV.

"Do I have to change?" Chloe asked, knowing full well she had to, and moreover had a pretty dress to wear, with tiny red dogs embroidered all over and red patent sandals that matched.

"Of course, you have to change," Bella said. "We are going to the theater."

"So!"

"When I was younger, we wore gloves to go to the theater."

Chloe heard many times all about the gloves and hats and uncomfortable underwear Bella wore, how she grew up without television, computers, or cell phones, and how she would never dare speak to her mother or her grandmother like Chloe did.

When they arrived at the theater, Chloe pointed out, "See, gran, there are people in jeans."

"More people make an effort, and when you make an effort, you feel better. Don't you feel nice in that pretty dress with those new shoes?"

"I like my shoes," Chloe admitted. They had the slightest heel and Chloe felt grown up wearing them.

Though Bella was sure Chloe would adore Kinky Boots, Bella did not expect to enjoy the play as she didn't like musicals. Nevertheless, she was aware of the smile on her face for almost the entire show.

"There was one scene that made me cry," Bella told Jessica when she returned from Poppy's party.

"That's what good theater is about. The two masks... comedy and tragedy," Jessica pointed out.

At Poppy's party, Jessica reported, "There were so many attractive men, but they were either married or gay. Still, I had a really good time."

The next day, whilst having breakfast and planning their day in the bar lounge, Jessica had a call from Poppy.

"Everyone said you were divine and Humphrey Beresford called me to ask where you are staying. He said he has some business venture he wants to discuss with you. I suppose it could be true, seeing as he is an antique dealer, but I know Humphrey. He can be very captivating." Poppy warned, "He's also very married and it's his wife who has the money."

Humphrey telephoned almost immediately. Jessica and Poppy ended their call. Jessica told him she didn't have time to meet him, but she did give him her email.

"Don't look at me like that, mother."

"I am not looking at you," Bella replied. "And if I am, it's because it's time to get going. We've only got one more day here to see The Frick.

"We never got to see the Frick," Bella sighed as the plane took off for Charleston.

When they checked in at their hotel, a very beautiful concierge – looking cool and unflustered – informed them, "It's the hottest day we've had in forty years."

"I believe it," Jessica said. "Global Warming, or Climate Change, whatever they want to call it, it's happening."

"It's August," the chief concierge – another beauty – corrected.

Jessica had her write down a list of good restaurants for them to try, and Poppy, too, had given Jessica some names.

Chloe flatly refused to venture into the steam bath outside the air-conditioned hotel for dinner and so Jessica and Bella left her with her kindle and TV whilst they walked to a restaurant recommended by both Poppy and the hotel concierge.

"It's *the* restaurant," Poppy said. "I looked it up in Andrew Harper's Travel Guide."

For those who don't know – and only rich, sophisticated travelers do – Andrew Harper publishes – for a fee – a reference guide to the world's most distinguished hotels and restaurants. Poppy was a subscriber.

The food at the restaurant was nouvelle Southern, which meant none of the delicious batter and a bizarre mix of ingredients that did not combine well. The waitress – yet another Southern Belle – was astonishingly good-looking. Her features were placed like jewels in a perfectly planed bone structure.

Bella complimented her, "You should be a Miss America or come to Hollywood."

"You've made my day," the waitress replied and pranced off to hand in their order.

"I see why they call them Southern Belles," Bella whispered.

Bella often complimented women. She was of the age when nobody wondered about an ulterior motive. It was the same with men. Bella thought nothing of complimenting men, young or old, although, from a few males' terrified reactions, they didn't always get it.

"Are you flirting with me?" One timid married fellow – proverbially tall, dark, and handsome – asked when she complimented him on his patterned socks.

"Yes," Bella replied. "I always compliment men on their socks, then I attack."

As they left their hotel for the restaurant, the friendly doorman, who looked like he'd been working at the job for many years, instructed, "Now, young ladies, when it's time for you to return, aim for the church with the clock."

"Maybe he thinks we'll be a bit drunk and will lose our way back to the hotel," Bella laughed.

However, on the way back from the restaurant, they managed to get lost. There was more than one clock tower in Charleston. Google's walking directions were not up to Charleston's streets. Bella's iPhone ran out of power. Jessica left her iPhone with Chloe in case she needed to call. A couple of young men were no help, nor were two different passing police cars. As they passed the third church with a clock and what seemed to be hours of walking in circles –

their clothes drenched – Bella and Jessica wondered what the hell they were doing in Charleston.

However, in the light of a new day, despite the global warming temperature, Charleston proved fascinating and when they set out and saw how close they were to their hotel whilst being lost the night before, they laughed.

The heat was oppressive even on the boat trip to Fort Sumter, where the tour guide explained it was here the very first shots of the civil war rang out.

"I had no idea." Bella's knowledge of American history was dismal. She never mustered the interest to find out much about the country she now called home, which she found strange, seeing as she was interested in so many other places; India, Russia, the Middle East, China, and especially African countries.

At Fort Sumter, Jessica left Chloe in the cool of the small gift store, where Chloe sat in a corner and read her kindle.

"I'm so tired. Let's go back to the hotel," Chloe nagged on the boat trip back, but her energy returned when they toured the Aquarium adjacent to the boat dock.

Bella liked Aquariums. They were dark and womb-like, and though she felt sympathy for any captured creature, ocean creatures were mesmerizing.

It was whilst she was marveling at two giant jellyfish, pulsing white translucent against their dimly lit prison, that she noticed, standing beside her, a Southern Belle holding a small black pig. It was the size of a poodle and happily nested in the woman's arms. Bella chose to make no comment. What could you say about a pig in an aquarium? The Southern Belle, in all her dark-haired, pale-skinned glory, stood for a while beside Bella and then moved on as children squealed with delight when they spotted the pig.

After they left the Aquarium, Chloe asked, "Did you see the pig?"

Bella replied, "You see all kinds of strange things when you travel."

Bella launched into one of her life lessons. "There is a saying that travel broadens the mind. You are a very lucky young lady. You have been to so many places and you are not even a teenager. I took my first ever plane trip when I was fifteen and that was to Durban."

Chloe had been to Durban – a coastal town in Quwa Zulu Natal – on the South Coast of South Africa, where the Indian Ocean washed warmer than the icy Atlantic Ocean, which lashed South Africa's more scenic West coast. At Ballito Bay, near Durban, Chloe and Jessica spent time with Debbie Bennet, Jessica's old school friend who owned a charming, rambling home with horse stables almost on the beach. Chloe rode a horse on the sand, which thrilled her no end. It was, she said, "My best, best vacation ever!"

"Most people have never seen some of the things you have. You have learned that there are many different…"

Before Bella could finish, Chloe interrupted, "Gran, you don't have to be always teaching me stuff I know already."

The next night Chloe threatened to again not join Bella and Jessica for dinner, but she was persuaded by the promise of a Pedi cab as Bella was adamant. "I am not walking." Her heel spurs were inflamed, and her feet ached. Her superior attitude towards walking those twenty blocks in New York had their revenge, not to mention circling blocks in Charleston in the heat of the night whilst being lost.

They chose to eat outdoors at the casual harbor restaurant, where, at the table next to them, two delightful female tourists from New Jersey complimented Chloe on her green eyes and bouncy auburn curls. The attention put Chloe in entertainment mode, and she chatted about how her parents were divorced, how she had successfully nagged her mother to adopt a cat and a dog, and now she wanted a miniature pig like the one she saw in the Aquarium.

"If I nag enough, I might get one," she whispered.

She went on to explain how much she loved horse riding and wanted to be a horse trainer when she grew up or else own a large dog rescue where she would have hundreds of dogs and employ a vet to take care of them.

"See what a nice time you had," Jessica told Chloe as they waited for the Pedi cab to take them back to their hotel.

"Those ladies were fun," Chloe agreed.

Bella wondered, as she often did, why there was occasionally an instant rapport with some people, as well as the opposite, an instant dislike. "Maybe we knew each other in a past life?"

This resulted in Chloe receiving a somewhat convoluted explanation about the concept of reincarnation as the handsome young Pedi cab driver – a student earning money and getting fit at the same time – peddled them back to their hotel.

"Can you come back as an animal?" Chloe wondered.

"What animal would you like to be?" Bella made a game of it.

Without hesitation, Chloe said, "A dog."

Jessica's choice was an elephant. "They are noble, care for their young and the herd is led by a matriarch." Jessica began to explain what a matriarch meant, but Chloe knew.

Even the Pedi cab driver had to choose. "An eagle. I'd like to be able to fly."

Before Bella could even think, Chloe answered for her, "Granny, I know what you will be."

"You do?"

"You'll be a little pig, like the one in the aquarium."

Chloe laughed so hard at the very idea, which started Bella and then Jessica, and eventually even the Pedi cab driver having one of those passage-clearing, pants-wetting laughs you can never explain to someone who wasn't present.

The following day, on a tour of a Southern Plantation, the guide explained how the land was once wild and needed clearing before there was anything at all. Even now, there remained huge trees, swamps full of alligators, poisonous snakes, and lots of mosquitos. Chloe – who'd been bitten badly – constantly complained of her inflamed, red bites.

Bella imagined how horrific it must have been for a person from Africa to be plucked from their family, tribe, and clan and plonked like merchandise – after a horrendous sea voyage – into a world so utterly different from the one they knew. They would not have known the language their captors spoke or what was demanded of them. They learned soon enough, mostly from harsh or amorous overseers and plantation owners.

The guide continued his tour as they chugged along the extensive winding waterways on a small train. "Slaves from certain places in Africa fetched the highest prices. When the settlers first planted rice, they were unsuccessful... then they found that if they bought slaves from rice growing areas in Africa, they knew what to do."

They stopped off the train to tour the tiny slave houses, which the guide told them were reconstructed. Bella remembered – with guilt and remorse – the servant's quarters in South African homes, which were also tiny and situated in the back yard, which was where the washing hung to dry. Service people came through the backyard. In apartment buildings, servant's quarters were situated on the roof. This only added to Bella's low opinion of architects since the top floor had the best view. Also, the architects placed the windows in the servant's rooms too high, so there was no view. Bella always found this disconcerting. It would have been so easy to make the window lower.

Chloe eschewed the tour of the main house and was deposited on her own at the petting zoo, where goats stood on mounds like statues and allowed themselves to be stroked and where a forlorn rooster sat on a pole and was quite passive when Chloe picked him up.

Thankfully the intense heat for their last day in Charleston and though Bella couldn't think of anything worse than going to the beach, that was what Jessica and Chloe wanted. Bella loved the ocean but hated the sand. Why the creator had combined, the two was not well thought out.

Going to the beach also meant buying a swimsuit. With a superior air, Jessica said, "I always pack one no matter where I am going."

Fortunately, there was a swimsuit boutique on the main shopping street, and even more, fortunately, they kept a make Bella already wore.

And so, Jessica, driving, they found a beach where there was a small restaurant, as well as toilet facilities. There was easy parking, also.

At the beach, there was a number to call to order chairs and umbrellas. "This is much more civilized," Bella said as the attendant arrived quickly with loungers and an umbrella. "I am impressed. Why don't they do this in California?"

Whilst Bella hated the sand, Bella loved swimming in the ocean. Here the undercurrent was so powerful it was dangerous to go deep and there were no lifeguards. Jessica and Bella had to keep an eye on Chloe, who spent almost the whole-time risking being swept away.

Later they did take a horse and cart tour around the old town, where in the area known as SOB (South of Broad), one house was more charming than the next.

"Some families have owned houses here since The Civil War and many were badly damaged during Hurricane Hugo," the guide informed them. "They had to build the outsides – according to Charleston law – exactly as they were before. Even the windowpanes. If you break a window here, it can't be ordinary glass. It has to be blown glass."

He was quite something the tour guide, having to maneuver his horse cart through the narrow streets as well as explain about The Powder Magazine, the oldest building in Charleston and the old slave market, now a museum of African American history.

"You can't get away from slavery here," Bella said solemnly.

"No, you can't," the tour guide agreed.

Bella said, "I think the government should have paid reparations. I've often thought about it. Maybe free university education?"

"It's a good idea, but it will never happen," the tour guide said. "What's past is past is what they think." And before anything further was said, they turned into a street where a gorgeous house changed the tempo of the potential discussion.

When Jessica spoke to her father, he suggested they go see the old synagogue. Bella wondered how Guy knew there was an old synagogue in Charleston. But then Guy constantly surprised her. The somewhat painful truth, she admitted to herself, was that she and Guy had been apart for decades, and Guy had been to many places and lived large portions of his life without her. However, his important memories were the times he was younger, newly married, with no money, and filled with ambition. He loved recounting these, knowing he'd told them many times before. Everyone, other than *Wife Number Two*, found this endearing.

An elderly docent gave them a tour, explaining the synagogue was a National Historical Monument and the country's oldest in continuous use. The experience was so pleasant, Bella said after they left, "I almost wanted to join the synagogue." Seeing as Bella neither lived in Charleston nor liked formal religion, this was something.

"I can't wait to get home," Chloe said as she read from her kindle whilst Jessica and Bella packed.

Jessica said, "I'd like to go on and on, somewhere else,

and never stop."

Bella agreed, "Where should we go next? What about Washington? I want to go to Washington and India, and I'd like to go to St. Petersburg. I wouldn't like to go to China, at least not to the big cities. I'd hate to breathe in that foul air. And maybe Japan?"

Chloe shouted, "I'm not going anywhere!"

"I have no desire to go to Japan," Jessica said. "I don't know why, but it has never appealed to me. And so, they went on, mother and daughter, dreaming about traveling, and as Bella drifted off to sleep, she was proud of herself. She had complained a bit. She had to admit, especially about her painful heels; she did complain about the sand on the beach and both she and Jessica almost cried when they got lost while walking to their hotel on the first night, but in the main, she had not complained about anything serious, and she and Jessica had not one bad word between them.

I am a mature woman, Belle reflected, and Jessica is too. There was something quite marvelous in recognizing this accolade. I am proud of my daughter and my granddaughter, and I think they are proud of me, too. I am a writer and writing my second screenplay and keeping up with my little life stories.

Chapter 21: Replacements

"Honey is the only food that never spoils."

The first thing Bella knew she had to do on her return from Charleston was to replace her faithful old dishwasher. Not because it didn't wash well, but because the baskets and shelves were rotted and the machine was so old, there were no longer replacement parts. Bella thought there was something analogous about the painful joints in her fingers and the worn-out spikes in the old dishwasher. The joints in her fingers were also very old, and there were no replacement parts.

Shelly offered to come with her, and Bella was more than appreciative, not only for her company but that Shelly offered to drive. Shelly always drove when they went anywhere together. Nobody wanted Bella to drive. Matthew English, her best male friend, now living between Nigeria and London, never failed to ask her when they communicated via email, "Had any accidents lately?" Bella didn't tell him about her recent two, which occurred during the same day, less than an hour apart. She was on the way to meet Nicole at the movies at The Westside Pavilion when she had the first accident. Her foot slipped off the brake at a stop sign on a slight hill. The man in the car in front of her wasn't amused.

"Don't you know what you're doing?" He was furious.

"I'm sorry. I didn't do it on purpose."

The second one occurred when she hit a pole whilst parking at The Westside Pavilion.

"Why I had to park between two cars when there was a whole bank of empty spaces on the other side, I don't know."

"That's why cars have bodies," Nicole repeated something Bella often told her about her own little accidents. But when Nicole saw the damage after they'd seen the movie, she exclaimed, "That's like bad, really bad!"

The Big Box store where Bella planned to purchase her new dishwasher was thankfully not busy when Bella and Shelly arrived.

"I want something solid but not fancy; one with baskets that won't get all rusted and bent," Bella told Monica, the most patient and charming saleslady, who showed off her wares as if they were jewels, and patiently explained the differences between models, like extra shelves and so on, all of which added more to the price.

"Who wants to actually watch their dirty dishes being washed?" Bella joked about a top-of-the-line dishwasher with a clear glass front. "Come into my kitchen and watch my dishes being scrubbed."

Bella didn't take long to make her choice. The model was not the cheapest and far from the most expensive, but Monica assured her about the baskets that would not rot.

Once it was installed, Shelly noted, "You must admit it looks better than your old one." Shelly had a fancy model, albeit without a glass door.

Bella replied, "Looks much the same to me. It was only the innards that were rotted. It's like this damned arthritis in my fingers, and my elbow and my knee. Now my other elbow is starting to hurt."

"Old age is not for sissies," Shelly quipped, as she often did, knowing full well she was a lot younger than Bella.

Bella sometimes said, "You're at least fifteen years younger than me."

"That's true," Shelly agreed with a superior smile.

Bella said, "With age, everything is relative. Nicole believes she's getting old. She's not yet thirty."

"I wish I was twenty-five," Shelly said. "But with what I know now."

"I don't remember being forty-five," Bella laughed.

"You know, what's that saying... youth is wasted on the young... it's true."

Bella agreed, "It's a pity nobody remembers being a baby. We're so adored and taken care of; rocked to sleep, fed and bathed. At least we don't remember being born. Getting squeezed out into the world must be one of the most terrifying things anyone has to face. There was a fashionable psychology thing going around long ago in the dark ages, before you were born, Shelly. It was called The Primal Scream. I read it on a beach and almost wanted to scream there and then and give everyone a fright. It was a load of hogwash."

Shelly grimaced, "God, Bella, you think of the weirdest things. No wonder you're..." Shelly was about to say, *alone,* but managed to stop herself before the words came out.

Bella didn't get upset, but she did state, "I'm not alone because I think weird things. I'm alone because I choose to live alone, bearing in mind the alternative, which is living with just anyone, or that someone you're always trying to find. Don't you think I could have a man if I really wanted to?"

"Of course, you could. I've told you, you should. Why don't you try Match again?"

Bella sighed, "I don't want anyone. I don't want that elusive someone you're always going on about. I'm not a misandrist. I like men. I've loved a few. I still love Guy. But

I'm a realist."

"You're so cynical."

"No, I'm not. There are times I think of how it was when falling in love was like diving deep into that uniquely painful state. Passion wafted in and out of my life, alternating with heartache. I've lived and loved and still love Guy, as you well know, in a way so odd it befuddles me. But there is something pathetic about a woman my age still looking for true love. At least that's how I feel about it."

"Miracles do happen," Shelly said. "If you work for them."

"You work for them!"

"I am," Shelly grinned. "I've gone back to Match, and I've got a date for Thursday night."

After decompressing from Charleston, a quick Sunday visit from Violet before she went to church brought bad news. Violet was concerned her daughter Gracie, was sick. This potential bad news sent Bella back to the darkness of the Dr. John Beadel screenplay.

When Greta arrived for Sunday brunch – Bella rarely locked her front door – she found Bella at her computer. She looked over Bella's shoulder at the screen.

"Are you still working on the AIDS script?"

317

Bella replied, "Yes, the only problem is everyone is bad. Movies have to have a hero."

Greta said, "Maybe you can insert a love story?"

Bella said, "Remember, all this happened during the time when apartheid was in full swing, and the government wanted to keep it that way."

Bella told Greta, "I want you to pay attention. There really was a biological warfare program created by The South African Defense Force. Nobody knew it, but South Africa was also conducting a secret war in Angola. It was part of The Cold War. The Russians were supporting one side and the Americans on the other. South Africa had compulsory two-year Army Training. My brother had to go. You know, one of the main reasons I left South Africa was so Ivan would not have to do service in the army. Once the compulsory two-year stint was over, there were two weeks to brush up every year. My brother said he did nothing much in the army and he never went to the brush-up sessions. Nobody bothered him. But when there was this secretive war, he was called up. We all went to see him off at the station. He was placed in what was obviously the alternative-scruffy company that'd never gone to yearly training. The train station was crowded, sort of like in those movies when wives send their husbands off to war. We didn't even know there was a war in another country. Josie was pregnant at the time."

Greta said, "That must have been hard, especially not knowing where he was going."

"The South African government made the Communist Gevaar (danger) the reason for all sorts of nefarious actions."

"How did you not know what was happening?" Greta asked.

Bella said, "You didn't know what was going on with The Vietnam War and you had a free press. We really didn't know what was going on. There was no internet. We didn't have television. The apartheid government didn't want us to know about the world out there. There was heavy press censorship. Newspapers came with blacked-out bits."

Greta said, "It's hard to believe, but your terrible story about AIDS has a ring of truth to it."

Bella said, "All the best stories are based on reality. Stories are truths dressed in fancy clothes. I am thinking of my characters, what they look like, and their backstories. That's something I have to do."

Greta said, "Don't forget you promised you'd come with me to the big art show."

"I won't. I have it marked in my calendar."

Chapter 22: Sven Be Damned

"A part can sometimes be better than a whole."

Bella didn't know what was going on with her long-time trainer, Sven. He was distracted. He was argumentative. She wanted to punch him, which she did the day he told her, "I looked up what you should weigh, and you are seven pounds away from being obese."

"Let's box," Bella said and did her best to pummel Sven's open palms as he deflected her punches in her red boxing gloves. Bella hadn't boxed for ages as her fingers were painful, but the pain was overtaken by the pleasure she got trying to make Sven's open palms hurt as he called out, "Right, left, right, uppercut, side, right left, uppercut, swipe, kick right, kick left."

Bella didn't think she was obese. A little chubby and mostly around the middle, but she was – for God's sake – over seventy!

Shelly suggested Bella try her latest weight loss method. "I order the food; I eat what they deliver and have no other food in my house. My fridge is bare; my grocery cupboard has nothing in it at all. I'm using it for purses."

Bella wanted to punch Shelly, too. In her opinion, Shelly

looked almost anorexic, and Bella was happy she could always rustle up a meal if anyone showed up unexpectedly.

"Your diet might make you thin, but it also makes you bad-tempered," Bella told Shelly.

"Jealousy will get you nowhere."

At the next session with Sven, Bella enquired about Rachel Rosenstein, one of his clients she'd met.

"She finally dumped her loser boyfriend," Espen said. "He made her pay for everything. Now she says she wants someone younger. She wants a man who wants sex."

What Sven left unsaid was, "Not like you."

Good for her, Bella thought she sounded like a five-year-old.

Sven then inquired, "Have you been looking at Tinder?"

Some months prior, Sven showed Bella the Tinder site, and whilst they were in the gym, he got her to join.

Bella agreed it was sort of fun swiping past man after man, wondering who the hell would ever click 'yes to a man sticking out his bottom; a fool with his tongue stuck out like a teenager; a man posing with another woman; a man covered in tattoos; one wearing too short shorts, another wearing too long socks; one with so much beard his face could hardly be seen and on and on, so it became quickly apparent to Bella that Tinder was not for her. Tinder was for young people who wanted a way to hook up. One young man of eighteen clicked 'like' for Bella. She replied, "Did you notice my age?"

He replied, "I like women of all ages." Bella trashed the app.

Sven was not giving up. "So, I want to ask you something. Are you a yes person or a no person?"

"I am a 'yes' person," Bella declared.

"So, when I tell you to go on Tinder, you give up after one stupid guy says he likes you. What about Match? You could find someone."

"I've told you before, and I'm telling you again, I am not averse to a man. Bella felt tears sting at the back of her eyes. "You say I should find someone, Sven, but in all these years I've known you, have you ever said to me, 'I'd like to introduce you to a man I think you'd like.'" Bella knew she had Sven there.

"It's because of Guy you aren't interested," Sven carried on. "I know you want someone like Guy. Someone in good shape and handsome and… rich."

Bella added, "And in love with a woman young enough to be his daughter."

"There are lots of nice men out there," Sven wasn't going to stop.

"Well, find me one," Bella said. "With his own house."

"So, he has to have a big house?" Sven pounced.

"Did I mention the size of the house? I mean, I want someone with substance… a home, a position in life… not someone who has a roommate."

"What if he rents a place and has a lease on a car? Is that good enough?"

Sven rented his place and leased his car. Bella realized she'd hit a sore spot. "I don't care if he leases a car or rents a place."

"You're not going to find a man like Guy."

I don't want Guy. If I did, I'd have stayed married to him." Bella wished she was still wearing boxing gloves.

"I know for a fact there are men out there." Sven persisted. "I am going to find you someone," he shouted, unaware of how upset Bella was becoming.

At that point, Lionel Goode entered the gym.

"There's someone of my age." Lionel Goode was almost deaf. Bella once tried to talk to him whilst they were on adjacent treadmills and gave up.

Sven shook his head. "He's too old."

"No, he's not. He's seventy-six. Not much older than I am. He used to date a woman who lived here. They went to dinner and the movies together." Bella thought she had more than adequately proved her point.

"So... what's wrong with that?"

"I don't need a dinner companion who's hard of hearing, and I prefer going to the movies on my own." Bella felt tears well. She usually had no problem crying in front of Sven when she was upset or down or whatever bothered her, but she didn't want to do so now.

"That's his name, Mr. Good? Sven laughed.

"With an *e*."

"What about a younger man? Someone in his sixties?"

"A man of sixty wants a woman of forty."

"Not every man."

"Show me a successful, attractive and interesting man of seventy-five who finds himself choosing a woman his own age. Show me!"

"I know there are some," Sven replied. "I can't think of one now, but I know there are."

"Well, if you know there are, why is it you've never introduced me to one? It's because you don't know. You can't deny it."

Sven looked sheepish.

Bella could not stop the tears. "You're supposed to make me feel good about myself, and now you've made me cry."

"I am so sorry. I feel awful."

Repeatedly he told Bella how awful he felt until she said, "If you don't stop apologizing, I'm going to put on my boxing gloves again and pummel you."

What was it, Bella wondered, *even in this day and age, a single woman was an affront to society? Why?* Bella could understand this from a biological point of view when women were of childbearing age, but afterward, when women could no longer add to the gene pool. Bella wondered whether she was unusual in that she was fine and happy without a man. There were many studies on being a single woman and research was inconclusive. In one study, Bella found both men and women became more and more dissatisfied with their marriages over time, with women being dissatisfied sooner than men. A common opinion was that married men and single women were the happiest. Bella knew couples who seemed happy and those who seemed miserable. Sometimes it was a big surprise when a supposedly happy couple split up. Ren and Naomi Yellen were so in love when Bella was having marital problems with Guy. Bella was envious of their relationship, but their marriage exploded, according to Naomi, because Ren never stood up to his interfering mother. As it is said, nobody knows what happens behind closed doors. Then there were famous couples like Angelina Jolie and Brad Pitt who presented themselves as married mavens, then poof, divorce.

It wasn't as if Bella had NO interest in men. She was a willing participant in conversations when single women – of all ages – complained about the dearth of decent men. It was one thing to find a decent man in his forties, but not one in his late seventies or eighties. On occasion, a movie studio decided to make a happy movie for the forgotten older demographic. Of course, as in all movies, they didn't show the real indignities of aging; incontinence, high blood pressure, creaking joints, and the inability to remember shit. There was the rare old-age romance. People did win the lottery. And she did admit to the occasional heartache when she thought of the powerful pleasure of being desired and tenderly loved.

Bella complained about Sven when she and Nicole walked Charlie that evening.

"Let's go have some ice cream," Nicole suggested. "Sven is like… don't pay attention to him."

"Ice cream is a cure for most things," Bella agreed. "It's a gorgeously warm night."

Bella and Nicole were enjoying their ice-cream at the outdoor tables at the local Gelataria when the 'terrorist' from across the road and his girlfriend arrived.

"It's the night for ice cream," Nicole said.

After they'd all complained about the day's heat and how pleasant it was now, the 'terrorist' and his girlfriend declined to join Bella and Nicole and sat at another table. Bella was pleased as she wanted to talk to Nicole about her screenplay.

"You know how truth is stranger than fiction. Well, there was a real biological warfare department in South Africa. It all came out when in 1996, two years after Mandela and the ANC came to power, South Africa did something amazing. They instituted a Truth and Reconciliation Commission."

"What did it do?" Nicole asked. "I mean the commission."

"The Truth and Reconciliation Commission was meant to heal the nation. Victims of apartheid gave statements and described how they were abused and how members of their families were murdered. Abusers could admit their deeds and ask for forgiveness. They could request amnesty only if they admitted what they'd done. It was not supposed to be one-sided, either. The commission also heard evidence from anti-apartheid fighters who'd been severely punished when they didn't toe the ANC party line. Some people accused each other. They used the commission to settle scores. There were horrible things done in the years before apartheid officially ended. I remember reading how young thugs posing as freedom fighters made a poor old black woman eat soap powder because she bought from a shop they were boycotting. Mob mentality brings out the worst in humans. You've heard of the necklace?"

"No, what's that?"

"They throw a car tire over a person's neck, fill the tire with petrol – that's what South Africans call gas – and set it alight."

"That's like so gruesome," Nicole shuddered. "It's amazing how cruel people can be."

It was at this moment Bella noticed Mr. Dragozetti pull up in his Mercedes and claim a parking spot outside the Gelataria.

Mr. Dragozetti was a fellow resident of Portland. Keisha, the receptionist, once told Bella he'd be nice to her, which always upset Bella to think anyone would think Mr. Dragozetti, with his dyed hair, cheap Italian shoes and belt, and worst of all, a thin mustache, was the kind of man she'd like. Probably he was a decent person, or maybe not? Bella didn't care to find out, and when she saw the kind of woman

Mr. Dragozetti was with, she knew he wouldn't care for her, either.

Mr. Dragozetti was an old-style gentleman in that he ran to the passenger door to open it for his date, who looked vaguely like Dolly Parton, with a black dress too tight, silver high-heeled sandals and garish makeup. Mr. Dragozetti pretended not to notice Bella as he protectively held his date and then opened the door to the Gelataria to usher her in.

"That's who Keisha wanted to fix me up with. He lives in my building," Bella huffed.

"He looks like your age," Nicole said.

"Do you think every man around your age is right for you?" Bella asked, thoroughly annoyed.

Nicole shrugged, "He's not in bad shape."

"I am not interested in his shape."

"And he drives a nice car."

"You can't kiss a car. He wears horrible little shoes, and I detest that thin mustache. It reminds me of my stepfather. Not to mention his dyed hair, Men can't get away with dyeing their hair to hide the grey. I don't know why but they just can't. And look at his date!"

"Maybe it's his sister," Nicole laughed.

"No, it's not." Bella was certain of that.

"Anyway, forget about them."

Bella told Nicole, "You know De Klerk, the white President and Mandela shared the Nobel Peace Prize."

"That's rad. How come?"

"They thought the actions F. W. de Klerk took were astonishing. He gave up power. He freed Mandela and unbanned the African National Congress. De Klerk went against his party. He did what he thought was the best for the country. That's why he won the Nobel Peace Prize. He and Mandela – both showed true leadership – together they prevented the expected blood bath."

Mr. Dragozetti and his date exited the Gelataria, each with an ice cream cone and sat at an outdoor table as far away from Bella and Nicole as possible, with Mr. Dragozetti still pretending he hadn't noticed Bella.

"Amazing," Nicole said.

"What?"

"I've never had these two flavors together."

Bella said, "It's a bit like what happened in South Africa. The two colors, black and white, shook off the shackles of apartheid. It wasn't that simple. There were vicious internecine fights and violence between different groups of blacks vying for power. It was mostly The Zulu against the rest. The Zulu at the time didn't even want to be part of the rest of South Africa. They consider themselves a warrior nation and superior to the other tribes. You've heard of Shaka?"

Nicole hadn't.

"Shaka is generally known as the King who conquered nearby Bantu tribes and forged them into The Zulu Nation. His life story has been written about and made into a movie. He was a brilliant and cruel warrior. His story is Shakespearean; he was murdered by Dingane, his half-brother. Dingane is famous for inviting a party of around one hundred Boers who wanted to negotiate the ownership of some land and then killing them all after he made them leave their weapons outside his kraal."

Nicole said, "That wasn't a good start for race relations."

Bella added, "The Boers then defeated the Zulu at The Battle of Blood River. But the Zulu persisted. They lived mostly in what we then called Zululand. Some migrated North to Zimbabwe, where they're known as the Matabele."

Nicole asked, "Which tribe is the biggest in South Africa?"

Bella replied, "The Zulu is the biggest tribe in South Africa and then comes the Xhosa. Then there are Ndebele…

they're the ones who paint their house walls with geometrics. There's Sotho, Pedi, Venda, Tsonga, and Pondo. Remember, they might be black, but they come from different tribes, which is like coming from a different country. Nobody thinks the Swiss, Italians, Poles and Scottish are alike. They have different languages and cultures and they're white, but we expect them to be different."

Nicole said, "I love how their names sound. Pondo, Ndebele…"

Bella said, "South Africa also has its indigenous people, the San. They were there before blacks and whites. They were decimated, first by the invading Bantu tribes from the Congo and then by Dutch settlers. The poor San, also known as Khoi San, also bushmen or Hottentots, were massacred. It's a bit of history black and white South Africans barely acknowledge."

Nicole said, "A bit like our Native Americans?"

Bella said, "I suppose so. But that's the way of the world; might wins. And then numbers win. It was inevitable South Africa could not be ruled by white people forever when they were the minority."

Nicole said, "Statistics count; I have to watch them in my job. The agency has all kinds of statistics, not only about the models but like who sees them in print and on social networks. We have computer guys who do that."

Bella said, "Before South Africa's first democratic elections in 1994, there were white Afrikaners who were not on board with change, but the blood bath – the massacre of whites by hordes of angry and bitter blacks, which had forever been prophesized did not occur. This says something about the good nature of black South Africans."

"Awesome. I mean, it's really amazing."

"Yes, it was. I see it as lucky. In fact, I think South Africa is a fortunate country."

"Why lucky?" Nicole asked.

Nicole had her back to Mr. Dragozetti and his lady. Bella faced them and could not help noticing how he and his date exchanged licks of ice cream with undeniable sexual undertones. What irritated her about Dragozetti? It wasn't as if she had a secret crush on him. Just the opposite.

Bella averted her eyes and told Nicole, "By the time South Africa became democratic, The Cold War was over. Communism failed in Russia, and they had to give up their destructive meddling in African affairs. And South Africa avoided the disastrous nationalization of resources, which ended up causing so much corruption in other African countries. They also instituted a brilliant constitution with protection for minorities. It's said the South African Constitution is the finest in the world. But aside from all that, South Africa is lucky because it has great mineral wealth. It's physically beautiful."

Nicole said, "I think South Africans are the nicest people in the world. I wish I could find a South African boyfriend."

"I'm not sure they're so good," Bella laughed. "From my experience."

Chapter 23: What's Going on in Honduras

"Why bother to ask questions when you have a gun?"

Bella complained to Sven about the struggles with her new script, even though she knew he wasn't paying attention to anything other than the word 'write'."

"I have trained many writers," he said.

Sven had trained someone in just about any profession that came up in conversation.

He'd trained stars, musicians, actors, doctors, and politicians. He listened to opinions and life stories and problems of all kinds. Maybe he was paying attention, maybe not, but he kept Bella moving whatever it was she was going through. The TV in the gym gave Sven a smattering of news. He often asked Bella, "What's going on?"

"I have no idea. That's why it's called The News. We have to listen to it now to find out."

Sven said, "I don't watch the news. It makes me miserable. I rely on my clients to tell me what's happening in the world."

What Sven did pay attention to was the newscaster if she

was female and his kind of pretty.

Sven went for a look, a flattish face and darkish skin. Surgically enhanced breasts were fine. In fact, Sven probably didn't even know what real breasts looked like, not to mention what they felt like.

"I can tell exactly what kind of women you go for," Bella teased

"And you?" Sven asked. "Guy can't be the only man for you."

At that very moment, a tall and very handsome black man entered the gym. Bella had seen him before on the treadmill, but his earphones precluded conversation. She didn't know his name or how long he'd lived at the Portland, which were the questions Bella would have asked out of both curiosity and friendliness.

The man gave a perfunctory hello and glanced up at the TV, which was showing for the hundredth time a video of a black man running away before being shot by the policeman.

"That brother was not thinking this was going to be his last day on Earth," he said, at which point Bella decided to introduce herself.

Byron Potts was visiting his sister, who lived in the building. Bella had never met her. Her condo was accessed by another set of elevators on another side of the building's large marble-floored foyer. The people who lived on one side almost never met those who lived on the other. It was a bit like two different countries separated by a large lake.

Bella thought Byron Potts looked around fifty. He did have a girlfriend; she lived in Florida. He lived in Las Vegas. He did something in sports entertainment. What that was, Bella didn't manage to find out. Like so many people who come to live in Los Angeles, he was vague about his occupation. His sister loved living in Portland.

"It's so nice and quiet," he said.

Bella wondered why it was people who liked quiet. She liked a bit of noise. The noise made her feel as if life was going on: garbage trucks, leaf blowers, mowers, dogs barking, fast cars, the odd motorbike, helicopters overhead and people talking, laughing, and sometimes shouting. In general, Bella didn't care for silence. Silence forced her to listen to the fridge, buzzing fluorescent lights and the various discussions in her brain. But then Bella was used to noise as she grew up on a busy street in Johannesburg.

Louis Botha Avenue – named for the first prime minister of the Union of South Africa – ran all the way from Hillbrow – an area filled with high-rise apartments that South Africans called 'flats' – to Alexandra Township, which was one of the only places where black people were permitted to own land.

Originally planned for a population of around seventy thousand, Alex presently housed around four times the amount, with thousands of renters living in tiny over-crowded shacks set up at the back of the original homes.

The township was named after the wife of Mr. Papenfus, who, in 1912, planned but failed to turn the land into a white suburb.

Whilst googling to find out more about the history of Alexandra Township, which Bella wanted to share with Nicole, Bella discovered in the same year as the founding of Alexander Township, New Mexico became the 47th State of The United States of America, Arizona the 48th and the Marines invaded Honduras.

On her computer, Bella scanned through the complicated history of Honduras. Over the years, America seemed to have done some of its usual meddlings; now, gangs terrorized ordinary people. Easier to comprehend was the weather in Honduras – like everywhere on the planet – was changing. The sweltering summer was becoming drier and hotter, and cool spells were more frequent. This especially affected banana, which was an important agricultural crop for Honduras.

Having discovered the list of yearly events on the

internet, Bella wondered what events would go down in history as important this year. She asked Nicole what she thought would become history worth remembering.

Nicole didn't take this seriously, "I broke up with Undrew."

"You didn't have a thing with him to break up," Bella teased

"I wanted to," Nicole then added. "The year isn't over. Maybe this is the year you'll find true love?"

"I have a true love," Bella said. She had taken to openly confirm her ongoing affection for Guy.

"Guy doesn't count," Nicole retorted.

Wanting to change the subject, Bella went back to The Truth and Reconciliation Commission.

"I want to find a way to include this in my new script. There was one individual, Dr. Wouter Basson; he was dubbed Dr. Death for a good reason. He refused to admit to doing anything, though others working with him admitted to horrendous acts."

"Like what?" Nicole asked.

"I don't think you want to know."

Nicole insisted, "I can take it."

"Animals – monkeys, baboons, pigs, dogs and rats –

were tested with a variety of toxins without a care for their suffering. They experimented on humans whom they dubbed *Enemies of the State*. In one horrendous case, three men were poisoned, and their hands and feet were tied. They were shackled to a tree to see what would happen. They were still alive the next day and were injected with a muscle relaxant, loaded onto a plane – more than likely still alive – and dumped into the ocean."

Nicole said, "I wish you hadn't told me."

"You insisted. I thought I'd do a similar scene in my script. But I can't seem to get down to it. It's making me sick, too."

Nicole said, "I've told you a hundred times and so has Undrew. Write a comedy, or maybe a love story." Nicole thought the love story idea might annoy Bella, but it didn't.

Chapter 24: eBay

"To buy or not to buy, that is the question."

Greta arrived at Bella, as she usually did, on Sunday morning. "It's still nice weather. We can sit on the patio for a while. I've brought my book, so you don't have to talk to me."

"I like talking to you."

Greta ignored this, "Even about my latest?"

"Yes, I am fine with whatever you want to talk about. Lovers are fine, though you're not the best advert for such endeavors, I might point out."

"Don't mock trying. In case you have never heard, life is about not giving up. If you don't take a ticket, you can't win the prize. Isn't that something you say?"

"You're right, darling. I admire your perseverance; truly, I do. But I don't have that… whatever it is that you must have to stare disaster in the eye and make it sparkle even for a while. It's a talent."

'You could see it like that, seeing you are not into men."

"I didn't say that. I said there were no suitable men interested in me. There's a big difference."

"You should start painting again."

Bella said, "I don't have the space. Artists must paint big now and I don't really have the inclination to find a studio and all that. And galleries only want young emerging artists. I asked one gallerist if she'd take an old emerging artist. She didn't think it was funny at all."

"You're such a good artist. It's a pity," Greta said. "I know you love your writing, but you have a God-given talent with your art."

Greta had a point. Bella lay on the patio swing contemplating what she was hoping to accomplish by writing an AIDS conspiracy story. What was done was done! Nothing she wrote could make a difference to the outcome if, indeed, it was deliberately encouraged.

Nobody would say, "Oh yes, we infected people with AIDS on purpose."

Was Violet the inspiration? The disease had certainly affected her family and now there might be a possibility that Gracie, Violet's daughter, was infected by her late husband.

When Violet showed up earlier – as she also often did on Sunday before going to church – she told Bella, "I am worried about Gracie. She says she is getting very thin."

Bella said, "She must go to the hospital."

"She doesn't want to go to the clinic. She says they will

do things to her if they think she has AIDS."

"What kind of things?"

"Where they live, they can chase her and Patricia away. Or go to the witch doctor for some bad muti for her."

"She must go to the clinic," Bella insisted. "There are medicines to help her."

Bella carried on along these lines until Violet said, "I have to go. I am singing in the church choir and another choir is also coming to sing."

Violet loved being part of the church choir. She could sing beautifully, as so many Africans could. Bella remembered the singing of chain gangs walking from the prison in Hillbrow; they sounded like a trained choir. The prison was known as The Fort. It was converted by imaginative architects to become The Constitutional Court in the new democratic country. They left some cells exactly as they were.

As for Violet's beautiful singing voice, nowadays it was politically incorrect to deem any people good or bad at anything; nevertheless, the Swiss were neat and tidy and superb at keeping time and nobody thought it racist if anyone said so. Italians were flirtatious and good at design. The Danish were good at modern design, not flirting. The French were snobby and chic, the Argentinians gorgeous, and Indian women had marvelous hair.

By the time Greta arrived, clouds had blown in. "Let's sit inside," she said.

Greta settled down into her favorite chair. Her neat head swiveled around Bella's eclectic living room. "I've got an idea. You know how you love collecting. Maybe you should start selling on eBay; you can make a business of it."

Bella understood Greta – with her minimalist taste – couldn't fathom some of the things Bella acquired.

"Maybe one day they'll be valuable?" Bella always ventured when Greta made a mockery of various odd bits, like the collection of shelf sitters perched on top of the Chinese cupboard, which, without its doors, was perfect for Bella's television set.

"That's wishful thinking," Greta said. "You could start off by selling your collection of Pekingese dogs. You don't have Pekingese now, you have Charlie. He's not a Pekingese."

Almost as if Charlie could hear, he jumped up at Greta, who gingerly patted his head.

Greta was more of a cat person.

Charlie was a mix of poodle, Maltese and perhaps a

smidgen of Tibetan terrier. When people asked Bella what kind of dog he was – for he did have a pedigree appearance despite his hybrid background – Bella conjured up fanciful breeds. "He's a 'Vietnamese terrier,' or a 'Tibetan Maltese,' or 'Tibetan poodle.'" Nobody questioned her veracity, nor did anyone make further comments, such as, "I have never heard of that breed." It was one of those dead-end conversations Bella found so common in Los Angeles.

Bella thought quite seriously about Greta's suggestion. She'd always found it thrilling to peruse antique and junk stores. Her friend Serena, who had the best taste in the world, said admiringly of the way she furnished her first home after her divorce from Guy, "You turn that into treasure."

Bella took this as a compliment, though when she moved to London, shipping a few of her favorite things, they didn't look quite as handsome in the city filled with truly fine old objects – available in flourishing antique markets – which made her treasured Yellow Wood cabinet look like what it was; a roughly made old cupboard.

When she lived in London, Bella wished she had more funds to buy from the treasure trove of antique markets, and when Margie Buckles, Bella's first English friend, asked her to attend a weekly auction and bid on old paintings – which Margie sold on to clients who frequented her stand in the antique market in Chelsea – Bella was in heaven. She soon developed a camaraderie with both the auctioneers, as well as other regular buyers. One – Angus Cookedge – was for a brief time a lover. Angus wore a gold hoop earring in one ear and a red printed kerchief around his neck. With his glossy, long, black curly hair, he could be mistaken for a gypsy, which he sort of was, as he moved on to live in Spain, Portugal, Germany and then to Morocco all within a year. His postcards to Bella said nothing more than, "Wish you were here." Then they abruptly stopped, and Bella never thought of him again though she did continue to help Margie, which gave her the opportunity to bid on the occasional well-priced piece for herself.

After Bella arrived in Los Angeles, she discovered an auction house where she bought a few things for her new abode at The Portland: a pair of Biedermeier chairs, a fancifully carved occasional table, and an elegant bench with turned legs. However, the pickings were slim in Los Angeles, where anything over twenty years old was considered antique. "And that includes women," Bella said. Then along came eBay, and Bella could find all sorts of artifacts with a bit of history: 40's jewelry, English china, old French linens with thickly embroidered monograms, shelf sitters, china Pekingese dogs, Dorothy Thorpe barware… some of the things she found to collect. Bella had difficulty curtailing her enthusiasm, for eBay was like falling into a vast emporium of potential.

Sven was also a devotee of eBay. He sought out things Bella didn't even know existed. When he won the one rare beer tap eluding his collection, he was ecstatic. Sven bought his latest Burning Man outfit on eBay; an outrageous studded black leather and pink fake-fur biker jacket, matching gloves and chaps included.

Since its inception, Sven had attended Burning Man, and he regularly told Bella how much she'd love the event though she knew – detesting crowds, heat, and dust – she would hate it. "It's for creative people like you." Though, Sven did now complain about how his beloved underground festival was changing.

"Billionaires arrive in their private planes and helicopters, with chefs and vehicles designed by professionals. It's starting to be about showing off, which isn't at all what Burning Man is supposed to be. But it's still amazing. You'd love it."

Bella was never going to Burning Man, not even if a billionaire offered to take her there on his private plane and house her in a luxury camp with a private chef and a bed with high thread count sheets.

Bella asked Shelly what she thought about making a business buying and selling on eBay.

Shelly said, "I want to see what I buy. I must feel stuff in my hands. I need instant gratification. I can't wait around to see if I win. And after that, I must wait for the delivery. I am not a collector like you, Bella." Shelly's eyes swept accusingly across the exuberance of Bella's living room. Shelly wasn't the person to ask. Her only internet expertise was dating.

Nicole thought starting an eBay store was "An amazing idea," and thus encouraged Bella to spend a lot of time on the internet finding out more about Staffordshire, Mason, Coalport, Transferware, Majolica and other types of vintage china, which resulted in a rapidly acquired collection of decorative plates, which, when they arrived, one by one, during the following weeks, Bella decided were so beautiful, she found a place to hang them, herself.

"Now, what have you done?" Jessica rolled her eyes when she saw her mother's plate collection hanging on the only wall retaining a bit of unadorned space.

Jessica tended to be less than supportive of her mother's money-making ideas, and for a good reason, seeing – over the years – Bella's schemes lost rather than making money. Bella could still summon a giggle when she thought of some of them, like the raffia no-shoe shoes she and Marina Painter crocheted, which were good sellers for about a month during the sixties; the bespoke patchwork scatter pillows Bella and Marina made in the eighties, or funniest of all, the broccoli gnocchi business Bella started with her Violet before she left South Africa to live in Los Angeles.

The broccoli gnocchi venture was inspired by Peter English, an artist friend who gave Bella his recipe for the divine spinach gnocchi he served at a dinner party. Bella – being creative and never managing to exactly follow a recipe – decided to make it with broccoli and gave the recipe to Violet, who was a naturally good cook. Violet's gnocchi was so successful that Bella decided she and Violet should go into the broccoli gnocchi business. "I will provide everything; you do the cooking. We share the profits." Thus, Bella invested in a large cooking pot, plus five hundred plastic containers.

The first order was a great success and Hilary Friedman, a friend of a friend who catered luncheons for executives, re-ordered a large quantity for an event. However, this time something went wrong and when Hilary heated the gnocchi, they fell apart, which infuriated Hilary and made both Bella and Violet realize catering wasn't their thing and they'd rather cook only for friends.

When Greta saw Bella's plate collection, masterfully hung on a section of wall flanked by two African Kuba cloths – made from fine straw – she said, "You're supposed to sell, not buy."

"I could not resist seeing how they looked."

What Bella didn't tell Greta was that she was up all night, not researching how to make a business of buying and selling, but rather looking at secondhand purses for herself. Why she, who didn't care about designer handbags and didn't have one due to a certain inverted snobbery, was suddenly into using Chanel, Prada, Louis Vuitton, and Gucci was something she didn't understand. She thought of calling Dr. Feather, who had moved to Florida, and whilst they did agree it was possible to talk on the phone or even on Skype, Bella hadn't availed herself of Dr. Feather's offer. Also, every time she thought of calling Dr. Feather, the time difference made it impolite to bother her old therapist.

Bella also didn't tell Greta she'd bought a couple of old handbags by lesser-known designers, whose low prices were a bargain. Bella was to await gold, pink and burgundy cross-body bags, all for less than $20, none of which she needed, and worse still, all made from leather.

Bella was nevertheless somewhat inspired by her purse search. She told Greta, "I'm still thinking of designing a handbag. The purse to end all purses; not too big or too small, with space for everything and not heavy. The perfect purse."

"There is no such thing as the perfect purse. That's why we keep buying them," Greta said, "I know a man who made millions selling handbags to ladies having their nails and hair done. I wonder what happened? I don't see him or his replacement any more."

Bella said, "I've never been good at selling. It's a talent, you know, to be a good salesman. It's like any talent, God-given. I'd have to hire a salesperson."

On this point, Greta agreed and added, "You first need to have them made. Probably in China."

The thought of traveling to China, breathing in their foul air, as well as the costs to get the project going, gave Bella another sleepless night. "I'm going back to being a writer. It's less stressful," Bella said to herself, trying not to admit she might be working on a screenplay nobody wanted to know anything about. Apartheid was so long gone young people didn't even know what the word meant, but Bella was by nature persistent. Once she started something, she finished.

Bella finished knitting projects and embroideries. She finished writing books she knew would never be published.

She finished what she started, even if it took her forever. She finished failures. She was – like her Chinese Goat sign – the kind of person who slowly and steadily climbs the mountain, finally reaching the summit, even if there was nothing to eat up there.

Thus, she was anxious to finish her screenplay and get on to something less disturbing, for even though Dr. Beadel was Bella's invention, there were people like him, and it seemed no country or people were immune to racist hatred.

Bella made some notes in the book Greta gave her;

Was Dr. Beadel a sociopath, like Winston Agadees, the anti-hero of her first script, The Lions of Amarula? Yes, he was. How will Beadel get his comeuppance?

That first script had come to Bella easily. She'd mulled over the plot for years. This one was different. She wondered why she founds sociopaths so interesting. Bella was aware her new screenplay was fiction, but the truth was stranger than fiction. She told Nicole, when they walked Charlie, "Some of the things I've put into the script are inspired by what really did happen."

"It's like so rad," Nicole replied

"Those responsible for biological warfare really did plant deadly toxins in cigarettes, umbrella tips, drinks and even in clothes. All that came out in The Truth and Reconciliation Commission. Those who came before the commission – in the hopes of gaining amnesty – told of discussions of eliminating entire black communities. The trouble with my screenplay is I don't have a hero. Nobody comes to save all those thousands dying of AIDS. Knowing about something bad doesn't make a hero. Heroes must act. They must do something about the situation. They must improve things… or die trying. I suppose those people who work in the HIV AIDS world are heroes."

Nicole said, "You are my hero."

After getting into bed – after taking Charlie for the last walk – she opened her notebook and added to the delicate doodles on the inside cover. Then she became more serious and printed out an email Marina had sent in response to some of Bella's inquiries.

Marina wrote,

I asked Kelly Morganstrum about AIDS. She's very involved in a program on how to stop transmission from mother to child. She thinks it is quite possible there was a conspiracy to infect black South Africans with HIV. She says almost 20% of the population is HIV positive. You already know that in South Africa, AIDS is an equal-opportunity disease. Both men and women get it; more women, as the men don't like condoms and many believe it's the white man's plan to stop them from having children. She says many of those who think they have AIDS do not seek help, as they will then be ostracized by their fellows. Even being seen entering a clinic is hazardous.

Marina ended her email, "What are you up to now, Bella?"

Chapter 25: Rules and Regulations

"Rules are made by the broken."

Whilst attending a meeting of The Homeowners in The Portland Party room, Shelly whispered to Bella, as the two of them sat on adjacent armchairs, "Do you think they're going to discuss anything important?"

Zara Tizbee, sitting in the chair on Bella's other side, said, "I've asked to make the pool warmer. So far, they haven't."

Bella said, "I agree. The pool should be warmer in winter. I suppose heating the pool is expensive; hardly anyone swims."

Bella thought how fortunate she was to live at the Portland, where there was a pool, albeit not hot enough for either herself or Zara Tizbee, who, with her two young boys, was new in the building.

Like all Boards, the Portland Homeowners Board was bureaucratic and power-driven. When they thought they should make a show of being inclusive, they appointed a committee. Hence, The Architectural Committee, The Gardening Committee, and from time to time, a committee for something less permanent.

The Gardening Committee's main job was to decide what flowers and what colors the flowers should be in beds strategically placed at the front of the building. Their choice invariably caused complaints; too much pink, not enough red, too colorful, not enough color. However, nothing got the Portland homeowners more up in arms when one year, the impatience planting was all white. White was boring, worse, and got dirty. Bella didn't agree with either adjective, but she was aware many people in Beverly Hills believed fallen leaves were 'dirty' and not merely evidence of nature's ongoing processes. Hence the constant leaf blowers utilized by Mexican gardeners without care for the noise and pollution they cause.

Bella decided long ago not to bother with what happened outside her condo. So long as the flowers bloomed, and they always did, she loved all the color combinations. Bella appreciated The Board, much as she dissed them. Who else would worry about the cost of light bulbs, the ever-present leaks judging by the frequent visits from the plumber, and all the mundane things needing attention, all of which made a living at the Portland so pleasant? That is until Cecil Gabor was voted chairman of the board. Gabor replaced Max Yudelman, who finally resigned after being chairman for years.

Cecil Gabor was going to make his mark. He was a stickler for rules and discovered the existing signage at the pool and adjacent Jacuzzi was inadequate. And so, placards of rules and regulations in triplicate – were installed.

- No diving. No lifeguard on duty.
- Children under the age of 14 shall not use the pool without a parent or guardian in attendance.
- Step-by-step instructions on cpr/artificial respiration.
- Caution: elderly persons, pregnant women, infants and those with health conditions requiring medical care should consult with a physician before entering the pool.
- Immersion while under the influence of alcohol, narcotics, drugs or medicines may lead to serious consequences and is not recommended.
- Do not use the spa alone. Long exposure may result in hypothermia, nausea, dizziness or fainting.
- Please use the restroom and shower before using the pool or spa.
- Persons currently having active diarrhea or who have

had active diarrhea within the previous 14 days shall not be allowed to enter the pool water.

- The pool deck is slippery when wet footwear is required.

- No smoking.

- No food, drink, glass or animals in or on the pool deck.

- Spa capacity is 6 people; maximum use is 15 minutes.

- The maximum water temperature is 104 f.

- Spa hours are 8 am – 10 pm.

Bella told Shelly, "I think I'm going to put up one more rule."

"What?" Shelly asked.

"You'll see," Bella replied mysteriously.

It was Sunday evening when Shelly returned to Portland with her date. Ewan Ackerman was a contender for husband number three. This was their third date and they'd been to see an exhibition at The Los Angeles Museum of Art.

Ewan was a collector of contemporary art. He had a boxy, modern home in the hills above Sunset Plaza Drive, where he showed off part of his art collection on vast white walls. The rest of his collection was in storage.

"Why buy art to put in storage?" Shelly asked Greta, who, being in the art world, might know of such things.

"Ewan Ackerman is a well-known collector. That's what collectors do."

"I can't imagine buying a piece of art to place in a warehouse. But he did say he'd take me to see his art one day."

Ewan Ackerman was divorced and had been single for years. He told Shelly he didn't like young women and added, "I appreciate how well you take care of yourself."

This odd compliment resulted in Shelly dyeing her hair blonder, rejoining the fashionable gym she once frequented, deciding to stop eating anything white, and retaining a personal shopper at Nieman Marcus to help update her wardrobe.

"I hope the personal shopper makes sure her dresses are not so short and her jeans not so tight," Greta told Bella.

Bella told Greta, "I can't imagine what Ewan Ackerman and Shelly Davidson have in common. But I suppose there's no accounting for sexual attraction."

To this day, Bella could never quite get over what it was

that attracted her to JP, whom she called – always garnering a laugh when she did – 'my gangsta lover.'

First, he had a mustache. It was a thick full mustache partially covering his top lip. It hid his uncared-for front teeth. Bella detested mustaches, especially when unaccompanied by a beard. She didn't like beards either. At one point during their crazy romance, he called her to come to pick him up outside a five-star hotel. He'd been involved in a fight and his front teeth were knocked out. He didn't fix them. He had a dreadful accent, one that clearly showed he didn't come from Bella's world. He was a liar, an unscrupulous con man, and a very bad alcoholic. He often carried a magnum revolver in a cross-body holster. On more than one occasion, he acted threatening toward Bella, putting his gun close to him, and looking at it, then at Bella. He was almost never without a drink – scotch in a long glass with lots of water – and an unfiltered Camel cigarette. He smoked two packs per day. He became addicted to Rohypnol, which he obtained from a doctor who lived across the road from him. This is in one of the many houses he moved to when his wife kicked him out. She took him back and kicked him out again. Such was the magnetism of the man to certain women, like Bella and JP's wife, that these two intelligent, educated women fought for him.

"There's a story!" she often thought, but the circumstances of her attraction to JP were unbelievable. She knew this to be true as she'd sent a draft of a novel she wrote about the mad passion to a few agents.

They all replied with the same comment, which went along the lines of, "This is not a believable story. Why would an intelligent woman (such as her heroine) take up with such a man?"

As time went on, and JP was finally felled by his addictions, Bella could not believe it was she who wanted JP more than anything. Only much later, she did understand the passion and drama-filled romance allowed her to ignore the failure of her brief second marriage to the closeted Phil Varelly, whom she called "my mistake husband."

Dr. Feather, her old therapist, thought JP was also a reaction to Guy marrying *Wife Number Two*.

"I went mad as a result of two husbands who no longer wanted me," she told Greta, who did understand the kind of insanity passion can induce.

On that balmy Sunday after the museum and dinner, when Ewan brought Shelly home, he suggested instead of going inside, they should enjoy a glass of wine by the pool. "It's a full moon tonight," Ewan said.

Shelly and Ewan had barely begun sipping their wine when Marco, the valet, came outside.

"You are not permitted to drink wine at the pool. And no glasses allowed," Marco added sheepishly.

To say this interrupted the romantic moment was an understatement.

Shelly went into instant fury mode. "I hate living in this fucking condo," she yelled at the moonlit water. "What's the difference to fucking anyone?"

"I'm sorry, Mrs. Davidson."

From Marco's expression, Shelly knew he truly was. "Who even knows we're here?"

Marco said nothing, but his eyes darted toward the Gabor condo overlooking the pool. Shelly glanced up to see Cecil Gabor move off from his vantage point.

Shelly screamed, "Why don't you and your wife come down and join us? Come on, come down, have a drink. Lighten up. Find something better to do than stand there and spy on your neighbors."

"I'd better be off," Ewan said and scuttled away, leaving Shelly at the pool. With wine and glasses in hand, Shelly banged furiously on Bella's door.

"I mean do people have nothing better to do than

complain about two adults drinking wine!"

"Yes," Bella said. "At Portland, there are lots of people who have nothing better to do than bother other residents with minor infractions. But who even saw you?"

Bella answered her own question. "Someone with a condo overlooking the pool."

A few days later, as he was taken to doing, Cecil Gabor was sitting in the Portland manager Mrs. Barkley's office when Bella walked in to ask if Mrs. Barkley could send a fax for her. Though Bella's do-all printer was supposed to be able to fax, Bella never worked out how to do this. Cecil had taken to spending copious amounts of time in Mrs. Barkley's office since he'd become Chairman of the Board, and Bella wondered whether there was some flirtation taking place, seeing she'd noticed Mrs. Barkley had, of late, taken to wearing dresses instead of her usual dark suits.

Whilst Mrs. Barkley worked on sending the fax, Cecil Gabor began, "I saw a baby in the pool. She was with... I think it was her nanny. And she was wearing a diaper." Cecil expected Bella to be as shocked as he was.

"And?" Bella knew what was coming next.

"I came down and informed her that we don't permit diapers in the pool."

"And?"

"Then I went back up to my condo and you know what? I see her remove the diaper and put the baby in a swimsuit," Cecil grinned victoriously.

"So, the baby can't swim with the diaper on or off? What must she do?"

"What if the baby pees in the pool, or worse?" Cecil looked to Mrs. Barkley for affirmation.

"It would be such a small pee," Bella declared.

"What if it's not a pee, you know, something else?"

Bella shrugged, "I thought you didn't want diapers."

Cecil Gabor tried another route. "We have people living here with compromised immune systems. What if they are affected by the baby's pee, or worse?"

"That's a bit far-fetched, don't you think?"

"It's a salt pool now, with no chlorine. If it was my own pool, I couldn't care less, but this is a public pool." Gabor was satisfied with this justification.

It was at this point Bella decided to let fly the arrow she had been keeping sharp in her shaft from the moment the conversation began.

"I pee in the pool," she said with a huge smile.

Mrs. Barkley burst out laughing. Even Cecil Gabor

couldn't help himself from a repressed, though horrified, guffaw.

Afterward, Bella researched salt pools and urine. She discovered that urine was sterile and saltwater pools did have chlorine, which worked like a normal chlorinator, making the likelihood of anyone catching anything from a swimming pool extremely unlikely, and if they did, the building was not capable, as there were all those signs denying responsibility.

Bella decided to make a sign: NO SWIMMING PERMITTED IN THE POOL.

She wrote it clearly in large black letters on a piece of stiff drawing paper. Then – it was night, and nobody would be at the pool – she went down to the pool and stuck her sign beside the largest of the three signs. It barely stood out, but she giggled to herself until she fell asleep.

"Go look at what I've done at the pool," she told Shelly the next morning.

"You pulled down the signs. They'll fine you."

"Just go look," Bella said again. "You'll see."

"I'll go before I go to yoga," Shelly said. "I'm not getting up, specially to see what you did."

Afterward, Shelly told Bella, "I couldn't see anything. The signs are all still up."

Go look again," Bella laughed. "Really look."

Seeing Shelly was expecting the signs to be pulled off the wall, she didn't notice one more sign, which made Bella realize the importance of expectations when it came to perception. It took two weeks before the sign was removed.

If only it was as easy to feel victorious about working on her AIDS script.

In that regard, Bella felt impotent. What was done was done. No script could make what happened not to happen. And from the general response to the subject, it was no longer of interest.

There were new pills to cure AIDS and the panic was over. There were other diseases, like Ebola, to worry about.

Bella decided to call Peter English, who now lived mostly in Tanzania. He always cheered Bella up.

Peter was one of those people who made friends easily. They were once almost lovers, but without saying anything, they decided to rather be friends.

When Bella was involved with JP, Peter did all he could to warn Bella off. "He's bad news," he said, which was nothing Bella didn't know.

Peter once owned a detective agency. He worked for various insurance companies and traveled the world uncovering fake insurance claims. Like Bella, Peter was a night owl, so she had no problem calling him at his time, midnight.

Peter was thrilled to hear from her. He was one of those friends who didn't need a bunch of niceties before getting to what mattered.

Bella asked, "What do you know about doctor Wouter Basson? They call him Dr. Death?"

Peter told Bella, "I know all about him. I followed the case. It made the daily news. Believe it or not, the bastard was acquitted of all charges... murder, fraud, you name it. He reminded me of an evil gnome; bald, mean little beard, grim smile and zero empathy."

"That's a perfect description," Bella said.

Peter continued, "They tried to get him, but the judge found him not guilty of all charges... murder, fraud, drug possession, drug trafficking, embezzlement, hundreds of murders."

Bella asked, "Do you think he was purely evil, or truly thought what he was doing was for his country?"

Peter said, "Witness after witness – scientists, doctors, decent men who were prepared to admit their part – gave evidence about what went on. It was the longest trial South

Africa ever had. Cost the state a bloody fortune. Nobody could believe the acquittal. The judge had no bloody business handling that case. He was so bloody biased."

"I know." Bella had read the entire transcript of the case.

Peter said, "It was a bloody, fucking disgrace."

Bella didn't like cursing; 'fucking' was such a lazy description, but it was indeed a fucking disgrace, and she reiterated, "A fucking disgrace."

"He will end up losing his license," Peter said. "But the fucker, he knows how to work the system. He was found guilty in 2013 on four counts of unprofessional and unethical conduct as a doctor when he headed the apartheid's biological warfare program, but he didn't have his medical license revoked. He has good lawyers who managed to extend his appeal."

The next day Peter sent Bella an email directing her to a short film he managed to find wherein the toxins were tested at a facility run by Dr. Wouter Basson.

The video was chilling. Even more so than the script she was writing, where her imagination could run wild. Basson's lab was no gleaming white lab but a derelict low-slung face brick with a tin roof, set back in large grounds so no neighbors could see or hear what was going on. What bothered Bella most was photographs of walls lined with animal cages and drains on the floor. The thought of how animals and even humans must have been tortured was sickening.

Bella showed the film to Nicole. "I wish you wouldn't have shown it to me," Nicole said. "I mean, I am glad you did, but like, it's so dark."

"Dark" was quickly replacing Nicole's "awesome." Bella bought a secondhand Thesaurus on Amazon and planned to give it to Nicole.

Having watched the video a few more times, Bella felt an infusion of energy and went back to her notebook. Again she made one of her lists, at the same time reminding her to purchase a decent ink pen. She'd once collected a few ancient models, but though they looked pretty, the ink flow was off.

- *Dr. Beadel is murdered, but his death is made to look like suicide. He was murdered because he knew too much.*

- *His widow Ilene remarries. Her twins are adopted by their stepfather and change their last names.*

- *Mabelell comes to America with her child, who is now a teenager and very beautiful. She wants to find out more about Beadel. She finds out he's dead and, for a moment, thinks of finding his wife and telling her what she knows he did but decides against it. Nobody she knows in South Africa wants to follow up.*

- *Mabalell meets and marries an American doctor who lives in Los Angeles, whom she met whilst investigating Beadel's company. The doctor invested money in the biological firm still run by Ilene and Beadel's partner*

- *The company has long since changed names and moved and is doing very well with a line of facial products.*

- *Mabalell and Ilene Beadel, who now has a different last name, meet inadvertently at a barbeque.*

- *Mabalell doesn't ever find out Ilene was married to John Beadel. It is something everyone wants to forget.*

- *Ilene also has a daughter with her second husband, who is a little younger than Mabalell's daughter.*

- *The two girls meet and immediately bond and become friends.*

- *They attend the same private school.*

When Peter called to find out if she'd watched the video he sent her, Bella's initial excitement had faded.

"This screenplay of mine does not make sense. It's a sort

of dead-end situation. I am trying to uncover a happy ending."

Peter laughed, "There are a lot of dead ends when you're a detective. And I should know. It was once my business."

Bella asked Peter, "I wonder if Wouter Basson would take a call from you? He'd give meat to my script."

"You've got to be fucking kidding," Peter laughed. "He didn't admit doing anything wrong during the longest session at the Truth and Reconciliation Commission. He claimed he did nothing bad during his criminal trial. Do you think he's going to tell Madam Bella Mellman anything?"

Unable to sleep after talking to Peter, Bella got out of bed and went to her ever-faithful big-screen iMac.

She opened Facebook to take her turn on Words with Friends. She'd never beaten two of her fellow players. Their monikers were Robbie and Aron. Was there something in that, she wondered? Robbie was devious. He made words she'd never heard, like LEV and OHM, but she was learning to be as sneaky. Bella and Robbie connected on Facebook. They discovered they knew each other and were once part of the same teenage crowd in Johannesburg. From Robbie's Facebook postings, he and his third wife were happily married and lived in Canada. Maybe Shelly was right? "Third time's the charm," Shelly always said before yet another new date.

In her game with Aron, the other male player, Bella, made the word FOLLOW, which got her just past Aron's score. She'd almost beaten Aron a few times. With her word ZONE on a triple word, she was about to win unless he pulled off something brilliant, which was unlikely. In the game with Ronnie, she played DOWAGER, which got her ahead of him by fifteen points.

She then looked at her emails; politicians were asking for money, charities asking for money, 20% or more off on just about everything she'd ever shown any interest in, ever, a message she'd been outbid on a pendant she was thinking of buying for Jessica.

Then she wandered to The New York Times online and read a couple of opinion pieces before going to their Fashion and Style pages. "I should have been a fashion designer," she often thought, remembering how she made books of fashion drawings as a young girl. One time when Bella contracted encephalitis and was bedridden – it seemed for ages – she drew fashions for women who lived the kind of life she imagined fancy people lived; outfits for the cruise, breakfast, lunch and dinner, fancy balls, glamorous cocktail parties, going to town, which was what the city was called when central Johannesburg was filled with elegant department stores and top echelon offices. She wished her mother had kept them, but Joyce wasn't one of those kinds of mothers.

Online Bella clicked through clothes for the new season from Paris, New York and Milan and she both admired and scorned the exquisite, sometimes comical and rarely wearable couture offered by designers. She marveled at models – tall, thin, and always young in all their elongated perfection – and felt the mixture of envy and disdain she always felt when she paged through fashion magazines, even though she was aware that without make-up and hair, lighting and computer-generated alteration, the girls could look quite ordinary. Nicole once sneaked home a book from the agency to show Bella what models looked like before and after their photographs were touched up; breasts were lifted, necks elongated, waists slimmed, and color evened out. It was comforting to know perfection was achieved by technology yet at the same time disquieting for Bella knew she didn't want to see reality in Vogue Magazine.

Bella moved from fashion to news and came across a photograph of a group of men gathered around a harbor before they embarked on a trip to Africa, a reverse Atlantic passage, which they thought would help them understand something more about slavery.

Bella – always thinking about what to write – wondered

whether she should write about slavery, not from the perspective of the slave – but as a white Slave Master.

The silence of deep night made her contemplate the discrepancies of her own thoughts. How could high fashion, slavery and dark AIDS conspiracies simultaneously take up space in her brain? She could own a deep appreciation for the unabashed beauty of high fashion whilst at the same time mocking its undeniable excesses.

"I am in conflict with myself," Bella said out loud. Then she saved the photograph of the reverse slavery passage with its accompanying caption in a file of writing ideas and decided to go back to bed.

Before she shut down her computer, she heard a ping. Aron, who was winning by 20 points, had entered a word and it was now her turn.

Bella looked at her letters. So many vowels and no E. She moved her tiles around on the screen and then saw it; a seven letter that would fit on an open S. She moved her tiles to make the word OFFICIOUS.

"Beat that, Aaron," she sent him an instant message.

Chapter 26: Cryptic Species

"Some differences don't deserve celebration."

It was one of those unseasonably warm Sundays with a light cloud cover. Bella hoped it might rain. She loved the rain. However, the likelihood of rain was nil. Los Angeles' summers were dry and hot and getting hotter. The winters, when it was supposed to rain, were becoming dryer. *Global Warming*, now called *Climate Change,* as if a name change would make what was happening not as bad, was the culprit. Or rather, humans were the basic problem. "Too many people, that's the foundational source," she would argue. Too many people want to eat, drive, travel, heat and cool their homes, and so on and on.

Bella, Greta, Shelly, and Nicole sat on Bella's patio, all of them half-reading the Sunday papers. The conversation moved from the usual contemplation by Bella of how to finish her John Beadel script to the latest atrocities committed by one of the many Islamic terrorist groups.

"I could not cut off another person's head," Bella said. "Or an arm or leg."

"What if your life depended upon it?" Greta asked. "What if you had to do it in order to live?"

Bella said, "That sounds like one of those idiotic questions; would you rather be burned alive, killed by a shark or eaten by a lion? Hobson's choice."

"Whose choice?" Nicole asked.

"It's a saying; one choice is as bad as the other. But it's not the same as people being killed and maimed. They have no choice."

"It's like those people who do it aren't even human," Nicole added. "Maybe they're not. Maybe they're from another planet?"

Greta snorted, "Now you're starting like Bella with her conspiracies."

"Now listen to this," Bella whooped as she found something appropriate to the conversation. "There's a thing called Cryptic Species."

"That's a real thing?" Shelly laughed.

"It is. It's when a species looks the same but isn't. One moth can look exactly like another, but their DNA is not the same; also, salamanders and they can't interbreed."

Nicole piped in. "Like if a donkey and a horse... did it."

"Fucked?" Greta felt like annoying Bella, whom she knew hated crude language.

"Maybe people who are capable of great evil have

different DNA?" Bella stated, and when no one said anything, she went on, "Conversely, maybe exceptionally good people have different DNA?"

Greta rolled her eyes. You're treading on thin ice."

Bella came up with, "Hitler didn't breed.

Maybe he couldn't?" Greta retorted, "Neither did Mother Theresa."

Nicole flung out, "She was a nun. They can't have sex."

Bella couldn't imagine herself beheading anyone, nor could she imagine doing anything as noble as treating Ebola patients with blood seeping from their orifices. She felt faint when she cut herself. Her brother Derek passed out when he saw blood. She'd seen him do so when he cut his finger changing a light bulb. "I think I'm going to faint," he said before tumbling off the stepladder on Bella's shoulders as she held the rickety old ladder steady. Bella didn't pass out if she cut herself but barely looking, she immediately covered her injury and – with half-closed eyes – stuck on a bandage.

Nicole said, "I think we can, like, all be evil or good. It's part of us. We are different but the same."

Bella replied. "Don't give me that politically correct bla. There are bad humans: thieves, pedophiles, embezzlers, killers… they know what they are doing. Their brains permit them to be untouched whilst they do their dirty."

Shelly changed the subject, "I freak out if I see a spider."

Bella said, "I'm not scared of spiders, but I'm terrified of insects, those ones with feelers and big legs, like locusts or those horrible big roaches we have here in LA."

"I don't like them either," Shelly agreed.

Bella announced, "I have a theory about this. Why we're so scared of bugs when we are so much more powerful than they are."

Greta sighed. Bella was about to explain one of her odd scientific theories. "Scientists think the coelacanth – a fish with fins that acted a bit like legs – could be a precursor of us. I was a child when one washed up on the shore in South Africa. I remember the excitement. Huge headlines in the newspapers." In a subtle admonishment addressed to Shelly, Bella added, "Everyone read the newspaper. We had a morning and an evening paper. Not only one. It was an enormously important discovery because scientists believed the coelacanth went extinct with the dinosaurs. Now they had evidence this was the kind of fish that could have made the transition from ocean to shore and they were still living."

Then came Bella's theory; "I see how insects swarmed

over fish with rudimentary arms who were trying to heave themselves onto the shore. Being eaten alive by insects must have been a slow lingering death. The fear remains embedded in the DNA of those of us who go back to coelacanths who had no defenses against the marauding insects. Not all creatures who landed up stranded on shore were attacked; that's why some people aren't scared of insects."

Greta said, "I'm dead scared of rats and mice."

Bella said, "My mother was so afraid of snakes, she couldn't stand even looking at a photograph of one, and her sister, my aunt, was the same. I thought she overdid it. But that was my mother. She tended to exaggerate. Maybe her line went all the way back to a creature being killed by a snake."

Both Shelly and Greta rolled their eyes, and so Bella went back to reading about cryptic species for a while before finding something she thought might interest her friends. "Do you know forest elephants and bush elephants look the same, but their DNA is different, and they can't breed?"

"I can live without that information," Greta teased. "Maybe that's why some people can't have kids. My friend and her husband couldn't have kids. They would have made horrible parents, so I think nature fixed it."

Shelly said, "Well, there are people who should not have children and they do, lots of them. They don't care about bringing them up. They only care about popping them out. It's a disgrace and we're too scared to say anything. And I'm not racist, in case you're about to say I am. It doesn't matter what color they are; some people should not have kids. I think if one kid is taken away to be fostered, the mother and the father should be neutered. I'm equal opportunity… not just the mother, but also the father."

"A little Hitlerian, don't you think?" Greta did not take Shelly seriously, but she did remind her of the words written by Hannah Arend, "*The banality of evil.*"

Greta, who read copiously about the Holocaust, said, "Mass killers like Eichmann said he was merely following orders. He could have just as easily been planting cabbages instead of planning and executing the destruction of the Jewish race."

"He was a cryptic species," Shelly announced happily. "He seemed human, but he wasn't. Anyway, I don't think we are all the same inside and out. Some of us are plain stupid and some are geniuses. I can't even work out my accounts."

Greta said, "I can spot a fake Hermes a mile off."

Bella could see the conversation going the way she'd

rather it didn't. However, Shelly decided to prove she was not racist.

"You might know Bella, seeing as you didn't grow up here, but we had lynching, and not so long ago. A black man could be lynched for looking at a white woman the wrong way. White people watched black men being tortured and then lynched as entertainment. I've seen pictures. Can you imagine? What kind of people did that?"

Nicole shouted out, "Cryptic species. One of my uncles like collected postcards they made of lynchings. He did it like because he was a professor and he wanted to show his students."

Greta didn't want to get into lynching at this point and neither did Shelly, who was going on one of her dates. Nicole was off somewhere, and Greta was late for an exhibition. She said, "At least us ladies are trying to do good, and Bella if you want to be a very, very good person, you'll come with me to this gallery opening. I promised Oona – she owns the gallery – I'd show up. You'll like her, she's quite a character. And afterwards, we can go for ice cream at that new place I told you I found. My treat. We can be very, very bad together."

Bella replied, "I can't stand gallery owners. They're a pretentious cryptic species, but I'll come with you anyhow."

"You can take photographs," Greta said.

"I wouldn't come unless I could," Bella replied.

Bella discovered the perfect pastime whilst having to attend social situations, like art shows with Greta. Without alcohol to liven the tedium of occasions where she had nothing to say to anyone, nor anyone to her, she took on the role of society photographer and pranced around saying things like, "You look so fabulous. Can I take your photograph?"

People were thrilled to have their photograph taken and Bella had never been refused and people were far too cool to ask where the photograph might be going, which was just as well as the only place it went was to Bella's iPhone.

The crowd at Oona's gallery was young and arty and – as usual – were thrilled to be chosen for a photograph, not only because they imagined themselves online or in the pages of a fashionable publication but because Bella's sincere compliments were encouraging. Like Nicole, she found herself repeatedly saying, "You look amazing." It was true; this young art crowd did look that way with their tattoos, piercings, extreme hairdos, and overtly art-driven outfits.

As she passed by Greta, interrupting her intense conversation with the artist, Bella whispered, "I'm the oldest person here, by twenty years at least."

"There's someone your age," Greta pointed out, a frail, bent creature closely peering at one of the artworks. Bella wasn't sure whether Greta meant to be witty, but she went up to the man who looked as if he had possibilities for conversation, only to discover he was extremely hard of hearing, and after a few tortuous minutes – during which Bella found out he was a retired lab technician and liked gallery openings for the free wine – she gave up and integrated herself with what looked like a fascinating group she'd already photographed. Anchored by a milk-skinned redhead who wore a wisp of repurposed kimono, they were discussing where to find the best hamburgers in Los Angeles.

Unable to contribute to the conversation, Bella moved on to a couple with multiple piercings. After duly posing for their photographs, Bella discovered the woman was a third-grade schoolteacher, and her long-time live-in Nigerian boyfriend was in IT. They also never want to get married.

"Marriage sucks," the woman pronounced. Her beau nodded in agreement. Both being from Africa, Bella and the IT boyfriend from Nigeria managed a bonding conversation about what they did and didn't miss in The United States until they were interrupted by another couple who joined in.

"I'm Chandler," the woman introduced herself.

"I'm Brian, artist and nihilist," the man shot out an uncovered forearm covered in dense, abstract patterned tattoos.

"So, you don't believe there is good and bad?" Bella challenged, but before the nihilist could answer, he allowed himself to be whisked off by a purposeful, young creature with stringy blonde hair dyed to look grey.

"I love your grey hair, you can see I love grey," the grey-blonde giggled, throwing Bella a compliment as she dragged the nihilist off into the crowd.

By this time – as they always did when Bella stood for too long – her heels ached. "I have to sit down," she said, excusing herself to sit on the only chair at the back of the gallery. There, quite happily, she waited out Greta's meanderings. And when Greta finally wanted to leave, Bella told her, "I'm craving salted caramel," in case you've forgotten.

When they arrived at the ice cream parlor, the couple who didn't want to get married were also there and they sat together. Her name was Jubilee, and he claimed the name Storm. Storm was not a Nigerian name and Bella thought Jubilee was probably not her given name either. They chatted first about ice cream flavors which segwayed – as

384

many casual LA conversations go – into movies, and finally, how difficult it was to be in a relationship.

"Seeing as I'm happier than I've ever been without one, what can I say," Bella laughed. "Of course, I'm older." Bella forced herself not to add wiser. "I've been there, done that more than I'd like to recall."

"What about desire?" Jubilee asked.

Bella had a reply, "Desire's like a waterfall. After it's fallen, it's just like regular water."

Greta said, "Don't mind her. She's a world-class cynic."

Bella was not to be stopped. "We shouldn't live in pairs. It doesn't work. How can any one person satisfy all one's needs? It's impossible."

Storm nodded and, addressing his comment towards Jubilee, said, "I'm not the only one."

Bella further explained, "Primitive people knew better. The women lived together; the men went out hunting. They got together at night. But afterwards there was no "what are you thinking", or "do you love me?" or worse, "do you still love me?" And the next day, they went about their separate ways. Women gossiped whilst they did the hard work of making a home, and the men went off hunting and got drunk. The kids helped, played and learned to be independent."

Storm said, "That's how it still is in many places in Africa."

"So, go back there," Jubilee taunted. "If that's what you want."

"Did I say I wanted to live like that?" Storm asked.

"You're always simplifying things," Greta told Bella.

Storm said, "Us Nigerians, we have gone away from traditional living. It has made many problems. Divorce, drugs, and corruption. My grandfather, he says, when he was a young boy herding cattle, things were better." He paused, then added, "But he does love his TV and his cell phone. And he didn't want me to grow up like he did. He wanted me to be educated and when I came to work in The United States of America, well, he was very proud. We often talk on Facetime."

Jubilee said, "Storm hates it when I even like talk with my girlfriends on the phone. He says I'm talking shit." Noting Bella's slight wince, Jubilee said, "Sorry, but that's what he says. He could spend all day and night watching football, or drinking with his buddies, or going to the gym and working out for hours."

"You work out, too," Storm accused.

Bella ignored this. "It was also nicer when generations

and families lived together. There were other people to talk to besides your partner... an aunt, an uncle and a grandparent. It's no wonder marriages don't work."

"We're not married," Jubilee pointed out.

Bella said, "I know, but you live as a pair."

Greta interjected, "Communes failed, too."

Bella said, "I think it has to be relatives; family, people who are close. It can't be a random bunch of individuals with different societal backgrounds."

"Back to the clan and tribe?" Greta said.

"And war!" Jubilee exclaimed.

Bella stopped herself from going any further with this and admitted, "I don't know what works. Some people are happily married forever and ever. All I know is that we must get rid of the idea you have to be married or have someone with whom to share your life to be fulfilled."

Greta grinned, "Have you ever thought, Bella, that you may be a cryptic species?"

"What's that?" Storm asked.

Greta explained as best she could. "It's when one species looks exactly like another, but their DNA is different, so they're really not at all the same. Like my dear friend here who, unlike most people, likes living on her own."

Storm said, "I am able to live on my own. I have, many times."

Jubilee glared at Storm. Bella was certain their night would end badly, but then, being young and more or less in love, it could end well, too.

At this point, they'd all finished their ice creams, and saying how much they'd enjoyed their interaction and how they hoped to one day repeat it, they went their separate ways.

In the car driving back, Greta said, "I'm not joking. I think you truly are a cryptic species. Maybe you can have your DNA checked. I went out with a man who did. He said he found out he had a bit of Neanderthal in his DNA. I told him I wasn't one bit surprised."

Back at the Portland on Charlie's nightly dog walk, Nicole joined Bella. She said, hopefully, "Undrew might not be gay. He says he loves me, and I know he like does, but it's not sexual. But we get on so like well with each other. He says he's never been with anyone who understands him like I do. Maybe he's The One?"

Bella smiled, "I've been mad about many Ones that weren't The One."

Nicole also told Bella she'd decided to go to cooking

school and handed in her notice at the modeling agency."

But the next day, she came to Bella to tell her, "They want me to like stay, and so they're giving me like more money and I'm moving up. I must like train someone to do my job. So instead of like full-time cooking school, I'm doing like part-time classes. And I have like to give up my writing group. Anyway, I cook better than I write."

"I counted six likes in what you just told me. You have to concentrate."

"I know, it's hard. But I have been thinking. I've been thinking you should write a love story about you and Guy ending up like together. I can see the ending. This old couple." Nicole almost said, *cute old couple,* and thanked her lucky stars she managed to stop herself, for if there was one-word Bella hated combined with old, it was 'cute'. "It would end like with you and Guy on a boat, going around the world."

Bella almost exploded. "Firstly, Nicole, it's a ship, not a boat. Secondly, Guy is still puppy-eyed with his Irina."

Nicole interrupted, thinking this would please Bella, "Who is young enough to be his daughter!"

"And I am still content on my own; sleeping, eating, doing, thinking, reading, watching, feeling, or not, without having to consider Guy or any other man! Plus, I am a writer. Or at least trying to be one."

"You're epic!" Nicole said

Chapter 27: Vows

"Vows aren't guarantees."

Bella opened the thick cream envelope, an invitation to the fiftieth wedding anniversary of Phoebe and Allan Schmook to be held at their daughter's mansion in Bel Air.

Bella spoke to Phoebe maybe once a year and no matter what was going on in Phoebe's life, everything was just fine. Allan had a heart attack, their oldest daughter had turned into their son, Phoebe had shoulder surgery, but to Phoebe, it was Bella, poor unmarried Bella, whose life was difficult.

Phoebe always started off the conversation with, "Have you found someone?"

"I'm not looking," Bella always replied, with which Phoebe gave a strangled sigh. "You brave thing."

A few days after Bella received the invitation, Phoebe called. Bella worked out the reason for her call immediately, though Phoebe took a while to come out with it; "I hope you don't mind, but Allan felt we had to ask Guy."

Bella said, "Guy and I have long ago worked out how to handle being together in social situations."

This was true. Since they both lived in Los Angeles – and even before – Bella and Guy found themselves attending certain events at the same time. This elicited compliments; how mature they both were, being divorced and yet able to treat each other so amicably. Bella never let those people know how hard it was for her to see Guy – at first with a variety of beautiful younger women he dated after their divorce – then with Wife Number Two at his side. Not that Bella wanted to be at Guy's side. She'd been there and done that and being at Guy's side was not where she wanted to be. However, he was the father of her children, and she still loved him in a way both profound and inexplicable even if she didn't want to be his wife, it pained her when he had anyone else.

Now, with Wife Number Two gone, she'd learned to deal with Guy's lady, the European mongrel.

Irina was also the same age as Jessica. Bella understood why Guy wanted an unencumbered, fresh-fleshed woman to share his bed. Had younger men found Bella desirable, she wondered whether she might do the same thing! But she didn't think so. Women were different, or at least she was. Her hormones didn't budge at the sight of a good body. There were times she missed the affection and attention of a man who loved her, but she'd learned to accept and quell the occasional longing to love and be loved. She was grateful she was not like so many single women who felt anguished and incomplete without a partner. Though, lately, she'd noticed the desperation women used to feel if they weren't married was lessening. This was a good thing, a very good thing.

Men were different. They needed to be able to have sex to prove themselves male, evinced by the explosion of erectile dysfunction drugs, the abandon with which they were advertised and the billions the pharmaceutical companies made producing and selling them. In Bella's opinion, men didn't have erectile dysfunction. They weren't meant to have erections at a certain age. It was the same evolutionary path women took as their periods stopped and they could no longer bear children. For heaven's sake, there was so much advertising for dysfunctional erection medications that both Jessica and Bella were forced to explain Viagra and Cialis to Chloe as soon as Chloe could read the TV ads. Bella's explanation was convoluted; however, Chloe and her friends got the gist.

Bella recently read about a women's drug for so-called sexual dysfunction, but she had never heard anyone of her sex mention it, and she wondered if it could be successful.

Women – due to their anatomical design – were at least able to have sex at any age. The fact that they might not want to was another story.

Shelly asked Bella, "So, who are you going to take to the Schmook party?"

"Nobody. I am quite capable of going out on my own."

"It's a big event, like a wedding. Look at their invite!" Shelly held up the important-looking invite, which Bella placed amongst the glasses on the wet bar.

"Why don't you find a handsome young man and ask him to come as your date? I know this actor…"

Bella stopped her. "I neither need nor want a fake date. I'm not like you."

Shelly didn't pay attention to Bella's barb, for it was true. But as far as she was concerned, she'd no more think of going to a big event like a wedding without a partner than allowing her hair to go grey as Bella was doing. Shelly didn't tell Bella – at the time – she too had been invited to a wedding and was wondering what to do about a partner and contemplated the actor for herself.

Shelly's wedding was in Stockton – the Northern California town where she used to live before she came to Los Angeles. The very idea of showing up alone at the wedding was giving her nightmares. She wanted to show off how well she'd done in Los Angeles since she left her boring husband, especially as he'd found a much younger

Philllipino companion almost the second the divorce became final. Her name was Munni, and Shelly's daughters told her she was good to their father and made him happy, and thus they accepted her. This made Shelly want to throw up.

"I also have to go to a wedding," Shelly finally told Bella. "I haven't got anything to wear, and my ex is going to be there with Munni. My girls have also been invited and they're both going. It's going to be fu… so awkward, but I have to go."

"You don't have to do anything," Bella replied.

"It would look bad if I didn't go."

Bella suggested, "What about taking one of your old beaux?"

Shelly was emphatic. "No, I want to make them all sit up and notice."

"What about that actor?"

"That's stupid."

"It was good enough for you to suggest him for me."

"I was joking."

"I wish my friend Karen was invited; she's the old friend I'm staying with, but she hasn't been. She left her husband a couple of years ago when she decided she was gay, so he's the one invited to the wedding with his new wife."

"Bingo!" Bella shrieked, "Karen can be your partner!"

But she's..."

Bella interrupted, "Not a man. So what! Who cares? Men marry each other and so do women. Why can't your date be a woman?"

"People will wonder."

"They'll wonder if you're gay?"

Shelly gave a sly smile. "It'll give everyone something to talk about."

When Shelly called Karen to broach the idea, she said, "I'll wear a gorgeous black St. Laurent suit I bought at a resale store. So far, I've never had the occasion to wear it. I'm your man!"

And so, Shelly filled in the little box on the reply card accepting two.

It was as if the heavens were playing *here comes to the bride* for the next day; Greta called Bella to inform her she was invited to a wedding.

"Remember I told you about my new commission to find art for Mervis and Trunk's new offices. Well, Freddy Mervis is getting married and has invited me to his wedding, his fourth marriage."

Bella asked. "How old is he?"

"Rich enough for it not to matter. She's an ex-sportswear model, gorgeous, like one of those Victoria Secret girls. My invitation says, 'and partner'."

Greta thought of taking Frank Maxwell. Asking him to accompany her to a public event would be a test. Frank Maxwell only saw her during the week, only called her during office hours and though he swore he was separated from his wife, she had her suspicions, which were confirmed when he said he would be away on a business trip at the time and couldn't make the wedding. This was the final straw and Greta decided that she wasn't going to see Frank again. She was glad she hadn't told Bella about Frank Maxwell. She could almost hear Bella teasing, "Another Glen!"

Though Frank couldn't come, Greta – knowing many artists – had no problem finding another partner. Saul Pipe was her choice. "He's one of the best-looking men I've ever met," Greta told Bella. "He's such fun too, and of course gay. All the best men are," Greta sighed.

A few days later, Nicole told Bella she'd been invited to attend the wedding of her friend Abby in Boston.

Bella met Abby on Valentine's Day when she was miserable, having been dumped by her boyfriend. However, the dump hadn't lasted, and he'd returned to claim her as his bride.

"Boston's a beautiful city," Bella said.

"I will hardly have time to see it. The whole weekend is wedding stuff... dinners and breakfast and cocktails. And I don't even like being with Abby anymore. She's like a different person now."

"In what way?"

"She acts like everything's perfect, but I know it isn't. Her fiancée Brandon's so controlling, and Abby does whatever he says. It's like they filter each other. I've seen it with all my married friends. It might not be obvious, but I notice. They look at each other whilst they talk; a side glance, a demeaning chuckle. They like know each other so well that any slight change in their way of speaking or even walking or standing and they're suspicious and all jealous. And they're like kind of scornful of each other. She fills in a bit of a story, and he corrects her and vice versa and I can see they get irritated. It's sort of ugly."

Bella said, "That's what happens when you're a couple. They speak the language of Bickering."

Nicole said, "It's such a like dreary experience watching my friends gradually join the orchestrated wedding wall. I've been to so many weddings by now and they're all cookie-cutter."

Bella said, "A wedding is a wedding. Whether it takes place in a palace or the beach, they all have the same well-defined configuration: a venue, a color scheme, table centerpieces, flowers, food, make-up, hideous bridesmaids' dresses and all the family variables. The bride is queen for a few days. The groom only needs to show up, not drunk. At a Muslim wedding I attended in Johannesburg, the bride wore a red sari trimmed with gold. She was exquisite. The groom wore an ivory Maharaja's suit. There were so many guests; some were seated in the corridor and by the elevator to the ballroom. Then I noticed jugs of cool red drinks, so no alcohol. At my table, where I knew everyone, someone had the foresight to bring a whole lot of those little bottles, like we get on the plane."

Nicole said, "Can you believe it? Abbey's ordered and sent back seven pairs of white heels already. She says they're not the right white. I mean, like white is white."

Bella laughed, "No, white isn't white. Go to the paint store and see how many shades of white there are."

Bella felt for Nicole. She didn't want to be married and she did at the same time. She scorned the wedding brouhaha yet found it impossible to ignore its attraction. She believed in true love and finding a soul mate, and she – like most young women – imagined marriage was more like a fabulous extended date rather than a legal contract to live an often-tedious co-joined life.

"What are the chances of me, you, Shelly and Nicole being invited to a wedding on the same weekend?" Bella asked Greta whilst they dined at Café Angelino, one of their favorite local restaurants.

"Mine isn't exactly a wedding, but a fifty-year anniversary is more or less the same."

Greta replied, "Maybe good things happen in fours? Usually, it's threes. Three deaths, three plane crashes."

"God, Greta, you are a killjoy." Bella did not like flying one bit. Any mention of plane crashes was unwelcome, even in jest.

Greta trilled the first bars of the song, "Love is in the air..."

"You can't sing," Bella sometimes found Greta thoroughly irritating.

After having found an 'awesome' dress and towering gold high heels to wear, Nicole happily went off to her Boston wedding after she discovered Atticus Cohen – a long-time crush – would be there.

Shelly spent far more than she wanted on a plain black sheath covered in palettes. "I hope Karen and I will look good together," she smiled weakly, still nervous about how things would look.

Greta shopped in her closet for a simple, long, subdued-gold, pleated skirt and sculptured white satin blouse with elbow-length sleeves. She'd worn the outfit before and felt good in it.

Bella couldn't make up her mind about what to wear. She decided on a kaftan made from a vintage sari. It was comfortable, didn't need a constricting pantie to flatten her stomach, and was original. She'd wear the kaftan with low-heeled gold sandals. They weren't fabulous; shoes made from manmade materials weren't.

"Perhaps I should become a no-leather shoe designer," she ruminated.

Prior to the respective celebrations, Bella checked the weather. It was cold everywhere, especially in Boston.

Bella sometimes checked the weather in distant places, which helped her understand better why countries were like they were. This was easy to do on her iPhone, where she recorded several cities' daily temperatures. She knew what the weather conditions were in Johannesburg, Sydney, where she had dear old friends, New York, just because, and Nice, France, because she thought that was where she should live, that is, if she made a fortune and learned to speak

French.

During the Iraq war, Bella added Baghdad. Summer temperatures were usually well over 110 degrees. "Politicians should have to spend one day in Baghdad in soldier uniform, carrying gear before making the decision to go to war." She'd sent a letter to the LA Times suggesting this. But it wasn't published.

Bella thought it was a sweet idea to have Nicole, Greta, and Shelly to supper the day after they'd all had sufficient time to recover from their respective celebrations. She was sure they'd have tales to tell.

Hers was poignant and she hoped she wouldn't begin to cry when she described how Guy asked her to dance when the disc jockey played a rock and roll oldie. Nobody else got up and Guy – fancying himself a mover and remembering how the two of them both loved dancing – swirled her around over and over again until she was so dizzy she held onto every shred of control to stop herself from falling flat out on the dance floor. As she concentrated on staying upright, she imagined everyone gossiping about her and Guy. "Poor Bella, still in love with Guy: how old she'd got, how fat, she still looks good, Guy looks better, how can she stand being in the same room with Guy and Irina?"

Bella thanked her God that by the time the number

ended, she hadn't disgraced herself in front of the crowd and dashed off to the bathroom just in time to hide her uncontrollable tears.

"And then I snuck off from the party. I didn't say goodbye to anyone. At least I didn't have to wait long for the valet to bring my car."

"Awesome," Nicole said. "I mean, like, so emotional."

Nicole looked the worse for wear. Her weekend was – as expected – alcohol-fueled.

"Actually, I had an awesome time," she said, looking bravely at Bella. "I hooked up with Atticus and he's coming to LA in a few months."

"Hooked up as in 'made a connection' or had sex?" Bella asked.

"Sort of both." Nicole grinned. "Don't tell Undrew!"

Shelly said, "Even though I've got three daughters, I still don't understand this hooking up. Is it sex or almost sex or dating?"

Nicole tried her best to explain, "It's definitely not like dating."

"So, is it sex?" Shelly persisted.

"Sort of, but more making out. It's like casual."

"So, you had casual sex with Atticus. What's his last

name?" Shelly was suddenly taking an interest in Nicole's morals.

"Cohen. Atticus Cohen."

"A nice Jewish boy," Shelly quipped, "Make your parents happy."

Bella never told Shelly that Nicole's mother committed suicide and she blanched. However, Nicole took it in stride and showed no emotion when she replied, "My father doesn't care what I do, so long as I'm happy. And my mother's not alive."

Thankfully that shut Shelly up.

Afterwards, Bella told Shelly about Nicole's mother.

"I feel so bad," she said. "I didn't know."

"Why should you? She didn't tell me for ages. I think she doesn't want anyone to feel sorry for her. Maybe she will tell you herself one day."

Greta's wedding venue was in Malibu. The ceremony took place under a flower-bedecked canopy at the bottom of a hill, after which guests negotiated a steep and stony stepped walkway to the top, where the reception took place.

"Apparently, the bride once attended a wedding there and always dreamed of having her own at the same place. It would have been fine if she married a man her own age, but

Marvin's friends are old, and negotiating that uneven path to the top of the hill where the reception took place wasn't easy. It wasn't easy for a woman of any age wearing heels, though I saw some young models – obviously friends of the bride – prancing up the path without a problem. But they had hardly any body weight to pull up with them. At least I wore wedges, but they were high and not made for negotiating irregular stone steps. My date sort of helped, but the path was narrow; one person at a time."

"How did the bride look?"

"Between the feathered bottom half of the dress and shimmery beaded top, she looked like a cross between a mermaid and a baby albino chicken. Still, she looked beautiful. I don't believe I've ever seen a bride look anything but, no matter what dress they wear. There's something about bagging your man that brings out the best in whatever you do to yourself."

Everyone agreed and Greta continued, "There was a pond with swans and koi and after the ceremony was over, Marvin pretended he was about to fall in and almost did. The non-denominational priest looked more like a bodybuilder and really did have to save him. And the vows were strange. She promised to take care of him, and not the other way around. She might have to, she's at least thirty-five years younger than Marvin and he smokes cigars and drinks like a fish."

"She'll be a rich young widow," Shelly quipped.

Greta said, "Or a rich divorcee. Marvin's been married three times. He can't be easy to live with, and he's not easy as a client, either. But then none of my clients are easy."

"What food did they serve?"

"There was every expensive creature you can think of served on the buffet table, including huge bowls of caviar. It's all I ate."

Shelly said, rather triumphantly, "I thought you were being a vegetarian?"

"Bella's the vegetarian, not me. But even if I was, and I am thinking of giving up meat, I don't think I'd be able to resist real Russian caviar."

Bella agreed, "I'd definitely have the caviar."

Shelly's wedding went off better than she imagined.

"Munni – that's my ex's girlfriend broke up with him the day before, so he was put at the table for the aged singles. Being polite, he took turns dancing with all the ladies at his table, including Aunty Fay, whom I know he can't stand. I danced with Karen, but separately, like all the young people. The worst thing was that nobody even seemed to notice she was meant to be my date. She was just another woman in a black pantsuit. I guess even Stockton's got more modern."

Bella asked, "And your daughters?"

"I barely saw them and when I spoke to them the next day, both said they'd had the best time."

"That must mean they hooked up," Nicole observed.

"Whatever that's supposed to mean," said Shelly.

Chapter 28: What's In A Name?

'Why is it Amen and not Awomen?'

"I almost called you Juanita," Bella's mother, Joyce, told Bella when she complained about not liking her name.

Joyce said, "Bella is a good name. Do you know the painter Marc Chagall's wife is named Bella? Chagall was so in love with her. He painted the two of them in the sky."

Bella looked up Bella on the internet.

Bella Absug was a leader of the American Feminist movement of the 1960-1970s. She was a founder of the National Women's Political Caucus and a Member of the United States House of Representatives for New York's 19th and 20th districts. She was on Nixon's official list of political enemies. This pleased Bella.

"Do you like your name?" Bella asked Nicole as they walked Charlie one evening.

"Yes, I love my name. I love your name also; you know Bella Swan is the heroine in one of my favorite TV series."

Bella said, "I found out Bellum in Latin means war. You know how Americans use the word Antebellum? That means before the Civil War."

Nicole said, "That's so awesome! I mean, interesting.

And Lady Antebellum is like an awesome country music group. And you know Bella is beautiful in French, and I like to think in Italian also and Isabella like a popular name now. Two of my friends have called their babies Isabella."

Bella said, "I think I'd like to have been named Jessica, so that's what I called my daughter."

"I don't see you as a Jessica or anything else but Bella."

When Bella once told Greta she didn't like her name, Greta said, "Well, it's a bit too late to change it. It's a good name. Bella Freud is the great-granddaughter of Sigmund Freud and the daughter of the famous painter Lucien Freud. I think she's a dress designer. You know who Lucien Freud is?"

"Of course I do," Bella said. "Do you think I'm a philistine? And I don't like his paintings. They are brilliant, I know, but I don't like to see all those veins."

Greta said, "Hollywood likes Bella. Mark Ruffalo, Billy Bob Thornton and Eddie Murphy are dads to Bella."

"How on earth do you know that?" Bella asked.

Greta replied, "You aren't the only one whose head is filled with useless information."

As something of a joke, Greta presented Bella with a book titled Cousin Bella – The Whore of Minsk. "I found it in a second-hand bookstore and I had to buy it for you," Greta laughed her head off as Bella tore off the sophisticated black and white gift wrapping and read the title. The book was written by American playwright Sherman Yellen and was the true story of his cousin, Ida.

The author took the liberty of changing Cousin Ida's name to Bella, as there were other Idas in his family history. Ida – an unfashionable name these days – was derived from the German 'work' or 'labor'. Bella searched the internet for a while, uncovering various Idas; the most inspirational was Ida Strauss, a first-class passenger on the Titanic who refused to board the lifeboat without her husband Isadore, resulting in the couple meeting their watery fate together, which made Bella remember why she was in an uncommonly desolate mood.

Being fired from a volunteer job at a shelter for women with substance abuse problems – which she'd done one afternoon a week for over ten years – was a good enough reason.

"We don't want you to come back," the new supervisor, Worthy Zhelish, said, flexing her recently acquired status. "You upset a member of our permanent staff and insulted him in front of our girls, and we can't have that."

Worthy Zelish offered Bella no thanks for volunteering

for so long; no chance to explain she couldn't do what she was supposed to do with the floor fan blaring away from the next-door room where the staff member was pretending to work. He refused to even move it to the other side of his office. When she sat down to begin the session, she said, "That man's an idiot!"

Bella could not help the tears, and she was glad Worthy Zelish couldn't see her over the phone when she asked, "Can I tell you what happened?"

"No." Worthy Zelish was emphatic. "You cannot come back here."

"I'm really upset," Bella could not hide the tears in her voice.

"I understand you're upset, but I'm sorry, that's the way it has to be. Goodbye."

Fortunately – as planned – Greta showed up shortly after the phone call ended. "You couldn't have come at a better time."

Bella sobbed, "I didn't even like going there anymore."

Greta was uplifting. "I don't know how you did it for so long."

Bella agreed, "I should have volunteered for a year or so; that's what most people do."

Greta pointed out, "I've noticed you stick at things you don't like doing. I don't know why."

"It's my nature. I'm a Capricorn and Capricorn is the Mountain goat climbing slowly and steadily up the rocky mountain, never giving up."

"Well, it's time to change," Greta said firmly.

"You're so right. I should be learning Spanish, not French. What use is French in California? I'm the worst student also. I am really bad at languages."

Bella promptly canceled her long-standing French lessons. She was an abysmal student, didn't do her homework to the poor teacher's chagrin, and realized she would never speak French unless she lived in France, which did remain a flitting fantasy.

"I feel so much better," Bella declared.

Greta said, "Quite frankly, the only way to learn French, other than living there, is to have a French lover. And I can't see you with a man who doesn't speak good English, as a language – with all its nuances – is important to you. I've heard you say that even Americans don't understand you. Now, let's go for our dinner. I'm hungry."

"I'd also be miserable if I was fired," Jessica tried her best to make Bella feel better when she called the next morning and heard the tears in her mother's voice. "It's horrible to be fired."

"How do you know?" Jessica had never been fired, as far as Bella could remember.

"I've got lots of friends who've been fired. It's awful."

Bella's tears increased, "But I'm glad I don't have to go there anymore. God did for me what I couldn't do for myself."

"God had nothing to do with it." Jessica found it annoying when her mother invoked God or, for that matter, any spiritual reasons for life's random events. Jessica was more like Bella's mother, Joyce, who declared, "I don't believe in God or life after death. What's here is here and that's it."

When Shelly showed up later that day for a quick chat, she noticed Bella's eyes were swollen.

"Are you sick?"

"No, I've had a big weep," Bella explained. "I was actually fired from my volunteer job."

"I don't know why you bothered with that place," Shelly said.

Shelly didn't press Bella for details, but Bella volunteered, "I don't feel like rehashing the situation. It's not just being rejected," Bella complained. "My neck hurts, my jaw hurts, my fingers hurt."

Shelly was used to Bella complaining about her arthritic fingers, her sore neck and she recently acquired TMJ.

"And please don't tell me about something else you heard that helps one of my ailments because I've tried everything."

"You're fine," Shelly said.

"I know I'm fine, but aside from being fired from a volunteer job... I mean, who gets fired from a volunteer position... the world is in a terrible state. It's depressing."

Shelly was also used to Bella going on and on about the problems of the world, and she'd learned to listen and make clucking noises when Bella complained about things she couldn't possibly fix, like India, China, Africa, Russia, The Middle East, not to mention drug cartels, the ivory trade, deforestation, oil spills, plus general corruption everywhere and in everything. And, of course, there was the screenplay with Dr. John Beadel and South Africa and HIV and AIDS.

Bella looked bleak. "Do you have any idea how many wars are going on in the world?"

"At least a dozen," Shelly hazarded a guess.

Bella didn't know herself, so she let Shelly's count pass,

making a mental note to find out.

"Can you imagine in a country like India, half the people poo outside," Shelly had a factoid of her own, seeing as she'd heard the startling statistic on her car radio whilst driving back from her yoga class. "That's put me off going to India!"

"You never wanted to go there anyway. You said not even the fucking Taj Mahal could make up for the fucking dirt and the beggars you'd have to contend with." A trace of a smile appeared on Bella's face.

Knowing that Bella almost never swore, especially twice in one sentence, Shelly said, "You need to go shopping."

"You sound like George Bush."

"What's George Bush got to do with it?"

"He said we should go shopping after 9/11, don't you remember?"

"Retail therapy lifts the spirit. Everywhere!" Shelly stressed. "I am sure even terrorists' wives like shopping. You know the biggest customers of Paris fashion are from The Middle East. Under those ugly black things, they wear it's all haute couture! Get yourself ready. I'm taking you whether you want to go or not."

Bella was not sure why, but the tears flowed again.

"I miss my mother." The words sprung, unexpected and out of context.

"I know," Shelly hugged Bella. "I miss my mom, too. She's been gone over twenty years and I still miss her. Now give me ten minutes. I'll be waiting downstairs. I'm driving."

Bella adored her father, Speedy Mellman, as much as one can adore a man whose life went belly up due to a severe case of alcoholism. She could talk to her father and his opinions didn't annoy her, as did those of her mother. Speedy Mellman might have been drunk, he might have slurred his words and blamed his long-suffering wife – Bella's stepmother – for everything bad that happened to him, but Bella found Speedy's transgressions amusing. One therapist – whom Bella saw when she was still living in South Africa – told her, "Finding an alcoholic father amusing is a valuable coping mechanism."

Bella's mother, Joyce – basically a solid citizen who fell for Speedy and then counteracted that mistake by marrying a bore after she divorced him – managed to irritate Bella with a few words. "Do you really need that?" after Bella purchased something, or, "I prefer your hair off your face," after Bella cut bangs. There was also the way Joyce's voice rose an octave and took on a posh tone when she spoke to people she wanted to impress. In her retirement home, Joyce deemed most of the ladies beneath her worldliness. "They are not sophisticated," she lowered her voice when she explained this to Bella.

As Joyce aged, and particularly after her second husband died – fifteen years before her – Bella realized what a fine person her mother was. Her accomplishments, considering her impoverished upbringing and attempts at being inclusive, were admirable. She worked when it was not the norm for women in her social class to work, firstly because she had to, but Joyce loved working and was the only mother of Bella's friends who did. She never complained – at least to Bella – about her tedious second husband as he became more and more neurotic about his health. When she retired, she became active in the anti-apartheid group 'Women for Peace'.

Bella frequently heard daughters complain about their mothers. "My mother didn't support me. My mother was tough on me. My mother was judgmental. My mother was disapproving." Joyce was all those things, but she was the one Bella wanted to talk to now when she was gone.

There were times Bella believed she found glimpses of Joyce. One night as she walked Charlie thinking deeply about life and death and how much she missed her mother, a young girl sitting on the curb asked if she could pat Charlie. Her name was Joyce, and Bella saw in this message. Someone called Bella "Joyce" in error, and that was a message. Bella was always looking for messages: from God, from her dead mother, from the great unknown. She saw God in the way the wind blew, in birds, feathers and shiny cents found lying anywhere. "God is a search," was Bella's considered opinion. And when she searched, she felt closer to accepting the mystery of life and death, even though for Bella, it was a death that was the real mystery too terrifying to comprehend.

Shelly – waiting outside in her car – called up. "What's taking you so long?"

When Bella felt bad, she made an effort to look as good as possible. She learned that from Guy. She could almost hear his bold laugh as he faced risk, disadvantage and near disaster as part and parcel of his role as self-made success.

"At least I look like a million dollars." She could see him as he shook his arms to fit better inside his bespoke jacket.

The Grove was an agreeable, therapeutic shopping center. In tasteful quasi-Italianate-Spanish surroundings, The Grove contained an amalgam of offerings catering to the melting pot of Los Angelino residents. The outdoor area was popular amongst almost everyone, though there were some

– like Wife Number Two, Guy's ex-wife – who judged the re-imagined old square 'fake.' It was snobs like Wife Number Two who had no problem wearing strategically worn brand-new leather purses, boots and belts and furnishing their homes with shabby-chic style, but the Grove was "fake."

The central fountain at The Grove splashed in tune to Dean Martin singing *Volare,* which took Bella back to her teenage years and perked her up as she and Shelly strode into the scented air of Nordstrom's, where Shelly wanted to show Bella a dress she was thinking of buying.

Bella tried to suppress a laugh when Shelly tried on the dress. Even Shelly – who saw herself at least fifteen years younger than she was – giggled at the tutu-style black lace and net confection that a week ago seemed perfect.

"I needed your eyes," she told Bella.

"Maybe you need new glasses. I mean new contacts." Shelly would rather be blind than wear glasses.

After trying a few more gowns – all of them far too short in Bella's opinion – Shelly decided this wasn't the day for finding a dress and they should rather check out the latest activewear at Athleta, which Bella always called Aletha for some reason which irritated Jessica who always corrected her mother, just as Bella corrected her mother when she consistently mispronounced certain words like 'comment' as 'co-mint'.

"You'll be invigorated when you work out with a new outfit," Shelly said and Bella agreed. And so, with the world's woes temporarily forgotten, Bella struggled into elasticized bottoms and tops, which felt like a workout in of itself. Finally, encouraged by an extraordinarily patient young saleslady and a cheery Shelly, she decided on a psychedelic-colored bottom and navy top. Shelly bought a cover-up jacket, and both Bella and Shelly decided they could not resist the brightly colored socks, which they declared they needed but didn't.

Afterwards, they enjoyed an iced coffee overlooking the outdoor fountain and watched mothers and young children, shoppers, lovers, and tourists enjoying the day.

Shelly didn't say, "See now, don't you feel better," and Bella was grateful, for to acknowledge the value of retail therapy seemed shallow, despite its obvious if transitory efficacy.

Later in the afternoon, when Bella took Charlie for his walk, a red-tailed hawk flew low, sweeping but a few feet from her face. When there was one, there were two as red-tailed hawks mated for life.

She wondered what hawks could find to eat in Beverly

Hills and when she got home, she cracked an egg, opened a tin of sardines and a tin of dog food, and placed the offerings on a tray on the patio. Hawks ate mice and snakes and even squirrels as well as other birds, but if they nested in Beverly Hills, perhaps they'd developed a more sophisticated palate.

Julietta, Bella's long-time housekeeper, clucked and removed the food when she saw the repast, untouched by hawks but swarming with ants, the next day.

She told Bella, "The rats come to eat, not the birds."

When Bella told Lu, her manicurist, about the hawks, she said, "It's a sign of good fortune when hawks nest nearby."

"How do you know?"

"I know. It's what the Apache say." Lu was Vietnamese.

"Oh, so you're Apache now," Bella laughed.

"I hear things in the salon. Many things. The hawk appears, and after, you have much good fortune. Your prayers will be answered. Big time!"

Though the hawks were impossible to spot amongst the leafy trees, Bella could hear their characteristic whistle-woops for two more days. And then, just as they arrived, they were gone. Bella hoped to leave some good fortune behind.

A week later, whilst walking Charlie, Bella found a single red-tailed hawk feather. She looked around for more, hoping that the single feather didn't mean the bird had been killed, but there were none. She placed the feather in a small sling bag she wore when dog walking. The bag held her iPhone, poo bags, lip ice and a handkerchief. Bella knew what she couldn't be without, even on a ten-minute dog walk.

Nicole saw Bella and came running out, "I have to tell you something. I did something I should never have done."

Bella waited for some dire news, but instead, Nicole told Bella, "I went to a fortune teller."

"And?"

"She told me that Bellamy would never be mine."

"Who's Bellamy?"

"Remember I told you about the British photographer, the one with the twins? The one I went with to Laguna for the weekend."

It was hard to keep up with Nicole's men. "The married one?"

"No, I told you he's separated."

"And where is he now?"

"He told me he like couldn't get too close to me or anyone. He's too like hurt by his wife leaving him."

"Fortune tellers can't see the future. They're good at

reading people."

"I know," Nicole nodded.

"You go see a fortune teller when you're unhappy, in love, rejected, or don't know what to do. I've done it myself. I remember going to see one in London. I still remember her name; Joyce, like my mother. She said, "I see a man whose name begins with 'B' trying to contact you. I told her that the only man with 'B' I could think of was my ex-husband's late father and I couldn't imagine why he wanted to contact me. She looked all serious and said, "He says he's very sorry for what happened. He still loves you." Bella chuckled. "She mistakenly assumed by my answer, we didn't get on. She wasn't very good at fortune-telling. At least your woman was smart enough to tell you a separated man – who can't get close – isn't in your future. I could have told you that for free."

"I know… but he was so awesome."

"No, he wasn't." Bella fished in her bag. "Now, here's something that will definitely bring you good fortune, and I'm giving it to you only if you promise to cherish it because I am giving over my good luck to you."

Bella handed Nicole the red-tailed hawk feather. She told her all about the red-tailed hawks she'd spotted. She told her what Lu told her and embellished the power of the feather somewhat, realizing that she was no better or worse than the fortune teller, only she did it with love and for free, and that was what real friendship was about.

"You're the best," Nicole said as her tears began to well.

"No, I'm not. I'm a failure."

"Lame! You are not a failure. Not at all!" Nicole said. "You're the least failure I like to know."

Bella said, "I've given up on the John Beadel script. It's not as if I am giving anything to the world by finishing it. If a movie was made about it, it would make people angry, and they are angry enough. And even though something like this probably did happen, it doesn't help those with AIDS one bit. I should rather write something about how a person can live with HIV now that there are cures."

Nicole said, "When I was going to my writing group, I wrote something I never finished. I don't think the other people finished what they were working on, either. It's a smart woman who knows when to give up and when to go on."

Bella laughed, "Where'd you get that smart phrase?"

"My boss uses it. I've heard her with models who don't make it, not because there's anything wrong with them. Mostly they haven't the right look for the moment, so it's hard to book them."

Bella said, "I did learn a lot doing my research, but I don't feel right giving up. It makes me feel like a fraud, not a real writer."

"You do so many things for…" Nicole almost said, *an old woman* but stopped herself.

Bella laughed at Nicole's discomfort. "It's okay, darling. I don't mind being called old. I am old. I don't know why being old is something we are supposed to be ashamed about."

"You're the coolest old person I know. I want to be like you when I get old," Nicole said. "I've told you that before."

"There are better role models," Bella said. "Writers, artists, scientists."

Nicole said, "You are a writer! I mean a real writer."

"I used to make a living being a copywriter, but now I'd starve if I depended on my work."

Nicole countered, "Van Gogh was a painter and he made hardly any money painting."

Bella said, "He's an exception."

Nicole replied, "No, there are like lots of people who are like brilliant, but they don't make money. You can't make that a rule. I know a woman who is awesome. She does these amazing things with the computer, and she doesn't make money and doesn't care if she doesn't. She says she does it for the love of it. And I think like you do too."

Bella knew Nicole was trying her best to make her feel good.

"Think of women like Jane Goodall," Bella said. "She's a hero. Or Ingrid Newkirk of PETA. She's astonishing; she didn't give up on her difficult course. She's done so much good in this world that she deserves the Nobel Prize."

Switching to one of Nicole's areas of interest, "What about Julia Child?"

Nicole said, "I don't know famous artists or writers or scientists, or Julia Child. I know you, and I think you're like awesome and I don't care if you don't like me saying, awesome."

Bella was uncomfortable being so complimented.

She changed the subject, "How is Undrew since he's moved?"

"He's fine. I still like him, but he's... I don't know. He's into his career. And so am I. My cooking classes are awesome. I'll have my own restaurant one day."

"Why not?" Bella said.

Nicole said, "I love your stories. And my friends do, too.

Undrew says you're grand."

Bella didn't feel grand. Of late, she had been alternatively berating herself and feeling fortunate. What could she do to be a better person?

When Shelly showed up at Bella to ask her opinion on her new boots, Bella told Shelly how useless she was feeling. "I have the extra bedroom, which is rarely used. I could foster a teenager or take in another unwanted dog or a cat. The rules at The Portland permit two animals. Instead of buying the crimson lipstick that promised not to stray into the fine lines above and below my lips, why don't I forgo such vanities and donate the funds to charity?"

Shelly said, "I refuse to allow you to have buyer's remorse over lipstick. As for fostering kids, how old are you? And cats ruin the furniture. I've had them, and no matter how many scratching boards you give them, they prefer the fabric of the chair's arms. Now tell me, do you like my new boots?" Shelly swirled around, feeling good.

"You look fabulous," Bella said and she meant it.

Since Shelly's brief but meaningful time with the art collector, she remained a client of a stylist at Nieman Marcus. "It costs to look good," she told Bella, who replied, "It's so worth it."

Then Bella told Shelly what she thought was the real reason for her feeling bad about herself. "I've given up my AIDS screenplay."

Shelly said, "I never understood why you were so interested in such a vile idea. Why don't you try dating again?"

Bella replied, "If you have anyone with my specifications, let me know."

Shelly laughed, "If I found someone with your specifications, I'd keep him for myself."

When Bella next had supper with Greta at their favorite neighborhood restaurant, Bella said, "You'll be glad to hear I'm giving up my AIDS script. It's a sad subject, and a script making out it was deliberately introduced does nobody any good, even if it's true."

Gretta said, "Do you know what I think?"

"What?"

"You're not going to like this, but I think you did this all to impress Guy. To show off, you're still smart, even if you're older and especially smarter than his Irina, who, because English isn't her home tongue, doesn't understand nuances or humor. You want Guy to be impressed by you. But he is impressed by you anyway. You don't have to do anything. He loves you; he admires you; he is impressed by you, and he always has been and always will be. It's because you are you, Bella Mellman. You don't have to change yourself into some serious investigative screenwriter. Why do you think he's kept you so close all these years since you divorced? It's odd, I know, but you really are in sync in some way. You know how sometimes both of you show up in similar colors. Coincidence or connection? Life can take myriad routes, but only one at a time?"

"Schrödinger's cat theory thinks otherwise."

Greta said, "Don't you go quoting things both of us don't understand. In your case, as in the case for us all, you took one route and that's all you can ever experience. It's the road you're meant to be on. It's karma."

Bella said, "I thought you didn't believe in all that."

For once, Greta conceded, "Maybe there really is something to reincarnation? Maybe we are born over and over again until we work out all the kinks. Maybe you really were Guy's mother, at least in one of his lives? Maybe he was your father in another? I can see you both inhabiting both roles… funny that."

Bella said nothing. She felt the connection between her and Guy was engraved by the master engraver. And she wanted Guy to feel the same way, at the same time knowing

– even if he did – he'd neither allow himself to think nor admit it. And then, though she tried to stop them, a few tears rolled down her cheeks.

"Don't cry, Bella. You'll ruin your appetite."

"Don't worry about my appetite," Bella said.

Greta almost suggested Bella might try doing a children's book, seeing as she could both do art and write, but she wasn't sure if Bella would think it a good or terrible idea, at least at this moment, seeing she knew Bella had toyed with the idea and rejected it. Instead, she asked, "How's your handsome trainer, Sven?"

Greta met Sven a couple of times at Bella. She'd met his child Adam and the child's Asian mother.

"He's fine. He's got such patience with Adam's mother. I so admire him. He doesn't lose his temper with her, and she's truly difficult. He puts Adam's happiness first. I wish I could say I did that with my children."

"There you go again, rubbing salt in your wounds. If you were such a terrible mother, your children wouldn't want to be with you. And I think every single daughter blames their mother for everything. Mothers are dart boards. It's their role. That's one of the reasons I never wanted to become a mother. It's difficult enough to berate oneself without a child doing it."

Bella laughed, "Sven is the best father I've ever known. Also, he's getting older. Clubs and loose women don't interest him any longer, but he still nags me to come with him to Burning Man."

"Oh, you'd hate that. Dust and dust and more dust. And some half-clad young humans and drugs."

"I know. I hate camping. I've only been once, and for only one night when I was in Botswana, in The Okavango Swamp. Our group was ferried to a small island known as Lion Island. After the barbeque dinner, we were all given sleeping bags. We even had mosquito nets. Then once we finally settled down in our bags, it began to drizzle. I could not sleep as the pilot of the small plane, who was with us the whole trip, snored so loudly. His snoring reminded me how most men snore and require constant pokes to turn on their sides. Guy snored. My second mistake husband snored. My gangsta lover snored. And now I snore, but I can't hear myself."

Their food arrived, and as usual, Bella had pasta and Greta a salad. Bella could not believe Greta was so disciplined when it came to food. When Bella picked a desert, which wasn't often, Greta wouldn't even have a spoonful.

Bella said, "I think Gracie, Violet's daughter, is HIV positive... but at least Violet did convince her to go to the clinic and get herself on the meds. It took a lot of courage for her to admit her daughter is HIV positive. I know a conspiracy movie would not make things any better for her; the disease exploded and that's that. Why? Nobody can prove a conspiracy to deliberately infect people. My script would not promote peace, it would only promote more discord and there is enough of that already."

Greta said, "That's such a wonderful way of putting it. Remember when you told me I had to move on when Glen died? I'm telling you the same thing. Move on!"

Bella said, "I have another story that might inspire a screenplay." Bella ignored Greta's eye roll. "This one happened in Zimbabwe."

Greta said, "I am not sure I want you to tell me."

"I know, there's no point to this story either. It's also a mystery and there's no uncovering what really happened."

"What happened?" Greta couldn't help being curious.

"A powerful man who might have displaced Robert Mugabe – the long-time, evil president of Zimbabwe – was burned to death in his large sprawling single-story house on his farm, a might add, a farm taken from a white farmer after independence. The house was a single story, there were French Doors and windows, and anyone could easily escape a fire. The fire department arrived conveniently too late, and the poor man was burned to a frazzle. It's rumored he might have been tied to a chair and been shot first. Nobody cared enough to pursue the obvious crime. And his wife became Vice President until she was fired. Nobody was held responsible."

Greta agreed, "You'd have to travel to Zimbabwe and ask a lot of questions. You would not be safe."

Bella said, "It's true. Anyway, it's also a dead-end story. Why am I drawn to stories where the truth can never be known?"

"What's truth?" Greta said. "Now I'm being existential. Seriously, Bella, why don't you carry on writing about what you know? Write about your life. We all love those Bella stories."

"I'm still doing that, but Nicole says I should try to write a love story inspired by the relationship between Guy and me.

Greta smiled lovingly at her friend. "Isn't that what you've been doing?"

The End

Made in the USA
Las Vegas, NV
17 April 2023

70720994R00243